King of Hearts

"I have yet to teach you who is master," Raoul growled. He raised his hand, then lowered it. "No, not violence. There is a better way. Come here and let me offer you a taste of the joys you can expect as my mistress."

Scarcely a sound passed Gweneth's lips before Raoul covered them with his own, his arms crushing her to his velvet coat, locking her in his fierce embrace.

"This is what you want . . . what you have always wanted," he muttered.

"No! No!" Gweneth cried out wordlessly as his mouth pressed defiantly on hers. Angry, insulting, he dared her to find warmth or feeling in his lust. She must never, never give in to his demand. But how much longer could she resist?

Silks and Sabers

Laura Parker

A DELL BOOK

Published by
Dell Publishing Co., Inc.
1 Dag Hammarskjold Plaza
New York, New York 10017

*To Chris
for the time,
the space,
the love,
that allowed this to be*

Copyright © 1980 by Laura Castoro

All rights reserved. No part of this book may be
reproduced or transmitted in any form or by any
means, electronic or mechanical, including photocopying,
recording or by any information storage and retrieval
system, without the written permission of the Publisher,
except where permitted by law.

Dell ® TM 681510, Dell Publishing Co., Inc.

ISBN: 0-440-17950-5

Printed in the United States of America
First printing—March 1980

CHAPTER ONE

"Bind me tightly, Renée. I do not wish to present the capitaine with any unnecessarily tempting targets. It is enough that his strength, his height, and his reach are all superior to mine."

Gweneth's young voice was firm and confident, but her concentration was not upon the vigorous tugs applied to the corset strings by her sister. Rather the image of her tormentor claimed her attention. His masculine, wind-sculptured features animated with amusement were those of an animal, Gweneth decided, coloring her vague recollections with the prejudice of her anger. But she was not a daughter of the famous master-at-arms Jacques Valois without reason, and the capitaine would learn the truth of that.

The deck beneath their feet buckled suddenly, throwing the girls together. For the third time in as many hours Renée complained, "I hate the sea! How I wish with all my heart that we were home again."

With a sharp command and a scurrying of feet above them, the ship settled back into an even roll. Renée bent her head into her hands, hoping to hide the telltale signs of her fear now that her task was complete.

Gweneth drew on the pair of cotton breeches she had commandeered from the captain's laundry. Their malodorous state brought a wrinkle of distaste to her nose as she considered the probability that lice or something worse were embedded in the grimy folds. But then she would not likely live long enough for such things to matter, and they were much to be preferred to a woman's hobbling skirts and petticoats.

"Those breeches are so big. You may use my sash," Renée offered as Gweneth gathered in the waist. "This is madness. What can you hope to win? The capitaine will kill you like that!" she cried, snapping her fingers. "Or worse. Suppose he merely disarms you and then gives you to his crew once he has ravished you? *Mon Dieu!* What will you do?" Renée wailed.

Gweneth shook her head impatiently. "He shall not find that so simple a task. What do you know of fencing, you of so little faith?" A slip of a smile deepened the curve of her lips. "If the capitaine should be victorious, then it shall be because I am dead, or nearly so. *Quant à ça*, it matters not," she remarked with a philosophical shrug.

"Oh Gweneth, you must not die. If he kills you, I swear I shall avenge you!" The look of savagery accompanying Renée's outburst was so out of character that Gweneth quickly gave her sister's shoulders a gentle shake.

"Such a face, Renée. Madame Bourgeax would be horrified. Just think of the wrinkles she would have said you are encouraging. What a sad second you make, filling my head with doubt. Next time I shall have a care to keep you miles away," she teased. Yet a quiver of misgiving sped through her as she studied the flawless oval face in its wreath of black curls, and Gweneth suddenly regretted her sister's beauty for it was a curse in their present situation.

"If fate should betray us once again, it may be you to whom the capitaine looks for his pleasure. Do not fight him, little one. He fancies himself something of a gallant, and if you ask him to be generous, perhaps he shall be." Her voice was purposefully hushed, but Gweneth could not keep the fury of her thoughts from her eyes.

"*Mère de Dieu!* I cannot bear the thought of this!"

Renée sobbed, throwing her slender arms about Gweneth's neck.

"Hush, *ma petite*. Have no fear. The man must deal with me first, and I promise you I shall make him pay dearly for all the villainy he has perpetrated. There are ways of dealing with even the likes of our Monsieur Capitaine. If you had but paid the slightest attention to Papa's lessons, you would know this. I shall dazzle this clumsy Englishman with my skill and send him to hell as payment."

With a gentle shrugging free of Renée's embrace, Gweneth turned away to put her arms into the white linen shirt drawn from the captain's chest. Of finely woven cloth with a frill of lace at neck and wrists it caused Gweneth to comment aloud her surprise that a miserable pirate should take such pains with his attire. The men to whom such garments usually belonged were men of breeding and rank. "Bought with blood," she reflected with a shiver.

"Put your mind to something practical, and braid my hair," Gweneth directed sharply when a look told her that her sister's brimming eyes forewarned hysterics. There was nothing she could do for either of them if Renée were to undermine her confidence. "And do be quiet, for I must think," she added self-righteously.

The present held only the knowledge that an enemy must be defeated, but the past had been one of peace and happiness, and Gweneth could not prevent herself from straying to memories of what had been.

Until two and a half years ago their lives had been full beyond measure. Jacques Valois was an artist, the critics exclaimed, perhaps the best master-at-arms of the civilized world. Even through the first tumultuous years following the onset of the Revolution, it had not been imagined that he would be arrested for treason.

Monsieur Valois welcomed noble and commoner alike; their own peculiar political sympathies were left behind when they stepped into his brilliant salon. Here fencing became an art. Its fascination for the master lay in the grace, the discipline, the execution of a perfect set; a form separate from the mindless, bloodthirsty thrashings on the battlefield or the clumsy brawling of young hellions bent on destructive pleasure or personal redress.

Beyond this his future was assured with his three sons. Phillip, the eldest, and Benoit, the youngest brother, took after their father: dark and slim in their courtly appearance. Adolphe, like Gweneth, was a replica of their English mother. And while the once fair heads darkened to a rich red-brown as the years passed, the cool, peaceful green eyes remained.

Adolphe hated his generous sprinkle of freckles, thinking they kept him from true masculine beauty, and Gweneth found no greater love for hers. Yet the countless scrubbings and bleachings with lemon water and occasional bouts with veils and umbrellas at last gave way to a begrudging acceptance of the nasty little spots when Gweneth discovered that lounging about in shaded pavilions thoroughly bored her. For as long as she could remember, she had chased after three older brothers, and the trappings of femininity only stifled her joyous freedom.

She proved to be more than a handful for Madame Bourgeax, who waged a fruitless battle aimed at proper behavior. For a time Gweneth would truly try her best, but no sooner did she suppress one raging desire than did she find another temptation under her nose.

What a contrast then was the final addition to the household, Mademoiselle Renée. A full three years younger than Gweneth, Renée's care fell to the formidable nurse on the death of Madame Valois. Of amiable disposition and ever eager to please, Renée took well to the lessons of ladylike conduct.

Gweneth's aspirations were of a different nature, and it came as a rude blow when even her father decided that a fencing school was no longer the place for a thirteen-year-old young lady. Still, with only six years separating her from Phillip, their home was often filled with youthful gallants who were ever willing to flirt and compliment Gweneth's ability with a blade as she postured with them in the sheltered privacy of the family garden.

The end to this life came one warm April evening. What had begun as a cautious evening's pleasure, bolstered by the first glimmer of salvation since the death of King Louis XVI in January of that year 1793, ended in frenzied terror. It was never known who tipped the rioters, or if, indeed, it was not pure tragic fortune which led them to the Valois residence on this particular night. The ugly cries for blood disrupted the gathering in the garden, and Monsieur Valois had barely ordered his daughters into the tiny alcove behind the library wall when a battering ram stove in the gate and an army of pig-tailed sansculottes, sporting the tricolor cockade, burst through, smashing every hint of resistance with lead-weighted cudgels and staffs.

With no more damning evidence than the fact that the Valois Academy had once been an informal meeting place for minor nobility and held, upon occasion, exhibitions for members of the royal family, the Valois men, bloodied and defeated, were swept up in a night of mass arrests and interned in the conciergerie.

Terrified nearly out of their wits, the girls nonetheless remained hidden. Later, when the house had been quiet for hours, sixteen-year-old Gweneth and thirteen-year-old Renée picked their way through the rubble of what had been a fashionable townhouse. Those members of the staff who had not been bludgeoned to death by the mob had fled. It seemed that they were entirely alone until Renée tripped over an inert body. Madame Bourgeax lay unconscious, but they were able to revive her sufficiently for her to order them to gather whatever they could find to eat and, after a night of shivering in the dark, they set out on foot for Madame Bourgeax's home in Brest.

Months passed as they waited in ignorance for some

word to reach them of the fates of their kinsmen. Nearly a year later, they were informed by the local magistrate that Jacques Valois's life had been forfeited.

Madame Bourgeax died a few weeks later, having never fully recovered from the head injury which had rendered her speech increasingly garbled with each passing month. The girls remained in Brest under the watchful eye of Madame Bertin, the housekeeper's sister, and they took up her trade as laundress. It was not difficult work, and it kept the girls indoors, beyond the baneful eye of the local authorities.

The arrest and death of Robespierre in July 1974 ended the wanton executions, but the Valois brothers remained shut away, their futures hardly less uncertain. Then Adolphe was set free, bringing with him word that Phillip had died from the fever in prison. Of Benoit there was nothing, yet Adolphe preferred to hope that, like himself, Benoit had found his way to freedom.

With the help of his remaining friends Adolphe was able to secure passage for his family out of France. They would not go directly to England and seek asylum with their English grandfather, for with the rumors of renewed war, the French were shipping spies across the Channel under the guise of escaped prisoners, and these men were caught and jailed as often as not. The thought of prison so alarmed Adolphe, still ill from his experiences, that they embarked instead for the West Indies and the home of their mother's sister.

The *African Star* was an English privateer of dubious reputation, and her captain proved to be an enterprising sort who respected the gleam of gold more than the law. He asked no questions of his three French passengers dressed in peasant garb and bound for service in the Americas. Even so, the girls kept to their cabin during the day, seeking only short walks on deck in the late evening under the protective eye of Adolphe. But sorrow still followed them.

The night had been cool, the fog gathering in veiling wisps, before they heard the startled cry from the mizzen lookout of an approaching vessel. The first volley came as a total surprise: the orange and blue flame of the cannonade on that far deck and then the flurry of explosions and stunned oaths as the fire found its mark on their ship.

"Pirates!" Gweneth heard the captain shout. "To your posts, me lads. 'Tis a bit of our own powder we'll be forcing down the swines' throats afore long!"

Adolphe shepherded his sisters between the smoldering timber of the damaged ship to deposit them in a life boat. Though they pleaded with him to come along, Adolphe would not abandon the fight but promised to retrieve them once the marauders turned tail. They were quickly joined by two other women passengers whom they had not met, and the boat was hoisted and dropped into the gray sea.

The tiny craft bucked wildly, and only a supreme effort of self-control brought Gweneth and the elder of their two companions to the oars. Cloaked in the concealing fog, its presence undetected in the tumult of the battle, the little boat vanished in the night to the unsteady pull of its terrified crew.

Hours later, when they had drifted out into the darkness, Gweneth spotted a ruddy glow against the ashen sky. The *African Star* had been torched, and its conquerors were gliding away with their sails showing blood-red in the flames' light.

There was no fear for her own life as Gweneth sat huddled with Renée and watched in agonizing helplessness as her last hope for happiness burned itself out, taking Adolphe with it.

Perhaps she should have been grateful for the sight revealed by the morning's light, yet the vision of that stately, graceful ship slipping easily through the quiet sea filled Gweneth with hatred. There was no escape as the ship came alongside, and Gweneth steeled herself to confront her brother's murderers.

Cries of jubilation arose from the seamen as they

handed the castaways on board and discovered them to be women.

"Well, well, look what the sea has seen fit to spill upon our decks. Four mermaids, each more comely than the next. My compliments to the Mistress Atlantic," declared an appreciative voice as the throng of half-naked men made way for their captain.

Half a head taller than most of those about him, he presented a striking contrast in black velvet and fine lace. He did not even bother to introduce himself or, if he did, Gweneth did not hear it, rendered deaf by the arrogant dark blue gaze of the tall, dangerous-looking stranger. As those eyes covered her slowly from head to foot, Gweneth felt her entire body blush, for he missed not a line nor curve exposed by her damp gown.

"Your servant, ladies," he added. "Welcome aboard the *Cyrene*."

"Anglais," Renée murmured breathlessly, and Gweneth knew that she, too, had heard the voices of their attackers which carried so clearly in the morning mist.

Hearing her voice, the captain said, "French? *Etes-vous Française*, mademoiselle?"

"I am French, monsieur. So are we all," Gweneth offered in his language. "Is that why you sank our vessel last evening?"

The captain was not taken aback by this forthright question but answered smoothly. "I do not sink ships, mademoiselle. Not even for so rich a prize as this." And his gesture included them all. "What was the name of your vessel?"

"You know it very well, Capitaine," Gweneth replied coldly, but the captain merely shook his head.

"I do not recall the name being spoken, but I admire the luck of her crew to be graced by your lovely presence."

"You lie, Capitaine," Gweneth exclaimed flatly. "And there is the proof." The captain followed her direction to where several barrels stood lashed to the main mast with their fronts chalked in the *African Star*'s name.

"Salvage, my sweet," he replied with an untroubled grin. "All that falls into the sea may be retrieved by any hand. The casks and their contents are now mine. And so," he added with a pointed look, "are you."

The remark drew hefty laughter from his compatriots as they pressed in on the women to view more fully the prize.

Renée drew back against Gweneth with a shriek, but Gweneth stepped boldly forward, too angered to care. "Must your men gape at us?" she questioned resentfully. "I am aware that the bulk of the English are sadly lacking in manners, but I find this exhibition disgusting."

The captain's glossy smile cracked a trifle, but he said almost pleasantly, " 'Tis you who present the exhibition, mademoiselle. Your clothing leaves little to the imagination, and we have been at sea many months. If you did not tempt us so openly, perhaps you would find our attentions more—ah, discreet. As it is, you are lucky they have not set upon you before now. Particularly you, mademoiselle . . . ?"

He left the question incomplete, but Gweneth did not answer. He could well wonder who they were, she thought, for it might make him hesitate to be as rash as he threatened. She could not know that it was her deep green gaze that gave him pause, for in a second he had turned to the others.

"And who are you, my lovely?" he asked Renée warmly.

Renée's eyes grew round as she looked up into his face, and a flush daintily shaded her cheeks as she replied, "I am Renée Valois, monsieur."

Gweneth stiffened at her sister's reply, and the captain smiled in satisfaction. The younger girl was a beauty, but there was none of the challenge of the first girl's eyes, only fear.

"And you, my beauties, are we to have your

names?" The two who had hung back from Gweneth's confrontation now bobbed in curtsy, each supplying her name and addressing him as "*monseigneur.*" The one called Amy gazed with frank admiration into his amused blue eyes, whispering, "*Magnifique!*" when he turned away.

"Now, mademoiselle. What am I to make of you?" he asked, returning to Gweneth's side. When she did not answer, but held his glittering sapphire stare, he leaned nearer to murmur, "How delightful you are. And may I return the compliment in your eyes. Were you to grace my bed as beautifully as you do my deck, I am sure to be more than repaid for having saved your life."

Stung by his crude invitation, Gweneth rounded on him with a flurry of words. "*Diable!* You are a madman as well as a rogue if you believe I desire anything more than a knife with which to slit your throat!" she cried and lunged at him bare-handedly.

But he merely caught her to himself and swung her off her feet, laughing heartily at her outraged expression. "Careful, mademoiselle, or I shall be forced to silence that tirade. I yearn to know if your lips can be as tender when purring with syllables of endearment as they are hard when spitting venom," he teased and pulled her closer until his sun-weathered face was within inches of hers.

Abruptly his embrace fell away, and Gweneth landed unceremoniously at his feet to guffaws of approval.

"Alas, duty awaits me, my sweet, and I cannot postpone it even for you. Take this one to my cabin," he ordered the man at his side, "and secure the others below." Without a backward glance, he strode away.

"What did you say?" Renée asked as she completed the braid.

"Only that the capitaine has given me one more reason to see him dead," Gweneth replied, putting an end to her reflections. "There, I am ready."

"No, I do not think so! I drag that spitting kitten up from the sea, and how does she wish to repay me? Slit my throat, will she?" Raoul grumbled. "Damn, if I don't have her purring under my touch by nightfall. Now mind your own business, you prying old sea dog."

"Aye, Cap'n," Daniel replied smartly and crept away, realizing it was best not to press Captain Bertrand when his eyes shone so overly bright. It wasn't the first time he'd seen that look when some particularly pretty skirt took his captain's fancy. Still and all, this temper had been abrewin' long afore he'd seen the girl.

Raoul ran a careless hand through his dark wavy hair. "Blast the wench!" He had learned nothing from questioning the other women. The two claimed the girls were sisters, and though he believed them when they said they were servants, it did not follow that the same was true of the Valois women.

"As good a lie as any," Raoul mused aloud for, though he had denied it, he knew enough of the *African Star* to suspect the nature of any passengers she carried. Then too he realized the danger of having come upon the survivors so quickly. Had not the emerald-eyed chit accused him of piracy straight away? "Servant, indeed!"

No domestic possessed a temper like that. Nor half the looks. There was the aura of a temptress about her, and the perfect French she spoke had not been learned in a scullery. No, if they were not spies, then the sort of employment she sought was of the kind that filled a rich man's bed and provided jewels and fancy gowns in return. Whatever their true identity, it was clear the women were destitute, and there was none to take exception if he were to avail himself of the charms of the russet-haired girl. The desire to know if her vivid gaze mellowed to soft sea-jade when slaked by love brought a smile of speculation to Raoul's lips. Yes, he might just be persuaded to set her up for a time as his own mistress if she pleased him. He would certainly be able to afford it after this run.

"Helmsman, put her about. We've done a proper morning's work, and there will be an extra profit in every man's pocket when we've disposed of the salvage."

Gweneth surveyed the bundle of rapiers propped together in one corner of the large paneled cabin. The best of the lot no doubt hung from the captain's belt, Gweneth thought as she extracted one after the other to test the relative merits of each.

"*Voilà*, this one looks promising," she cried, pulling it free. The blade was two inches longer than the others. "It will help even my reach," she observed to Renée. In spite of its weight the well-balanced length gave a smooth performance as she swung it aloft and made several figures. "And now, Capitaine, you shall pay for the death of my brother," she called with a salute.

"Confound this sea. It is nearly noon, and yet the morning chill persists," Raoul murmured to the man near him and shook off the tremor of his body as a droplet of sweat raced across his chest. Impatient with his own discomfort, Raoul leaped the balustrade of the pilot deck with ease and landed before the steps to his cabin.

"Prepare yourself for death, Capitaine," Gweneth warned with a leap forward.

"What the devil?" Raoul muttered in exasperation but fell back a step before the advancing figure with sword in hand. One eyebrow shot up quizzically as his gaze swept the breeches and shirt and came to rest on the furious expression of the lady-cum-sailor.

"You make a most fetching cabin boy, my lady, but

I prefer my women in skirts—when clothes are necessary," he continued gamely, recovering from his surprise.

Gweneth stepped forward guardedly. "I offer you the chance to defend yourself, Capitaine, which is more than a rogue deserves. On guard, monsieur."

"Surely you jest, mademoiselle. I have no intention of drawing against a woman. Put that dangerous weapon aside before you come to harm," Raoul answered contemptuously and turned his back.

"You shall fight me, or I shall kill you where you stand," Gweneth threatened boldly and placed the tip of her blade between his shoulders. She had known she must provoke him in a manner which would not allow him to decline.

Raoul turned back, arms outstretched, but the expression on his face was still that of simple annoyance. "What madness is this? We have no quarrel, you and I. In truth, I have been considering a more intimate association with the greatest of interest," he announced, presenting her with an engaging smile. Instantly his arm shot out to disarm her, but Gweneth, expecting this, retreated and lunged, catching his velvet coat full across the shoulder. A smile of satisfaction flickered over her features as the tip slipped neatly through the material and left it hanging from the sleeve.

"You affect the frippery of a gentleman when it would serve you better to study the manners of one. There, monsieur, I supply the quarrel," she suggested confidently in English so that all might understand her challenge.

"Why you bloodthirsty little minx," Raoul hissed, her mockery having sent his own blood boiling through his veins. His hand came swiftly to the hilt of the sword at his hip. "If you insist, then I see I must teach you proper humility. However, you should be warned that few men have dared be so rash in facing me and"—a slow grin spread across his bronzed face—

"they were quickly dispatched into the bosom of eternity to rue their folly."

"You do not frighten me," Gweneth replied over the pounding of her heart. He would fight!

"Not yet, mademoiselle," Raoul countered and with a single fluid movement his weapon flashed into brilliance. "But, by God, I shall!"

"Lookee here! The cap'n's gonna have a go with the Frenchie, a girl at that," shouted one of the sailors.

"Aye, Cap'n. Set her back on her heels, or let me be doin' it for ye," added another. "I reckon I could do with a bit o' sport."

Lewd offers and remarks came from every quarter, but Gweneth's eye never strayed from her prey.

"Gweneth, *ma soeur*, I beg you! Give this up!" Renée pleaded urgently as she hung uncertainly in the galleyway.

"Give heed to your sister, mademoiselle, or I may decide to leave your fate to my men," Raoul jeered.

"Afraid, Capitaine? Or is it that your bravery is kept for those who are defenseless? Any dastard can threaten a helpless woman, but you are not half so anxious now, I fear," Gweneth baited recklessly. He must fight, she told herself. She must settle the account of her brother's death—even if it meant her own.

The muscles of Raoul's jaw flexed menacingly, standing in sharp outline under his darkened skin, but he was slow to answer. "Yours is a wickedly barbed tongue, my lady, but I cannot believe that you are so eager to die."

"Then believe this!" she spat back, and only just in time did Raoul grasp her intent and raise his weapon to deflect her deadly attack.

"Enough!" Raoul growled as a dark light kindled into flame behind his eyes. Now he, too, felt the warm flush of the promise of battle, wanting nothing better than to vanquish that disdainful look in the girl's eyes and render her at his mercy.

"If it is a duel you desire, fair one, a duel you shall

have. Make way, you fools, and let no man move to interfere until I give you liberty. Come along, mademoiselle. Let us have proper space." Raoul marched out onto the deck newly cleared by the eager spectators.

Gweneth moved forward, noticing the powerful muscles of the captain's back and shoulders, and the first measure of uneasiness prickled her scalp as she observed that latent strength soon to be unleashed upon her slight frame. A quiver pulled at her lips as she realized that he could snap her wrist like brittle kindling if given the chance.

"Curious?" Raoul called, finding her discomfort encouraging, and with a sweep of his hand he opened his shirt to the waist. "I am gratified by your eagerness to see more of me. If you would simply forgo this reckless scheme, it would be my pleasure to show you things of even greater novelty. But first, if you insist—" And he lay aside his blade to shrug free of his coat. "I do not relish losing any more of my wardrobe to your lucky marks. Forgive my nakedness," he added and drew off his shirt, revealing a deeply sunburned chest.

"If I were you, Capitaine, I would not display so ample a target, for I may not be able to resist the urge to carve my name in that wide expanse." Gweneth's laughter bubbled forth at the temerity of her own words, but she blushed slightly when it was answered in kind by the seamen.

Damn the girl, did nothing frighten her? Raoul wondered angrily. She dares cut my coat to rags and shows no fear at the sight of my superior strength. "Have a care, mademoiselle, for I intend to quell that proud defiance and bend it to my will."

A gust of wind drew a rippling shiver over his exposed skin, and Raoul cursed. He did not like the anger this *jeune fille* provoked within him, but he shrugged off his lightheaded mood and grabbed up his rapier. This was not the moment for weakness.

"Your obedient servant, my lady—for the present." Raoul bent slightly from the waist, saying, "Shall we begin?"

The play of steel on steel sounded sharply in the extraordinary silence as the blades met, engaged, and arched free. The captain's unsuspected skill as a swordsman became apparent in these first moments, and Gweneth found herself gaining respect for his knowledge with every movement. Free but not careless, careful but effortless, there was more here than the brute force of a brawler. His was a cultivated facility, and Gweneth drew a long breath in understanding that she had chosen her own death.

Raoul watched Gweneth in equal amazement. He had meant to ridicule the child hiding behind the sword, and here he faced a fencer of some experience. If she were a man, he would have found himself sorely pressed for, even now, he was ever on his guard, parrying her tentative thrusts but hesitating to follow through with the riposte. He was half again her weight and a head taller, leaving him to feel a complete fool but for the fact she danced about him like an angry bee, ever ready to sting her prey. Who was this girl that she advanced so fearlessly upon him and did not retreat at the threat of his thrust? Well, he knew how to take care of that.

With a swift parry and lunge the clang of metal rang loudly as the blades slid along one another and locked at the hilts. Gweneth threw her full weight against the captain when their shoulders met above the crossed rapiers, but she knew that he would send her flying across the boards when he shoved back.

Raoul leaned near and reached out his free hand to brush a sweaty tendril from the girl's face. "There, chérie," he crooned sweetly, "I would much rather caress that lovely body than carve it up." Suddenly he had a handful of her hair and he jerked her face against the cold steel. "You see, I could quite easily scar that beautiful cheek with a nasty welt, but I do not want that—but rather this." And he bent over the blades and covered her trembling lips with his own, crushing her mouth against his teeth until she tasted blood.

A tormented cry rose in Gweneth's throat as she struggled to free herself from his blatant mockery, but this maneuver brought wild cheers of approval from the ring of men.

"I wager half me pay the cap'n can take her down with the blades still betwixt 'um," one shouted and, as if to prove the bet aright, Raoul's other hand came up to rest on Gweneth's shoulder and then slid along to the small of her back to arch her against him as he continued to force punishing kisses on her mouth across the barrier of steel.

Incensed to the point of madness, Gweneth kicked out frantically, catching the captain just below the knee. He cried out, momentarily freeing his grasp, and Gweneth jerked away. Miraculously her rapier remained in her hand while the captain's slithered to the floor. When he reached down lazily to retrieve his weapon, Gweneth lunged, and the thrust of her blade cut deeply into the captain's left shoulder.

In that awful instant when the flesh resisted the tip, the blade bent slightly, and Gweneth experienced with horror the full impact of her action. Never before had she scored more than a courtesy mark with buttoned foil. This time she knew what it was to wound a man, and her stomach retched in response.

"Damn you, vixen! Pull back!" Raoul raged in blind fury, for her blade still lodged in his flesh. It came free with a jerk, and Gweneth let it fall from her hand, the sight of its red-tipped edge draining the blood from her head so swiftly she swayed.

"Pick it up," Raoul demanded. "Pick it up or I'll run you through unarmed." A muttering restlessness stirred the crew, but none sought to interfere.

More angry with himself than her for having lowered his guard, Raoul watched uncertainly as the girl bent slowly and put her hand to the hilt of her weapon. It was now necessary to force her to withdraw, or he would never overcome the humiliation before his men in having been wounded by a woman.

"Gweneth, *mon Dieu*, give up," Renée pleaded once again but found the way blocked by a burly seaman when she moved toward her sister.

"Best let 'em be, missy. The cap'n will decide the proper end," he said and pushed Renée none too gently behind the circle of onlookers.

Gweneth gazed in bemused fascination as the captain's rapier flashed into position, and her own trembled wickedly as it crossed in answer. The next time steel seared flesh it would be her blood gushing forth, and her startled eyes flew to the place where the captain held a hand to his wound and scarlet rivulets flowed between his fingers.

A twinge of pity caught at Raoul, but he frowned in rejection of the girl's conscience-stricken face. After all, 'twas no more than expected that one of them might be wounded. Had she not struck him deliberately? Yet she appeared ready to sacrifice herself to his blade if she saw no alternative.

Abruptly Raoul lowered his rapier and signaled for his shirt. He thrust his arms into it and pulled it together. "You promised to carve your name. You have done little more than dot the 'i,' chérie. Come now, do not be frightened by a healthy letting of blood. I played unfairly and deserve the lesson," he conceded with a smile and approached her unarmed.

Gweneth stared in wonder. He had not sought to kill her, as he might easily have done, but she could utter no words of apology for having struck him in Adolphe's name.

"*Ma belle*," Raoul whispered, coming nearer still. "You may quit this battle even now. Why must it be the life of one of us?" And he gently placed his fingers on the tip of her blade.

Gweneth gasped and sprang back from the face growing larger than life in her fright-widened eyes.

"You killed my brother," she whispered faintly, releasing the weapon.

A thousand thoughts rushed over her, and then she felt her knees give way but not the moment when the deck soared upward to meet her.

CHAPTER TWO

The room brightened slowly and behind closed lids Gweneth saw the nursery in her home on the rue St. Germaine. Her mother was there, pressing cool, soothing towels to Gweneth's feverish cheeks. *"Ma mère, ma mère,"* she whispered in greeting and reached out for the comfort of motherly warmth, yet the feeling under her hand was hard and prickly.

"Hardly a mother, mademoiselle," came the reply, deep voiced and filled with humor.

Gweneth's eyes flew open and focused in disbelief upon the *Cyrene*'s captain, bare to the waist and leaning over her. It was his cheek she had touched. Gweneth snatched her hand away, and her eyes darted about the cabin for some assurance that they were not alone. But the recesses of the paneled room revealed no one, and Gweneth recoiled from the man above her.

"Easy, my lady," Raoul cautioned and pushed her head back against the pillow. "You fainted, and before I could catch you, your head hit the deck, quite hard I'm afraid," and he carefully folded a damp cloth and laid it on her aching brow.

"You!" Gweneth cried miserably. "I would never believe you attempted to aid me."

"Ma belle," how can you say such a thing? After all, getting you into my arms has been the object of this entire folly. You have made a damnable mess of it, fair one. You might have finished me off or been killed yourself. As it is, we both fell wounded, bereft

of any consolation." Only Raoul's smiling assurance kept the sting from his jest.

Gweneth opened her mouth to protest, when her attention turned to the captain's bloodied shoulder, which was not yet dressed. With a stab of guilt she bit her swollen lip, saying instead, "Does it hurt terribly? I am sorry."

Raoul looked at her sharply, then grinned. "Why I believe you are. In that case the wound was well worth the price if it earned your sympathy and concern. It is only a scratch. You are quite a hand with a blade. Where did you ever learn such skill?"

Gweneth did not reply but watched as the blood swelled from the cut and coursed down his chest. Without hesitation she removed the cloth from her head and applied it to his wound. "You still bleed, monsieur. There could be infection if you are not properly attended. You must lie down," she admonished and pushed up on one elbow.

"Are you suggesting that I join you in my bunk, chérie?" Raoul asked with eyes full of mischievous delight.

Gweneth shook her head in quick denial, but the sudden movement set her senses spinning wildly, and she pressed her hands to her temples in distress. The cotton coverlet slipped from her shoulders, and looking down, Gweneth gasped in astonishment and jerked it up.

"You have undressed me! You had no right to touch me!" she cried, her eyes dark with accusation.

"Gently, mademoiselle. You cause yourself needless grief. That ridiculously tight corset was the probable reason for your fainting spell. How could you ever hope to keep your wind in that condition?" Raoul put his hand to the sheet, and Gweneth gave a frightened whimper, but he merely tucked the sheet securely under her chin. "The clothes in question were mine. Naturally I helped myself to them. If you are left without, my lady, it is my benefit and your loss." The laughter which followed was long and strong and merciless in its meaning.

"You are despicable," Gweneth retorted and rolled away from him, dragging the bedding with her. He had undressed her, and she knew he had lingered long and hungrily over her exposed body, for the blood from his wound had spattered the sheets and smeared her limbs. Had he touched her intimately or . . . no, she could not bear to think what might have happened. The very thought of his touch left her burning with shame.

"Your suggestion of rest pleases me," Raoul said after a moment. "My bunk is a very tempting place at this moment."

The mattress sagged under his weight, and Gweneth turned to face him on the narrow confines of the bunk. "Please, you would not, you cannot—" she pleaded but heard the panic in her voice and quieted. Whatever else, he must not have the satisfaction of her fear.

"Oh, I can and I would," he echoed pleasantly, "but I shall not—yet. Now hush so that we may both sleep." Raoul stretched out full beside her in his breeches but, to Gweneth's relief, he did not seek to share the bedding. His eyes closed and yet Gweneth knew him to be every bit as aware of her as she of him.

"My sister, the others?" What had he done with Renée?

"They are properly quartered, unlike you, *ma chérie*. We reached a compromise, their honor for yours." Raoul's eyes opened now, and he raised up, turning to her. "You shall stay with me. I won and yet have shown mercy. Do you not find that a fair arrangement?" The dark-lashed lids lowered a trifle, veiling his expression though a smile lifted his features.

"You did not win," Gweneth countered hotly. "I forfeited the victory. That is different. If you force your will on me, it is still rape, and I shall yet see you dead." The defiant words gave her courage despite the fact she had not the strength to resist him.

"Quiet, woman, you talk too much," Raoul replied with an almost irritated edge to his voice. "I am weary of the battle. Take this reprieve to gather your strength, for you shall soon need it. It is not my habit to take a woman who is not fully conscious of what we are about, else she would be unable to thank me properly afterward," and, drawing close, he kissed the top of her bare shoulder.

Gweneth could not move and simply closed her eyes against his affection. She must get away, she thought frantically, but where could she go? He had taken her clothes, and all that lay beyond the cabin door was a vast gray sea. Miserably weak, Gweneth pulled the covers tightly about her and gave the captain her back. She must have time to think.

Raoul looked down at the tangle of cinnamon-brown hair splayed upon the pillow by his face. She was quite a woman, in more ways than the obvious ones she had displayed when he undressed her. The delicate coloring of her skin, not the alabaster of many fair-haired women, was a sweet apricot mellowed with a blush of rose. Studying the soft curve of her shoulder peeking over the sheet, which hid the fine sprinkling of freckles upon her full-swelling breasts, Raoul sighed softly in memory. He had not been able to resist covering them with tender nibbling kisses in spite of his urgent desire for revenge.

Raoul shifted and grunted at the sharp burning sensation in his arm. She had driven her blade into his flesh, but there was soon to be a time when he would return that favor in his own way, with her full knowledge. Oh yes, that he would do. Chuckling to himself, he turned away to relieve the weight on his sore side.

Gweneth slept long and soundly, and her head felt much better when she awakened, but the serenity vanished abruptly. She was not alone. Turning slowly so as not to disturb her bedmate, Gweneth came round to find the captain dozing peacefully beside her. The cabin lay in deep shadow, all but hiding the desk and shelves of charts and books. Nothing else had changed since the morning. Nothing but the realization that her clothes had disappeared, and she was more vulnerable than ever to the man at her side.

Contemplating his face for the first time, Gweneth found to her amazement that he was decidedly handsome. Now that he could not intimidate her, she took some pleasure in studying him. His features were sharply etched: the eyes deep set and pleated in the corners like those of all sailors, his mouth wide with well-shaped lips.

Gweneth's breath caught in her throat as she remembered the taste of his mouth. It was not her first kiss from a man, but neither was it like any in her experience. He had made her aware of his lust in a way she could never forget, but there was no tenderness in it, none of the finer feelings.

Gweneth shook her head and looked away. What could she expect? He was a stranger. A pirate. Why should he wish to woo and gently court her when there was no need? He had left no doubt as to his intentions, and now she was simply to wait for him to awaken and take her.

Gweneth pulled up straight and leaned against the wall, putting all the distance she could between them, for his length cut off any possibility of maneuvering past him. She was trapped, and as she stared down at his wound, the old anger crept into her fear, and she wished her sword had struck three inches lower. No, she did not wish that. In spite of all, Gweneth realized, she could not have deliberately killed him. Only her grief had fostered that brief insanity and, merciful heavens, she had come so close!

The open wound drew her curiosity, and Gweneth came to her knees with one hand clutching the covers to her body as she reached out and touched him gingerly. The fingers of her hand crept up to the skin of his neck, the heat from it seeming to scorch her fingertips, and as they settled in the hollow of his throat to measure the too rapid pulse, Gweneth gasped softly in surprise. The captain was ill. She bent lower to try and detect the point of entry of her blade. It appeared to be too high to have pierced the lung, but what else would explain the sudden sickening?

A hand came up swiftly, pinning Gweneth's face to the captain's blood-spattered chest. *"Ma belle,"* Raoul purred. "So you could not wait for me to awaken. I am flattered." The words were slightly slurred, but they struck terror in Gweneth nonetheless. She strained against the force pressing her face to him but discovered that she could not free herself without losing the bedding, which she was certain would inflame him more, and so gave up the battle.

"Better, much better," Raoul remarked approvingly as Gweneth's wary gaze slid round to his face, but his eyes remained closed. "Your breath is cool and sweet upon my flesh. Will your kisses be equally provocative?" Raoul's eyes opened now, and Gweneth stared into their bright blaze until it seemed she knelt before an open hearth.

Raoul's broad hand caressed her hair and encircled the nape of her neck. "Let us test your spirit, mademoiselle," he whispered and tilted her face up to his.

Gweneth strained against his embrace, but her squirming brought a grunt of pain when she struck the captain's injury. She went limp, unable to endure his agony, and let him drag her cheek over the coarse curls of his chest and settle her head in the curve of his neck.

Raoul lifted his head and touched his mouth to hers. The heat from his lips caused her to tremble, and he chuckled, murmuring against her mouth, "Ah, you like it, my lady."

"Non—" Gweneth began, but he pulled her tighter until no more words could escape their kiss. Gently he nibbled and probed her soft mouth, and Gweneth reluctantly tolerated his kisses, for they were not rough and rude like the first. Yet they made her uneasy in other ways, for part of her was beginning to enjoy the intimacy of his mouth on hers and the gentle whirlwind it stirred within her. "The blow to my head surely dazed my sense," Gweneth thought in confusion. "I hate this man. He is responsible for my brother's death."

Raoul released the girl's mouth at last and took a deep breath, surprised by the weakness that pervaded his limbs. This young woman fanned his desire, but his body hardly responded. She had not continued to fight him, and yet he sensed her antagonism in the tense muscles of her neck beneath his fingers. She interested him, she did that. If only this confounding weakness would pass.

"You may have a way with the rapier, mademoiselle, but I as your lover shall teach you how to respond agreeably to my own very personal thrusts," he said huskily in her ear and put a possessive hand on her bare thigh under the sheet. Too late he realized his mistake in teasing her, for she jerked free, and he was too weary to drag her back.

Gweneth sat up, grabbing the covers to herself, and pushed the streaming masses of hair from her flushed face. "I have had no lovers, monsieur, and you shall not be the first. When I am ready, I shall choose for myself, and I have every confidence that I can find a man who is not so easily laid abed by my sword."

Her laughter sounded too loudly in her own ears, but it goaded Raoul beyond endurance. He bolted up, encircling her shoulders with his right arm and crushing her between himself and the wall. Gweneth screamed, twisting frantically within his arm, but failed to push him away.

"Quietly, chérie, unless you would have an audience for our love play." Raoul leaned his full weight on her, and Gweneth felt his taut muscles press her from shoulder to hip. "If you do not fancy my style of fencing, perhaps you shall find my ability in bed more to your taste. If not, we shall keep trying until your pleasures find a match in mine. I am most versatile." With that he caught her about the waist and pushed her down on the bed under him.

Abandoning the protection of the sheet, Gweneth shoved both hands against his chest near the hollow of his throat. "I shall fight you," she warned, her eyes narrowing in challenge. "You are wounded, and I will use that to my advantage. I will hurt you and forever hate you for forcing me to do it." The false calm in her voice was born of a fear past censoring the truth. What could it matter? He would defeat her anyway. Still it served to steady her fluttering heart to wave this declaration of war before him.

Raoul slipped his arm from under Gweneth and sat back, bracing himself against the wall with her caught between. Astonishment shone in his face as he looked down on her, for the tilt of her chin and the determination in those green eyes bespoke her dislike and fear of him. He had played this game many times before, and each time the lady had acquiesced in good humor when put to the final test. Of course, it was always the case that they were not the chaste ladies they claimed. He prided himself on his ability to choose such women, saving himself many a shilling. What woman would expect payment after having been seduced against her will? No, this open defiance and unguarded aversion displayed before him now were not what he had bargained for.

Gweneth struck his hand aside from the stray curl he fingered, and Raoul's brows came together in a deep frown. She had spoken with the cool-edged finesse of a courtesan, leading him to believe her the recipient of many a man's company. And yet she spurned his advances with the artless fear of an innocent. It came as a rude discovery to learn that she was a virgin. Just who was this beautiful young woman who drove him to duels and violence?

"You are a mystery, little one," Raoul sighed. He should have remained still under her touch when she had thought him asleep, for he had been aware of her gaze as it traveled his body and had warmed to her hand's pressure. It was when she leaned close enough to kiss his bared chest that he could not resist touching her in return. She had come submissively into his arms and even allowed him to kiss her repeatedly. Why had he not been content with that for, by Jupiter, his head ached sufficiently for two men, and the stiffness in his shoulder spread with every moment. Unable to defeat the constricting spasms of pain climbing his chest, Raoul groaned and gave up to a violent shudder.

Gweneth, who had long since closed her eyes to the captain's inquiring stare, now looked up at the sound of his distress to see the glistening perspiration quiver above his pale lips before his head nodded forward, jerking his shoulders free of the wall, and he pitched over onto her.

Though she raised her hands quickly to break his fall, the impact of his weight extracted a startled cry from Gweneth. Raoul stirred slightly, his head lolling in the generous curve between Gweneth's breasts, and whispered, "You win, my darling. Poisoned by Cupid's wicked arrow."

For some moments Gweneth lay listening to the hammering of her heart and, under the fingers of her hand, the fevered pulsing of the captain's. Somewhere above their heads a seaman dropped his burden with a thud that reverberated through the cabin. An explosion of oaths followed and then a grunt of pain from what Gweneth guessed was a booted kick. Savages, all savages, she thought angrily, but the incident did not rouse the man with her.

Cautiously Gweneth raised her hand up to the captain's face and wiped the thick mahogany hair, damp with sweat, from his brow. She had been right in thinking him ill. But poison? What could he have

SILKS AND SABERS 33

meant? And if he should die, what would become of
Renée and herself? "A fine time to think of that!" her
conscience responded accusingly. Whatever the consequence, she must get help.

Gweneth pushed against the captain and managed
to slide his right shoulder onto the bed. Raoul moaned
again but, when no words came forth, Gweneth threw
her modesty aside with the covers and, easing out
from under him, rolled him onto his back. Raoul's lids
fluttered, and Gweneth drew back in expectation, but
he did not seem to see her. When he did not move
again, Gweneth scrambled over his inert body and
put her bare feet on the floor. She looked around
frantically for something with which to cover herself
and spied the captain's chest. Tripping lightly across
the cold undulating boards, she bent and lifted the
lid.

There among his clothes lay her gown and petticoats. Even her chemise had been neatly folded away.
He had been so sure that she would nestle snugly in
his bed, she thought resentfully as she hastily pulled
on the chemise and then glanced over her shoulder.
The captain lay as if asleep, and she shook out the
gown and drew it over her head, not bothering with
petticoats or corset. Her hands could reach the fasteners only half the way up the back, but that would do
for now, she decided.

Returning to the captain's side, she picked up the
cloth he had used to ease her head and, rinsing it,
gently wiped his face. In the next minutes his wound
was washed clean with a sliver of soap Gweneth
found by his razor. The chest yielded up many possible garments which could be used to make bandages,
but Gweneth reluctantly chose her own petticoat of
pink batiste. It had been her one concession to fashion that remained. Not even for Adolphe had she been
able to part with it, but it was clean and would be an
excellent bandage.

Her actions were careful and methodical, but

Gweneth's fingers trembled and she chewed the corner of her lip as she prepared to cleanse the injury with whiskey. "Capitaine, you must survive," Gweneth murmured to herself. "I find I do not like the reality of your blood on my hands after all." She pulled the cork from the bottle and firmly pressed the cut open to receive the liquor.

Raoul jerked awake under the hurtful pressure and reached up, wrenching her hand away.

"Let me be!" Gweneth commanded in alarm. Then, more gently, she said, "You must be still, Capitaine. I shall not harm you. Trust me." Her wrist stung where it was confined within the steel trap of his fingers, but Gweneth made no attempt to free herself.

"I am at your mercy, mademoiselle. Do not take advantage of my helplessness." A wobbly smile twisted his mouth, but Raoul's eyes were dull with pain.

"Rest easy, monsieur," Gweneth cautioned and continued her task when the captain released her arm. Though he paled and closed his eyes, Raoul did not move to prevent the flow of smarting liquid into his wound.

Gweneth wrapped the dressing tightly to stem the bleeding when he raised up on one elbow with great difficulty, and she offered a silent prayer of relief when done, for he had not cried out with the agony she knew her ministrations had caused him.

"*Oui*, Capitaine?" Gweneth asked, bending low to put her ear near his moving lips.

"Daniel. Only Daniel must know," Raoul repeated weakly and then, as his eyes rolled up under his lids, he fainted.

Gweneth touched the feverish cheek gently in comfort before arranging his head on the pillow and covering him. This sickness was more than a simple wound. If he were truly poisoned, then she must seek help. Such matters required a skill she did not possess. Yet . . . the captain's command had prevented his seamen from making sport of her and the others but, if he were to die or even if they knew him to be helpless, what could she expect? Was it not better to wait?

Gweneth nibbled the fleshy part of her forefinger in thought, a habit that Madame Bourgeax deplored with lengthy castigations and to exactly no effect. In moments of great stress Gweneth knew no hesitation, but in matters requiring niggling decisions, the rogue finger inevitably made its way to her mouth. To wait and chance the captain's life or brave a ship of lecherous, barbarous seamen: this was the choice. Gweneth crossed the floor and drew back the bolt.

Garnet ribbons of light from below the horizon streaked the violet ocean and azure sky of late evening. The deck appeared deserted but just as her waist came even with the deck, a tall, spare-bodied sailor stopped to peer down the hatchway. His greedy eyes, sunk beneath black thatched brows, swept down Gweneth's face and fastened on her bosom which was unrestricted by proper foundation, bringing an ugly sneer to his loose-lipped mouth.

"Cap'n's had his fill, aye, girlie?" he snickered and offered his gnarled, leathered hand. "Come here and give us a fair chance. Could be the cap'n's not to the likin' of a spitfire such as ye. He be a mite too much the gentleman, me thinks. Shoulda smacked the daylights outta ye for marking him the way ye done." The man's insulting stare seemed to strip her naked, and Gweneth put a defensive hand to her neckline as he added, "Looks to me like he done no more than was necessary." Satisfied with this judgment, he bent down to grab for her.

Gweneth fell back, all too aware of her half-fastened gown, and stumbled down the stairwell. "Do not touch me," she ordered as one hand groped behind her for the door latch. What could she say to keep the man from coming in after her?

"I should keep my hands off the capitaine's *chère-amie* if I were you, or you may find a taste of the whip to his liking," Gweneth blurted out as he reached the lower step. "I am sent to fetch Daniel. Find him for me this instant, or I shall report your insolence to the capitaine."

The threat of his commander's displeasure brought the seaman up short and he backed off slightly, but there harbored a gleam of resentment in his eye. For her, for the captain, or for the pair of them, Gweneth wondered anxiously? She knew instinctively that she had made a dangerous enemy.

"No need to get yer wind up, girlie," he grumbled sulkily. "I'll be seein' to Daniel. Ye best get below afore the cap'n comes aseekin' ye. He's known to entertain his crew with a wench for less aggravation."

The look of maidenly astonishment on the French girl's face produced a hoot of glee from the sailor's lips. Serves her right, he thought, if she chose to believe him. Perhaps Cap'n Bertrand had given her reason to fear such an action, and the man turned away in crude speculation of just what might have taken place behind that cabin door.

Gweneth jerked open the door and stepped inside, slamming it after her as she whirled round to glare at her captor. So he had provided entertainment for his crew, had he? She gave his boot a vicious kick where it lay discarded on the floor. And to think she had tried to save his life, feeling guilt and sorrow for her part in his illness. Gweneth marched over and stood before the captain with arms doubled across her chest. "Pirate! Blackguard! Rogue!" she railed in an anger-shaken voice.

The captain did not answer. He lay silent, his face an unearthly gray beneath the sun-bronzed cover and his lashes forming a long shadow on each cheek. Seen thus, it did not seem possible that he was a brutal, evil man. His mouth held no cruelty nor mocking sneer now, but the lips were soft and slightly parted, sucking in shallow breaths. Quickly Gweneth reminded herself that she must not be so naïve as to imagine that fairness equaled goodness.

The knock at the door startled her from the silent brooding, but Gweneth glanced at the captain's quiet form again before turning to the door. "Who is there?" she questioned without drawing the bolt.

"It be Daniel, missy. I bring supper for Cap'n Bertrand and ye."

Opening the door a crack and peering into the dark, Gweneth saw the silhouette of a short thin man. Cautiously she dragged the door back and allowed him to enter.

Daniel's eyes swept the disheveled lady quickly, then went to the desk, but the captain was not there. With a slow grin he turned to the bed. Dropping the tray on the table, Daniel cried, "Ah, missy, what o' ye done?" as he hurried to his captain's side. He put an ear to the bedsheet covering the man's chest and then a hand to his burning brow.

"Oh, monsieur, he is very ill," Gweneth said when she had replaced the bolt and joined the steward at the bedside. "I have done what little I know how, but I know nothing of curatives for poison." Daniel turned on the girl with a look of pure malice and made a move as if he would strangle her. "I did not do it!" Gweneth replied as she backed away. "How could I?"

The man's hands fell to his sides slowly. "Mercy's sake. Nothin' good will come of this. Women," he muttered. "They near done him in times afore but never—"

"I am not to blame!" Gweneth insisted, nearly in tears. "If he is poisoned, then it was by other hands. He himself told me of his distress."

"Phew," Daniel exclaimed and ran the back of one hand over his lips. "Well, this be not the best o' crews. Some o' 'em be the slimiest, thievinest . . ." And a few words unknown to Gweneth followed until he remembered the lady by his side. "E'scuse me, missy. I forget meself. Hell no, none o' them have anythin' to gain by it. It ain't poison what's ailin' him. Not if ye ain't—"

"*Mais non*, monsieur. I swear it!"

Daniel shook his head and stared at the man on the bed, but Gweneth could feel that at least part of his anger was still directed at her.

"What are we to do, monsieur?"

"I don't rightly know, missy. There be a multitude o' ailments that plague men on the seas. We can work to bring down the fever but—" His voice trailed off, and Gweneth knew his thoughts had turned to the worst.

Her own anger faded watching the concern deepen in the old sailor's expression. Here was one who thought a great deal of the captain. "Monsieur Daniel, the capitaine asked that no one else be told that he is ill."

"Rightly so," Daniel nodded. It were bad enough they'd had to take on women, but he didn't like to think on the possible trouble to come were the crew to know the captain was helplessly ill, not with the women aboard.

Seeing the older man's brow knitted in worry and spurred by her own concerns, Gweneth offered, "Perhaps no one need be told." She looked down at the captain. "I could care for him, if you would allow it. If, by morning, he is no worse, we can hope that he will recover with time, *n'est-ce pas?* Perhaps you might tell the others that the capitaine fancies his new lady so much that he . . ." She began but stopped, blushing full before Daniel's suddenly keen gaze.

Daniel gave her a sly wink. "I think I be knowin' how to put it to 'em. The cap'n's always had time for a pretty face and, to my way o' thinkin', the sight o' ye is more than enough answer to why he's abed. They will believe every word and curse his devilish good fortune."

Gweneth avoided his smile and made a great business of smoothing the folds from her skirt. "It is not so, monsieur. I am not . . . he has not— That is, what you say to the others, it is a lie," she said so softly Daniel barely heard her.

Daniel's brows rose skeptically, but he replied tactfully, "Well, I be known for me tall tales. They will listen to me and ask for more."

Gweneth frowned, her delicate brows drawn to a peak. If even this man did not believe her, who would? "I shall need clean linen for bandages and fresh water," she said finally. "Oh, and he will need broth and, perhaps, tea."

Daniel shook his head. "We have only coffee. The water's limited on account of rationin'. Cap'n's orders, and how am I gonna explain the need for broth? Only the bandages will raise no questions, for they all know ye cut him."

Gweneth sighed and said, "*Alors*, with some salt and biscuits I could make broth from whatever you bring at mealtime. It will taste horrid, but the nourishment will be there. *Eh bien*, it is the best I can manage."

Daniel smiled at the girl with new respect that she should go to such trouble for a man she nearly killed a few hours before. And here she was showing positively masculine reasoning in an effort to uncoil their problem. Women were uncommon strange creatures, to be sure. "Aye, missy, whatever ye say. Still and all," and with a sidelong look at the captain, "it seems a shame to change his dressin'. I kinda like the cap'n all trussed up in pink."

Gweneth looked down at the demolished petticoat strapping the broad chest. "Do you think he would truly hate it, monsieur?" she asked, her face brightened by the first smile Daniel had ever seen there.

"Aye, madder than hell if he knew. Wrapped up neater than a bloomin' present, that's what!" Gweneth giggled and Daniel laughed with her.

Well, well, he thought, she had a sense of humor too. Full of surprises was this young girl. Could it be the cap'n had bitten off more than he could comfortably chew? Daniel wondered, finding himself casting an appreciative eye where her gown gaped away from her shoulders as she bent to replace the cloth on the captain's brow. Too bad the cap'n was abed alone.

"Monsieur Daniel, is your capitaine truly the scoundrel he has shown himself to be thus far?" Gweneth questioned, her smile now gone. "The man I sent for you said—" And she paused, feeling the warm rush of blood to her neck and cheeks. No, she had to know. "He said that your capitaine had done such terrible things."

"Whatever Gibson said be a pack o' lies," Daniel announced loudly. "The rascal's a—well, he was more than unhappy with the cap'n's orders that the other women be let alone, seein' as how he took ye for himself," Daniel replied, but his own color stained his finely wrinkled cheeks as he met Gweneth's inquiring look. Hell, why should he care if the girl's sensibilities were trod on? She had tried to kill Cap'n Bertrand and, wounded or no, there was no missin' that look in the cap'n's eye when he carried her limp form into his cabin. She deserved the punishment and if she were a maid, then she had no right to go strutting about the deck in breeches before his captain. Still Daniel could not help responding to her shame.

Gweneth considered Daniel's reply. "But you do not know—"

"No, missy. Whatever he said ain't so," Daniel objected. "I'd stake me life on it. Cap'n Raoul Bertrand is as fine a man as I have ever sailed with. A pure gentleman of . . ." Daniel hesitated as if he were about to say more but thought better of it.

Gweneth brushed the hair from her face and looked from the steward to the captain. Something in his face made her want to believe Daniel.

Daniel moved away and had reached the door before Gweneth remembered Renée. "My sister, where is she?"

"Cap'n Bertrand had the women bunked together in the forward cabin. They be safe and havin' their supper. No need to fret for yer little sis. Ye be wantin' me to give her a word, missy?"

"*Oui*, tell her—" Gweneth paused. She loved Renée but knew her for a loose tongue. It was better that she not know the truth, however much a comfort it would be to her. "Just say that you have seen me and that I have not been harmed. That is all, monsieur. Oh, and tell her not to leave her cabin for any reason." Renée might be foolish enough to venture out in search of her if not instructed otherwise. Thanks to Madame Bourgeax, Renée would not think of disobeying her elders.

Daniel nodded and withdrew after a last glance at his captain. He could do no better than the girl, and he liked to think the cap'n would rather be cosseted by her than any old stubble-faced sea salt.

CHAPTER THREE

Evening passed very slowly into night while the captain stirred restlessly from time to time but never roused himself to consciousness. Gweneth placed a chair by the bunk and worked steadily to reduce the fever by gently dabbing the moist cloth on his cheeks and brow, then stroking his chest with slow, smooth motions. The feel of a man's hard body was a new experience for her but, at least, he was no longer a total stranger.

Captain Raoul Bertrand. How strange it was that this Englishman should have a French name. His looks were not Gallic nor was there any trace in his English speech that French was his native tongue, though he spoke her language well. So well, in fact, that she hardly realized till now that nearly all their conversations had been in her tongue. Intriguing questions of every sort occupied Gweneth's fertile mind as she nursed her patient until the brass lantern nearby flickered unsteadily. Sprouting a curling plume of smoke, it swung rhythmically to the ship's wambling.

Much later, when Gweneth momentarily dozed, a finger touched her hand where it lay slung over the armrest. The gesture brought her fully alert, for someone had spoken.

"Marianne? Is it you, Marianne?" the captain whispered once again with incredible sweetness as his fingers closed over her wrist.

"Monsieur?" Gweneth called doubtfully and leaned near. His laughter was gentle and joyous as he struggled to sit. "Non, non, you must not. You are ill," Gweneth said, rising to her feet to push him back.

Raoul's arms came up at once, his hands settling firmly about her waist. "Marianne, you did not leave me." There was a wistfulness in that phrase that made Gweneth frown at his fevered countenance with trembling lips.

"I am Gweneth, Capitaine," she replied and, catching up the cloth, lay it on his febrile brow. But he reached up to remove it. "Use your hands, Marianne. I long for the tender caress of your delicate hand." He took her hands in his, rubbing them on either cheek. "Ah yes, they are soft and cool."

Gweneth slipped her hands free, somewhat embarrassed by his affection, and put the cloth back to his brow. "Please, Capitaine, let me use the cloth. You are so feverish."

"Not feverish, my darling," he sighed, "but on fire for you, and only your sweet kisses can quench the flame."

Gweneth compressed her lips in annoyance. He thought her some other woman, a mistress perhaps? "My sweet, just a single kiss." His tender pleading disturbed her, for she had not thought him the sort to beg for favors, but she continued to bathe his face without reply.

"Marianne, it has been so long. Do you not love your husband any longer?" he asked poutingly.

Gweneth's eyes grew round, and she pulled back from the hands seeking to fondle her. "Your wife?"

"Marianne, please come back!" he cried, the ache so plain in his hoarse voice that she stepped forward without thinking. "Sweet one," he whispered and took her hands in his, bringing them to his lips and covering them with fervent kisses.

"Capitaine, I am not your wife. Capitaine, no," Gweneth objected as he drew her closer. "You are delirious from your wound," she said and touched his dressing. "See, you are injured. Please lie still."

Raoul stared at her, momentarily confused. "Are you but a dream? Am I dying?" he asked slowly.

Gweneth ran a finger along his rough cheek and smiled. "Capitaine, you are ill, but that is all. I am real. You shall not die, you must not. You are safe with me, I promise you."

Raoul sighed and blinked the fresh sweat from his eyes. "Ah, Marianne, tell me that you love me still. I can die in peace with your tender words of love in my thoughts." His fingers clutched her shoulders with such intensity that Gweneth flinched. What should she do? He was addled with fever and believed her to be his wife. Poor woman, Gweneth thought absently, did she know how casually he filled his bed when at sea? Still he appeared to harbor sincere feelings for his Marianne and so, likely, would she.

"Darling, a word, a single line of affection that I might hold in my heart for all time," Raoul begged and pulled Gweneth down on the bed across him. As his bearded cheek brushed hers, her lips parted to touch the scalding skin by his ear. "Your Marianne loves you, I am certain," she whispered unsteadily and found that tears filled her eyes.

Raoul cupped her face between his broad hands and studied it with mistrustful eyes. "Who are you?" he asked suddenly.

Gweneth covered his hands with hers and squeezed them impulsively. "I am whoever you believe me to be, Capitaine."

"And you do love me? You do?" he asked in fierce urgency.

"I love you."

The words stumbled out over her pale lips in a breathless whisper of a lie.

"You will not leave me again?" His hands convulsed beneath hers.

"Non, I will not leave you. I swear it," Gweneth answered in a stronger voice. "When you awaken, I shall be here. Now rest, my Capitaine." She brushed his

SILKS AND SABERS 45

lids closed with her fingertips, and he smiled dreamily, releasing her as he fell into a peaceful sleep.

Gweneth sat down wearily and pressed a palm against her lips to stop their quivering. He was so desperate, did he know that he would die? Gweneth shook her head sharply and gulped back the stinging tears. Was it wrong to lie to him? It was such a small thing, and yet it rocked her to her very soul; she had never said those words to a man, and now they were given to a stranger on behalf of his wife.

"I am merely tired. I must stop this foolishness," she said to herself and stripped the moisture from her face with the back of a hand. She would pull the captain through his illness, if that were possible, and send him home to his wife and, perhaps, children.

Raoul dreamed now. It seemed he burned alive. He had once seen that happen in the islands to a woman the people suspected of witchcraft. He could not save her single-handedly and had turned away in disgust and revulsion while the agonizing screams of that wretched soul pierced his heart and mind. For weeks afterward he had awakened in an icy sweat with her wails rending the pattern of his dreams. Now it was he who writhed in the blaze.

"I would have saved her if it had been possible," he cried out to the nightmare repeating itself again and again. The images swirled and faded, to be replaced by another.

Marianne now stood above him, her dark eyes filled with hurt and fear. "You left me with child, Raoul. You promised never to sail again, you promised!" she accused.

Raoul moaned and reached for his beautiful, delicate wife, big with child. "Marianne, why did you not tell me? Is our child a boy or girl?" He longed to touch the firmly swollen belly, but Marianne twisted from his embrace. "Our child is dead," she sobbed. "Just as I am dead." One arm came up with a finger pointing in blame. "You let me die. You let us both die!"

"No, Marianne, I did not kill you," Raoul whimpered and caught at the cold slender hand to lay it to his heart. "I loved you!" But the shadow failed and vanished.

A cold shower bathed his face and arms. "Quietly, Capitaine, quietly." Was it Marianne? Yes, she would quench the flames, for she loved him.

"It be a bad omen, Cap'n, the bloody sunrise. We sail into a gale for certain, sir," cried Daniel as new visions pressed in on Raoul's bewildered wits. "My God, how dark grows the sky!" he shouted in reply. "We sail into the bowels of hell!"

The sea swelled before him, rising like an angry, gleaming serpent, and curled over the bow of his ship, drenching him with its frigid waters until his mind and torso quailed before the lash of the salty whip. "It is so cold, Marianne. I am so cold!"

Gweneth stroked the captain as he tossed about, his words jumbled and senseless. "Monsieur, you must lie still. Remember your shoulder," she cautioned, but his flailings increased until Gweneth lay full across his chest in an effort to keep him from totally destroying the bandage, which oozed with renewed bleeding. Her hair fell in tangled masses over his face and hers, blinding her as she groped for his arms.

Raoul muttered a curse and shoved the body grappling with his away. He groaned with pain as a spasm shook him and then fell silent. Gweneth, who had been thrown to her knees by the bed, rose and felt frantically for a pulse. The captain's heart still beat, but both he and the bedding were soaked with sweat and blood and, even as she stared helplessly, he began to shiver under her hands.

She needed help, but there was none to be had. Daniel had returned earlier with fresh linen but suggested that it would be better for all if he did not come again until morning—"Seein' as how the cap'n was so well entertained," as he put it.

To her increasing horror the shivering became a series of violent, involuntary spasms; the captain's breath sucked in with a trembling hiss. "The cold, so cold," he stuttered between chattering teeth.

Gweneth ran to the trunk and returned with two wool blankets. As she leaned over to tuck the edge of one under him, the captain spoke. "Please stop the cold."

"I am trying, monsieur. The blankets will warm you," Gweneth assured him.

"Come a little closer," he whispered. "You are so warm and soft. Share your warmth with me for a little while." His injured arm came up and, locking it with his other behind her, he pulled her down onto his chest. Gweneth gave in to his embrace lest she hurt him.

"Capitaine, the blankets will warm you, and I shall stoke the fire for you," she promised gently, but Raoul could not hear her and his fingers were busy at the back of her gown. "Non, non, Capitaine," she protested and raised up but, to her great surprise, the bodice of her gown came loose from her shoulders, and he pulled it down to her waist.

Gweneth snatched at it, but the captain smiled with relish and held it fast. In the glimmering depths of his eyes he saw the figure of his wife. "Ah, Marianne, you are more beautiful than I remember. A woman grown now, no longer a child. Let me drink my fill of your beauty," he murmured and reached out for the lush roundness of one breast.

"Monsieur!" Gweneth cried and would have backed away had she not been trapped by her gown. The captain's hand traced the circle of her silky firmness, then cupped it with a gentle squeeze. Truly alarmed, Gweneth squealed and grabbed at his hands.

Raoul's brow puckered in displeasure. "Come, my sweet. You were ever the reluctant wife." His voice grew coarse and husky. "Come and share your delicious favors." His grip fastened on her waist and he lifted her toward him.

Gweneth could not break his hold, but a loud knock on the door sent her spinning within his grasp. "Who is there?" she called, hoping for Daniel's answer.

"It be Peckcum," came the rumbling reply, gruff and discourteous.

"Away with you, mate. Can you not tell when a man is engaged?" was the unexpected rejoinder from Captain Bertrand himself.

Gweneth turned to look into the momentarily sane gaze of Raoul. "Do not touch me! Please let me go!" she cried quickly for the sake of the man beyond the door.

"Aye, aye, Cap'n. May you make port safely through the storm," Peckcum hailed and added a rude remark about the luck of some men. His laughter made Gweneth's skin crawl, but at least it was punctuated by the clomp of bootsteps as he departed.

Alone now, Raoul jerked the young woman in his arms back to face him. "Where did Daniel find you? You are not the sort I usually bed." Gweneth jumped at his words. He was not as aware of the circumstances as she had thought.

"I am Gweneth, Capitaine," she replied in her own language.

"A French wench," he said approvingly. "Very well, *ma belle,* come here and—" But the violent shuddering began again, and he fell silent, hugging his aching shoulder. "You are a wicked girl. You cause me such pain," he rasped and, turning away, his lids fluttered closed.

Gweneth pulled her dress up and fumbled with some of the fastenings.

Turning to the blankets which had fallen to one side, she picked them up and began stripping the old bedding with no other thought than that the captain must be dried and comforted. The events of the last moments might never have occurred. She worked and pushed until she had removed the dirty sheets stained with blood.

The captain moaned unintelligibly, lost in his dreams, and after some consideration Gweneth thought it best not to disturb his bandage. His breeches were another matter. They were soaked with sweat and clung to his hips and thighs, leaving nearly nothing to her speculation. They must be terribly uncomfortable, and he would be warmer without them, Gweneth told herself. And, having thrown the first of the blankets over him, she reached under it to loosen his waistband.

What seemed a simple job was not. She had not reckoned with his weight, and it took several minutes of very undignified tugging to peel the tight, skin-hugging material from under his hips and over his thighs. The blanket slipped down more than once, and Gweneth's face was a mortified shade of red by the time she jerked the breeches free of his feet, but the captain never gave any sign that he was conscious of her actions.

It was beyond her how a man ever found his way out of such a garment in a hurry, and she had to surpress the urge to laugh aloud when she finally claimed her trophy. The leather breeches could easily have been his hide, she reflected as her eyes strayed back to the captain. He was strongly and handsomely made, she conceded, not unlike some wild beast with his rich brown mane and tawny pelt. "Shameless, shameless," a voice in her head scolded, recalling the words of love he had spoken to his wife, and Gweneth dropped the garment as if it had bitten her.

The soothing lap of the waves against the ship's hull and the even roll of the cabin were her only companions in those next hours as she worked to keep the fire blazing in the grate. But it was woefully inadequate to chase away the shivery drafts in the small cabin, and even Gweneth's body stiffened with the cold.

Grown too weary to think properly, Gweneth finally gave up that task and sat down. The captain slept, but his body jerked beneath the covers, swept by an icy chill from within. Gweneth touched the haggard face which now found no repose in sleep. He turned and mumbled into her hand, but the only word audible was "cold."

Gweneth sighed and made her decision. The fastenings came loose quickly, and she drew the gown over her head to replace it with the captain's nightshirt from the chest. Then she turned back to the bed and, bending low, whispered in the captain's ear as she rolled back the covers, "Can you move a little, Capitaine? I wish to join you." The captain's head moved against the pillow. "Move, mon Capitaine, just a little," she encouraged and his eyes opened.

"Mother?" he questioned drowsily.

"Hardly a mother, monsieur," she replied with a chuckle and put a hand under his shoulder to urge him over. His brows lifted in wonder. "Do I know you?" he asked softly.

"Non, Capitaine, I think you do not," she said and slipped down under the blankets beside him.

His arms opened in welcome and pulled her near. "You are warm, so very warm." Gweneth felt him move firmly against her and remembered too late that he was naked. She shivered at the touch of his skin, his thigh pressing insistently along the length of hers, but he merely placed a kiss on her brow and seemed content to hold her to him. Soon his shivering abated.

Gweneth relaxed slowly and let her head rest on his shoulder, finding that she could sleep in spite of his disturbing nearness. And as she drifted off, from somewhere there came gentle laughter. *"C'est très bon, ma belle."*

"Cap'n, you up?" The voice was familiar, and Gweneth's heart sank as she scrambled from the bed and hurriedly pulled the covers over the captain. The knock was repeated, and the voice came more insistently. "Cap'n? Peckcum to see you, sir."

Gweneth brushed her loose hair back and looked down at her attire. She must not let the man inside, and yet she dared not step out of the room in this condition. At the third pounding the captain stirred with a feeble moan and, afraid that he would awaken, Gweneth rushed to the entrance. "*Oui*, what do you require?" she asked through the door.

"It be the cap'n I am to speak with," Peckcum replied.

"Your capitaine is asleep. Come back later," she urged and stealthily fingered the reassuring bolt.

"What are you about, wench? Open this door afore I break it in. Cap'n? You there, Cap'n?" Peckcum bellowed.

"Silence, you fool!" Gweneth yelled back without thinking.

"Eh? What say you?"

Gweneth bit her lip and hugged her arms to herself to fend off the cold penetrating the thin gown.

"The capitaine sleeps," she repeated quietly and then added, "Please, monsieur, let him rest. He has been awake most of the night. Let him be."

"How's that?" Peckcum asked, then cleared his throat. "Aye, I kin your meanin', but what of me orders for the day?" The gruff tone was now buoyed by high spirits. Not a man Jack among them could resist enjoying her humiliation, Gweneth noted glumly.

"Can you not see to this ship for a day without orders from your precious capitaine?" Gweneth retorted. Let them think she despised their leader and yet feared him, both of which were probably true, she thought absently, if there were but time to put her exact feelings into focus. His high-handed tactics had cost her her reputation, if not her virginity, and she was bound to be the source of jest and rude remarks for the remainder of the voyage because of him.

"O'course, I run a smart ship. When it comes to sailing, few men be me equal, but we sail for Cap'n Bertrand's pleasure and mind his orders. I'm a mind to know if he still means to put in at the Indies."

"Which Indies, monsieur?" Gweneth held her breath.

"The West Indies, if it be your business. St. Thomas or Antigua, most likely."

"Are you certain?" Gweneth asked quickly, for it seemed too good to be true.

"Lookee here, mam'zelle. You mind me words to the cap'n and be addressin' your questions to him though, at the sight o' you, he is liable to entertain other ideas." In the silence that followed, Gweneth heard him retreat. Daniel had done a good job. They treated her like a mistress.

Gweneth lifted her chin haughtily and turned her back, thinking it much too early for such problems. She raced back to the bunk, intending to snuggle down into that delicious warmth again until a sweep of the blankets revealed the captain's state of undress. The covers flew back up in a hurry, and Gweneth gingerly crept away, her enthusiasm for the venture squelched.

"At least you live, mon Capitaine." He had not regained consciousness during the night, but there had been no more delirium. Gweneth turned from the bed and stared beyond the cabin.

The view from the porthole was of a blue-gray dawn, all difference between sky and ocean absorbed in the leaden sea mist. Gweneth stirred uncomfortably as the crisp sea breeze wafted under the door and curled in chilly eddies about her bare toes. She tucked the folds of the nightshirt protectively close, but it provided little comfort as there was a clammy streak from shoulder to hem along the side that had touched the captain during the night, his fever warming her skin to the point of perspiration. Guiltily Gweneth plucked the clinging fabric from her body, remembering how brazenly she had slept in his embrace, well-contented by that heat.

Having pulled a blanket from the bed and wrapped it around her, Gweneth shoved the captain's chair before the pot-bellied stove and sat down to dry herself. She had slept a precious few hours. But after months of troubled days and tortured nights, those hours were the most peaceful she had known. She bent her knees and tucked her feet under the edge of the bedding, thinking it ironic that she should lay so comfortably in the arms of her enemy. But, perhaps, that was the answer. In all the three years before she had never known the faces of her enemies.

"*Mais non*, mademoiselle, you are simply a wanton," Gweneth decided in amusement as she nodded off.

"Cap'n Bertrand, it be Daniel with breakfast for ye and the young miss."

It was well into morning, the cabin awash with sunlight, and the chill was fast evaporating. Gweneth yawned with the barest sigh and stretched her arms up over her head, every muscle stiff and cramped. Never again would she sleep curled up in a chair, she decided.

"Come along, Cap'n, and be a good fellow. Allow the little lady a bite to eat." Daniel's voice was a welcome sound, and Gweneth hurried over to let him enter.

The door swung wide upon his entrance, and the delicious aroma of hot food set Gweneth's stomach churning in anticipation, for it had been two days since she had eaten a full meal.

"Oh, Monsieur Daniel, *c'est delicieux!*" she cried in rapture only to be jolted by the expression on Daniel's face when she looked up from the tray.

Daniel's poorly disciplined features betrayed his thoughts at the sight of the girl standing before him dressed in the captain's bedclothes. His glance shifted to the bunk. The captain didn't look to be the cause of her undressed state but, before he could think of a thing to say, Gweneth scurried away and snatched up the blanket, wrapping herself in it.

"Pardon, monsieur. It is most unseemly, I fear, but it was such a long night and then Peckcum came before daylight and then . . ." Her words fell over themselves in explanation.

"It be aright, missy," Daniel assured her matter-of-factly. "I reckon I know what a young girl looks like. Ye be close to the age of me eldest daughter." He grinned and set out a plate.

"Have you many children, monsieur?" Gweneth questioned, glad for the change of topic.

"Me name's Daniel, missy. Aye, I've sired a fine brood, three sons and three daughters. Me eldest boy is aboard," Daniel said proudly.

"How lucky you are, Daniel," Gweneth replied wistfully and placed herself before the empty plate. "I have—had three older brothers."

"That so? Then what ye young ladies be doin' floatin' about alone on the sea?"

The story poured out of Gweneth easily in the beginning, but the last words betrayed a tightness in her throat. "And so there is only Renée and myself. All is lost . . . and for nothing . . . a few barrels of cargo delivered into the grasping hands of English pirates."

This was madness. Here she sat discussing her brother's death with one of the men responsible, she realized too late. Well, at least he was one of the crew, for Gweneth could not imagine Daniel harming anyone for a few pieces of gold. No, not he. But the captain? Yes, she could believe him capable of destroying anything which stood between him and that which he desired.

"Well now, missy, don't be thinkin' on such things if they upset ye," Daniel said gruffly at the sight of her shining eyes. "English? Do ye say Englishmen attacked yer vessel?" he questioned suddenly.

"*Oui*, Daniel. I heard your voices carrying over the

water. You see, I have known all along," Gweneth said frankly. "There was no doubt in my mind from the beginning."

Daniel let his compassionate heart win out over his loyalty as he thought it no wonder the poor child had set out to do to death for the captain. He had not been topside when the women were first brought aboard, and by the time he saw them, the captain was at drawn swords with this girl. He wondered now if the captain was aware of the girl's beliefs or if he had even sought out an explanation.

"Missy," he said softly. "We didn't scuttle yer ship, if that is what ye be thinkin'. Cap'n Bertrand be an honest man who don't hold with piracy."

"Non, he would only seek to force himself on helpless women," Gweneth returned angrily and took a deliberately vicious bite of a biscuit. If the captain were innocent of one crime, there were many others to be laid at his doorstep since boarding this ship, she reminded herself.

Daniel cast a sympathetic eye her way, having the experience of many years under his belt to recognize that her defiant tone hid fear. And yet, in spite of her malice, she had taken care of the captain. A truly gallant spirit, had this one.

"Ye eat yer fill, missy, and I'll be a seein' to the cap'n awhile."

Gweneth dug in heartily, finding herself ravenous. Madame Bourgeax's exclamations of disapproval aside, Gweneth filled her plate to overflowing and tucked a hefty forkful into her mouth. Fully engrossed, she looked up only when Daniel cleared his throat. Her gaze shifted sideways to see him holding the pair of breeches aloft, and she swallowed carefully on a dry crumb, then reached quickly for the mug of coffee, avoiding his inquisitive look.

Daniel shook his head and chuckled. He would dearly love to know just what had transpired during the night. He bent over the captain and discovered with satisfaction that, whatever had happened, the French girl had done right by him. Out of tact he refrained from inquiring as to the reason for Cap'n Bertrand's nudity but found a pair of loose drawstring trousers with which to cover him.

Raoul awakened to the discomfort of callused hands dressing his wound. "Daniel?" he asked groggily.

"Aye, Cap'n. 'Tis fair kind to hear yer voice. Just ye lie quiet till I fetch ye a bit of coffee."

Raoul's features convulsed in rejection. "No. Some brandy, Daniel. Just brandy."

"That is not what he needs," Gweneth objected from the table, having overheard the captain's mumblings. "He must have something more substantial than spirits." And she rose. Within minutes she had prepared a simmering broth of dried beef from the breakfast tray, adding bits of bread and potato.

Daniel propped the captain's head in his lap while Gweneth spooned the gruel into their patient. His dark blue eyes regarded her wondrously, but he said nothing and accepted the food at her gentle urging. When he no longer had the strength to swallow, Daniel lowered him carefully to the bed and covered him. Soon the captain slept.

"A fair mornin's work, mam'zelle. I am much obliged. Had I been alone, I'd have gotten nothin' more down him than a shot o' whiskey. The cap'n be the most bullheaded man ever born when he's angry or ailin'." Daniel grinned and patted Raoul's inert arm.

"It is a good thing I am with you," Gweneth answered then, and realizing the irony of that statement, she smiled wryly.

"Now, don't ye go bein' sorry for yerself. I kin how it was for ye, thinkin' we done yer brother in. Still ye done more than many a one would. Seein' as how it was between ye and the cap'n, mebbe he had it comin'."

"Daniel, do you know the capitaine's wife?"

Gweneth asked, for thoughts of the woman had been circling in her mind all night.

"Wife?" yelped Daniel, his eyes flaring in brief astonishment. "The cap'n ain't married."

"But this Marianne he spoke of—"

"Ye best be forgettin' whatever ye heard, missy. That's me advice to ye," Daniel cautioned and gave his shaggy head a vigorous wag. "A man oft times talks out o' his head in a fever." The cap'n would have his hide if he were to find out that they had discussed Marianne. "The cap'n won't take kindly to yer repeatin' what ye heard."

Gweneth pursed her lips in annoyance, realizing that she would learn nothing from Daniel. "Whatever you say, Daniel. *Eh bien*, it was mere curiosity, nothing more. Poor woman, she really did marry a rogue." But Daniel did not rise to the bait and merely grinned. It did occur to him, though, to speculate if the mam'zelle's interest were as general as she claimed.

"Another matter, Daniel. Should the capitaine's tremors return, is there nothing I can do for him? The stove does not warm him sufficiently and the blankets do no good, even though I warm them before the fire."

"Tremors, did ye say?" Daniel stroked his chin. " 'Tis the miasma which ails him then," he announced in conviction. "We lost more than a few men last voyage. 'Tis why some o' the crew be new to us. That's what's been comin' on him for days, only he's too stiff-necked to admit it. I have such spells meself when me ague acts up. 'Tis but one sure cure for the shivers, but I don't rightly see as how we can—I mean, me missus, she always has a remedy for it. O' course, I don't expect, seein' as how ye be a gently bred lady, that ye might see yer way clear to . . ." A short dry cough interrupted his rambling.

Gweneth shook her head. "You make no sense, Daniel. Simply tell me what must be done."

Daniel scratched behind one ear and hitched a thumb through a belt loop while studying the floor. "There be nothin' to warm a body like the heat from another," he ventured. "I'd do it meself," he added, "only the boys would become a mite suspicious if I stayed the night here. They allow the cap'n his head in these matters, but if they was to think—well, I ain't rightly dead yet."

"Oh," Gweneth said in a tiny voice. "You are right, of course. It is not so very much you ask, and I risk nothing I have not been near forfeiting all along." Gweneth looked quickly away. "Besides, I did the same last night. I do not suppose that the capitaine has any memory of it. In that case, it does not signify."

"Aye, missy. It does seem so. The cap'n be owin' ye a great deal, and I aim to see to it that he knows all ye done."

Gweneth's gaze swung back to Daniel's leathered old face. "Oh no! I do not want the capitaine to know anything of this." She raised her hands expressively. "I wish only to forget all that has occurred. Let him think whatever he wishes. Promise me that you will say nothing of my willingness to aid him."

"Whatever ye say, miss. I'll be a leavin' ye for now." Daniel nodded and left, his amusement barely contained behind his lips. "Yes sir, the cap'n has quite a surprise in store when he finally does awaken," he chuckled to himself.

CHAPTER FOUR

On the morning of the sixth day after the duel Raoul awakened to a tropical sun which poured through the uncovered portholes and pooled in huge gold coins on the floor. He breathed deeply of the salt air but could not recall putting out to sea. Was he still in port? No, the gentle swell and low of his bed could only be the roll of the sea. What's more, he was not alone, a head lay on his shoulder and his arm encircled a comfortable softness.

Raoul squinted against the bright light which stabbed his sensitive eyes, and his stomach turned over as the ship dipped sharply. Fighting the nausea took all his determination. Damn, that the captain should become seasick like a new seaman, and here with a wench beside him! The sensation passed slowly, and he was dimly aware of pain in his chest and head.

Never, after any night's revelry, had he fared this badly from the effects of women and drink. It must truly have been an uncommon spree to have left him so sickly. He felt as limp as a ragged edge of sail in a calm.

Raoul peered down at the half-hidden features of his bedmate. Cinnamon tresses spilled over his arm and onto the bed and below her smooth brow the tip of a small straight nose was visible. The mouth was full and naturally blushed, but nothing about her was familiar save the faint scent of her perfume. Strange, the fragrance was an expensive Spanish concoction, not the sort of luxury to be indulged in by most street women. Perhaps he had given it to her himself. For services rendered, he thought and chuckled.

Raoul raised his head for a better look. One slender hand rested lightly upon his chest. This was no ordinary barmaid, the hand was too soft and her features too refined. Who was she?

"Ugh!" Raoul groaned and fell back listlessly on the bed.

Gweneth moved into the space now between them, moaning in sleepy protest at his defection, but the rejoining masculine laughter jarred her awake. The captain's arm held her fast, but it relaxed as she pushed up on an elbow, and he watched in bemused silence while she scrambled out of bed and stood. The nightshirt reached to her knees, but her slim legs and trim ankles received his full consideration.

"And who might you be, my sweet?" Raoul asked thickly, and a lopsided smile drew up one corner of his mouth and nestled in a stiff patch of whiskers.

"Capitaine Bertrand?" Gweneth replied with a frown. "How are you?" A quick hand to his cheek told her that his fever had broken at last.

"Do you always exact such a considerable toll when a man beds you?" Raoul questioned of the lovely girl with weary-worn smudges beneath the greenest eyes he'd ever seen. She seemed the worse for wear than he in her crumpled gown and tangled masses of hair falling to her waist.

"You have been ill, Capitaine. Do you remember nothing? You were wounded also. You must be aware of the pain in your shoulder. That is the result." Gweneth answered. "Non, non, do not try to sit," she admonished. "You have been sick with fever for six days and have lost a good deal of blood besides. You must be quiet until your strength returns. I will heat something for you to eat," she said and turned away.

Raoul lay back and watched as she padded about his cabin in bare feet, her natural grace and beauty fascination enough for now. He noted that she wore nothing beneath the gown and remembered with satisfaction that she had slept cozily within his arms the night long.

But his wound. Raoul put a hand to the bandage covering his left shoulder. He could not remember how that had come about. Had he fought some man for the girl?

The dull pain in his head grew steadily worse with the effort of thought, and Raoul soon gave up the exercise. For whatever reason, he was alone with a most fetching young woman, and he wanted nothing more than to coax her back to his side. In spite of his aches he would dearly love to press her to him and feel the yielding of her tender body to his.

Gweneth set the kettle on the stove for coffee as Daniel had shown her. If the captain were truly recovered, there were new problems to be faced. She had come to accept his home as her own, using whatever she wished; his comb and brush, his mirror, even the cake of gardenia-scented soap wrapped in tissue and tucked into a corner of his trunk. She had read his books and even done a bit of mending, anything to fend off the loneliness while the captain lay racked with fever and chills. Perhaps it was better to pretend that there was nothing unusual in her presence, Gweneth decided, and poured a fresh cup of water for her patient.

"Slowly, Capitaine, or it may make you ill," Gweneth cautioned as she braced his head with one arm and held the cup for him. Raoul wrapped an arm around her waist for support and drank thirstily. She was lowering him back to the pillow when he turned quickly and brushed a kiss over the tip of the breast crushed to his cheek.

Gweneth dropped his head, moving back, and Raoul cursed the sickening thud as he hit the pillow. "Either you behave, monsieur, or I shall leave you to your own devices. I see your illness has done nothing for your manners, and I will not be mauled by you. Keep your favors for someone else. I shall have none of them. *Comprenez-vous?*" Gweneth's voice delivered the rebuke in clear, crisp French, but her eyes flashed in bright anger.

Raoul stared at her as the sting of her words recalled something to memory. "You are the one who cut me!" he cried in realization and pushed up on one elbow. "Why you ungrateful little wretch! I saved you from becoming shark bait, and you repay me with this," he continued and thumped the dressing. "You shall pay for this, mademoiselle, that I promise you!" he thundered.

"I have paid," Gweneth answered softly and, turning away, went to retrieve the boiling kettle. Her lower lip trembled now that she was shielded from his arrogant gaze. He would never understand to what degree she had paid and, for her safety, it was better that he not know exactly how. It was ridiculous to have hoped that his attitude toward her might have changed. Anger and resentment gnawed at her as she prepared the steaming brew. She would never forgive him. Never!

Raoul sat up groggily and braced himself against the wall. Remembrances clarified: the sighting of the castaways, the salvage, and this young thing who thought she was defending—what? She was a fair hand with a blade but not stout of heart, for she had fainted at the sight of blood, and he had brought her here to be put to bed. He could recall now undressing her and then the feel of her under tentative kisses, but the rest was lost in the raging of his fever.

Raoul swore softly and rubbed his bearded chin. To recall so little of what he had paid so dearly to achieve, it was as if the fates sought retribution for his mishandling of the deed.

Gweneth brought a cup of coffee to the bedside and cautiously handed it to the captain with a warning glare. Raoul took it, running his palm over the back of her hand before closing his fingers about the mug. He blew across the smoking surface and took a long swig. The swallow would not go down, and he choked, spewing the liquid back into the cup. "Mercy, this is the worst coffee I've ever tasted," he groaned and handed it back to her. "Would you poison me, mademoiselle?"

"That is a shame," Gweneth replied, not the least bit regretful that she had botched the brew. "I suppose I did not actually hear every word of Daniel's instructions. Me, I like cocoa." She finished with a shrug and a barely governed smile of amusement.

". . . damn if I don't!" shouted the unpleasant voice that Gweneth had given daily battle through the door. "Wench or no, there is a ship to be run, and the cap'n's needed!" The knock was of such an explosive nature that even Raoul started.

"Aye, man, speak up," Raoul called in full commanding tones.

"It be Peckcum, sir," the first mate mumbled in something close to surprise. "Will you be seein' me today?"

"But of course. For God's sake, woman, let the man through," Raoul ordered, but Gweneth stood her ground. The captain did not look nearly as able as he sounded.

The fractional silence was shattered by a girl's cry and, in an instant, Gweneth sprang for the door, dashed the bolt, and pushed past the bulky form of the disgruntled first mate, trailing her blanket up the stairs. She had recognized that voice and knew only that Renée was in danger.

A knot of seamen had gathered on the main deck, but they broke apart as Gweneth advanced on them to reveal Renée's slight frame held in forcible restraint by the one Gweneth knew as Gibson. His grimy hands clutched at Renée's body, and she screamed again as his slack lips descended upon her exposed throat.

Gweneth stopped short, oblivious to the curious

stares of those about her, and grabbed up the first likely looking weapon, the mop from a pail nearby. Why oh why had she not thought to arm herself before now, asked one part of her while another whispered, "Too many, Gweneth. There are many too many this time."

Fear trickled through her veins in agreement, but she did not act on it. Swinging the mop up like a mace, she landed it squarely across Gibson's back with a smart whack. "Take your filthy hands from my sister this instant," she cried and leveled a look of pure malice at the sailor who moved toward her.

"Gweneth! No one would let me pass. I thought you dead!" Renée cried in near hysteria.

Gibson spat and cursed, rubbing the place on his neck that had born the attack with one hand, the other hand firmly gripping the girl. He swung round to face his assailant and came face to face with blazing green eyes and a riotous tumble of chestnut hair partially veiling a blanket and nightshirt. A slow sneer spread over his repulsive features as he said, "Well, well, if it ain't the cap'n's baggage and fresh from the night's work, looks like. I been awaitin' for ye, but I'm a mind now to seek me ease with another of ye fancy wenches. One be as good as another, most times."

Gibson lifted Renée off the deck in one motion and heaved her slight frame over his shoulder. Gweneth's breath came in one long gasp of alarm as she drew back to swing again, but Renée struggled with her captor like a wildcat, pummeling his back with her tiny fists and thrashing about with her feet. Gweneth held back the next blow lest it strike her sister.

Gibson laughed at Renée's useless efforts and turned to move away. In desperate calculation Gweneth swung low, the wooden handle snapping sharply in two over Gibson's shins. Taken unexpectedly, he howled in pain and dumped his burden on the deck.

"Let her be or I'll see to it the capitaine has you

flogged," Gweneth threatened but did not try to force her way past Gibson when he stepped before Renée who sat weeping on the boards.

Gibson snickered and advanced a step. "Will ye now? And just how is it to come about?" Gibson turned to the men close by. "Any o' ye seen the cap'n once he shut himself up with the whore? I'm a mind the girlie done for him," he continued when the others shook their heads. "She cut him, ye all saw it. Maybe he was worse off than we figured. Peckcum ain't even talked to the cap'n. And there ain't a man among ye who ain't itchin' for a taste o' these women. I say we take what we want, for there be none to stop us," he shouted as the crew mumbled among themselves in assent, ogling the girls while the idea became desire.

Gweneth matched their gaze in unwavering defiance, though her heart doubled its already rapid pace. If they were to come after her, she might be able to make at least a few of them wish they had chosen other sport before they overpowered her, and she grasped the mop handle tightly between her spaced hands in warning. But a whimper from Renée struck a fatal blow to Gweneth's militant spirit. She could fight for herself but Renée . . . and Gweneth's thought sickened and died in misery.

"Go along, me hearties. 'Tis but a wench who defies ye," Gibson taunted and reached down to jerk Renée to her feet.

A scream of impotent fury broke from Gweneth's throat, and she flung herself at Gibson, grabbing him about the neck with both hands, but she was caught up in turn by a foul-breathed man who was squatting nearby. Gibson pulled free of Gweneth's strangling grip and gave her a stiff shove that sent her and the man holding her sprawling onto the deck.

Gweneth and the sailor struggled in the tangle of the blanket, but the seaman gained his footing first and, with the help of two others, forced her to her back while greedy fingers tore at the gown in search of the young flesh beneath.

"Merciful Mother of God, was I spared once only to be humiliated more horribly this time!" she wailed as she lay unable to prevent the many insulting hands from defiling her.

Other men gathered to join in, looking on in eager anticipation as the first man unbuttoned. None heard the shout, but all looked up in alarm as a shot rang out. There stood Captain Bertrand with a smoking pistol.

He came forward in the immediate silence and placed a booted foot in the man's back who crouched over Gweneth, sending him spread-eagled across the deck.

Tears of relief blurred her vision as Gweneth stared up into the face of her savior. He had dressed quickly and wore only his breeches and boots but, though his face was pale, his features were steeled in anger.

Raoul reached out his left hand to Gweneth, but she rose alone after gathering the blanket to shield herself. His attention switched to his crew.

"What is this, Gibson? Would you seek to disobey your captain's orders beneath his very eyes?" Raoul asked when, from the corner of his eye, he saw Gibson slink away.

Gibson spun around and grinned foolishly. "Aye, Cap'n, but here we are athinkin' ye come to some bad end. The boys and me been in sore need of female company and"—his smile grew bolder—"seein' how it was with ye and the girlie, well, ye'd be understandin'."

Raoul let the pistol hang loosely in his hand, and a thin smile straightened his mouth. "I fail to see how it is that you would disobey my order, whatever your personal discomfort."

His eyes shifted to the other members of his crew. "Are there any others of you so disposed to challenge my command?"

Not a single man replied, and Raoul's disdainful smile deepened as he glanced back at Gibson. "No one else has a quarrel." The smile hardened further. "I guaranteed the safety of these women, and yet you would seek to make a liar of me. I will not tolerate insubordination of any sort aboard this vessel. Take him below, and you there," Raoul said, indicating the man who once straddled Gweneth, "take that one in hand too. There will be full attendance on deck at dawn for a flogging." To Gibson he said, "You are free of my service at our first port of call, but if you so much as cross my shadow beforehand, I shall have you flayed alive. Now begone before I reconsider the leniency of my actions."

Raoul dismissed the men with a wave of his pistol and turned to the girl half hiding behind him. "Your servant, mademoiselle, and my apology," he said with a brief bow.

"Liar," Gweneth whispered darkly into his startled face. "Do not expect my thanks, for I fail to see the difference between you and them. What does it signify which man does the violating? The result is the same, *mais non?*" Her fright-widened eyes searched his briefly before she ran past him and embraced her sister. They spoke together in hushed phrases and then turned toward the far deck.

"I'll be damned!" Raoul grumbled irritably and tucked the pistol in his belt.

He strolled the deck in long quick strides which cost him greatly, but he realized the danger in letting any man think him less than fit. These seamen were new to him for the most part, and he never sailed comfortably with a strange crew.

Of all the miserable luck, he thought in annoyance, to be saddled with a green crew, a bout of ague, and now four exasperating women. If his luck held, there'd be a typhoon any minute. That speculation brought him up short to cast an appraising eye about the horizon. He gave orders for the securing of a slack sail and brought the ship round closer to the wind before going below to collapse in exhaustion on his bunk.

"Gweneth, please. It has been days, and still you will say nothing to us of what has happened to you. Are you ill? Did the capitaine hurt you terribly? Oh Gweneth, say something!" Renée pleaded and stamped an impatient foot before her silent sister.

Gweneth answered with a tolerant smile. There was nothing else to do. The truth was better hidden until they were free, and she could not see the point in fabricating lies to serve the imaginations of her fellow captives. Besides, she suspected the girl named Amy of more knowledge than she herself possessed of the amatory arts. It was she who had enhanced Renée's fears with such vivid descriptions that Gweneth was caused to cry halt when Renée began suggesting the possible cruelties to which she might have been subjected.

"Dearest sister, I say what I have said before. I am well. The capitaine did not harm me—" Her eyes flickered to the others. "No more than a little, and now it is over. I do not wish to think of it. Daniel says that we should be making port in a few weeks. We shall disembark, wherever it is, and find someone who can send word to Governor and Lady Dillingham."

"Mademoiselle Valois, you must make sure that this man is made to pay for his outrageous behavior," counseled Sarah. "What if you should be with child?" She blushed, saying softly, "*C'est possible*, mademoiselle. Your uncle is an influential man? Then he shall see to it that the capitaine makes an honest woman of you."

Gweneth's young jaw dropped. She had not considered her lost honor to be more than a private matter and that her uncle might, indeed, seek revenge. But the captain had not accomplished his intent, and it was better that the matter never arise.

"Non, non," Gweneth said slowly. "I am certain that I am not in that way." She jumped to her feet and paced the tiny space. If only she could be sure that no word would reach the captain, then she would confess all. "If it is as you have said, that my uncle would be forced to seek amends, then we simply won't tell him."

"*Mon Dieu*, Gweneth, do you know what you are saying?" Renée replied.

"*Oui, ma petite.* Do you think I would have my shame spread across the seven seas?" exclaimed Gweneth dramatically, rising to the tone of her story. "Please, you must swear that you will not breathe a single syllable to anyone about what has occurred." Her voice rose in such anguish that the women agreed quickly to do their mistress's bidding, for that is how Sarah and Amy perceived Gweneth.

"We have no money, no possessions, no home, and you contract the services of two lady's maids, Renée," Gweneth whispered in halfhearted disapproval when told on the first day of their reunion that her sister had engaged the two.

"Think of it in this light, Gweneth," Renée answered patiently. "They are unemployed. We have no chaperon, no decent clothing, nothing at all to give the impression of respectability to our situation. If we must move among strangers, would it not be of value to have some sign of gentility at our disposal? Who will doubt our position if we are accompanied by two attentive servants?" she asked brightly, obviously enjoying her own brand of logic.

"Ah, the hand of Madame Bourgeax," Gweneth murmured sagely. "But how shall we contrive to pay them?"

"*Quant à ça,* you shall manage something. I absolutely believe it," confided Renée. "Why Madame Bourgeax often pronounced upon your uncanny ability to extract yourself from every sort of contretemps."

"Did she?" Gweneth murmured and fell silent to wonder if that were, indeed, a compliment.

The days lengthened to an endless stream of unrelieved hours, each much like the last. The captain had given strict orders that the ladies were to be kept below and out of sight of his men. Daniel dropped in often between his duties, bringing a bit of cheer to the hour with a wild story of the seafaring life or a book, and once he taught the girls how to play mumblety-peg, tossing the tip-balanced jackknife off his finger with a flick of his thumbnail. He filled several afternoons with pleasure which, otherwise, would have grated on their nerves with boredom.

Daily it grew warmer as they sailed southward, the ocean now dyed turquoise beneath brilliant clear skies, and the tiny cramped quarters steamed at midday where only days before they had been dismally dank.

Whenever Daniel ventured to speak of the captain, a closed, withdrawn look came over Gweneth, and she appeared not to hear a word but, secretly, she was relieved to know that he was recovered. Once Daniel went as far as to hint that she might be welcomed were she to offer to visit the captain. Let him wait, she reasoned, and know that she would ask for nothing, not even the sight of sun nor breath of fresh air. She did not require his thanks nor want his attention for he had been nothing but a source of irritation and an unaccountable dread which gripped her whenever his sapphire eyes engaged hers.

For days now he invaded even her dreams, his bold advances and enticing smile beckoning. She knew the feel of his mouth on hers, warm and tenderly moist one instant, hard and brutal the next, crushing her lips till the taste of blood ran onto her tongue. Awakening each time to the darkness, Gweneth shivered in fear that he had actually shared her bed. She understood herself not at all for, to her shame, she had responded to the captain's entreaties and caresses, ready to give all in hopes of attaining a pleasure she could only imagine. Each time he betrayed her, and yet the next dream of him was no less seductive. His eyes, his lips, his hands sought her, and she pressed herself brazenly to his strong muscular frame, filled with a longing to be possessed by him. Yet in the daylight she felt nothing for him. How could she? He had a wife. Marianne waited somewhere for him.

So it was with some mystification that the ladies found themselves accompanying Daniel up on deck one evening before supper. The night crew came up soon after and positioned themselves about the ship amid boisterous camaraderie, but not a man made any reference to them as they stood leaning over the railing to watch the setting sun.

The brisk sea breeze pinked Gweneth's cheeks, and she licked the salty spray from her lips and lazily trailed her fingers over the rough surface of the hull, the sour tepid climate of their cabin forgotten for the hour.

Gweneth noted when they came up that the captain stood on the poop deck eyeing them with interest, but she had not allowed herself to show the slightest concern for his whereabouts though she was certain that he followed their every movement. Later, when she lifted her head in laughter at one of Renée's witticisms, she saw with great uneasiness that he had shifted his position and now stood within easy reach of them.

"*Bon soir*, mademoiselles," he greeted them when at last they turned back and faced him. "I trust you are enjoying your outing." His voice was conciliatory and his wide smile included them all. "I am truly sorry for the seeming callousness of my orders, but it was necessary to take my crew in hand after your most upsetting appearance, however pleasant a diversion it seemed at the time. Say that you forgive me and let me make amends by offering the hospitality of my table for dinner." His invitation was made to all, but his gaze sought Gweneth's. "I can promise a most delightful repast."

Gweneth gave him her haughtiest look. How dare he be so congenial and placating! As if nothing had occurred! As if they were friends! "*Merci*, Capitaine, but I have no appetite," she replied, but the look of disappointment on the three faces turned to her caused her to add, "But, of course, I speak for myself. I believe the others would welcome the change. If you will excuse me . . ."

"I shall not!" Raoul announced with a scowl. "Mademoiselle, you would spoil my dinner with your uncivil conduct and compel your friends, by their sense of loyalty, to deny themselves the joy of good society and a fine meal. That I cannot allow. Is there no side of you which does not bristle with prickling thorns at every gesture of friendship?"

Gweneth moistened her lips carefully. It was not the captain's words which tempted her but the thought of "fine food." She had consumed nothing but suspiciously riddled biscuits and dried beef these last weeks, and the offer of an alternative was not easy to refuse.

"Gweneth, have pity," coaxed Renée with a quick tug on her sister's sleeve.

Perhaps the captain's good conduct should be preserved for all their sakes, Gweneth reasoned. The others had suffered confinement because of her, and it would cost her precious little to spend an evening in the captain's company in return. Surely he would behave with propriety. "Capitaine, if it still meets with your approval, I believe that you shall find that we all wish to join you," Gweneth answered with self-surprising graciousness.

And her desires were met. There were golden-fried crescents of fish, griddled potato cakes with bits of onion, a tin filled with crisp biscuits, and two jars of preserves, and dried figs with filberts and squares of chocolate for dessert. The hour passed quickly with the unaccountable luxuries laid before them, and though they replied to the questions put to them by their host, only Amy made any attempt to engage the captain's notice. She chattered on continuously, undaunted by the presence of her employers or Gweneth's annoyance, and the captain seemed to welcome her flattering conversation, bestowing on her many an appreciative glance and smile.

"Perhaps you will tell me where you are bound that I may lay a course in that direction," Raoul suggested at the close of the meal. He spoke now in English though the conversations before had been in French.

Gweneth lay her napkin on the table. "We plead no favors on our behalf, Capitaine," she replied in French. "Your next port of call will serve our needs amply. From there we should be able to make our own way. We are not totally without resources."

"How can you be so certain of this when you do not know where my course lies?" Raoul asked with a mischievous grin. He was glad Gweneth had been the one to reply, for the sound of her voice was salve for his wounded pride. No woman had ever treated him with so little regard. She spurned his every advance and gave him no more due than the lowliest swab.

"Monsieur Daniel has told us that you seek the West Indies," Renée chimed in. "We shall—"

"We shall be happy to be put ashore there," Gweneth finished with a squelching look at her sibling. She had no desire for their final destination to be known, as much for her own peace of mind as for the possibility that Sarah's warning concerning her uncle could prove true.

Raoul set an elbow on the table and leaned his smooth chin on his knuckles. Gweneth found herself admiring the finely wrought features again bronzed and healthy. By comparison she felt quite gauche with her wind-blushed skin and hair hastily raked back from her face and braided. She could not know that it was her eyes, magnified by lantern light, which held Raoul enthralled.

"I sail for the Caribbean, that is true. It is Tortola in

the Virgin Islands I seek. Does that meet with your requirements?" Raoul asked politely but the mischief remained in his expression.

Gweneth's eyes lowered beneath his gaze. "I suppose there is a fair-sized town with a government there, Capitaine?"

"There is a town of sorts, mademoiselle. Road Town is its name, but the government is scanty. You would do better at Antigua. St. John is a proper government seat, British government that is. Guadeloupe and Martinique are our French neighbors." A fearful glance by Renée in Gweneth's direction told him they were fugitives, after all, just as he had assumed.

Gweneth looked up and met his facile smile. "Are you including St. John as one of your ports of call, Capitaine?" She watched as his lids lowered a trifle, veiling his marine-blue eyes in thick dark fringe.

"I should be delighted to include St. John in my itinerary if you but request it, mademoiselle. In truth I should be glad to comply with any request you make of me." His brows raised in arch amusement.

Gweneth answered his invitation with a smile of her own. Oh no, my clever capitaine. You will not deceive me into becoming indebted to you again. I could never elude your required payment twice. *"Merci,* Capitaine, for your offer, but we are content to disembark at Tortola." Gweneth rose to take her leave, but the captain had not yet conceded the loss.

"Mademoiselle Valois, I should like a few private words with you," he said easily.

Gweneth shook her head. "We have no matters between us which require discussion, Capitaine. The past is better forgotten, the future . . . there is none," she answered firmly.

Raoul rose now and came to her side. "I will speak with you," he said confidently. "Either willingly or unwillingly. The choice is yours. Allow me the right to detain you courteously." The pleasant tone did not disguise the threatening sense of his words, and three pairs of eyes turned her way, two wide with alarm and one narrowed in speculation. "If it is that important to you, then I suppose I should remain a moment," Gweneth replied noncommittally and reseated herself. She nodded to the others, but her heart beat more swiftly when they rose to leave. She knew it would not do to have the captain suspect her fear, and so she drained the last of the wine from her goblet while they departed.

"There, this is better," Raoul said when the door was shut and he came to sit by her side. "I have sorely missed your company," he said sweetly and took her hand in his. "We should be very good friends and not bitter enemies. I have only the fondest memories of you and hope there is some small part of you which returns the affection."

Gweneth blinked in disbelief. "How could you expect me to ever feel anything but the severest dislike for you?" she questioned and freed her hand.

"You were most kind to me when you might have done your worst, *ma belle*," he reminded her. "You—but come in, Daniel," he greeted when the door opened.

Daniel addressed them politely and then went about the matter of the dishes though his gaze held Gweneth's in brief understanding. Gweneth sighed in relief at his timely appearance and found the courage to rise and take her leave again.

"If you wish to apologize for your abominable behavior, monsieur, then save your breath. We are sworn enemies for all time. You have slandered my reputation, humiliated me before a sister whom I cherish, and sought to take from me the one thing that was mine alone to give. I do not wish your good feelings nor repentance," she said shortly and glared down at him in defiance.

Raoul's brows drew together. "A moment, mademoiselle. I have no intention of apologizing for collecting what was fairly won. You bristle self-righteously with accusation when it is you who owe me the apology." He smiled with deceptive ease and rose to walk about. "You forfeited your sleeping arrangements for the length of the voyage in submitting to a spell of the vapors. Yet for nearly three weeks you have not honored your part." He turned to fill his sight with every tempting curve and swell of her body. The dress was a near rag, but she was still an inviting vision.

Gweneth reddened before his insulting leer, but the words came easily. "How dare you suggest that I come back here! After all that has happened, how could you ever believe that I should agree to such an outrageous proposal? You must be mad, monsieur!" She turned and hurried for the door, but the captain caught her by the arm and gently but firmly turned her back to him.

"*Ma belle*," he murmured in mock reproach, "do not fly from me. You were not always so reluctant for my company." His eyes found hers and searched their depths. "You slept willingly at my side each night of my illness. I did not dream the soft pressure of your body to mine the night long, and I do not recall that I forced your arms about my neck nor your head upon my shoulder each time I awoke to your embrace."

Gweneth paled as sickening thuds pounded her ribs, for she had not realized that he was aware she had shared his bed, though the memory of it haunted her still. Her gaze flickered to Daniel, but his back was to them.

Raoul touched her cheek, and she flinched. "Do not be ashamed before Daniel, mademoiselle. You are not the first woman to be brought here," he said honestly, "but I shall find it a most difficult task to ever equal your spirit and beauty." Raoul chuckled softly and ran a forefinger over Gweneth's lower lip. "I would, of course, see to it that you are generously cared for. To begin with, would you like a new gown, perhaps of the finest ivory silk? No, I think emerald satin, to match the color of your eyes. They hold such promises, *ma belle*," he whispered and moved to her, but Gweneth eluded his kiss and pulled away.

Had the exchange not been in French, Gweneth would have denied her own ears. "A gown?" she breathed incredulously, shaking her head to clear dazed senses. "You would substitute my honor with a bolt of silk?" She turned with deliberate intent upon the man who barred her path. "*Mon Dieu!* Do you think me some tart a shilling can buy? Or is it that you believe any lady would spread herself on your bed because you wink and grin? Is your vanity so great you fail to understand that I find you totally resistible?" Gweneth's voice shook with barely contained emotion, and she clenched her fists till the nails puckered the skin of her palms.

"Are you finished?" Raoul asked impatiently and moved away from her damning gaze. She had surprised him with the venom of her dislike.

"*Mais non*, monsieur, there is a great deal more I can say if even a little of it will seep beneath your thick hide and touch your heart, providing you possess such a thing." Her eyes smarted with unshed tears, but she had the presence of mind to back toward the door. "I am not for sale, Monsieur Capitaine. One small dose of your company is more than sufficient—"

"Enough!" Raoul shouted, and his fist came down hard on the corner of his desk. "Enough, woman. You try my patience sorely. You shrew about like a wife, and that is the very last aggravation I need. Be gone if you cannot bring yourself to give to me some of the comfort which is the nature of your sex!" But the door slammed shut before he finished.

"Damn the wench!" Raoul cried with feeling and dropped into his chair. "Daniel, keep that swishing skirt out of my sight, or I shall not be answerable for my actions."

"Aye, Cap'n, but I would not fret the point. The

way she flew when ye opened the cage, it don't seem likely she'd seek ye out again. Ye put the fear of Beelzebub himself in the poor mam'zelle. Showed her exactly what she can expect from ye, ye did." Daniel nodded to himself and scraped a dish loudly. "She'll not be needin' me to stave her tears again," he added above the racket.

Raoul did not miss the jibe. "How's that? What do you know of her unhappiness, Daniel?"

Daniel turned a sorrowful eye on his captain. Many a thing he could tell the captain had the girl not pledged him to silence. "Only that it were not her intention to kill ye—not really, I'm athinkin'—and that there were moments when she regretted . . . but never ye mind, Cap'n. I'll be akeepin' the little French girl outta yer path." He placed the last dish on top and lifted the stack. "Ye be knowin' the ways of women better'n me, only don't it seem that the mam'zelle is a mite different than them others? Them street women I come by for ye, they be had by any man for a coin. But this here missy, I hear a different tune when she waltzes by."

"Daniel," the captain drawled. "If I did not know better, I should say she had bewitched you. Waltzing, indeed. What she deserves is a—"

"I'd say ye took care of that bit o' business a'ready, Cap'n," Daniel broke in. His loyalty knew no limit in most cases, but he did not care to hear the mam'zelle bad-mouthed, even by his captain.

Startled by the reproach in Daniel's tone and then drawn into a steadily blackening mood, Raoul asked, "Did she speak to you of that, Daniel? Did she win your sympathy by weeping onto your shirt front, wailing about my cruel and inhuman treatment of her?"

"Kept her thoughts mostly to herself, she did, Cap'n. Took no guff from this scurrilous crew of ours though, did she, sir? She be a proud, headstrong young thin', a genuine lady. And it be much to her credit that she's still able to bare her claws when need be. Who'd be expectin' it of that bit of fluff?" Daniel asked in innocent reflection and began scrubbing in the dishwater.

Raoul grumbled under his breath. He had offered her what any man offered a woman to whom he had taken a fancy. A maid's wages, if that is what she truly sought, were not for a beauty of her temperament. The master of any household who employed her would make fast work of her, one way or another. Why then had she refused him? She could have a great deal from him, he reflected. He was not a stingy nor poor man, but she had yet to accept the rules. He could not understand her reluctance to renew their association once the deed was accomplished, for the women always came round after a romp under the covers with him.

Raoul smiled to himself. He knew his worth, having been complimented many times by the sort of women who would know. But this one, had he begun wrong with her? Brutality never appealed to him, certainly not where a woman was concerned. He had been so angry with her for having cut him. Could he have taken her cruelly, not caring that he discovered her to be a virgin? With the fever and his violent temper unleashed, who was to say what had occurred?

Raoul shied from that conclusion, for it left him uneasy, and yet . . . He picked up his quill and dipped it repeatedly in the inkwell, then applied it to a sheet of his log.

"Did she say I hurt her, Daniel?" he questioned in an uninterested voice, but the quill halted on the paper in anticipation of the reply.

Daniel paused before answering. "She said nothin' to me, Cap'n. There was no need. We come to an understandin' that first night." He looked over his shoulder to the man hunched over his desk. "Do ye remember nothin', Cap'n?"

"Precious little, Daniel, precious little," Raoul muttered and laid the quill aside. Daniel hummed to himself, convinced at last that the mam'zelle had been spared.

CHAPTER FIVE

"If I must wear this gown a single day longer, I shall scream! Non, I shall rip it into tiny pieces and—" A cry from above broke in on Renée's daily laments as the girls prepared for their evening stroll. Renée jumped to her feet and opened the door. "They've sighted land!" she cried and slipped out through the portal.

Sarah and Amy quickly followed, but Gweneth remained behind. For weeks she had prayed for this very day, but now her fingers shook as she finished her braid and her knees were treacherously weak when she stood. The captain would be on deck, but the temptation to see the green fertile beauty of land won out.

Gweneth put her arms into the sleeves of the cotton shirt Daniel had loaned her, her gown having been worn beyond mending in several delicate places. If the captain were above, she would stay just long enough to glimpse the island and then return. He had not spoken to her since the night of his insulting proposal. Perhaps he would refrain permanently.

Squinting against the rapidly dissolving sunset, Gweneth at last detected a thin dark sliver on the horizon. For the first sight of land, this was a disappointment. Still it represented the end of the voyage as Daniel told her they would enter the bay on the morning tide.

Raoul watched Gweneth from his perch once his eyeglass convinced him that this, in truth, was Tortola. The nearly lawless territory had been chosen with purpose, for he did not mean to leave Gweneth beyond his reach until he had satisfied his need of her which occupied more and more of his daydreams. He had deliberately set himself at a distance from her, seeking to ease his frustration and anger but to no avail. Now he would force the issue once and for all. She would need a protector, and it might as well be he for, in spite of Daniel's opinion to the contrary, there was a wildness in her nature which defied a respectable background. Away from prying eyes she would be more amenable, he was certain.

The knock on his door an hour later surprised Raoul, but the sight of Gweneth lightened his spirits. He could guess the reason for this visit and welcomed the chance to put his plan to the test.

"Come in, Mademoiselle Valois," he encouraged and drew up a chair for her by his desk.

Necessity alone brought her to this meeting, and Gweneth watched closely for signs of displeasure that he had been interrupted. There was nothing overtly threatening in the captain's appearance though his clothes were dusty and he was in need of a shave and brushing. "Capitaine Bertrand, I have been told that we shall make port in the morning and have come to request that we should be allowed to go ashore as early as possible." She shrugged and looked down at her ragged gown. "We shall hardly present a formidable entourage, but surely some authority will hear our plight and offer aid."

"I have offered repeatedly—" Raoul began, then smiled the thought aside. "But no, allow me to assist you this one last time. If you will but inform me of the name of your friend—or is it employer? Ah, no matter," he said, retreating again. "The name is all that is needed, and we may both rest easy. I would not have you stranded in this port for weeks if that is not required. It would prove a greater hardship than the time you have spent thus far aboard my ship." Raoul sat back and crossed his legs. "For all I have been told, you may be no closer to your destination than before you were rescued."

"Non, non, monsieur, we are very near," Gweneth replied before thinking. She smiled at her blunder and saw it reflected in the captain's face.

"In that case, mademoiselle, you should allow me to escort you personally. Your employer would certainly wish you to be taken care of, and I would rest a great deal easier if I knew you had been delivered into the proper hands," he said and sat forward to reach for quill and paper. "The name, mademoiselle?"

Gweneth's expression soured. "So now you believe my story, *n'est-ce pas*? Could it be that you sense another sale to be had? Is it that you believe that your pockets will weigh a little heavier for the effort of relinquishing us in person?" she scoffed. "You have considered that possibility, mon Capitaine?" she continued and held his look squarely. "Then consider this. What tale will you tell to keep your neck from being forfeited when it is known how you have mistreated the nieces of a colonial governor?" All these weeks Gweneth had waited to wager this last desperate stake, and now it was played.

Raoul's expression remained unchanged, but the knuckles of his hands turned white where they grasped the desk top. He had not believed anything but that the girls were destitute and bereft of adequate protection but, damn the ill luck, the look in those fathomless green eyes did not lie. Not only was she all that she claimed, but it seemed he had slipped his own head through the noose.

"And, of course, you would not hesitate to whisper that lie to your uncle," he said slowly, but her provoking smile proved too much and he bolted to his feet and strode round to pull Gweneth to hers.

"In that case," he said bitterly, "I may as well enjoy the plunder if I am to suffer the consequences. Then, too, we must be certain that you have all the facts aright." He yanked Gweneth to him and not even the full force of her hands against his chest could prevent the inexorable advance of his lips to hers, silencing her cry of protest.

Raoul held her writhing body close and exalted in the still strangely new taste of her mouth beneath his own. His hands slipped beneath her shirt, questing the soft velvet patches of skin exposed by the tattered gown and, as the material shredded in his fingers, the blood quickened through his veins. Soon all would be unveiled for his delight, her soft smooth shoulders, tender full breasts, and nicely rounded hips, and he would kiss and fondle every inch of her until she begged him to love her. The devil take the morrow; she was his this night.

Gweneth thought she would smother in the captain's steel-tempered embrace, but when she gasped for air, she was acutely embarrassed by the indecent advantage he took of her parted lips. His hot breath seemed to wilt her resistance, dragging all strength of will from her with the knowledge of the unrelenting passion which possessed him, and she soon hung limply in his arms. There would be no mercy in his victory, for his anger drove away the ardent lover, and she shrank inwardly from the cruel taskmaster.

Raoul lifted his head and chuckled in satisfaction. "You are learning, *ma belle*. If you would but forego this pretense of aversion to me, I should teach you to enjoy it."

Gweneth grimaced, gulping in painful breaths, and turned her face away. "You are dirty and unshaven. It is not pleasant to be near you," she said huskily and pushed free of his slackened grasp. "We are both in need of a washing, Capitaine, but do not force your hot sweaty self on me again, or I am certain to be violently ill." She pulled the shirt together over her ruined gown and then wiped her mouth with trembling fingers.

Her barb might not have found its mark on any other man aboard, but Raoul, who prided himself on his appearance, was abashed by her frank statement. He could feel the perspiration trickling down his back even as he stood there, and he reddened in chagrin.

God's blood! There seemed no end to her mockery of him. He had known he was not fit company for a woman, having crawled over nearly every plank of his vessel these past two days to assess cargo and the need for repairs and supplies; but that consideration had flown when she threatened to present him with his head if he should seek to accompany her to her home.

"You had better go back to your cabin," he said crisply and ran a knuckle over his mouth to remove the taste of her kiss. "This is not the night for such foolishness. We will talk again tomorrow when I have returned from Road Town. No, you may not accompany me," he said and raised a silencing hand. "These islands are little better than ports for thieves and scalawags of all nationalities. The government exists of little more than title. If it is peaceful this year, I will allow you to disembark. If not," he shrugged, "you must leave that judgment to me."

Raising her head in mute surprise, Gweneth looked long into his still passion-fired stare. She had not expected to defeat him, least of all on such a minor consideration. He was a strange man, comprised of unexpected points of honor. "Are you of noble birth, Capitaine?" she asked on absurd impulse.

Raoul grinned and placed his hands on his hips. "Simply the bastard of one, mademoiselle. My father was unable to sire a son legitimately, and so brought me up with nearly all the advantages of a true heir. I might have gotten the fortune, after all, had I not made a costly mistake. You see, I do not handle well under the whip and bit." Raoul's features hardened a fraction, and his eyes glazed in thought but, in a twinkling, he was smiling again. "There, now you may add my disreputable beginnings to your growing list of charges against me," he said self-mockingly.

"Non, I think not. I am indebted to your background just now, Capitaine," she replied sincerely but turned from him. He had given away a little of himself, and she was naturally curious, but it would be risking her escape not to leave now.

Raoul's hand touched the bolt before hers, but he opened the door and followed behind her without further word. Gweneth crossed the middle deck confidently but paused at the rail to search the horizon once more for that thin stretch of earth between sea and sky. The captain came to stand by her and leaned over the side, his elbow just brushing hers.

"Are you familiar with these islands?" Raoul asked softly but kept his eyes fixed on the land.

"Non, Capitaine, I have never even been aboard a ship before," Gweneth confessed and was relieved by his choice of this impersonal topic though she would have preferred to be alone to recompose her tremulous emotions before returning to her sister.

"And yet you have not become ill once," Raoul thought aloud. "That is a feat few could boast about their first time at sea. Your friends were quite bilious those first days, Daniel says." He half turned to look at her when suddenly he turned back. "Here, look, on the horizon," he whispered urgently, and his finger pointed to a place just off the starboard bow.

In the dim light of late evening Gweneth spied a flash of light at the water's surface and then it disappeared. No sooner was she certain it was only her imagination than the black water split and a silver iridescent form leaped high and arced back to slice the surface cleanly.

"What is it?" Gweneth cried. "Look, there again," she whispered and tugged the captain's sleeve in excitement.

Raoul sucked in an inaudible breath at the touch of her fingers. She had forgotten her anger quickly in childlike awe, but he was still keenly aware of his craving for her.

"Yes, I see them," he replied quietly. "They are dolphins, known to the ancients as mermaids. They are our safe passage in and out of these waters, for many of the islands are surrounded by coral reefs. A mistake, and a captain may find his ship stranded, or worse, without an underbelly to buoy his vessel. These little darlings will guide us through to safe harbor. 'Tis not known why they should choose to do it, but they have been with us since morning and have come out to play now that we are riding anchor till daylight. 'Tis a good omen of a journey fairly met. The sea can be a blessed benefactor as well as a demanding mistress."

Raoul glanced down at the girl by his side. Gweneth was leaning over on tiptoe to glimpse the silvered figures in the indigo waters. The breeze whipped long strands of hair back from her scalp but a few spread across her expectant face and clung to her parted lips. Raoul looked up and away to his shortened sails. The girl was more provocative than ever with the wonder of nature reflected in her beautiful eyes. He simply would not let her slip out of his hands without knowing where she could be found. But if she were the niece of a governor, he had better find some way to amend her impression of him before he let her go. Otherwise he was certain to find a bounty on his head one day soon.

Gweneth glanced up cautiously at the captain, but his eyes were searching the riggings. She studied his profile, the features in sharp relief to the sailcloth behind. He had spoken lovingly of the sea and of its creatures, but he had no such tender words for people. He cared nothing for her company save toward one purpose and, no doubt, he was itching to be back to his logs and charts.

Gweneth grabbed a finger of hairs from her face and gnawed her lower lip. It made no sense that she should even wonder what his thoughts were, but she felt something, perhaps gratitude that he had given her her freedom when she did not expect it.

"Are you ready to go below?" he asked when he looked down and found her eyes on him.

"*Oui*, Capitaine," she replied softly and dropped her gaze before he could guess her thoughts.

Raoul followed her to the steps and even down the tiny corridor. "Sweet dreams, *ma belle*," he intoned deeply and placed a swift light kiss on her cheek. Gweneth shrank back, but he turned and left her there alone.

Gweneth rose early and watched as the ship rounded the island to find a passage through the reefs. Their aquatic friends from the night before kept pace with the ship's prow, darting in and out of the waves with nymphlike grace and speed. The island was much nearer now, and Gweneth found its softly undulating, green-shrouded peaks more to her expectations of what an island should be.

The other girls stirred when the activity above their heads grew frenzied. There were excited cries from every quarter, but over them all rang the decisive orders of the ship's captain. His voice rang clear and vibrant, echoing with an excitement which matched that of the others. Gweneth, too, became infected with an impatience of her own. "Tonight there will be hot water, clean clothes, and fresh food," she murmured aloud.

Yet, when they had been anchored within the bay for an hour, not a soul came to give them any word. Daniel had brought breakfast before the piloting of the reefs, when every man's eyes were required at his post, but he had not returned.

Just when Gweneth was ready to brave the crowded deck, there came a shout, followed by a "heave-ho" and the splash of a boat into the sea. She ran to the porthole to see the captain casting off with a small party. Her delicate brows drew together in a frown, and her lower lip trembled ominously. He meant to keep them prisoners until whatever diabolical scheme he had planned was satisfied, she decided angrily. Well, she would see about that!

She dressed rapidly, urging the others to ready themselves to follow, and a party of four set forth. However, Daniel and Peckcum were coming below at just that moment and when the door opened, six pairs of eyes met in surprise.

"Mornin', ladies," greeted Daniel. "Cap'n Bertrand's orders are that ye be havin' the use o' his cabin for the day. There be hot water for bathin' and a washtub for yer clothes. A stiff breeze like today's will dry anythin' in an hour or two." He smiled and stepped aside to let Peckcum through. The first mate doffed his cap uneasily.

"The cap'n said I was to make a list of whatever it is you be needin' in the way of—" And he cleared his throat and put a finger in his collar. "Thin's of a personal nature, you might say. You make known what you need, and I am to fetch it from town," he finished and looked over his heavy shoulders rather helplessly at Daniel.

"Does this mean we shall not be allowed to leave the ship at this port?" Gweneth questioned quickly, her fear and anger vying for control of her emotions.

"I ain't privy to the cap'n's thinkin', missy. Best do as you are told and speak to him when he returns." Peckcum heaved a thumb in the direction of the stairway, and the girls followed the men after Gweneth grumbled in very unladylike French and conceded with a shrug.

The joys of a real bath awaited them. Fresh hot water, not sea water, filled the tub, and another of the captain's pungently fragrant balls of soap lay waiting. There were towels from the captain's cabinet and sheets to wrap up in while waiting for their laundry. "This capitaine, he thinks of everything," Renée squealed in appreciation.

Gweneth took a needle and thread to each of her garments to darn the worst spots, patching them with cuts from the hem, and was content to be the last to bathe. She frowned over the work, but the concentration was not for the needle which moved swiftly in her hand. Thoughts of the captain and the meaning of this delay occupied her. He had warned her that this was a rough frontier and that the authority might be lax, yet he should have taken her along. She alone could speak the names and positions to bring an air of urgency and respect to their plight.

"*Mais non*, the capitaine must have things his way. This is his ship, we are his prisoners, our lives are in his fickle hands. *Diable!* May I ever be spared the sight of that swaggering cock when once we reach land," she muttered and promptly stuck her finger. She put it quickly into her mouth and looked about sheepishly, but no one had heard her tirade. Amy helped Renée shampoo her hair, and Sarah was busy scrubbing the first of the gowns.

In due time Gweneth slipped into a hot tub and the pile of wet clothing was left on the doorstep for Daniel.

"Imagine, Gweneth, the *Cyrene* waves our petticoats about like banners," Renée giggled. "I wonder what the other ships must think?" she asked, peering through the porthole with brush in hand.

"Are there many other ships in this harbor?" Gweneth questioned over one soapy shoulder. Having been so lost in her own miserable thoughts, she had not allowed herself to cast a hopeful eye toward the island just out of reach.

"Oh, oui, mademoiselle," answered Amy. "There are several small boats and one splendid ship all gold and black, every bit as grand as this one. I should like to know if her capitaine is as magnificent as his ship," she said breathlessly.

"Hush, Amy," Sarah scolded under her breath. "The way you go on about men it is a miracle any of us is safe. We would not be here now save for you. Make eyes at the capitaine once more, and I shall pinch you black and blue, I swear it!"

Amy blushed furiously and glanced at Gweneth's back. Certainly her mistress was lovely, but she had heard that sailors preferred women of experience and racier appetites. Mademoiselle Gweneth had the looks, but her heart was chaste and full of chivalrous dreams of love, like all pampered young ladies. Surely a man like the captain desired something different. He had not even sought her out after the first time. Certainly it was because she had disappointed him, Amy reasoned.

Amy squinted into the tiny piece of mirror in her lap. She was as pretty in her own way, with her smooth pink complexion, clear blue eyes, and straight blond hair. And then there was that knowing slant to her smile. The captain could not have failed to notice that. No, she was certain that he had and nearly been persuaded to seek her out. But how could he, with Gweneth keeping such a sharp eye on them all?

Amy squirmed restlessly. She had hated to leave André though she should have known he could not be forced into marrying her, even if he were regarded as a mere *citoyen* by the new design. It had not been wise to threaten the family with scandal, the kind they as former aristocrats could so ill afford under the watchful eye of the New Directory. And the ardent lover had turned dutiful heir and allowed his parents to send his pretty maid and her sister Sarah from France.

Still, Amy admitted, she missed his hard lean body and smooth hands which had brought her such pleasure. No, she was no innocent, and she knew the captain must be all the better for his years of experience. She would welcome the opportunity to trade long, lingering kisses with such a man and stroke that hard-muscled body.

Amy cast a sidelong glance at the captain's bunk

and felt a twinge of envy for her mistress. It really was selfish of Mademoiselle Gweneth not to speak of her adventure.

By lunchtime the ladies were dressed. From spun gold to tawny auburn to mahogany to raven's wing, four heads turned their damp tresses to the blazing heat of the tropical sun as they lounged on the quarter deck under the protection of Peckcum.

Gweneth paced the small deck in quick, deliberate strides with her arms folded tightly across her chest. She had refused Peckcum's offer to buy new dresses for the others and herself. It would be the captain's money that went for such things and she could not, would not, accept his hospitality now that there was no cause. She even refused lunch and nearly came to insults with Peckcum over his lowering of a second boat without her.

"Blimey, Daniel," Peckum grumbled when Gweneth had retreated at last in defeat. "I have never known the likes in all me days. She's as wild as a tigress, and yet she apologizes for her black temper and then dismisses it with a shrug. I am only a wonderin' how the cap'n ever subdued that little she-devil."

"Oh, he has had his problems there," Daniel answered and snorted. "She be a real lady, that's the rub. Take a look, me friend. Ye'll never be knowin' a finer example." Daniel wagged his head and loped away.

Gweneth watched as the two small crafts shuttled between land and sea, carrying their loads of sailors to shore leave for the night, but it was late afternoon before she spied the captain aboard one of the boats. She had remained above board in the heat of the day, hoping to catch the captain should he sneak back, but now that he was within minutes of reaching her, she was no longer sure of what to say.

Gweneth crossed her arms and tapped her foot impatiently but found, in the moment the men heaved the rope ladder over the side, she could not bear another fight, certainly not where all could see and hear. She turned on her heel and fled, her long cinnamon hair streaming behind in the breeze.

Raoul's spirits were high as he deftly climbed aboard his ship. The British magistrate was away on business to one of the other islands. There would be no need to lie to Mademoiselle Valois, for the man was expected to be gone for nearly two weeks. What could he do?

A wide grin greeted all as he swung his booted feet over the rail and onto the deck. He had something else in mind for this evening. His luck was running high, and he meant to take full advantage of it. Mademoiselle Valois would see him in a different light tonight. He had watched the softening in her eyes when she heard of his noble, if bastardized, background. She wanted him to play the gentleman. Well, it was a part not unfamiliar to him though a trifle dusty from disuse. Tonight he would win the fair lady with seductively sweet wooing and cunningly exacted caresses. She would come to him of her own volition, and together they would share a rapturous joy not yet fulfilled in either of them.

So jolly was Raoul's mood that he slapped Daniel on the back most congenially. "How goes it with our gentlewomen, Daniel? Were they pleased with their baths and new frocks? Give a woman a bright new bauble with which to adorn herself, and she will come round every time," he congratulated himself.

Daniel slid a sidelong glance at the merry man walking by his side. Something good must be in the making, for Captain Bertrand was not a man given to lighthearted banter. Now how should he broach the matter of the mademoiselle's temper.

"Been a good day, Cap'n? Aye, that be fine news. Now the ladies be most pleased with their baths." He stopped to scratch the back of his left ear. "As to them frocks—well. The ladies were not wishin' to be puttin' ye to such an expense. Most polite and thankful they be, only they could not own to such extravagance for their sakes."

Raoul stopped in mid-stride and turned a world-wise look on his man. "In other words Mademoiselle Valois resisted the suggestion to the point of threatening to run Peckcum through if he brought back so much as a ribbon. Am I correct?"

Daniel's wrinkled face split to the sound of hoarse laughter. "Ye come close enough, Cap'n, ye rightly did. The girl had poor Peckcum nearly run aground more 'n once. He cast off more in self-defense than in resolve. That little missy could take on her weight in wildcats, I do believe. She did apologize," Daniel added thoughtfully, "but I'm amind she's awaitin' yer return, for I glimpsed her stewin' about on the quarter-deck just now." But when they turned to look, the starboard deck was empty.

"Where does she get it, Daniel? You would expect a gently bred girl to be terrified of this scalawag crew of ruffians, and yet she wades in over her head at every opportunity," Raoul said in exasperation.

"Could be somethin' she said once about her family, Cap'n. As well as I recollect, she has three brothers before her. The little missy would have learned early to hold her own in their midst. It would come natural to her."

Raoul mulled over this bit of information and then started forth. "I have plans, Daniel. Tonight Mademoiselle Valois shall be a lady because I shall treat her as such. 'Tis not a brother I wish to appear as in her eyes," he added with a chuckle. "Come along, there is a fair amount to be done." Daniel followed behind the captain's bold stride in eager curiosity to know just what his boss had in mind.

"This is yours, *ma belle*. A present, if you will."

The captain had entered their cabin unbidden and now slung a red satin gown across Gweneth's lap. "I shall return within the hour. See if you cannot arrange your hair more pleasingly. I would have the pleasure of introducing you to my acquaintances, but they are people of some quality and style and, in your present condition, you would be bound to be an embarrassment." He turned and strode through the doorway before Gweneth found breath for words.

"Oh, mademoiselle, *c'est magnifique*! The lines, certainly Parisian. The material!" purred Amy as she rushed forth to finger the gown.

Gweneth sat staring at the open door. What peculiar game was the captain fashioning this time? The girls held the gown up between them for her view, and it captured her attention. It was of a bright rich crimson, nothing that Gweneth should ever seek to own, but she could not help admiring the fashionable cut and obvious quality of the fabric. The bodice was encrusted with tiny pearls and cut sparingly to fit a slender waist. The skirt ran full to be caught up in places with beaded lace doilies, revealing an underskirt of white lace ruffles.

An expensive gown, if not in especially good taste, it reminded Gweneth of the courtesans who had occasionally graced the arms of the fashionable lords attending exhibitions at the Valois Academy. Yes, that was it. The gown had been designed to a man's specification and tastes; the neckline too low, the waist too tight. The frock of a *chère-amie*.

Gweneth jumped to her feet, shaking in anger. "Non! Non! Non, he cannot make me, and I will not wear it! He wishes to make a spectacle of me before his friends, and that I will not tolerate!" More and more Gweneth found herself venting her anger in English, though she was well aware of the captain's fluency in her own language.

Amy and Sarah looked to one another in puzzlement. They had not understood her words though they knew her to be furious. Every time that fine strutting male came near her, she flew into some rage, Amy observed sagely. Sometimes their altercations were in French but most often they were not, and the girls would, as they did now, press Renée for an explanation.

Amy brushed the gown lightly with her hand. "He is a most generous man. Mademoiselle Valois could do much worse. Look how he seeks her out," she whispered covertly to Sarah. "If he displayed such interest in me, I should curl up happily in his bed and—"

"Oh, do be still," replied Sarah. "You must keep your eyes from the capitaine. He is the sort who would gobble up a tiny morsel like you without a second thought. Mademoiselle Gweneth has shared his hospitality, and just look how afraid she is of him. His fine eyes may promise happiness, but I hear the mademoiselle cry into her pillow each night. You had best keep a distance. He is a savage."

"He can well find someone else to accompany him!" Gweneth finished at last, unaware of the conversation that had gone on behind her. She whirled around, snatched the gown from Amy's fingers and turning back, flung it out of the door.

"Mademoiselle!" thundered that deep voice Gweneth had learned to dread. And then he was there, filling up the small doorway. Scooping up the gown, he held it out in one hand.

"This gown cost me well over one thousand francs, and I will not have it used to swab the decks. You will put it on because I demand it, and you will wear it and smile and come with me wherever I should see fit to take you." Raoul's voice rippled with barely contained—what was it?—anger or amusement, Gweneth wondered.

"And, furthermore, you will be ready in exactly one hour, or I shall take the liberty of seeing to your toilette myself. In which case it may be that you shall not need the dress after all." The wicked gleam in his eye suggested that the last idea appealed to him the best, and when Raoul took a step toward Gweneth, she shrank back with an involuntary shudder.

"Blast it all, woman. Do you really think I should strike you? Take this and put it on. Daniel will bring a trunk, and you may take from it whatever you may need." He held the gown out, and Gweneth would have reached for it had she been certain that her fingers would not fumble and drop it.

Raoul scowled at her but then shrugged and handed the gown to Amy before heading for the door. "One hour, is that understood, mademoiselle? *Une heure*," he translated for emphasis and though he could not see it, he must have taken her silence as consent, for he left without a backward glance.

In the hour following Gweneth brushed out her hair and selected a white silk chemise and several lace-edged petticoats from the trunk Daniel delivered as promised. Studying her face in the mirror, Gweneth could not help wishing for a faint covering of rice powder. The smelly grease Daniel had given the ladies to ease their sunburn had done its job, and the little mirror reflected back a smooth complexion. Still her blush was too pronounced by half for a genuine lady. Well, there was no help for that. "After all, it is only the capitaine and his kind who shall see me," she sighed.

Sarah caught up Gweneth's hair in a wide band of black velvet ribbon and arranged row upon row of long curls down her back. Given more time, she assured her new mistress, she could do better, but Gweneth's indifferent reply satisfied her. For the captain she would do no more than a minimum, but her feminine pride was pleased with the results.

"I wonder whose dress it is the capitaine bids me wear?" Gweneth questioned aloud as Sarah and Amy slipped the frock over her head. "A trunk full of women's clothing; they must belong to someone." And her thoughts strayed to the mysterious Marianne. "Perhaps the gown is the wrong size, and I cannot wear it at all," she said with perverse delight, but the dress was a remarkably good fit, as though it had been made for her. Its whaleboned bodice fit sleekly about her waist and forced her bosom up so high it threatened to spill out over the very low neckline.

Gweneth looked down in dismay when the gown was fastened and crossed her hands over it to shield herself. "*Mon Dieu*, I cannot be seen in this! Every man with breath left in him will be at my heels!" she cried in despair.

"You forget the capitaine, mademoiselle. He is not likely to let anyone else near you, for he fancies you for himself," replied Amy dryly and eyed her with great envy. "How beautiful you look, mademoiselle. The capitaine's eyes will pop right out of his head."

"That is not what I want, Amy. I do not seek his favor, anything but. I wish to be left in peace."

"*Mais non*, mademoiselle," counseled Sarah. "Think a moment. Is a man not more easily handled when he believes it is he who calls the tune? You have railed against him all these weeks and to what end? We are nearly at our journey's close. Why claw at him now and risk your safety after all this time?"

"She is right, Gweneth," joined Renée. "You must remember what Madame Bourgeax always said about catching more flies with honey than vinegar."

"Oh, Renée, Madame Bourgeax would say this entire nightmare is of my making. Why, she would charge me responsible for the pirates who attacked us and then chastise me for allowing Capitaine Bertrand to rescue us. I can hear her even now—" And Gweneth's voice rose high and nasal. "You, mademoiselle. Just what I should expect from our prodigal Gweneth. Swishing and coquetting about enough to tease a man from his senses. You always were one to hang about the young gallants. And do not think I have not seen you smiling and blushing in their presence. Serves you right that some rogue would seek satisfaction in your bold ways. Imagine the unseemliness of boarding a strange vessel, and with an English capitaine, no less!"

The girls broke into peals of laughter at her expert

miming, and Gweneth joined them with a sense of relief. Home did not seem so far away after all. They were not aware that someone had entered until he spoke.

"It is a very pleasant change, I must tell you, to hear the melodious sound of feminine laughter. Perhaps you will allow me to join in the jest?"

Gweneth spun round to face the intruder, her skirts dancing out full, and the captain's next words froze on his lips. His eyes widened in approval as they swept over the dramatic change in her appearance. The dress showed her off to every advantage; her smooth, slender shoulders, narrow waist, and the enticing curves of her exposed breasts.

A most exquisite example of her sex, Raoul found himself thinking. He longed to finger the curl nestling in the hollow of her throat and then his gaze went lower to the full swell above the neckline. A beautiful creature, better than he ever expected. The devil take it that he had so little memory of the feel of her and the rare satisfaction she must have given him. He would seek an opportunity to amend that fault, perhaps this very night.

Gweneth was no less startled by his appearance. Gone was the rough, unkempt sea captain. This man was a neatly turned-out gentleman, from the perfect knot of his immaculate white stock below the bronzed features to his cream-colored, velvet-collared coat. Even the ruffles of his shirt had been carefully starched, and the fawn-colored breeches stretched over his muscular thighs like a second skin. Only his thick dark hair, gleaming in the lamplight, remained untouched but for a brushing. How he put to shame those men who still clipped their heads and then covered them with powdered wigs. So intent was her study of him that Gweneth quite forgot her revealing gown and stood impassively when he came forward and took her hand lightly in his. With a grace which quite surprised her, he bent and brushed a bare hint of a kiss on her fingertips.

"*Enchanté*, mademoiselle. You make a most fetching partner. I begin to believe that you are all that you claim. It is my most fortunate luck to be your escort this evening," he voiced in most flattering tones.

Gweneth pulled her fingers free when he did not release them immediately and reached up to cover herself when she realized his eyes lingered there.

"Monsieur Capitaine, I cannot be seen like this. The gown is too revealing. I have never owned anything so—" And she hesitated, hunting for the appropriate term which would not spoil his momentarily good mood.

"So alluring, mademoiselle? Is that the term you seek?" he asked pleasantly.

"That will do, monsieur. It embarrasses me."

Raoul covered her wrist and drew her hand from the bodice. "Do not be shy, my sweet. The gown flatters you, nothing more. There is no shame to be had in that," he said though he, too, was beginning to doubt the choice, for he could see that every man present would have eyes for her and that he would need to watch over her every minute. Still, that in itself was not a displeasing task.

"Come. A carriage awaits us at the dock." He put her hand in the bend of his arm and spoke to the others. "*Bon soir*, mademoiselles. Would that I were four men and could escort you all. Alas, that is not the case, and you are safer here with Daniel." He bowed low and smiled charmingly at each of them, catching Amy's sly wink with a fractional hesitancy in his movement.

Gweneth hung back when he started forth and would not step out. "Monsieur, please. At least allow me a wrap, something with which to ward off the chill," she pleaded and managed to smile through the fear laying claim to her now that he was pursuing his plan.

Raoul saw the beginnings of trepidation in her eyes and halted, for it was not his intention that she should find him anything but a perfect gentleman this evening. He would need to win her confidence before pressing on to more intimate matters.

"Certainly, my sweet. Take what you need."

Sarah came forth and wrapped a white silk shawl over Gweneth's gown and whispered an urgent bit of advice in her ear. "Treat your capitaine as a *gentilhomme*, and he may find that it is a role he enjoys playing for you. He is your protection, remember that."

Gweneth murmured skeptically but allowed herself to be led away after warmly hugging Renée. Was she a fool to go, Gweneth wondered? But no, this way she would finally set foot on land, a foothold she could attain no other way.

CHAPTER SIX

"Where are you taking me, Capitaine?" Gweneth asked once they were on their way.

"I have friends on the island who are hosting a ball. After all these weeks at sea, I thought you might enjoy an evening out." They had been lowered into the skiff with helping hands, and Raoul drew Gweneth protectively to his side as they cast off, pretending not to notice her stiff posture.

He tapped the end of her nose with a forefinger. "I like those flecks of gold dust on your lovely face. They tempt me to bend and kiss each one." Gweneth moved nervously within his arm, and Raoul feigned a long face. "Never mind, *ma belle*. If you start at the mere suggestion, then we shall all find ourselves in the bay should I brave the attempt."

Gweneth smiled in spite of herself and did not contest when Raoul resettled her by his side. "How nice it is to see that you do know how to smile," he said, then raised a hand to point out various sites as the oarsmen pulled them toward the dock.

The island lay as a lush green mound against the darkening sky, and the cooling sea air, which still held the last heat of midday, brought the rich earthy smell of land out to greet them. Off to either side of the dock ahead, a thin stretch of pale ivory sand spread out to the water's edge. Gweneth's spirits rose in response to the lush tropical splendor as she reminded herself that she was going to a ball.

At nineteen she was old enough to be married. There should have been several balls by now in honor of her coming of age. There would have been gorgeous ball gowns and many attentive suitors, each vying for her favor. She would have chosen carefully, not looking for wealth or title but a man who would have seen in her someone of intelligence and élan. The man would have been clever and proud, bold and enterprising, and eager to introduce her to the ways of love with consideration and respect. She would not have sought beauty of face and form, but it was not to be rejected. A man such as she dreamed of would necessarily be lithe and agile, a man of action.

With something akin to begrudging concession, Gweneth reflected on the man at her side and found nothing lacking in her requirements save for consideration and respect. The capitaine was intelligent and obviously an adventurer, perhaps too much so. His pride exceeded her desire, but his swaggering bravado did have its attraction. Ah, but his voice, that was the best measure of the man. It could be rich and persuasive when wooing with seductive words but rang with the decisive timbre of authority when commanding the men under him.

Her brothers, would they have made him one of their own? Gweneth pondered, for it was from them that she had learned what she knew of men. They were great flirts but, when in love, there was no limit to the expressions of sincere intent in their manner.

Phillip would have been married and a father by now had he lived. There was a certain lady to whom he had become secretly engaged but in the uncertainty of the days of the Terror it was felt they should wait. That was a mistake. Now Phillip was dead, and Annette had been forced into an arranged marriage to some noble who secured her passage out of France.

Gweneth picked agitatedly at the lace of her skirt. Such thoughts were best forgotten. It was all gone and nothing, certainly not the cavernous sorrow which threatened to engulf her, could ever change a single line of the history.

Raoul knew he talked mostly for his own benefit, but he did not mind as long as Gweneth was near. Her faint scent of jasmine teased his nostrils and boosted his resolve that the evening would be a success.

After a short while they were handed onto the dock and into the waiting carriage. Gweneth sat forward to observe all the better the fascination of this new land. Along the waterfront stood several low-roofed, weather-distressed storehouses and nearby a sandy lane wound its way toward a row of shanties from which music and laughter could be heard. Gweneth wrinkled her nose in distaste and was glad when the carriage turned off that road and plunged into the thick of the jungle. The foliage pressed close in on them from every direction, all but shutting out the sky.

"You will find these islands a strange mixture of European culture and primitive life," Raoul said when she gave up her vigil and sat back. "There will be the stamp of civilization on tonight's affair, but I should like to show you the other side of life here one day. You would find it both enchanting and frightening. I wonder which would affect you the greater?" His voice was low and caressing in the dark carriage as he said, "It is quite easy to fear that which is new and different, but with time and familiarity it often becomes a pleasure." Gweneth did not answer, but his tone made her strangely aware of his nearness.

The carriage soon turned onto a dirt road lined with tall slim trees whose clustered branches gave them the look of giant feather dusters as they swayed in the wind, sweeping the night sky free of clouds. The lane threaded its way through fields of sugar cane, skirted a brief span of jungle, and then emerged onto a broad carriageway. Now the house came into view, a large white frame mansion with long columns bracing the veranda and a balcony which ran the width of the front. French doors opening onto the balcony allowed Gweneth a glimpse of the brightly dressed ladies and gentlemen who stood just within, and the rooms blazed in greeting with the golden light of hundreds of tapers.

"Oh, *c'est marveilleux!*" Gweneth cried. "There are gardens and even a fountain. *Je ne s'imagine pas—*" And she halted her rushing exclamations to laugh at herself. "I should speak one or the other, *n'est-ce pas?* Which shall it be, Monsieur Capitaine, English or French?" she asked.

"Whichever pleases you, mademoiselle. Either sounds delightful on your lips," Raoul replied. "I hope you shall forgive the informality of my dress. Wigs are deucedly difficult enough in England, but it would be sheer idiocy to attempt such tomfoolery on a tropical night. Oh, you shall see them but under them will be swollen florid faces drowning in their own juices."

Gweneth giggled and tossed her head back, sending the curls bouncing about her shoulders. Never had she imagined the wealth of plantationers to equal this. "Shall there be government officials present?" she asked, speaking the thought that had been on her mind from the start.

Raoul watched her expression brighten with hope and cursed under his breath. Their evening together had not yet begun, and she was thinking of leaving him. Alas, she was bound to disappointment, and he related to her what he had learned that morning.

Gweneth swallowed hard but then shook her head quickly to dismiss the defeat. "Weeks, monsieur? What are we to do? We can pay no one for lodging." She looked across at her companion and forced the next words aloud. "Will you be long in Road Town?" There, she had voiced her need of him at last.

"We sail with the morning tide," Raoul lied smoothly.

"So soon as that?" she whispered in dismay. Struggling with embarrassing helplessness, Gweneth folded her hands in her lap and wet her lips. "Where are you bound, Capitaine?"

Raoul smiled triumphantly and covered her hands with one of his. "Wherever you shall command, *ma belle*, but do not let us linger here when our hosts offer more pleasing surroundings." He leaned a little closer. "Or have you found a more interesting diversion?"

Gweneth's hesitation at the great double doors sprung from personal discomfort. She was not ashamed to be in the company of the handsomely arrayed man by her side, but her gown was another matter. She could not very well enter the dance floor with her shawl clutched protectively to her, but did she dare to reveal all that there was to be seen?

The answer came abruptly and completely from the captain. No sooner had he stepped with her over the threshold than he removed the silk cover from her shoulders with a flourish and handed it to the doorman, a Negro slave in livery, complete with powdered peruke.

Raoul lifted Gweneth's chin with the lightest touch of his hand and said, "Chin up, *ma belle*. No one shall dare less than complete respect for you. With such ladylike meekness as you possess, have you not always found it so?" he teased and put her hand through his arm to lead her into the ballroom.

By the time she had danced her third gavotte, Gweneth had lost all her fears. Their hosts, Squire and Lady Nicolson, proved to be a pleasant middle-aged couple who welcomed her warmly, if formally, into their home as Captain Bertrand's guest. The squire had escorted her out onto the dance floor for the first set and assured her that she would not lack for partners.

The squire was a broad, stocky man of impeccable manners who questioned her only briefly in regard to her voyage and destination. Captain Bertrand had introduced her as simply a passenger aboard his vessel whom he thought might enjoy the diversion and, without actually lying, Gweneth gave no true answer to any of her host's questions. There was no need, she told herself, to embarrass her uncle and aunt by admitting her strange circumstance. Moreover she hoped to be rid of the captain before she reached her family. With luck, her relatives need never know of this excursion.

Raoul stood apart after the required pairing with his hostess. Lady Nicolson was still a handsome woman, some years younger than her husband, and it was her invitation that had brought him here, but he was not of a mind to trade meaningless flirtations on this night. The suggestive squeezes of her hand and artfully contrived glances through lowered lashes left him cold. Friends of old, he might once have welcomed the temptation, but Squire Nicolson was one of his best customers and he would not risk business for a dalliance with his host's wife. It might have proved diverting for a lonely man but, tonight, Raoul felt himself to be anything but lonely.

Gweneth passed by on the arm of another, but she nodded in his direction and Raoul warmed to the delicious sensation that spread through his body as he gazed on her graceful form. Careful, Captain, he counseled himself, or you may make a spectacle of yourself before this genteel gathering that not even your custom-fitted evening coat can disguise.

Raoul chuckled low and lifted another glass of champagne from the silver tray gliding past on the arm of a servant. He must get Gweneth alone. Why, he had not availed himself of her company for even a single dance, and many were pressing close by her in hopes of the next. The lure of the gaming tables could not compete with the lovely figure in scarlet, he observed as he moved toward her.

Gweneth demurred the offers assailing her when

the dance ended. She had danced every figure and knew she would not become a wallflower in this setting where there were five men for each woman unless she claimed the right of rest.

"Pardon, messieurs. I simply must not neglect my escort a moment longer," she replied graciously to the proposals being put forth and extended her hand to Captain Bertrand as he reached her side.

"You are the belle of the ball, my sweet," Raoul observed when he had drawn her from the floor.

Gweneth looked up at his face for any hint of disapproval but smiled brightly under his approving gaze. "*Merci*, Capitaine, but I am sure it is only the novelty of a new face or, perhaps, it is the wrapping which attracts the admirers," she answered saucily and accepted the glass of champagne he held out.

"Not another face nor another figure would do such justice to the gown, mademoiselle. 'Tis your own sweet self which captivates them, as I foretold." His admiring gaze swept her again, and Gweneth found herself blushing.

"Perhaps a turn about the garden will restore your complexion," Raoul advised and led her through the open doorway and down the steps. "There is something out here you must see," he said when he had drawn her into the shadows beyond the house. "Sit with me awhile, and I promise you a treat." He helped her to a seat on a stone bench and joined her.

Gweneth fanned herself with her fingers and sipped the intoxicating bubbles. "*Merci*, Capitaine. I should enjoy a moment's rest." The night was warm and close but agreeably so, and she did not hesitate to linger alone with the man at her side. Past grievances forgotten, she allowed the night air and company to merge as one in tranquility.

Raoul sat back and studied her face, pale and beautiful in the dark, and marveled at his own reserve. The lady had ignited passion's flame within him from the moment he first set eyes on her, but there was something about her which disturbed him the greater now that they were alone and she had lowered her guard. There would be no coquettish words, no flirtatious glances from her, and yet he wanted her all the more because of this. Long forgotten words stirred in his mind and became thought.

> My Love is like to ice, and I to fire:
> How comes it then that this her cold so great
> Is not dissolved through my so hot desire,
> But harder grows the more I her entreat?
> Or how comes it that my exceeding heat
> Is not allayed by her heart-frozen cold,
> But that I burn much more in boiling sweat
> And feel my flames augmented manifold?

By God! The sight of her in the night invoked even poetry from the nether regions of his memory. Raoul snorted in mirth. That was unforgivable. No such sentimental rubbish was needed to beg excuse for his carnal hunger. Once burned—and he had been, gullible fool—he would never again dissemble with petty phrases of love the nature of lust. So, Mademoiselle Valois played a different hand than most women; the object remained the same. If she must be led patiently, so be it. Of course it would be of inestimable help to hasten the pace with a plenitude of champagne, Raoul reasoned, and drained his own glass with ease. Poetry! Good God!

"Your patience is rewarded, my lady," Raoul said in deep hushed tones and Gweneth looked up and away in the direction he indicated.

There, through the line of distant palms, came a faint glow just above the black water's edge. Gweneth paused, her glass in midair, and watched. The glow became silver-white just before the first edge of a full moon broke through the surface of the dark and rose clean and pure into the black velvet sky.

"Ah, *éclatant*," she breathed in awe and let the

empty glass be removed from her hand. Entranced by the moonrise, Gweneth had forgotten the captain and gasped in total surprise when he leaned forward and kissed her mouth soundly but briefly.

"'Tis good luck to steal a kiss from a pretty *jeune fille* at the rise of the full moon," Raoul stated when Gweneth turned a troubled frown on him.

"Capitaine, I have never heard such. You contrived it just now," she replied coldly and daintily lifted his confident arm from her shoulders.

"Just so, but it should be a custom, and I propose that we have just initiated it." His laughter was not in the least contrite. "More champagne, *ma belle*, for that is what you are, sweet one," he said softly and kissed her bare shoulder. "I shall not be long." And he left her alone.

Gweneth watched his retreating figure and thought, The night must be affecting my senses, for she had liked the feel of his lips and the flattering attention he had shown her.

Voices from beyond the nearby shrubbery arrested her thoughts, and Gweneth swiveled on the bench to see the passage of two people quite near.

"No, Andrew. Suppose we should be seen," a high feminine voice admonished halfheartedly.

"Now, Susanne, do not adopt the blushing maiden pose with me," came the amused reply. "We are not the only couple to seek respite from the heat and noise. Did you not notice that the captain brought his lady this way not long before?"

"Captain Bertrand? I should hope you do not cast me in the role of the girl who accompanies him!" she scoffed indignantly.

"What is this? She is nothing short of an exquisite trinket. I found her a most congenial young lady. You could do much worse than to pattern yourself on her manner."

"Really, Andrew? You would have me barter my affection?" the lady questioned stiffly. "I have heard tales of that man and his women. She may fool you with her blushing smiles but—that dress. Why, every lady here knows her for the courtesan she most definitely is!"

Gweneth's breath caught in her throat, and she held it lest they hear her strangled cough and know she was nearby.

"The deuce, you say?" the young man stammered. "Yet I suppose you are in the right. Though I do think your pique is most peculiar. Were you Lady Nicolson, our hostess, such viciousness would seem more appropriate."

"Poor Evelyn. Of course," came the agreeing reply. "Dear me, I had quite forgotten that episode. Why one devilish grin from that handsome rascal, and I'd be tempted to fall headlong into his bed just as Evelyn did. That is, if it were not for you," she finished with a flirtatious giggle.

"How droll," her companion replied sourly.

"Jealous, Andrew? Good, it becomes you," the lady teased.

The couple moved on, and the rest was lost, but Gweneth's eyes stung with tears from the pain in her chest. She had not fooled anyone with her formally correct bearing. The dress had branded her as a harlot as surely as the captain's reputation. And to think she had been so close to accepting his regard as genuine this once. Plummeted by shame and anger, she bowed her head to fight back the desire to weep.

"Here we are, *ma belle*," greeted the captain as he stepped from the shadows. Gweneth took the glass without meeting his eyes and quickly downed half of it. The sputtering and choking which followed effectively covered the reason for the tears which splattered onto her cheeks.

"Champagne always balks at disrespectful treatment, my lady," Raoul admonished humorously and dried her face with a handkerchief produced from his ruffled sleeve. "There, no more tears, mademoiselle, or the others will think you have come to harm at my hands." He raised her hand to his smiling face and pressed the palm to his cheek. "I should never harm you on purpose, *ma belle*. Never."

Gweneth regarded him with bright eyes full of mistrust. Would he now press the matter which must account for his having brought her into the garden in the first place? He believed also that she would be one more in the parade of women through his life.

"What is it?" Raoul asked solicitously and placed a kiss in her palm. "You were so lighthearted when I left you. Is the night's diversion not to your liking?" He reached out to touch her cheek but paused at her recoil. "What is it, *ma belle*? Have I offended you in some way?"

"Does it really matter what I think and feel, Capitaine? I am here at your command, spared none of the humiliation of being known as your paramour," she replied resentfully. "Not even the most heartless gentleman would force the company of a strumpet on his equals."

Raoul's brows shot up in stunned surprise, but his jaw set menacingly under compressed lips. "You think I would bring a street woman to this place? No, but I can show you exactly where I would take that kind of woman. Come!" He jerked her up from the bench and strode swiftly into the ballroom and across the dance floor.

Gweneth tripped and nearly fell, but Raoul was not of a mind to notice the embarrassment of his lady as he dragged her unceremoniously through the dancing partners. That several couples stopped to stare was lost on him. He had spent a better part of the evening trying to impress this little chit with gentle society. Well, she was about to be impressed with a very different sort of company.

He stopped only long enough to bid a curt farewell to his hosts, but Gweneth's breathless apologies were cut short by his impatient manner, and he swung her shawl over her gown and pushed her before him out of the door. He grasped her hand, leading her quickly past the startled faces of several late arrivals, down the steps, and along the line of waiting carriages until at last he stopped before theirs.

Raoul jerked the door open and, when Gweneth could not find the step handily, grabbed her about the waist and lifted her off the ground and into the carriage. He stepped in and slammed the door before she found a seat.

"Come here," he commanded, and Gweneth found herself propelled backward and practically into his lap. To the driver he gave some quick orders and then settled Gweneth in his embrace as the carriage sprang forward into the star-laden night.

The captain held her so firmly against himself that Gweneth felt he would crush her. "Please, Capitaine, you hurt me," she pleaded, but his iron grip did not relax.

Raoul glanced down at the girl within his arm. "My name is Raoul. That should not be so difficult for you. Say it."

Gweneth looked up in murderous intent until she met his half-amused, half-reckless expression. The beginnings of a smile softened his once grim mouth, but she did not return it. "Say it," he repeated less gently and tightened his embrace.

"*Oui*, monsieur. *Ra-ool, mais non?*" she inquired and his arm relaxed.

"And your name, that is English enough for me. You are Gweneth. I like my name on your lips, Gweneth. Say it again."

Feeling a bit irritated by his whimsical mood, Gweneth repeated his name singsong fashion. His other arm slid round her then, and suddenly his lips covered hers, and she was forced back until her shoulders nearly touched the seat.

His kiss was long and deliberately possessive, filling her with both exhilaration and dread, and Gweneth shivered from the effect of his proximity in the dark. Why could he do this to her? Gweneth wondered. Was it that she really wanted him this way? Part of her rebelled. Yet, as if to answer her question, her lips moved beneath his, timidly returning the pressure.

"There," Raoul said huskily and raised up, freeing her at long last. "That should teach you to make sport with my name, mademoiselle." He pulled at the lace of each cuff and lifted the collar of his coat to correct his attire and then glanced up and out of the window.

Dazed by this abrupt change, Gweneth rose awkwardly, as he offered no assistance, and mentally cursed his high-handed tactics. It was not the sort of treatment she had expected after his ardent embrace, but it was just the sort of thing the captain would do, she scolded herself in disgust at her folly.

She tugged the front of her gown up to the more respectable height from which it had slid and jerked her tangled skirts from under his legs, pushing herself into the far corner. "*Une vailliante geste,* mon Capitaine. *Merci.* Do you treat your wife, Marianne, with much the same dignity, or do you save it for the other women in your life?" she inquired angrily.

Raoul jumped visibly, and his head snapped around to her. "What did you say?" His voice cut through the close quarters like a blade, and in the half shadow of the moonlight his eyes gleamed like those of a jungle cat.

"I only inquired as to your gallantries toward your wife," Gweneth replied boldly but, having realized her mistake in uttering Marianne's name, a quiver of apprehension threaded her words. But no, if he allowed her no dignity, then his own wife was not sacred either.

"What do you know of my wife? If Daniel has been filling your head with rubbish, I shall—"

"It was you who were the source of my knowledge," Gweneth interrupted. "In your delirium you spoke of her often and even thought I was she." She could not resist taunting him, for he had shamelessly embarrassed her. "It was very touching, I assure you. Does your poor wife know how casually you seek other women while she waits at home for your return?"

Raoul grunted ominously, adding to her impression of him as a predatory beast, but he simply said, "My wife is dead. We shall speak no more of it," and turned back to the window.

Gweneth was strangely disturbed by his answer. He had rambled on about a child and murder for hours at a time, but the words never came to any order she could follow. At least she was not in the forced company of a married man—if that was a real comfort.

Gweneth nibbled her lip for, in finding respite in the fact that Raoul was a free man, she had admitted to herself that it mattered, if just a fraction.

As if he had read her thoughts, Raoul turned back and said, "Does that alleviate your qualms, mademoiselle, to know that the man you kiss so warmly is fair game?" His mocking voice trembled with laughter, and it was Gweneth who looked away this time.

The night had been relatively pleasant till now. Had she worn one of her own gowns and been in the company of family and friends, she should have reveled in the sensuous warmth of the tropical night where the stars nestled just above the treetops. In that moment in the garden when she had watched the great splendid globe rise wet and luminous from the sea like a single perfect pearl, she had experienced a feeling of ecstasy. But now as they retraced their path along the palm-lined lane, Gweneth bitterly regretted her decision to come with the captain. He sat in the dark enjoying an aromatic cigar, totally absorbed in his own thoughts, uncaring for the torment which racked her. How wonderful it must be to be a man, Gweneth reflected for the thousandth time, secure and dominant in a world of his own making.

Raoul took a long slow draw on his cigar, his features momentarily lit in the amber glow, but he knew Gweneth would detect nothing there. Years of training masked his emotions when necessary, but he could not hide from his thoughts. He could kick himself for not using the opportunity he had sought to gain an advantage with her. She had held her mouth to his with no reluctance for the very first time, and it was he who had backed away like a frightened lad with his first wench. And him, a veteran for nearly half his thirty years, quaking in his boots from a simple kiss stolen from a blushing maiden. His mind flinched. No, a maiden no longer. He had seen to that, and yet her innocence remained.

That was what had frightened him. She had no right to tempt him so openly with the soft perfume of her hair and supple tender body only to tremble so helplessly in his embrace. He had wanted her desire to match his own, forthright and freely given.

Just look how prettily she pouts, he thought as he stole a glance at her. The moonlight silvered the tips of her curls and lashes, and she might have been a dream. Yet when his eyes lowered to the place where her shawl fell open to reveal the smooth texture of her breasts, his breath caught in his throat and he choked on the smoke.

Gweneth looked across at the sound of his sputtering, but the captain gazed out, mindless of her existence.

Raoul sat forward suddenly and flicked the cigar out of the window. What had he said of Marianne? Had he murmured her name even as he made love to Gweneth? That would explain a great deal, but he could not ask her what had happened. A man could not simply apologize for a mistake like that.

The devil take it! He could use a good stiff drink. It would not be much longer now for he could see the gleam of inky water on the horizon. Soon he would show her how real men lived, a place where the joys of life were crammed into a few short days until it was time to set sail again. He was familiar with her way of life, but now she would have a taste of his.

CHAPTER SEVEN

Gweneth sat forward as they entered the lane at dockside. "Are we going back to the ship?" she inquired hopefully.

"Do I frighten you so that you would be so easily rid of me? I should never have suspected it a short while ago," Raoul answered with a smile. "Do not despair, *ma belle*. You shall have the honor of my company a while longer and, perhaps, you will learn a valuable lesson."

Gweneth opened her mouth to reply, but the carriage came to an abrupt halt before a rather ill-kept two-story house. Lush vegetation ran riotous over the iron fence, spilling its heavily laden branches of fuchsia and magenta blooms onto the roadway and saturating the tropical night with a thick honeyed scent.

Beyond the shadows of the garden, lamplight flooded through the open windows, and it was there that Gweneth's attention was drawn. Ribald laughter and music carried on the sea breeze from that place, the voices boisterous and coarsened by whiskey. Above them floated the notes of a woman's sultry song. Gweneth shrank back against the seat. Surely he did not mean to take her in there.

"Come, my lady. The night awaits us. By the sound of it I should say we have arrived just in time." Raoul sought Gweneth's wrist, and when she pulled back, he gave it a fierce tug, sending her forward across his lap.

"Tsk, tsk, *ma belle*. If you are not careful with that

gown, you shall soon find yourself wearing so much less." He lifted her by the arms and set her on the seat across from him, ignoring her attempts to hold him off.

"Listen and heed my words, Gweneth. This is no place for your sharp tongue nor lofty attitude," Raoul instructed as he rearranged her scattered curls. "You will stay by my side and do and say only as I command. This is no longer my ship and these men will not take kindly to insult."

Raoul drew out a handkerchief and dabbed her face, which was moist from the night air. "Now, let me look at you," he said, and his head wagged lightly as he held her chin between thumb and forefinger. "You may cost me my carousing, for I see I shall need to remain sober in order to protect my investment." Gweneth's features softened a trifle before he added, "I should not like to see my expensive gown ripped to shreds because you tempted some poor wretch to uncontrollable passion. Mind your manners, sweet, for I would not have you damage my reputation with an undignified display," he finished calmly and reached out in time to grab the hand that would have landed a slap on his cheek.

Raoul's grip tightened until a tiny cry of pain escaped between Gweneth's lips. "Heed this, mademoiselle," he whispered and thrust his dark, scowling face so close that she moved back against the seat. "You will be a perfect lady in there, or we shall both overlook your gentle breeding and remain here to have a little sport of our own. I have had more than enough of your priggish, high-flown ways. You were correct earlier when you said that you were here as my paramour. So be a quiet, docile mistress, and follow behind your master. Close behind."

Gweneth drew herself up against the leather-bound seat and answered his frown with a hostile look though her wrist throbbed badly. "It is always the same, Capitaine. I am obliged to do most anything which will save me from suffering at your hands." She tore her wrist free from his loosened fingers and, reaching under his arm, unlatched the door. "After you, monsieur."

Raoul's features darkened a fraction more, but then he shrugged and bounded from the carriage, signaling to the driver. Several coins passed between them, and now he turned to her, helping her down from the step.

Gweneth indifferently dropped her hand on the arm he offered and lifted her skirts free of the unkempt walk as they entered the gate. The steps were old and the newly replaced planks shone as pale white strips in the moonlight.

"This is where I should have spent the evening had I been alone, mademoiselle. Mind the experience, and you may learn a great deal," Raoul said as he opened the front door.

A scene of wild disorder rushed up over them in a tide of sound and light as they entered. Half-empty tankards of rum and trenchers of meat crowded every corner of the rough-boarded tabletops while people clotted the aisles and unfamiliar music pulsated through the close thick air, which smelled of men and sweat and liquor and tobacco.

Gweneth's hand tightened on Raoul's arm as he started forth, and she found herself being threaded through the midst of the shifting throng. Some men stopped to study her with undisguised interest, while others were so completely involved with the women hanging about their necks that Gweneth was rapidly losing her innocence as to what men and women found pleasurable in one another. The bodies of these strangers pressed her with such casual intimacy that more than once she gasped in astonishment and heard answering laughter. She closed her eyes and clung to her escort for dear life.

Raoul came to a halt so suddenly that Gweneth looked up in surprise to find his path blocked by the sprawling legs of a swarthy man in sailor's garb. The clammering voices about them died away slowly until all within hearing turned their attention to the confrontation.

"What ho, laddies. Look what the wind blows our way, a fine gentleman and—but let us see her, my lord." And the man reached out and whipped Gweneth's shawl from her shoulders. A roar of approval accompanied her unveiling, and he held it up high even as she reached out to snatch it back.

"Aye, my lord, but I do admire your taste in women. Come here, lovely," he beckoned and grabbed Gweneth's outstretched hand. Gweneth was pulled free of the captain's arm, and when she turned back to plead for assistance, she met his devilish smile. The captain inclined his head, and Gweneth stumbled backward into the sailor when he jerked her arm.

A gasp of fright accompanied her unceremonious spilling into the man's lap, and her pulse quickened as his arm slid round her waist to press her to him with the approving hoots of those about them.

"Faith, but you be a comely wench. A tender plump morsel just ready for the tasting," he continued and squeezed one bare shoulder while pressing his crisp sun-dried lips to her other. He smelled of a long voyage and cheap wine, causing Gweneth to shudder within his grasp.

"Cease that this instant," she demanded coldly in English, and with a tug on one greasy lock of his stringy hair she forced his head away.

The man yelped but did not release her. "A firebrand as well as a beauty, it makes the thought of you all the sweeter," he replied in coarsely accented English and reached up to give one of her own curls a sharp tug.

Gweneth squealed and swung her free hand up to give his face a full stinging slap. The seaman and his friends roared with laughter, much to Gweneth's confusion. "I understand perfectly the fascination you hold for your gentleman friend, but best mend your ways, me girl, for he does not seem to mind if you linger awhile to entertain us," said one of the other men around the table.

Gweneth looked up instantly in search of the captain. He had moved some distance to one side, his arms folded leisurely across his chest, and that same mocking expression animated his features. She stared at him in disbelief. Surely he did not mean to leave her in this scroundrel's embrace? Mingled fingers of dread and rage closed over her heart when his gaze slid from hers.

Raoul motioned to the innkeeper for a drink before allowing his attention to stray back to the man on whose lap Gweneth was perched. Let her ponder the possibilities of her future without his protection, he decided coolly. She should prove much more tractable after this.

"What say you, my lord? Is she mine?" The cocky tone of the sailor implied that he did not expect the fancy gentleman to decline, and Gweneth's hands clenched impulsively into fists.

Raoul took a long sip of his drink. "She is worth a great deal to me. What would you offer for her?" he inquired lazily.

The sailor's expression brightened. "Is she for sale? Well, well and all the while I am thinking she is a lady. They do fashion them prettier every year, do they not?" His liquor-glazed eyes dropped to ravish Gweneth's uncovered flesh with such open greed that she snatched up the edge of her shawl to cover her bodice.

"Libertine! Debaucher! Befouler of all that is sacred—" A gush of every Gallic aspersion she had ever heard rushed from Gweneth's lips as she turned her anger on Raoul. She hated him, she screamed, understanding now that he had brought her here to abandon her to anyone willing to take up her keep.

"Careful, lovely lady. Save your strength for the

coming hour," the seaman counseled with a chuckle, but Gweneth shoved away the filthy hand that sought to touch her and turned on the drunkard a stare of such venom and disdain that he hesitated to force the issue just yet. Instead he looked back to her owner. "What would you exact for an evening's pleasure?" he asked with a grin.

Raoul shrugged noncommittally. "The gown she wears put me back a thousand francs alone but, I suppose, you would return that undamaged? Then there is the need for me to find a new diversion, for I had looked to her to quench a thirst she has as yet but whetted. Five hundred pounds, I think that a fair price. You are not likely to ever again possess her equal."

The group of sailors nearby groaned disparagingly, and Gweneth's eyes narrowed in suspicion. No one would pay such a sum for a woman, even she realized. He had only sought to frighten her, the heartless dog. "Cheat," she murmured under her breath.

The sailor shook his head and spat on the floor near Raoul's boot. "Bah! I could fill my bed a thousandfold for such a sum, did I possess it. There must be a better bargain we can strike between us." Gweneth had eyes only for the object of her contempt, but she was attentive to the hand which moved behind her and then of the touch of cold steel on her upper arm.

With a strength she had not known was hers, she lunged free of her captor and fell on the captain screaming that she would rip that smirk from his handsome features with her bare hands. Raoul's brows shot up in amusement as he handily caught her by the wrists and hauled the dangerously poised nails up over her head.

"Beware, Capitaine. The man has a knife!" she whispered frantically in French as she struggled with his superior strength. Raoul's expression altered not a whit, but when Gweneth would have repeated her warning, he clasped a hand quickly over her mouth.

"Forgive me, sir, but I believe I shall keep her for myself after all," Raoul said courteously. "She is new to the game and needs a firm hand." He twisted Gweneth around and held her back against his chest. "Tell the man that you prefer my company, mademoiselle."

Gweneth murmured to herself and gave his shin a sharp kick with her heel, well aware of the admission he meant her to make to this room of interested parties, but nodded reluctantly when his grip tightened. She would get even, she promised herself. Oh but she would choose her moment to exact a suitable revenge!

"Now, if you will detain us no longer," Raoul said and made to pass the man. A loud scrape of his chair accompanied the sailor's rise to his feet, and then he was brandishing a long fine-honed blade in his right hand. At once Gweneth was thrown free and landed on her knees as the others made room with shouts of delight at this new turn of events. Her heart raced wildly as she scrambled for a footing, but the scene before her eyes when she spun round on her knees steadied her fright.

Raoul stood with feet apart, and in his right hand he held a pistol, no doubt lifted from his open coat. The sailor raised his knife menacingly but his face had flushed and his stance was unsteady.

"My man, why should we come to blood over the affections of a simple wench when both of us could spend our energies so much more profitably? She is but a female, after all." Raoul spoke amicably, but the barrel of his weapon was lowered to the man's midsection. "What difference which chit relieves the discomfort of a long voyage? It all comes to the same in the end." He smiled, yet Gweneth detected the tension in his voice and the glint in his deep blue eyes. He would kill without regret if the need presented itself. It was as if he wanted this fight.

The man's grip flexed on the handle, but the wariness in his face betrayed his reluctance to engage the gentleman.

"Capitaine Bertrand, my friend!" The voice belonged to one of the crowd, and Gweneth glanced toward the door. There stood a man dressed in an elegant red velvet coat heavily embroidered with gold. "But, what is this, *mon ami*? Would you rob me of a first-rate seaman? And to what cause?"

The imposing figure made his way through the spectators until Gweneth found herself gazing with widened eyes up into his fiery black stare. His features were unusually pronounced, with broad cheekbones and a wide sensuous mouth beneath a heavy drooping moustache. And when he removed his broad-brimmed hat in salute, he revealed a head of unclubbed raven hair falling in shiny waves about his shoulders.

He had strolled between the two contestants as though they held nothing more dangerous than a pint each, his eyes fastened on the slender girl in the crimson dress which billowed out about her. A single fragile flower among the thorns, he mused to himself and smiled slightly. "Mademoiselle," he greeted her and held out his hand. Gweneth took it, feeling the warm reality of him as he assisted her to her feet, and he gently kissed her fingers.

"Are you the cause of this point of honor?" he asked in perfect French, and Gweneth's legs felt less steady when he smiled, broadly and enticingly.

"*Oui,* monsieur," she replied and dropped her gaze in uncommon shyness, but she did not resist when his hand lifted her chin again. "*Exquise,* mademoiselle. *Enchanté.*" His voice was both flattering and appreciative, and as Gweneth blushed in response, a hint of satisfaction crept into his smile. His gaze swept the rest of her quickly and then he tucked her hand into his arm and turned back to the two men whom all had seemed to have forgotten.

"Would you two braggarts fight like a pair of rutting stags?" he asked and shook his ebony mane. "I believe the *jeune fille* is quite capable of making her own choice. In fact, it would seem she has." He looked down into Gweneth's face and pressed her hand in the curve of his arm. "Therefore, gentlemen, whatever the outcome of your squabble, I believe you shall find that the little quail has flown both your lures." He bowed low with a flamboyant sweep of his plumed hat and turned his back on them to guide Gweneth away.

"Music, Inez! We must not let those fools spoil our evening," he instructed. The crowd was silent a fraction longer, and their disappointment was palatable when they turned their backs, grumbling now that the entertainment had been curtailed.

Gweneth allowed herself to be led away after a single backward glance, and her heart skipped a measure. Raoul's confident smile had dissolved, and in its place was a grim line. Could it be that her tormentor was left agape by the man who treated her with respect and obvious interest? A slow smile of mischief spread across her lips as an idea came to her. The opportunity for revenge had presented itself in the very person of her rescuer.

The gallant stranger shepherded her to a table near the edge of the room, a quiet, partially enclosed area reserved for the more important visitors to the tavern.

When he had seated himself beside her on one of the faded velvet chairs, he spoke. "I am Laurent Lavasseur, capitaine of the *Christobel*. And who might you be, *ma petite?*" He leaned near and put a hand over hers, which were laced in her lap.

"I am Gweneth Valois, Capitaine. You were quite reckless to interfere, but I thank you for your bravery. I do not wish to imagine what would have occurred had you not," Gweneth replied sincerely.

Laurent felt her hands trembling slightly beneath his and smiled. " 'Twas nothing, I assure you, mademoiselle." Gweneth looked up in search of Captain Bertrand, and Lavasseur's gaze followed hers. "Are you so very worried about our friend? He shall return to you in a moment. I have put him in the embarrassing position of removing himself from a fight he was sore to press. You must be of great importance that he should seek to prove his bravery for you." Laurent's hand squeezed hers, and Gweneth turned back to him. "Is he important to you, Mademoiselle Valois?"

"He has brought me here against my will, but I do not wish to be abandoned, monsieur," she replied frankly and moved from the captain's very personal touch.

"Against your will? But I do not understand. Are you not bound to his company for the evening? He sets a great store by you, that is certain, but am I to understand that he holds you by duress?"

"He holds me for ransom, I suspect. He is a plunderer and a pirate and I wish now that I had held that knife," Gweneth whispered in angry tones.

"I see," Laurent replied slowly. "He is very important, *mais non?* But this talk of piracy—a term you should not bandy about in this place, *ma petite*—how is it that you name him such? He has always been a man of honor and quality in our associations."

"Honor is the last virtue I should ascribe to him. Is it honor that holds my sister and two maids prisoner aboard his vessel? Is it quality that drives him to mockery and ridicule?" Gweneth's chin began to quiver with emotion at these last words, and she bent her head in shame.

"This becomes more curious with each word, mademoiselle, but allow me to offer you some refreshment before I beg you to continue," Laurent offered gently and signaled for a servant.

"*Merci,* Capitaine, but nothing for me."

"But you must. Something, mademoiselle," Laurent encouraged. "A little brandy, perhaps, sherry. Yes, that will revive your blush. You are too pale. I should like to see more color in your cheeks and lips. A glass of your very best," he said to the man. "Now—" But he was interrupted by the arrival of Raoul.

"Damn you, Lavasseur. You cost me a round of drinks and, also, my sport. I was more than willing to test your man providing, of course, that we would lay the weapons aside."

"Ah, Capitaine Bertrand!" Laurent welcomed and stood to clasp hands vigorously. "In such delightful company, your choice of entertainment bewilders me. As it is, you are likely to lose a great deal more before the night is out." And his eyes dropped to Gweneth.

"I thought I warned you not to make a spectacle of yourself, mademoiselle," Raoul said sharply when his gaze, too, fell on Gweneth.

"You say so many things, Capitaine, I find myself quite unable to know what you expect. First you threaten to sell what you do not own, then you mock me cruelly to the whole world. It was not my decision to come here, and if you never present yourself to me again, I shall not regret the slight," she answered in icy tones.

"*Mon ami*, you have a most remarkable find in this lady," Laurent said and laughed as he took his seat. "And she tells me you have three more at your disposal."

"What bilge have you been spilling?" Raoul asked quickly and seated himself opposite them.

"Only that you are a rogue, Capitaine. A fact I am sure Capitaine Lavasseur has had ample time to discern for himself since you are already acquainted." Gweneth looked away and took a cautious sip of the sherry set before her. Her eyes widened in appreciation as the quality of the liquor settled on her tongue and warmed her throat. "*Merci*, Capitaine," she murmured and smiled at Lavasseur.

"Something for you, Bertrand? Rum? Brandy?" Laurent offered.

"Brandy," Raoul demanded of the servant.

"When did you make port, Bertrand? I did not see your ship in harbor yesterday." Laurent leaned back and crossed his legs.

"Only this morning. I noted the *Christobel* in the bay for I had hoped to catch you this trip, but when my man called, you were not aboard."

"There were business matters which required my attention on the far side of the island. I returned only this moment. And a handy thing it was. My man did not recognize you, and I apologize for his rash behavior, Bertrand. But I have never known the time when you needed to fight for the affections of a lady. Could it be that the notorious capitaine has lost his fascination?" Laurent questioned with a twinkle in his eye.

Raoul glanced at Gweneth. "It is only that I have chosen so poorly this time that the girl has not the sense to know the luck which befalls her."

"I know full well the disastrous fate with which I am met," Gweneth retorted. "And, as to luck—"

"Enough, mademoiselle," Lavasseur objected, abruptly but kindly. "Could it be that you have married this young thing, Bertrand? It would appear that I have trespassed upon a domestic squabble." The rapid sounds of denial which erupted from them both brought laughter from Laurent, who was enjoying hugely this contest of wills.

"God forbid that I should find myself shackled to the likes of Mademoiselle Valois. It were better that I should lose my desire for women entirely!" Raoul declared.

"I am in complete agreement, Capitaine. May your wish be granted," Gweneth concurred.

"Valois, Valois, the name is not entirely unfamiliar," Laurent mused. "I once met a Phillip Valois in Paris. A marvelous swordsman. *Ma vie*! Would that I should acquire such skill as is his. Do you, per chance, know of him, mademoiselle?"

"He was my brother!" Gweneth exclaimed with a softening in her voice that made both men desire that she should once say their names in that same breathless manner.

"*Ma foi!*" Laurent remarked, and a long whistle accompanied this. "Capitaine, you may soon find yourself at the business end of a rapier held by one of the ablest swordsmen in all Europe. It is her father I refer to, of course. And, if I am correct, there are three brothers. You take a rash course in absconding with a female of that household."

"It was the most unfortunate day of my life when I fished her up from the sea, Lavasseur. For weeks I have had this splinter under my flesh until I am rubbed raw by the agitation."

"Had you been a true gentleman, you would never have known anything but gratitude and courtesy from me. You cause your own misery, Capitaine," Gweneth corrected coldly.

Laurent looked from one to the other, and his curiosity could not be contained. "I must have the story. Mademoiselle, you must explain how you came to meet our mutual friend."

Laurent proved to be an excellent audience, and it was with some relief that Gweneth let the story of her flight from France and the reasons behind it pour forth to this stranger. "When we were sighted by the capitaine, it should have seemed a salvation, but I was soon fighting for my life," she ended with a defiant glare at Raoul.

"Not your life, mademoiselle. Never that," Raoul amended. "But why have I not heard this tale before? In all the weeks we have been together, you have never spoken so openly," he added in puzzlement.

"You never allowed the chance for explanation, Capitaine. I have never been anything truly human in your eyes. You ignored my needs with casual ease and only my blade prevented you from forcing your own on me."

"You fence, Mademoiselle Valois?" asked Laurent

when he saw Raoul blanch. "This gets better with the telling."

"Ask the capitaine, monsieur. He can answer better than I," Gweneth replied though a stab of fear shot through her, for she realized that it was a very dangerous thing to belittle the captain's ability before his friend. But he deserves it, she told herself. Too often he had made her the butt of his cruel humor.

"She boarded my vessel with all the airs of a queen, accusing me of piracy," Raoul volunteered. "That sharp tongue of hers led me to a foolish mistake and in allowing her to defend that which she seemed so sincerely to treasure, I found myself to be pricked. I do not have your head for names, Lavasseur, and it was after the mademoiselle was fully armed that I discovered her ability. Nothing of consequence you must agree, mademoiselle, for the debt was honored in full that very afternoon, was it not?" Raoul asked in a preemptive tone.

Gweneth bit off the retaliatory words that trembled on her lips and glared furiously at his self-satisfied sneer. Tears welled in her eyes in defense of his vicious attack but these, too, she blinked back, knowing that he cared nothing for her humiliation.

"But you might have injured her, Bertrand," Laurent said incredulously. "No gentleman should ever bully a sweet innocent such as this." And he lay a gentle, possessive hand on Gweneth's arm. "Had I been there, I should have spared you the degradation. I swear it!" His fingers closed firmly over the soft silkiness of her skin.

"Look here, Bertrand, could you not see that she deserved your respect and protection? You have dealt too long with the wrong sort, *mon ami*. Her appearance, her every gesture, they bear me out." Laurent let his hand slip down the smooth flesh of her arm and rest on her hand. "*Ma petite*, I beg your forgiveness on behalf of my foolhardy friend. He must have been struck with a moment of madness to have sought to harm you in any way." He raised her hand to place a kiss there.

Raoul chuckled deep in his throat. "Still the flamboyant courtier, Lavasseur. And you, chérie, so you have found a protector at last. But be careful you do not fall into his debt, or you may find that he exacts the same payment."

"At least it will be mine to choose for a change, *mais non?*" Gweneth replied but found she could not meet either man's gaze.

"I thought you had chosen when you warned me of the knife concealed by that fellow. You were eager then to see that I did not come to harm," Raoul taunted and sat back lazily with arms folded.

"It was my own safety which prompted my actions," Gweneth assured him. "I have discovered that there are still a few things I despise more than your unwelcomed attentions."

"Stop this, both of you," Laurent demanded. "This is an evening for revelry, not recriminations. 'Tis your first night in port, Bertrand, and it is my last. I would have the pleasure of your company, providing this childish bickering will cease. More brandy, Capitaine?"

Raoul nodded in agreement, and then his eyes strayed to the place where Laurent's hand rested in casual possession on Gweneth's shoulder. The obvious satisfaction in her face soured his mood further. She wished to play one against the other, he thought, and forced a smile to his lips. That is a very dangerous game, *ma belle*. Play it well, little one, but know that it is my bed you shall seek before the night is out. There are many things you do not understand, and one of them is that Lavasseur would never steal what is rightly mine. We go back a long way, and the friendship has stood the test of time.

"To you, *mon amour*," he intoned softly and downed the contents of his glass.

Gweneth pretended not to hear the intimate words

and turned to look over Laurent's shoulder to where the music played. The final bars of a tune ended and, in the short pause, from the shadows there emerged the figure of a young woman. Dressed in a skirt of bright colors and a thin blouse which fell negligently from one shoulder, she wore a single scarlet flower in her heavy black hair, which fell in a veil about her shoulders. And, young though she was, there gleamed the ancient invitation in her large dark eyes.

The music took up again, and she began to sway in time to the primitive rhythm, her body moving with the fluid grace of a serpent. Tiny cymbals tinkled on the bracelets she wore on both wrists and one bare ankle and, as the music grew louder, her dancing became more bold. She swirled out among the tables, lifting her skirt to reveal slim brown legs and a ruffle of black petticoats, but the sensual lines of her face remained impassive.

The sailors reached out, running their hands freely over her moving form, and several tucked coins into the front of her blouse, beneath which her rounded breasts swung freely. She teased and taunted them but never lingered long enough to be caught.

Gweneth's round-eyed stare seemed to amuse her as she danced their way, but it was Captain Bertrand who received her provocative, half-pouting smile. She ran a hand through his hair, her fingers brushing his cheek as she leaned near, and Gweneth was certain that nothing was shielded from his view when she dipped low before him. But she spun away when he put out a hand and beckoned.

On and on the music played, and she danced back toward the center of the room to hoist her skirts high in a dramatic finish. A shower of coins followed her curtsy and cries of appreciation reverberated through the close smoky air. She bent and scooped up a number of coins, dropping them one by one into the neck of her blouse, but her dark longing look was for Captain Bertrand.

Gweneth stole a quick glance at him and looked away in disgust. Never had she seen him thus, his face gleaming with a sheen of sweat and his breath slightly labored. Nor had there been that intensity of expression in his eyes when he looked at her. If that were the sort of emotion he had wanted her to invoke, then she was well rid of his consideration, Gweneth thought, but only halfheartedly. She swallowed back the sensation of queasiness rising in her and stifled the very impulse of jealousy.

The girl lifted her skirts with a quick toss and ran from the floor straight into the captain's lap. "Capitaine Raoul!" she squealed in glee and entwined her slender arms about his neck as she lowered her mouth to his.

She strained against him in such abandon as Raoul's hands boldly caressed her that Gweneth gasped softly, but they were meshed together in mutual desire, oblivious to all else.

Laurent had watched the exchange in amused detachment, but he was moved by the look on Gweneth's face when he turned to her. His hand tightened on her shoulder as he leaned near. "Do you always hide your feelings so well, mademoiselle?" he questioned lightly.

Gweneth started at his touch and looked up to meet that mischievous wicked black stare within inches of her own. Some of the same emotion in the captain's eyes was now reflected in his. "If you are feeling neglected, *ma petite*, I should be delighted to attend to the slight." And he bent forward till his lips touched hers.

He tasted of brandy and tobacco, but there was a warm sweetness in his light kiss which compelled Gweneth to respond, and when he moved back, she experienced an odd sense of loss.

Laurent arched a single brow. "There is much else I should like to know about you, mademoiselle. You are not the reluctant shrew Bertrand would have me believe."

Gweneth blushed hotly. "Forgive me, Capitaine . . . perhaps the liquor," she murmured and put a hand to her lips.

"Never apologize for giving a man pleasure, chérie. He does not want to believe that you really regret the impulse which he fostered," Laurent whispered in her ear and placed a quick kiss there. "I am glad to see the blush has returned to your lovely face."

Gweneth's thoughts jumbled together, bringing no order to her emotions. She did not regret the kiss, and yet, what must he think of her?

She found the courage to look across at Captain Bertrand, who was just now disentangling himself from the girl on his lap. "Enough, enough, Leila. You make me forget my companions. What a wanton you are. Have you no shame?" he teased and dropped a kiss on her slender neck.

"Not where you are concerned, Raoul," Leila replied saucily and drew him back into her embrace.

Releasing him at last, she giggled and said, "It has been too long, my capitaine. I will not let you leave me soon." She kissed his brow and turned to Laurent.

"*Bon soir*, Capitaine Laurent. I see you provide your own company this night." Her gaze strayed to Gweneth, smooth and distant. The dislike and mutual distrust was instant between them. "Is she one of your fancy women from New Orleans?"

Laurent shook his glossy head with a laugh. "May I present Mademoiselle Valois, a visitor to your island from Paris. A lady and a thoroughly charming creature."

"Are you truly a lady?" she asked. "Oh, but of course. That gown must have cost a fortune. Raoul," she pouted, "you promised me one like it. Have you brought something for me?"

The blood drained from Gweneth's face, but she forced herself to watch Captain Bertrand. So the dress belonged to the girl on his lap. If he was embarrassed, it did not show, and Gweneth decided that the evening needed nothing so much as another sherry as she stared down at her vacant glass.

Raoul dodged Laurent's shrewd look, but he answered easily. "I believe I may have something for you, you wicked girl, but that matter can wait a few days."

"You said that we would be leaving with the morning tide," Gweneth protested quickly and glanced up.

"Did I so? Then I have changed my mind," Raoul said, patting Leila familiarly. "I had forgotten the enticements this port holds."

"But you promised," she persisted.

"I doubt that I have ever promised you anything, mademoiselle. As you said before, you are at my mercy, and I no longer have the desire to sail with the sun. It is done."

"I do not know where you are bound, mademoiselle," Laurent said suddenly, "but I sail with the tide and would be honored to have you aboard my vessel."

"She cannot pay you. She sails as my guest and at the favor of my good nature," Raoul countered swiftly, but his smile stiffened a little.

"Whatever the capitaine has offered you, *ma chèrie*, you shall find me more generous a hundredfold," Laurent replied and smiled. To Raoul he said, "I have learned that you do not credit the lady fairly, Bertrand. She can be most accommodating when properly approached. *Mais oui*, mademoiselle?"

A frown formed on Raoul's brow. "Just what do you mean, Lavasseur?"

"You are not the only one to receive the affections of a young woman, *mon ami*. I have used my time as wisely as you." Laurent gathered a handful of Gweneth's curls into his hand. "If you wish to come with me, then I shall see to it immediately, mademoiselle."

"There are three others as well. They will cost no

small sum to closet and feed. I am not yet privy to the lady's destination. She may demand that you set sail for France again," Raoul warned.

"A most tempting idea, Capitaine. I should like nothing better than the opportunity of sailing with her indefinitely."

Raoul grunted and tossed back another full glass only to signal for a refill. The flush had not left his face, and Gweneth began to wonder if it were the brandy rather than Leila which caused it.

Leila stirred within Raoul's arm. "Capitaine, let us leave them alone. They seem content in one another's company, and you and I have much to say to each other after all these months." She bent and nibbled the corner of his ear, whispering words which brought a secret smile to his lips before she hopped from his lap and took his hand. "Lavasseur does not want us here. There, you see, he is not even aware of us."

Raoul gazed up to see Laurent tracing Gweneth's cheek with his fingertip. The devil take it, he thought and muttered a curse. That wily Frenchman had gotten further with Gweneth in an hour than he had in weeks. As he watched with set jaw, Lavasseur moved toward her upturned face.

Gweneth caught a glimpse of Raoul's piqued expression as Laurent bent to her, and she leaned forward to meet his lips, her fingers tentatively touching his satin tresses. Swiftly Laurent's arms encircled her and drew her from the chair into his lap.

Breathless and more than a little surprised by the fierceness of his second kiss, Gweneth made herself respond to his demand. Let Captain Bertrand know that she cared nothing for his caresses but preferred even those of a stranger. He had shamed her twice this night. She would show him how cheaply she held his regard.

"I thought I instructed you not to embarrass me with your licentious displays, mademoiselle!"

Gweneth drew back and cringed as though Raoul had struck her.

"You make a convincing whore, but I was under the impression that you preferred the part of coquette," Raoul jeered.

"That is unfair!" Laurent cut in and, to Gweneth's amazement, there was a tension in his voice that bespoke his displeasure. "You bring the *jeune fille* here and dangle her beauty before these whoring curs, even offering her the humiliation of pretending to sell her, and then fondle a new woman before her very eyes. What do you know of proper behavior? Do not address another disparaging word to the lady in my presence, or I shall be forced to overlook the fact that we are friends." Laurent's tone did nothing to blunt the warning.

Raoul stood, his blood churning with rage. Gweneth had managed to make him look a fool in the eyes of one of the few men he respected. He had counted on their friendship to keep that fancy bit of fluff in her place, but he should have guessed that she would not be meekly subdued. By God! How eagerly she had kissed Lavasseur. Raoul could almost feel again her kiss when he embraced her in the carriage, and the aching for her which was a constant part of him these days became agony. There was but one cure for it.

A bitter, contemptuous smile sprang to his lips. "Very well, Lavasseur, she is yours for now. For a friend there is nothing I would deny, but remember the favor for I shall collect on it one day." Raoul roughly jerked Leila to his side and stared at Gweneth as he drained his glass. "*A beintôt*, mademoiselle, but be ready when I have a desire to depart." He saluted in her direction, and Gweneth was left to watch in anger and hurt as they crossed the floor and mounted the stairs at the far end of the room.

CHAPTER EIGHT

"Have you supped yet, *ma petite?* You are so light in my arms that I fear I should hurt you if I squeezed hard."

Laurent was heady with the prospect of having Gweneth to himself. He could only guess at his friend's strange behavior. Bertrand displayed a frank dislike at her affection toward another man, and yet he sought a different woman to fill his bed. Of course Bertrand had always blown hot and cold where women were concerned, but to prefer a wayward gypsy to the prospect of conquering this *belle fille,* bah, he must be mad!

Perhaps, having bedded her before, he had grown tired of her. But no, that was not to be believed, Laurent decided as his practiced eye studied Gweneth's throat and bosom exposed by the daring cut of her gown. More likely the capitaine found himself caring much more than he thought wise. It would be a simple thing to fall in love with this delicious young ingenue. She demanded respect and unwittingly brought forth a man's desire to protect her with that sea-green gaze. He smiled self-indulgently. Beware, Laurent, or you may hear yourself promising that very thing as you hold her close in the moonlight.

It was physical agony for Gweneth to keep back the hurt she felt at being rejected, but she smoothed her features into an unreadable mask when she noticed her companion's eyes on her. What would he think if he should guess the extent of injury to her pride? She had behaved badly, and yet she had not been able to prevent it. Only a short while ago she had given in to Captain Bertrand's kiss and felt the quickening of her emotions. Now a total stranger had done the same.

You have escaped the capitaine as was your wish, so forget and enjoy your moment of freedom, a voice within her urged, and Gweneth heard herself say aloud, "I should like it above all to share a light supper with you, monsieur."

"Excellent! I shall order a special meal for us. There are private dining rooms upstairs where we shall have the peace to eat at our leisure, away from this tumultuous crowd." Laurent slid Gweneth from his lap and lay her hand on his arm.

He addressed the innkeeper in rapid Spanish, and Gweneth merely understood that he received a key and the man's good wishes.

The key opened the door to a small room, but the interior was too dark for Gweneth to judge its contents. The shutters of the windows were folded back to let in the night, and she crossed the darkened space to catch the breeze from the bay. The wind blew fresh from the sea above the treetops on this floor, and the room was cool and sweet. She stepped out onto the balcony and leaned against the iron rail to study the harbor where the lantern lights of the vessels were scattered and reflected on the backs of waves like shards of amber glass.

Laurent lit a single candle on the table and removed his coat before joining her. His hands embraced her shoulders as he stood behind her, and she shivered at the touch. "You are cold, *ma petite?*"

"Non, Capitaine. The night is warm and beautiful. So much has happened that it seems impossible that it is yet the same day," Gweneth replied. But she shivered again even as she spoke.

"Then, perhaps, it is I who cause your trembling," he said very near her ear, his warm breath caressing her cheek. "Do not be afraid of me, chérie. You are quite safe—for now." And he dropped his hands. He went on to point out his ship, the black and gold *Christobel* calmly riding her anchor, and so engrossed were they in a discussion of her merits and successful voyages that they were surprised by the knock which announced dinner.

Gweneth turned back with laughter on her lips which immediately vanished. The room was furnished with a small table flanked by two velvet armchairs. Straw mats covered the floor, and in one corner stood a tall bamboo birdcage partially covered to protect its sleeping inhabitants. But the most impressive and, by far, the least welcome sight to Gweneth's mind was a large brass bed. She looked away quickly—there was no reason to doubt its existence—and her heart leaped into her throat as the possible reason for her having been brought here came clear.

Laurent noted her mounting fears and sought to turn them aside. "Come and sit, mademoiselle. I challenge you to a match, your appetite to mine. You say you have had nothing to eat, and I am famished to the point of collapse. Let us indulge ourselves, and moderation be damned for the remainder of the meal." He swept Gweneth into a chair while the servant set the dishes before them.

A feast it was and, once begun, Gweneth no longer doubted Capitaine Lavasseur's statement that he could eat sufficient for two. There was not an ounce of fat anywhere on his long lean frame, but he dispatched enough food to keep Gweneth content for days.

Laurent kept their glasses brimming to offset the highly seasoned food and filled Gweneth's silences with talk of his home near New Orleans and his travels. When he sat his chair back at last, Gweneth was smiling dreamily. His voice was vaguely familiar and comforting despite the peculiar colonial intonations which occasionally crept into his excellent French.

This, combined with the abundance of wine, gradually evaporated the tension of the evening.

"Monsieur Lavasseur, I thank you—but then, that is all I have done all evening, *mais oui?* You saved me from that sailor and then from Capitaine Bertrand and now from starvation. I must seem the incarnate of the damsel in distress. And you, my Capitaine, were ever the gallant knight," Gweneth announced with gratitude. Candlelight, mirrored as pure green flame, shimmered in her brilliant eyes, and Laurent was no less immune to her attraction than any other man. He leaned forward and blew out the single light in the room. "Only too true, chérie, but who shall save you from me?"

Gweneth cast a wary glance at the bed and bit her lip. Who had turned back the covers? She rose quickly to her feet, but a dizzying weakness made them insufficient support. Laurent was at her side in an instant.

"You are not accustomed to so much wine, mademoiselle. Come to the balcony and get your breath," he instructed and led her to the open window with an arm about her waist.

With a deep sigh Gweneth leaned against his shoulder, closing her eyes. He was a good man, she thought anxiously, and though she was no longer certain of what was happening, she knew that she was drawn to him in spite of her fear. She raised her face when she felt him bend to her, turning her in his arms and pulling her close, and her fingers threaded lightly through his flowing locks and then clasped behind his neck.

His third kiss was different still. There was the need and fervent longing, but it was mellowed by tenderness and the desire not to frighten her. A rippling sigh sped through her, and Gweneth swayed against him, no longer wishing to escape his intoxicating ardor. This man cared for her, wanted her, and after the humiliation of this night she needed desperately to be found desirable. Oh, but it was not as in her dreams!

Laurent lifted her into his arms and crossed the distance to the bed quickly. Then, with her still in his arms, he kissed her throat and shoulders, murmuring enraptured words of desire until his mouth took hers again; and she learned a great deal from the kisses that followed. He was a gentle, experienced lover, patient until he stirred within Gweneth the helpless need to submit to all he demanded, and he heard his victory in the whimper which rose from the girl trembling in his arms.

"What do you say, *ma petite?* My name is Laurent. Your capitaine is busy elsewhere. You are safe with me," he promised. "Before the night is finished, I shall make you forget that villain. You shall be loved with such tender passion you need never remember his brutality. I swear it!" His voice was deep and hushed, and Gweneth felt more than heard his ardent expressions as he held her to his broad chest. He continued to caress her with an intimacy she had never allowed any man, gently pulling the gown from her shoulders to expose her breasts to his kisses. But when his hand slipped under her skirts to stroke the cool velvety flesh of her thighs, Gweneth cried out.

"Please, non! You do not understand, monsieur. I cannot do this! There has never been anyone else," Gweneth pleaded breathlessly. "I lied to the capitaine. He does not remember, and I lied to save myself. Please, listen to me!" she begged, and when Laurent's hand slid from beneath her gown, she poured out the story in short jerky sobs.

Gweneth drew his ear down to her lips when she was done and said, "I have behaved shamefully, and you have every right to force me to your will, but you must believe me. I speak the truth."

"*Sacré Dieu!*" Laurent exclaimed. He wanted to finish what he had begun but could not reconcile it with the prospect of seducing the virgin in his arms. No wonder Bertrand was at his wits' end. She was no cold maiden, devoid of any prospect of desire. No, she was capable of a passion she did not yet realize was hers, but he did not want her in this way, not here among these dogs. The devil take Bertrand's soul that the poor girl had come to him in this way. She would consider him no better than a knave if he took her now.

Laurent kissed her brow and then her eyelids which glistened with spent tears as she lay limply in his embrace. "Do you know, little one, that it was Bertrand's name you spoke in my arms. Is that who you desire?"

"Non! Non!" Gweneth pulled away and onto the bed beside him. "I hate him! My life is no longer my own because of him. He taunts and threatens me like a cat with a captive bird only to pick up with the first woman who comes his way. I would be mad to feel anything but loathing for him!" she protested indignantly.

"It is sometimes called that, chérie." Laurent's laughter was blunt but gentle. "What am I to do with you? I know what I should like to do but that can await some other time. Ah, *ma chérie,*" he sighed. "Come and let me unhook the rest of Leila's gown so that you may rest. Bertrand will not come for you before dawn, and you may as well be comfortable."

"You guessed?"

"Oh, I guessed many things, Gweneth. After all, Leila has been Bertrand's woman for several years. But not everything, not the most important thing of all."

Gweneth sat docilely as Laurent unfastened her gown and drew it over her head. He rose and tossed it over a chair while she wriggled free of her petticoats and hastily dived under the covers. When he came back to the bed and removed his boots and shirt, Gweneth lay still, clutching the bedding to herself, unknowing whether she would fight or give in to the man beside her.

"In a place such as this I cannot leave you alone," Laurent said matter-of-factly as he threw his shirt aside. "I will lay with you, and if anyone should seek to disturb us, they will find that you are suitably occupied. In the morning I shall return you to your capitaine, if that is still your desire." He swung his feet onto the bed and lay down beside her. "I shall not lay a hand on you. You have my word."

"I believe you," Gweneth replied in a whisper of relief.

"It is good that you do, otherwise I would be tempted to play a much different role for you. You try a man's soul, *ma petite*. You do do that." Laurent pushed up on one elbow and placed a soft kiss on her mouth. "I am determined to win you now," he said and lay back with his arms folded across his chest.

Raoul sat up and pushed Leila away. "In the name of heaven, have you no subtlety, Leila? It is the man who is wont to do the wooing. You claw and tear at me like some bitch in heat!" He rolled easily off the bed and reached for his breeches.

Leila's arms came round his waist from behind. "What is wrong, my Capitaine? Always before you have welcomed my advances. Many is the time you have said as much," she answered coyly, teasing his hard-muscled ribs with dancing spiderlike fingers.

"Were that ever true, it is no longer so. Here, cover your nakedness," he said curtly and hurled her blouse and skirt over his shoulder. Breaking free of her, he moved away.

"What are you doing?" she wailed when he stood to button up.

Raoul sat again and began drawing on his boots. "Since you cannot fill my needs, I shall seek solace somewhere else. Maybe there have been so many, Leila, that you are no longer capable of real emotion," he replied caustically and stood once more.

"Why you—!" And she let loose with an account of abusive Spanish worthy of the best of any of his seamen as she flung herself against him, biting and scratching his bare chest.

Raoul mastered the girl's raging assault quickly. "Enough, vixen." His arm shot out, pushing Leila back onto the bed, and he turned to retrieve his shirt. "If you are so eager for a man's company, then I shall send Lavasseur up to you. It could be that he will find your shameless behavior more to his liking."

Leila's mocking laughter caused him to turn back with a surprised glance. "Capitaine Laurent does not need me, Raoul. He has found a suitable woman to spread herself under him. That fancy strumpet he held so protectively in his embrace should have satisfied his lust by now." She raised up and touched Raoul's cheek. "Do not tell me you care a whit which whore he beds?"

Raoul grabbed her by the shoulders and shook her until the smile had faded from her lips. "Never let me hear you speak of Mademoiselle Valois in that manner. Do not think she peddles herself with the careless ease of your kind. She is a lady!" he shouted and dropped his hands before he could be tempted to throttle the smirk that returned to Leila's face.

"And you believe that?" she sneered and curled her slim legs under herself without bothering to shield her nudity from his angry stare. "Then perhaps you would like to know that they are occupied this very moment at the end of the hall. Rafael was bringing up dinner for them when I went to fetch more brandy for you." And the darkening fury in Raoul's eyes drove her to twist the knife a little more, for she could see that he cared very much, and she hated him for it. "Lavasseur paid for a great deal of wine and engaged the room for the night. I do not think your French girl reluctant. Rafael said she accompanied the capitaine quite happily. From the eager way she clung to him earlier, I should think their dinner may have gotten cold before they turned their attentions to satisfying less important hungers." But Leila's triumph was short-lived, and her eyes grew round with fright when

Raoul groaned like a wounded beast and reached for the pistol in his coat pocket.

Leila scrambled from the bed and threw her arms around him. "Raoul, Raoul, what is one woman more or less? Would you lose a friend for a harlot who cares not who satisfies her? No, I speak in jealousy. Stay here and let me ease your pain." She snuggled closer, lowering her hands to caress his buttocks. "I know ways of arousing your desire that a lady like she would never dream of. Oh Raoul, please do not—!" she cried, but he had torn free and staggered out into the hall.

Raoul's head roared from the effects of drink, and his chest seemed to burst with each sickening thud of his heart. He had never thought it possible that Gweneth would give herself to another. After the way she trembled in fright from a single kiss. . . . But Lavasseur, he could understand Lavasseur's urge to bed the girl. And he must seem a hero in her eyes after the way he himself had treated her. That adventurer was not above plying her with enough wine to render her resistance useless.

"It is my fault," he growled in a fury of self-loathing. "Had I accepted my need to possess her above all her protests, then I should be reaping the rewards of the night's labor rather than that clever Frenchman." Damn them both, he would soon put an end to their frolicking!

Raoul leaned against the wall of the hallway to collect himself and pressed a thumb and forefinger into his eyeballs. Gweneth's vision stirred in his mind; the sheer agony that possessed his soul wherever those jade eyes leveled that look of disapproval, the fullness of her lips, the tempting swell of her fully rounded breasts. Curse it all, he was a man, and he would take her this night and, rape or no, he would be released at last from the torment of wanting her.

He drew himself up and looked down at the weapon in his hand. He had no intention of killing

Lavasseur for having succeeded where he himself had failed. He had as much as given Gweneth to him, and she was but the innocent victim of his own—but, damn, he hated the thought of being at fault on every count. Well, so be it. He would be a blackguard if necessary, for he must be rid of this torture.

Gweneth awakened to the pressure of a hand against her mouth. She began struggling immediately for, in the dark, all memory of where she was or with whom was lost. "Hush, chérie. It is I, Laurent, and we are about to have a visitor." Gweneth relaxed, and the hand was removed. "Move closer, *ma petite,* for it is better that we leave no doubt as to our reason for being here," he whispered and eased himself under the covers as he pulled her near.

His arms enfolded her as his mouth covered hers in a deep proprietary kiss, and she reached out, embracing his muscular flesh as she heard the door open softly.

"Ah, *mon amour,* you make me dizzy with the intoxicating wine of your kisses. I tremble to your touch as I never have before," Laurent murmured loudly against her mouth.

The door was forced back with a crash that made them both jump, and Gweneth looked up cautiously over Laurent's shoulder to see Captain Bertrand swaying drunkenly in the doorway. The light from the hall threw his long shadow rippling across the bed and made the barrel of his pistol gleam wickedly. Gweneth caught in a long trembly breath and shrank from the man beside her.

"Well, well, if this is not a cozy scene. My faithful friend in the arms of my woman," Raoul drawled contemptuously.

"You do choose your moments most ill-advisedly, *mon ami,*" Laurent returned casually as he rolled over to face him. "What is this, a weapon? Surely you do not mean to kill us in a jealous rage, Bertrand. How would it look? And, besides, you are too late to play the avenging savior. The mademoiselle and I were beginning anew." Gweneth saw his smile in the dim light and wondered at the need for the lie. "If you have concluded your own business, then why seek us out? Is not one woman sufficient for the night?" Yes, Gweneth decided, let him believe anything that would make him suffer as she had. She moved into the inviting circle of Laurent's arm.

"You would do well to remove yourself while there is still the time, Lavasseur. If you require further satisfaction, there is a half-empty bed down the hall, and I believe your attentions will not be unwelcome—for a price."

"What, and leave the *jeune fille* alone? That is most ungallant of you, Bertrand. As to the other, I could never buy what I have found here tonight. It has been a most educational evening," Laurent said and placed a kiss on the swell of Gweneth's breast above her chemise.

Raoul swore under his breath. "If it is her needs which concern you, then know that she will not be left unattended," he replied tersely and put out a hand to brace himself in the doorway.

Gweneth lifted her lips to Laurent's ear, pleading in a tiny voice, "Please, you will not leave me? I fear what he will do."

"You frighten the girl, Bertrand, but then you seem to know no other way with her. It is a pity." Laurent brushed Gweneth's lips with his, murmuring, "I shall wait on the other side of the door. If you have need of me, just call, *ma petite*."

"There, you see, Bertrand," Laurent said, rising from the bed. "I can be as accommodating as you." He picked up his shirt and began dressing. "But know this. If any harm should come to her, you shall answer to me."

Raoul grumbled something unintelligible but lowered the pistol. When Laurent finished, he bent quickly and kissed Gweneth. "*Merci, mon amour,* you will ever be in my thoughts," he voiced warmly. "Trust me," he murmured softly and then scooped up his coat from the chair and approached Raoul.

"And thanks to you, *mon ami*. There are few who would allow even a friend such an exquisite opportunity." He chuckled and swept past Raoul into the hall.

"So, you have learned something of the ways of men," Raoul said thickly when they were alone and Gweneth knelt in the midst of the bed with the sheet held protectively before her.

"I have discovered a great deal more: that not all men are the the devils you would have me believe, that there is tenderness and comfort to be had as well as the violence you would inflict," Gweneth replied defensively and clutched the covers tighter.

"You prefer the fawning attentions of that clever-tongued Frenchman to the wooing of a full-blooded man?"

"Infinitely, monsieur."

"Then is it time to refresh your memory, mademoiselle. I would not have you forget me so easily. No, stay where you are!" he cried when she stirred. "I have precious little desire to chase after you, my lovely vixen. Pray leave the trap baited that I might be more fully enticed into your lair. I shall cool that hot blood that fires your eyes and barbs your tongue before the night has quit us, and you shall learn with the rising of the sun what it means to be fulfilled by a real man."

"Spare me your lies. It would serve you better to use the weapon in your hand for as certainly as you lay it aside, I shall find a means to use it. Think on that, my fine brave Capitaine," she spat back. "Go back to that—that gypsy you panted for so hotly a short time ago. Or did she find your advances equally detestable? Buy what you can and leave me alone. I hate you, despise you, loathe the very sight of you! But for you I should be dead and long past caring. Would that I had died in France with my brothers and father or drowned at sea. The agony of either could not possibly compare with the torture you put me to!" Sobs racked her body, and Gweneth fought for control. "Non, non. You shall not make me cry! Whatever happens, you will not make me cry!" she wailed as the thick tears blurred her vision of him. Shamed by this weakness, she covered her face with both hands.

Raoul heard the choked-back weeping and cursed. What had become of all his fine plans for this night? He had meant to flatter and charm her, to steal a few kisses in the dark and then when she was dizzy with wine and the nearness of him, to lure her to his bed. But it was his own head that whirled, scattering his thoughts. Whatever had possessed him to bring her here? If it had not been for that fracas with the seaman, she would never have had the chance to sneak away with Lavasseur. That was more insult than any man should be made to bear. He gave a shove to the door, leaving them in complete darkness.

"Will you cease that senseless sniveling? Saints above! Can a man find no peace in this whorehouse?" he groaned and lurched toward the bed.

Gweneth's head jerked up. "Is that what this place is? *Sacré Dieu!* Is there no end to the degradation you would heap upon me? Why do you hate me so?"

"'Tis you who abhor the sight of me, mademoiselle. What is there about me that you find so disgusting? I am young, virile, a fine figure of a man, and tortured with desire for you. What more do you require?" he raged in drunken self-pity.

"*Amour*," Gweneth whispered calmly and found it enough to ebb the tears.

"Love?" Raoul questioned scornfully. "What would you know of love? Have you found a lover in this Lavasseur? I doubt it. Or is there another man somewhere, someone you left behind in France?"

"Perhaps." Her answers floated across to him in the dark, and Raoul was no longer sure of where she lay as he groped toward the bed.

"Then you are a fool to deny yourself for a man who may well be dead." His thigh touched the mattress, and he dropped the pistol and shrugged off his coat. "We have of our lives only what there is at this moment," he continued and sat to pull off his boots. "Anyone who lies in wait for the future risks losing all, for tomorrow is promised to none." A single thud marked the loss of the first boot. "Only those who seek the richness of life in each day can ever know a complete lifetime. I am such a man. I think, I feel, my dreams and hopes are no different than any others, but I take some consolation whenever I can." The second boot fell.

He wrenched open his shirt. "You seem to me to be of the same thread, *ma belle*. Your spirit and courage are to be admired. But you are a woman, too, and such a desirable one at that." The shirt floated to the floor. Raoul stood and began removing his breeches but heard her soft gasp and sat back down.

"You are made for love, Gweneth. I see your beauty and wish to pay tribute. Is that love? If so, then you may find that I love you in my way." He fell back beside her but did not reach for her. "I want you, I need you, that is all I can offer. No, that is not quite true. I will be gentle and tender and bring you pleasure such as you have never known was possible. It was not my intention to frighten and hurt you. I have berated myself a thousand times for that first day. Had I understood fully your situation, I should have wooed you with such gentle words and caresses. I am ready to do that now." He paused to sigh from the exertion of his speech. "What say you, *ma belle*?" He could hear her quickened breath, and the knowledge sharpened his desire.

"I say you are the most flagrant, glib-tongued liar I have ever had to misfortune to meet," Gweneth answered and sprang from the bed when he lunged for her. She whirled around to face him in the unlit room. "You shall not win me for the gratification of your lust with pretty phrases, Capitaine. You must either show yourself for the rogue you are or pass this night without me."

Gweneth braced herself for his attack, waiting for the moment when she must scream, but nothing stirred in the shadows of the bed. In the long silence that followed, she came to hear his heavy breathing and then the first rumblings of snoring. "Oh, my Capitaine, you are a most negligent lover," she giggled and went to pick up her petticoats and gown.

From the moment he reeled through the door she had known, as Lavasseur must have, that it was merely a question of time till he succumbed. She had nursed enough of her brothers' besotted stupors to recognize the signs. He would awaken to a grand case of the megrims, and she wished him every jarring minute of it. "Please, Lavasseur, you promised you would wait," she said to herself and hurried into her clothes.

Laurent lit a cigar as he lounged in the hallway. He had given Bertrand something to ponder and, if he loved the girl, he would have to admit it, accepting the consequences. If not, then, by God, he would not get another chance to touch her.

There were worse things than being in love. Laurent himself tried to make a habit of it, for it seemed to make the play all the sweeter. Several times he had come close to slipping on the yoke of marriage, but his good sense had won out each time.

Yet the mademoiselle was not the sort one took and then tossed aside. She deserved better than either of them, but it looked as if she would have one or the other before this was all over, Laurent mused, and a broad grin broke over his features. Yes, he would not mind coming home each time to her arms. He might even be persuaded to end his roaming, and that was a posture he had never considered before: the true and faithful lover.

Laurent glanced at the door. He should never have given Bertrand the chance to win her back. But, if Gweneth did not appear soon, he might as well try his luck elsewhere, for she had inflamed his loins in a way that was difficult to ignore. "Damn be to all virgins," he cursed good-naturedly, then jumped to his feet as the door opened.

"Chérie," he greeted her appearance with relief and went to embrace her, but Gweneth pushed him away and looked at him warily.

"What is it? Did that rascal harm you in some way?"

"Non, non, he is sleeping soundly, monsieur," she replied.

"Then what is this, *ma petite?*" he asked in concern.

Gweneth looked straight into his puzzled face. "I have been a fool to both your wiles, and all the time I thought you, at least, sincere," she answered in disillusionment.

"What is this? *Ma foi,* I am sincere. Why should you question it? Has Bertrand been slandering me to his advantage?" he questioned testily.

"Ah, that is what matters to you, *n'est-ce pas?* Both of you care more for your own precious prides than the truth. You make love with the same words, offer the same promises, beg the same favors. There is no difference between you." She had not meant to say this but the sight of his self-satisfied expression recalled her embarrassment of her wanton behavior.

"Oh." Laurent smiled self-deprecatingly. Her anger had surprised him, but he understood the cause. "So the capitaine's wooing is a good match for my own. Well, there is no help for it, chérie. The words must be the same for any man."

"Then how shall I ever believe a man? The lies and the truth speak with the same tongue, and there is naught to mark the difference." She sighed and bit her lip.

"There you are wrong, *ma petite.* There is the woman's heart to tell the difference. A man ventures wherever he is welcome. It is the lady's choice to make the invitation." Laurent smiled and took her hand between his. "You see, you have grown a bit tonight. You have had two men plead the same cause to you. When you are able to know the difference, when there is one, then you will have won a mastery over all men," he offered encouragingly.

"Providing, of course, I am allowed the freedom. Till now, I have been given very little choice," she complained.

"And you are wrong in that too. I should say you held the night firmly in your possession. Twice you have been alone with a man who desired you very much, and yet you stand before me as innocent as before the experience, or nearly so. You are wiser in many ways, and I cannot help feeling the pride of having taught you a good part of it. For, when you do choose the man, I am afraid I have equipped you with sufficient knowledge that the poor fellow will not stand a chance against your charms. And, having lost the match, will be consoled with love's pleasure, some of whose secrets you have learned with me tonight."

A devilish delight fired his gaze as he continued to speak. "And, if I should not be the man, then I beg you allow me to at least complete the lesson beforehand, mademoiselle." He put a finger to her half-opened lips. "That is all for now. Come along, chérie, and I shall take you from this place."

As they walked along, Laurent wondered what she would think if she knew he had realized who was at the door before it opened and had deliberately sought to enrage Bertrand with his overly sweet expressions of love to Gweneth. She would say he was protecting his pride, and she would be right. At least Bertrand had the excuse of illness, but he had no such defense to explain his failure to seduce the girl.

She was afraid just now of the depth of emotion

that had nearly caused her to cast her virtue away, but he was quite certain she would have capitulated if he had persisted. And now that the taste of passion had touched her lips and poured through her veins, it would not be long before she sought again to drown herself in its heady brew. And he himself would pour the cup.

CHAPTER NINE

The *Christobel* cut through the deep blue of the open water, pushing an eternal wave before its bow, waves trailing out behind with the delicate ribbing of a lady's fan. The brass fittings of the ship sparkled mirrored images on the backs of the crew. A mighty fortress, self-contained and invincible, with its ruler rightly placed before the helm.

Laurent had donned the workday attire of a sea captain, dressed in dark brown breeches and simple white shirt with full sleeves, but he still bore a striking contrast to those about him. His half-open shirt revealed a gold cross glistening against his smooth, well-muscled chest, and his ebony mane had been securely anchored by a single black grosgrain ribbon. All that was needed was a black silk eye patch and gold ring in his left ear, thought Gweneth as she came up on deck and saw him standing wide-legged and arms akimbo. His fierce good looks and penetrating eyes announced him to be a formidable personage. One would not lightly cross this gentleman for, after all, that is what he was.

Gweneth stopped short to watch him give several brusque orders to the men under him. She did not regret her decision to accept his hospitality for the voyage to Barbados. She never wanted to see Captain Bertrand again and, though Renée and the maids were baffled by her seemingly frivolous whim to board a new vessel in the middle of the night, she felt it was the right choice. She could not face Captain Bertrand, and it was certain he would have discovered some means of restraining her.

She would have changed back into her own nearly destroyed gown before disembarking from the *Cyrene* but Laurent surprised her with a middle-of-the-night visit to a local seamstress and purchased a simple frock for her. The scarlet gown had been left for the captain. Leila could have it and the man who owned it, Gweneth determined.

She reached up to tame a wisp of hair tickling her eyes and caught Laurent's attention. "*Bon jour*, mademoiselle," he greeted loudly and waved her to him. Gweneth made her way past the curious stares and up onto the captain's bridge.

Laurent took her hand and saluted it with a kiss. "How delightful, *ma petite*. Have you rested well?" His appreciation of her was not daunted by the daylight nor the simplicity of her attire, and the black eyes studied her intently.

"I could not sleep for long," she admitted and looked a little past him. "When the drowsiness of the wine left me, I decided to come on deck before my restlessness disturbed the others." She had not realized until this moment how uncomfortable she would feel in his presence. The memory of her outrageous behavior and the allure of his blandishments were all the fresher in the morning light. She had nearly given herself to this man who had been a perfect stranger less than twelve hours ago. Were her senses to be trusted in light of that?

"Then you require some breakfast, mademoiselle. I have not yet eaten, for I meant to see that we were well under way by daylight. It would not do to be pursued, would it?" His amused expression caused Gweneth's face to color.

"I must seem an empty-headed child to you, Capitaine, after my impulsive and often unwise actions, but I thank you for taking us into your care," she said carefully. "That is all I would have you know and, if you will excuse me, I shall leave you to your business. I must not cause you any problem." She turned and would have left him had he not put out a restraining hand.

"Do not let your delicate feelings cause you to deny the hunger you must feel. If I recall correctly, you do eat, mademoiselle. Why not join me, if only to assure yourself that I am quite human and subject to the ordinary frailties of everyday life."

Gweneth forced herself to face him and was heartened by his infectious smile. One could not help liking him. She had only herself to blame for her embarrassment and guilt and, if he could be civil in spite of her aborted seduction, however unintentional, then she could do no less.

Daniel watched as his captain paced the cabin with a damp cloth held to his throbbing head. He had expected swearing and anger, but this tightly controlled rage was far more dangerous. It were better that the captain should rant and curse, heave a few things overboard, and then forget. But this, it was as though he were drawing the anger in on himself like a human typhoon: drawing in the heat and fury of a rising storm until it gathered itself into a bottomless vortex, only to be destroyed in the very venting of that frustration and wrath.

"I want to know where he has taken her, Daniel," his captain hissed in a deadly whisper.

"Aye, Cap'n, but I been a tellin' ye, they did not say. The mam'zelle come aboard with Cap'n Lavasseur sayin' as how ye gave her leave to go—"

"Did you really think me such a fool, Daniel?" he muttered in the first stirring of rage.

"Aye, Cap'n. I take yer point, only what could I do? It ain't as if she was yer wife, bound to ye legal like. She owed ye nothin'—"

"She owes me everything!" Raoul returned sharply, cutting across the pattern of Daniel's speech. "Damnation, Daniel, I shall have my due yet! That lying, cheating twit. When I lay my hands on her, she shall pay up in full. Get another man, and the two of you are to comb every stinking hole on this cursed island until you have found someone who knows where they are bound. Heed me, Daniel. You find out where that teasing chit has run off to or I shall have your skinny hide hung from the yardarm. By God, I shall!"

Raoul winced at the pain his raving cost his sore head and dropped into a chair. "Why, Daniel, why did she do it? I would have given her anything. Dear Lord, she could have had my very soul for a little deference and consideration. But no, she flirts and teases me until I should burst with the need of her, and then she skulks off with the first swaggering Frenchman who comes her way." He sighed heavily and closed his red-rimmed eyes. It was smarter to be silent. This raving betrayed too much.

Daniel would have loved to question his captain about the particulars of last night's adventure. Things looked so promising when they cast off together. The little mam'zelle were a beauteous sight, and every man aboard had shared in that covetous look in the cap'n's eye. Then this morning the innkeeper from the Casa Bello had sent for him to collect his cap'n. He had heard the talk of the mam'zelle's staying the night with Cap'n Lavasseur but, until the moment Cap'n Bertrand began swearing against the man, Daniel had held the talk in no account. Poor cap'n, poor mam'zelle!

"Find out where she has gone, Daniel, if it is the last thing you do," the captain ordered again, and though Daniel had weathered many similar threats, he beat a hasty retreat.

Raoul stroked his weary brow. When he awakened to Gweneth's absence, his spirits sank with the weight of an anchor. Not only had he lost the opportunity of possessing her, he had let her slip away with her lover.

A right round of swearing followed that thought and in the several minutes it took to abate the black fury in his heart, Raoul discovered something in himself which he had not credited. When at last he fell silent, it was to the realization that the gaping breach which rent his peace of mind was caused by more than the mere loss of a wench; he had lost a woman who was coming to mean more to him than he ever intended any woman to mean again.

Marianne. The name floated into his mind on the wind of memory. His Marianne, how he had loved her. He was young, only twenty, but she was younger still, barely fifteen when he took her to wife. After the death of her father, Raoul's mentor on the sea for the two years he had sailed, he had sought to keep the girl from an orphanage or workhouse by marrying her.

She was a frail young thing, timid and shy, frightened by his ardent displays to the point where they had been married a full year before he coaxed her into the act of consummating their vows. He had been at sea most of that year, and he knew her to be young for childbearing but, in the end, he had found it necessary to persevere, such was his need of her.

And to what disaster. Though he was ever the patient, gentle lover, she had screamed in the final moments, causing him to back away in fright from the deed now accomplished. She wailed and sobbed inconsolably throughout the night, starting at his every attempt to staunch or dissuade her tears. Never again, she had screamed at him finally. Never! There would be no children by her, she shouted into his dumbstruck face. He could whore about all he wished, but she would never again be so ill-used.

He had left her that next morning, and her advice he took in abundance. During the next year he drank and caroused with the wicked women who accepted him. Then he returned home to find Marianne far gone with child. She said it was his, begged him to believe it, but the wretched disgust he felt at the sight of another man's work nearly cost him his sanity. He, who had worshiped the ground on which she stood, had been soundly trounced for seeking his husbandly rights. Now his virtuous wife stood before him heavy with another's child.

A man possessed he had been, raging and threatening one minute to crumple sobbing like a babe the next. She pleaded with him to give up the sea. She hated the loneliness, sobbing that she had not meant the words spoken months ago. But he could not be in the same room with her without choking on the gall which heaved into his throat when his eyes fell on her belly.

Where he went and what he did for the next week he would never know but when the constable tumbled him out of a foul-stinking ditch early one morning, it was with the news of his arrest for the death of his wife. His beautiful, fragile Marianne had been found hanged.

The man never came forth to own up as Marianne's lover, and Raoul might have hanged himself had it not been for a village midwife who came to give testimony that Marianne had been to her in hopes of procuring an effective method for losing the child within her. She said the girl had taken a lover from among the gypsies whose caravan had spent the harvest season in the valley, and some weeks after their departure found herself to be with child. Loneliness was her excuse, but she feared her husband's wrath and hoped to be rid of the results before he ever knew. Yet the child had remained, and her husband had come back unexpectedly.

The people took a dim view of the nobleman in their midst, his misrepresented birth adding to their puritanical prejudices, but in the end they set him free. The admission that the child was another's made it seem fair justice in some eyes that she should meet a bad end, but Raoul understood that, in her shame and misery, she must have taken her own life.

Soon thereafter, Raoul's father, who felt himself to be much abused by his willful son, took it upon himself to deliver the final blow in deleting his notorious offspring from his will.

Bitter, barren of spirit, and nurtured by shame and rage, Raoul took to the sea again. Bastard and firstborn alike, men labored side by side, each for his own destiny. Raoul had done better than most. He was wealthy beyond immediate need in this his thirtieth year, and if he lacked, no man knew what it might be. But he knew, knew now that Gweneth was beyond him.

She is just another wench, he told himself and set to pacing the floor again. Lovelier than most, perhaps, but silky skin and intelligence mattered not that much when the need was on a man and a woman spread herself under him. So he had had the girl but could not remember it well. At least he had taken her before Lavasseur. Women were all the same. They lied and cheated, and to ravish one was the same as to love one. No woman would ever infect him with that disabling disease again, for he meant to give none the chance.

"Damn, it is not so!" Raoul cried and wrenched the cork from a bottle on the shelf. The amber liquid spilled down his parched throat and ran out of his mouth onto his chin, spattering his shirt front. Raoul cleared his throat loudly and ran a hand over his wet mouth. Gweneth had been different. He had wanted her with a passion not matched since the days of his youthful lust for his child bride. Now he must be content with the fact that she was his once and would have been so again had his temper not gotten the better of his judgment.

"To Lavasseur," Raoul toasted and raised the bottle. "May you ride her long and well." His laughter was dry, but he found he could not put the bottle to his lips behind that particular toast and, instead, cast it from him in disgust.

When Daniel returned he found his captain hard at work over his maps with measure and quill. The heavily scored lines of his face bespoke the anger which gripped him still, but the sore redness of his eyes had vanished, leaving them agleam with purpose.

"What ho, Daniel. Have you plucked the little bird only to lose the meat?" Raoul hailed when he spied Daniel's prize.

Daniel looked down at the red satin slung over his arm and then determined the meaning with a smile. "Not quite so, Cap'n. More like I bear the plumage the little partridge left in safekeeping for ye. The dressmaker in town had instructions that this was to be delivered into yer hands. When it came known I were seekin' a certain young lady, she sent for me and here I am direct to yer side." He came forward and held out the garment.

"And what am I to make of this gesture? 'Twas plain she desired not my aid nor gifts," Raoul replied in dry-voiced ire. "Away with it!" he stormed and brushed the satin rudely from his desk. "Burn it or lose it to the sea, it matters not, but spare me the sight of it."

Daniel coughed discreetly to hide his poor inclination to make light of his captain's ill humor. "There be more here than immediately comes to light, Cap'n. If I were ye, I'd be havin' a closer look." Daniel held out the gown once more to the now mystified man.

Raoul took the dress slowly from Daniel's arm and let it fall loose from the shoulders, its folds spilling free to the floor. For all its beauty, it seemed a mere rag in his eyes now that it no longer framed the comely form he so admired.

"I see nothing to inspire your cryptic—" he began but paused when he detected the edge of a paper tucked into the bodice of the gown.

Raoul gathered it quickly into his lap and sought to

unpin the attached note, his fingers lingering an imperceptible moment at the neckline which the night before restrained and caressed tender plump breasts. He cursed his own sentimentality and wrenched the note free to hide the effect his thoughts had upon him.

The thick rough paper was pressed with a common seal, but the neat feminine inked hand he would surely have recognized though he had just laid eyes on it. The note was written in Latin, but Raoul barely noticed, so intent was he upon the substance of the correspondence.

> Capitaine,
>
> Among your several other accomplishments, I should hope you may account Latin as one. It seemed proper that I be discreet. I shall not excuse my arbitrary behavior in securing other passage for our final destination. However, circumstances constrain me to offer my gratitude to you for having been the instrument of our rescue and maintenance these past weeks. So, too, must I offer my regret that you must now go your own way having wrought no payment for your dedicated labor.
>
> Lest my meaning be misunderstood, you may tell your steward that I have given my consent to an interpretation of my words.
>
> > Adieu
> > Mademoiselle
>
> P.S. Lest you feel the slight too pointedly, know that monsieur, your friend, fared no better last evening. I shall toast both your virtuous gallantries at the first opportunity.

Raoul studied the letter a second time and then a third, translating each word for clues. At first reading, it seemed an inordinately civil parting from one of whom he had expected the deepest resentment. Upon second reading there was superimposed the lilting stamp of irony. By the third inspection Raoul derived with certainty that she had offered this not as a friendly leave-taking but as a high jest, the butt of which was himself.

At last he turned his attention to his man. "She asks my forgiveness in setting off without me. She thanks me for my charity and then belabors the point of my lack of reward. It is to you I am to look for the answer to the riddle, Daniel. I quote her," and he repeated the fateful wording in loud, dry tones.

Daniel's weathered eyes grew wide in amazement, then shifted quickly away from the penetrating gaze of the captain.

"Well, man, what is the meaning of this?" Raoul demanded impatiently.

Daniel reddened perceptibly under the captain's unflinching stare and scratched at the spot which always seemed to tingle when he found himself at a loss for words. "Aye, Cap'n, I'm a ponderin' it. Bless the lass, she does me a bad turn this time, and after all I done in her behalf," he grumbled reluctantly.

"Get on with it, Daniel, or I shall wrest it from you with my bare hands," Raoul threatened and came to his feet.

"Steady, Cap'n. Here be the gist of it. The plain truth be the mam'zelle's still a virginal lady. Now hear me out!" he cried hurriedly when the captain's face flushed in fury. "It may be that ye'll be stringin' me up after this tale but give me leave to speak, Cap'n." That large menacing figure stood rigid before him for a short time while Daniel's Adam's apple worked furiously up and down his throat as though he could feel already the dangling coil; but then Raoul regained his chair. Daniel sighed, sucked in a fresh breath, and commenced explaining in halting, apologetic terms all that had occurred.

"So ye see, sir," he concluded, "it seemed best to let ye believe the lie. None was harmed by it. The mam'zelle went in dire dread o' ye. Only I don't rightly be knowin' what to think of her slippin' off to the bed . . ." The captain's wild-eyed stare pierced Daniel to the core. "Well, I ken she ain't the sort to do such a thing," Daniel finished weakly and dropped into a nearby chair, forgetting the added disrespect of this act.

Raoul stared long and hard at the letter as it lay open before him. The false petticoat had tried to cheat him of his last shred of consolation with this final insult, and the angry shame of it stained his cheeks an ugly shade of purple beneath his sun-darkened skin. And to think his own man had been a party to the deceit. His hands flexed into fists but just when the torturous humiliation might have driven him to violent retribution, he saw again the last line and, unaccountably, the muscles in his face twitched convulsively until he was overcome by boisterous mirth.

Daniel eyed his captain incredulously, for he shook with such laughter that he bent double to control the trembling.

"It be good ye see the humor of it, Cap'n," Daniel said hesitantly. "She was a lively thing, given to high-spirited—" But the captain roared on till Daniel began to fear the odd twist of mind which drove him to such glee.

"Aye, Daniel, a high-spirited minx, to be sure," Raoul voiced when he had mastered his fit. "The bold audacity of the revenge! How sweet it must lie in her heart. She played us all for the fools we be. Good God, I must either love or despise her for it. The subtle wit, the charm of it. Two bulls supremely gelded by one chaste maid!" He took a long breath only to chuckle the harder, and Daniel frowned in complete bewilderment. "Two bulls, Cap'n?"

" 'Tis all here, man," said Raoul, thumping the note and supplying the final line. "Lavasseur fared not a whit better than I. He sought to have me believe else but, as God is my witness, the girl must speak the truth. So she loves to sport with men, does she? I hope she rides the high wave of her success well, for I shall have my reward yet. Make no mistake, Daniel. I shall find her and when I do, the last victory shall be mine."

Raoul paused and shook his head to sober his thoughts. A fire blazed deep within his sapphire eyes, matching his determination to pursue Gweneth's challenge, and Daniel perceived in it a real danger to the lady, greater by far than the mere loss of her virtue.

"Just what are ye amind to, Cap'n?" came his troubled query.

"For the moment, nothing. While you have combed the waterfront, I have made inquiries of my own. It seems Lavasseur set sail in such haste he left half a crew behind with orders that he would return for them within a fortnight." He swung his booted feet up on the desk and laced his fingers behind his head. "I will wait for him, that is all. Simply wait," he said with cunning calm.

Lavasseur was surrounded by lovely visions of femininity at each meal, but the object of his interest rarely gave him a moment alone. How torturously Bertrand must have suffered, he thought, for in the four days since they set sail, Lavasseur himself came to know a fair amount of the same. His thoughts were ever in her direction.

He could easily have satisfied the urge with the sweet blond maid accompanying the lady, for she threw herself into his path at every opportunity. She stretched her duties to the utmost in this endeavor, seeking in his cabin a candle here, a quill there, all for *"mademoiselle."* Laurent had chanced to steal a kiss or two on those occasions, but to woo the one would be to lose the other. He advised discretion on Amy's part with the gentlest of hints that he would deny her altogether were word to reach her mistress of their interludes, and she agreed.

Gweneth spent most of her hours in untangling their difficult story into some manageable thread. At final evaluation it seemed prudent to negate all reference to Captain Bertrand, alluding to Captain Lavasseur as their rescuer and benefactor. When she put the question of his compliance to the captain on their final night at sea, he sanctioned her proposal heartily.

"A perfect solution, mademoiselle," Laurent complimented and turned his back on the porthole where he had stood listening to the full length of her plan.

"You show a wisdom beyond your years. To mention the villain's name is but to put you to the needless worry of explaining the necessity which brought you to seek other protection. This way the matter is skirted with sensible foresight." He came forward to where she sat and took Gweneth's hands in his. "What would you have me do, *ma petite?*" he asked charmingly and bent a knee at her feet.

"Simply say, Capitaine, that it was you who sighted our tiny craft and brought us across the sea. Is it conceivable that you have recently made such a voyage? I am reluctant to include you in my deceit. I seek to preserve my reputation at a compromise to your own," she replied with misgivings.

"Tsk! It is not a smirch upon my honor that I should uphold so fair a maiden's virtue at the expense of a near truth. For have I not saved you from trouble and dishonor? Had I found you upon the sea, I should have had the privilege in total," Laurent answered confidently and placed a fleeting kiss on one of her fingertips.

Gweneth gazed down at the glossy head bent in homage and smiled. "I do believe, Capitaine, that your chivalry is bettered only by your cunning skill with words." She laughed freely, but the merriment gave way to sudden disconcertion when he raised those dark penetrating eyes within inches of her own. Gweneth held his gaze unwaveringly, but her heart rose to pound insistently in her throat, so compelling was the look he accorded her. To circumvent the enticing invitation there, she freed a hand to brush away a stray curl, as though it were the cause of the discomfort she felt.

"Gweneth—I take the liberty of your name now that we are comrades in distress—I shall do all you ask of me and still more if you will but allow it." Laurent's velvet voice caressed her senses, leaving her less confident with each second. This interview should be brought to a swift conclusion, she realized, and rose to leave, but Lavasseur held her other hand and as yet knelt upon the floorboards.

"*Ma petite*, you must have some understanding of the depth of my feeling for you," he murmured. "Do not be so cruel as to leave me at your feet without any sign that you hold me in some esteem, however slight." This might have seemed a plea of distress on another man's lips but, from Laurent, Gweneth found herself at the disadvantage of offering solace to a superior force.

"Monsieur Lavasseur, you play unfairly upon a woman's sensibilities with such heartrending phrases," she answered lightly, if in slight reproof, and it affected the right result, for Laurent was on his feet in an instant.

"Mademoiselle, I would not toy with your most delicate and deeply felt emotions. My own happiness would suffer if I should take slight to your feelings. Rather I engender to have some measure of those feelings. That is all." But his simple reproach only heightened Gweneth's trepidation, and she fell back on the single defense at hand.

Straightening herself up to her full height, which fell far short of his towering presence, she asked, "Would you now have payment for your chivalry?" The rebuke came more sharply than was required, and she watched in regret as the warmth vanished from Laurent's eyes, leaving them cold as pitch.

"*Mon Dieu!*" he cried in injured affront. "Do not cast me in the role of that libertine Bertrand. Have I pressed you even once for that which you were hesitant to provide?" he asked indignantly, and the hurt mirrored in his fine eyes caused Gweneth's hand to tighten on his.

Quickly he continued, "Have I forced the least unwelcome attention on you? Do I call you to account for your passage, steal one unwarranted liberty, beg a single favor? If I am too abrupt in plying my case, it is because I lose you on the morrow. Am I not to know if I should seek your company again? Will no welcome await me should I happen to sail into your harbor with the express purpose of sharing your society?"

Gweneth's face flooded with shame for her unfounded suspicions. He deserved much better from her. "Monsieur, you shall always find welcome in my company. My recent experiences leave me unduly apprehensive. Pardon, Capitaine." Yet she looked away from his brightened countenance, feeling those words had been artfully wrung from her.

"*Voilà!*" he cried happily. "That is all I wish, *ma petite*. The words give me the hope I seek." He took her free hand and, together with the other, kissed them again.

He raised up very slowly and, when his head came level with her own, he leaned forward swiftly and kissed her smiling lips. Gweneth started in surprise but before she could withdraw, his hands found her shoulders and pulled her closer until she stood full within his embrace.

The friendly kiss became something more as his lips moved boldly over hers, but Gweneth no longer wished to be free of him, and for a short while she gave in to his fervent demonstrations until it became obvious that he would not willingly break off. Indeed he required more intimate favors, for his hand had come up to cup one breast.

"Enough, monsieur. Please," Gweneth breathed nervously and pushed him gently back.

With the greatest of reluctance, Laurent gave way. "As ever, *ma petite*, I am constrained to do your bidding," he replied with a shrug. Then the slyest hint of a smile touched his mouth. "Still you have bestowed upon me more than I expected, and I am grateful. My compliments, mademoiselle." The smile deepened into soft laughter when Gweneth's cheeks flamed with his dubious compliment.

"Let us depart, mademoiselle, before we find ourselves engrossed in the subject matter beyond our ability to forestall the conclusion. Like a good book, once begun, one is compelled to seek the final page." He gathered her to himself in a quick hug and kissed her brow, then whirled her around and gently urged her toward the door.

He had won a significant victory. In those minutes Gweneth had responded, Laurent knew. She was not yet fully aware of her blossoming need to find womanly fulfillment, but when that realization came, he would be there, ever the admiring suitor. Twice now he had backed away after pointing up her own enjoyment of their intimacies. The promise lay in their next meeting.

Gweneth lay awake through most of the night. Laurent's kisses brought her back to the thoughts and feelings she had shoved from her mind countless times since setting sail: thoughts of Captain Bertrand's chivalrous demonstrations on Tortola and then his evil unprovoked spite. He had betrayed her cruelly.

Gweneth rolled over on her stomach in the blackness and bit a corner of her pillow, clutching it tightly between her teeth so that the others would not hear her sobs. Why did she feel more desperately alone than ever? Bertrand meant nothing to her, and she certainly meant nothing to him.

Two large tears slipped down her cheeks from the huge lump lodged in her throat. There had been too many abruptly wrought good-byes in her young life, and she could not abandon this new man with expedience. Or was it fear of the unknown which prompted her response to this supremely self-sufficient man who displayed a great interest in her? Captain Lavasseur might still that fear if she but allowed it.

The tight aching left her slowly as her thoughts fastened on that hope, but it was Captain Bertrand who visited her dreams; gentle, tender, and with sweet laughter upon his lips as he held her body confidently to his own.

CHAPTER TEN

No committee of dignitaries appeared on the dock to meet the little party of travelers. No one knew that Governor Dillingham's nieces lived, much less had made the arduous journey across the Atlantic in flight for their lives. Madame Bourgeax wrote the girls' English grandfather when Monsieur Valois and his sons were arrested, but they had no way of knowing if the letter reached its destination and, as the months passed, no reply nor inquiry came in answer.

Captain Lavasseur had sent a man ahead to secure a carriage, and it was into this that he handed the ladies. The same low-roofed storehouses lined the waterfront as they had in Road Town, their canvased sides billowing in the steady breeze. Up the shore, however, lay Bridgetown proper and its small neat streets alive with people and traffic, which reminded Gweneth of nothing so much as her single childhood memory of an English country village.

It was toward the main section of town that the carriage turned, straight toward the municipal buildings. Her uncle would have his office there and, though he was related only by marriage, Gweneth preferred to present herself to him as courtesy as well as a formality. They were émigrés, without papers or sanction.

Laurent had dressed carefully for the occasion, wishing to present himself in the best light. He hoped to receive a warm welcome as the restorer of loved ones to the bosom of their family and, thus, earn an open invitation into their home. His black-clad body was relieved by simple touches of immaculate white lace at throat and cuffs; his only other adornment was the ornate sword belt buckled to his waist and heavily encrusted with gold. He appeared affluent but not ostentatious, a sober young gallant entrusted with the sacred responsibility of two gentlewomen.

Toying with one end of his moustache, Laurent enjoyed his uncommon good luck. The family would shower their gratitude upon him and, with meek humility, he would disavow any but the humble pleasure of having been allowed to serve so charming a group of young ladies. The added boon of the governor's influence could well throw further business dealings his way. Ah, Laurent, fortune smiles broadly upon you, he congratulated himself.

Gweneth sat between Sarah and Amy, mentally rehearsing the story she must tell. The others stared in awe at the exotic scenery which was no longer new to Gweneth, and she only half heard Laurent's narrative of the sights moving past.

She must throw herself on the mercy of an, as yet, unseen relative, utterly devoid of any means to ease the hardship of four mouths to be fed and bodies to be sheltered and clothed. Gweneth recoiled inwardly at this necessity. It was not only Captain Bertrand's charity she resented. Never had she sought the benevolence of anyone. Hard work was no stranger. She had toiled daily for months on end in Madame Bertin's laundry room until she fell exhausted into dreamless sleep. The work not only provided shelter in exchange for safety but it also gave her freedom of knowing all debts were paid.

This, at least, was a family matter, but she would seek to assure her relative that, were a capacity to present itself, she would be agreeable, nay, eager to become gainfully employed. That settled in her mind, Gweneth's attention was directed back to the deep vibrant voice of her host.

Within minutes of their arrival the five sat on a

velvet-covered bench in the great hallway of the magisterial office. The stamp of civilization in a primitive land would have been Captain Bertrand's appraisal, Gweneth mused. The white stone building seemed quite imposing beside the coral block shops and wattle and daub huts lining the rest of the street. But, of course, His Majesty's business would need to be conducted in proper surroundings whatever the circumstances. The deep mahogany wainscoting gleamed in the bright sunshine, and the several exquisite chandeliers which hung in the foyer tinkled in the relentless sea breeze.

One could almost imagine oneself in London at first glance; the drab-clad figures darted about with queues severely tied back or covered with heavily powdered perukes, their gold-buckled high-heeled shoes marking a quick staccato rhythm on the smooth marble floor. Yet the sultry air brought back the tropical reality as Gweneth shrugged to pull the slightly damp fabric of her gown free from her back.

The droning of a horsefly by her ear caught Renée's eye, and she squealed in fright even as Laurent lazily swatted it away. Her high-pitched cry echoed down the cavernous hallway, and several startled and not-at-all pleased heads swiveled toward the drab little group. On the heels of this followed the click of a latch along the hall, and one massive oak door swung open.

The slim black silhouette of His Excellency's secretary paused there and then approached them. The willowy-built man halted before Captain Lavasseur without any acknowledgment of Gweneth. "His Lordship, Governor Dillingham, will see you now," he announced in a dry formal voice.

Gweneth noted again his thin angular face, lined with arrogant self-importance, and felt the hair bristle on her neck as it had when his condescending look swept indifferently over her upon their arrival.

"That is most satisfactory. And if you will be good

enough to show us Monsieur Dillingham's office, we might alleviate the anxiety which your tarrying must be causing him," Laurent replied and met the secretary's haughty stare with one of his own.

True, the governor was no lord, but who was this impudent foreigner to point out such a matter, thought the man as he held the captain's gaze for two seconds before turning away in defeat.

Gweneth smiled her thanks in answer to Laurent's wink and took the arm he offered, signaling that the maids should remain behind.

They had been forced to put this most personal business in a note carried forth by the pompous man, and Gweneth had merely indicated the arrival of members of the governor's wife's family by ship.

Gaining confidence from the man beside her, Gweneth tucked a willful wisp of hair back and squared her shoulders. She must not appear the pitiable wretch her story would have her seem.

The door swung wide on a large dark paneled office filled with carefully arranged maps and charts. Massive furniture was sparingly placed about, and fine Turkish carpets covered the floor. But all eyes were drawn to the impressive desk flanked by high windows affording a panoramic view of the harbor below. A well-dressed man sat behind that desk, head bent upon the work before him.

"The new arrivals, Your Excellency," advised the secretary, and the governor begrudgingly lay his quill aside before raising his head.

He wore a magnificent white peruke, but the face beneath surprised Gweneth by its swarthiness and youth. It was a broad square face, prominent of brow and chin, with a straight nose and thin-lipped mouth. The effect was one of determination and stubbornness; but when his eyes fell on Gweneth and he rose, the lips parted in a cordial smile, belying his barely concealed displeasure at being interrupted. In build, as well, he was broad and square but the swell-cut coat and knee breeches gave him the appearance of solidarity and power. All together he was a handsome figure.

"Ladies?" he questioned as he came forth. "Whom have I the pleasure of addressing?" He took the hand Gweneth offered, and she curtsied briefly before replying, noting that his gray eyes lingered appreciatively on her face.

"Your Excellency, I am Gweneth Valois, and this is my sister Renée. And may I present our escort, Capitaine Lavasseur."

Surprise flickered across the man's features and then dismay. "Elizabeth's daughters?" he cried. "But why did you not say so before? Hollingsworth, bring refreshments for these people at once," he ordered the secretary who stood near the door. "Come come, my children, and have a chair. Dear Lord, we thought you all dead."

"Governor Dillingham, I hardly know where to begin our tale," Gweneth said when they were all served sherry. Quickly she related the story she had told Captain Lavasseur a week ago. The governor listened silently, sketching a note here and there but never interrupting until the matter of their rescue came to light.

"Then this is the man who accompanies you," the governor said when Gweneth hesitated at the name.

"*Oui*, monsieur, we owe our safe conduct to Barbados to Capitaine Lavasseur," Gweneth answered. That at least was not a lie.

Laurent had remained on his feet and at some distance, for he knew this to be a private affair. He sipped the brandy offered and perused the shelves of leather volumes until he heard his name pronounced.

The governor beckoned him forward, and Laurent shook the extended hand. "I am only glad to be of service, Your Excellency. Such lovely ladies should not be called on to make the sacrifices they have had to endure. It has been my most humble honor to be of assistance in any manner." He spoke sincerely, in spite of the artfully turned phrases, for the hearing again of Gweneth's plight and the remembrance of her dishonor in Tortola touched his romantic heart as poignant as its first telling.

"We are indebted to you beyond measure, Captain," the governor replied and waved Laurent into a chair. "Now, my child, what is it you wish of me?" he asked when he turned to Gweneth.

"*Enfin*, monsieur," she said with a slight shrug, "we are alone and destitute. Had Adolphe lived, we should seek only exile and safe conduct to England. It was our hope to throw ourselves on the mercy of our grandfather, but we dared not approach England directly. If you can find it in your heart to shelter us until we have contacted the marquis, we should be forever grateful," she said quietly and looked to Renée who lowered her eyes. How embarrassing it was to plead this case to a stranger, and her chin trembled in shame.

"Dear child, of course you must have our protection. Anything less should be tantamount to throwing out my own children," the governor exclaimed with feeling and came from behind the desk to press her hand gently. "Do not give the matter a second thought. You have been wise to come here, in any case." He paused to look deeply into Gweneth's eyes. "It is my sad duty to inform you that your grandfather died a year past. My wife and I hold the family office now, and you would have been sent here to my protection after all. So you see, it has all worked to the best advantage," he reasoned and smiled contentedly.

"But this is not the time for long conversation. You are exhausted. I shall have my carriage sent round at once to take you home." He walked briskly to the bell rope and pulled it impatiently. "I must send a note to my wife, for we should not wish to catch her unprepared," he added. An unaccountably harsh look rippled across those granite features and was gone before Gweneth was certain she had witnessed it.

"I should accompany you myself but, as you can see, I am overcome with business. I leave you in the care of the man who has already shown himself to be most dependable." He shook Laurent's hand again and led them to the door. "Now, ladies, if you will wait in the outer office, I shan't stay the carriage long. I must send word to Leonora first, that is all."

Gareth Dillingham closed the door behind them and paced slowly back to his desk, swearing under his breath but with little feeling. He was not the sort of man to be easily brought to real emotional display. A supreme actor, his own emotions he kept tightly coiled lest they provoke him to a mistake. A clear head and rational thought had brought him thus far; it must serve him all the better now.

"Curse the Terror," Gareth exclaimed as he sat and took a quill in hand. He had blessed that insurrection little more than a year ago, for it had meant the end of the Valois family and the old marquis was but recently dead. The old fool left Briarwood's finances to be carved up between his daughters' children, a full half going to those French papists his eldest daughter had whelped with that Gallic coxcomb. The title decended to the eldest male and that would have meant Phillip Valois. But how providentially the Revolution had intervened to lay the title and all the lands and monies within his reach if he could produce a son. Now the ocean had deposited the last of them back at his feet, endangering all his hopes. Damn the ill wind which steered the captain's vessel to harbor.

Gareth sat forward suddenly and tapped his forehead with the feather tip. No, no, perhaps not. Had they gone directly to England, the girls should have discovered themselves not forsaken and destitute but partial heirs to a great fortune. Perhaps providence still smiled on him, he thought, and a slow smile crept over his proud countenance. They would never know of the inheritance, not if his wife, Leonora, kept her own counsel.

He snatched a thick creamy sheet and scrawled a short but deliberately severe message to his loving wife. She had done so little of what he had expected of her, she must not fail him in this. Gareth had spent these twenty years of his adult life in preparation for the riches he was finally amassing. Leonora must be made to understand that it would bode very ill should she attempt to intervene now.

The note was completed quickly, and the governor's seal pressed to it. Gareth fingered the embossed shield absently and his lips turned down in distaste. How he hated these islands. All his life he had endured this island, the son of an indentured servant who'd bought his freedom, and he had used every bit of his wit to climb to the position of manager of the marquis's holdings in Barbados. Then his luck had come, marriage to the marquis's daughter and the ownership of the plantation outright. His hand went involuntarily to the bit of stuff in his pocket. Bought luck and superstitious nonsense maybe, but now the title of marquis would be his son's.

Within months of his planned resignation to take up the duties and pleasures of this new inheritance, he was now beset by a host of new circumstances. Still he had always enjoyed the complexities of intrigue in which the stakes were often men's destinies. Yes, he smiled, it might prove an interesting diversion to serve as his own kingmaker this final time.

Gweneth had last seen her aunt when she was four but remembered Leonora as a tall slim woman with the same English good looks of her older sister. They should receive a warm welcome here, at least. For all his civilities the governor seemed less than pleased by their unexpected preservation from the guillotine, Gweneth decided but quickly tossed that ungenerous thought aside. It was unfair to expect his utter delight at finding himself shackled with four strangers because of his marriage ties. He had been polite and unerringly sympathetic to their cause, offering the shelter they sought. That was all she had hoped. Their journey was at an end at last.

The governor's mansion was in many ways like that of Squire and Lady Nicolson's in Tortola, though larger and facing a lagoon. There were even formal gardens, a marvel that such splendor could be carved from the surrounding jungle, but the lush, gentle foliage of England was replaced here by the vigorous turgid greenery of primitive vegetation.

True to his word, Governor Dillingham had sent word before them, and his wife stood waiting on the carriageway. Gweneth remembered little of her mother, but the sight of that tall slender figure and tousle of shimmering red-gold curls beneath a white ruffled morning cap sent shivers of memory along her veins, and she tumbled out of the vehicle and into Leonora's outstretched arms before anyone could assist her.

Locked in that comforting embrace, Gweneth found herself giving in to the tears she had fought on every occasion since the death of Adolphe. There was no longer the need to be strong and supportive, no more fears to be faced down and opposed, no tangle of emotions and reason in the arms of her mother's sister.

"The Lord be praised, you have come back to us from the dead!" cried Leonora Dillingham. She lifted her niece's chin. "How you have grown, more beautiful than ever. And can this lovely creature be Renée?" she asked and reached out to enclose the other girl.

"Oh, but you are both too thin, and look how brown you are," Leonora added disapprovingly, then smiled at the color which rose in both girls' cheeks. "Two little ragamuffins, and I have just the solution. Nice hot baths with scented soaps and towels and then crisp clean sheets." Leonora began herding the girls toward the house when she glanced over her shoulder in remembrance.

"Where are my manners today?" she scolded herself and hurried back across the lawn, offering her hand to the captain. "Please forgive me. It is the shock, the absolutely delightful surprise which causes me to forget myself," she explained rapidly and smiled at the handsome stranger. "You are Captain Lavasseur. My husband mentions you in his note. We are deeply in your debt, and you shall not find our hospitality lacking a moment hence."

Laurent saluted her hand and said, "A thousand pardons, madame, that my presence puts you to any concern. By all means see to your gentlewomen. I can make my way to your salon with the help of a servant and, if you will allow, I should like a word with you before I depart."

"You are not leaving us, Capitaine?" asked Gweneth, betrayed by the intensity of emotion in her voice which culled a speculative look from her aunt.

"I would not make so bold as to interfere now that I have seen you safely to the bosom of your family," he replied self-effacingly but answered her concerned expression with a smile.

"Nonsense, Captain. You must stay the day and have dinner. Why I have a room being prepared for you, unless you have made other arrangements," Leonora answered. "Come, someone will see to all of you, but now I go with my girls."

The late-evening light poured through the cracks between the shutters, striping the floor in shimmering gold bands. Gweneth's head stirred against the bolster, and her lids fluttered open. Above her hung a gossamer curtain falling in folds about the bed. The delicious sensation of complete rest spread through her languorous body, and she stretched fully with both hands over her head, arching her back and pointing curled toes until every fiber was taut. The goose-down mattress and cool linen sheets were a luxury nearly forgotten.

She could only guess the time, but the low-riding sun gave notice that it was late. The events of the day hardly seemed real once she had been held by her aunt. There had been servants to help her bathe, two young black women, and then a leisurely tea while she was massaged with a thick fragrant lotion and her hair combed out. Then she was put to bed.

What was said or who might have come and gone were blanketed in the stupor which overcame her upon entering the house. The weeks at sea, the terror and apprehension, had disappeared, leaving her mind a corridor of empty shadows. Sleep came unbidden, really before she ever touched the sheets.

A light rap on her door preceded the figure who then slipped through. The mosquito netting obscured all but the general form of a woman, and it was not until Gweneth sat up and pulled the curtain aside that she recognized Leonora.

"Good, my dear. You are awake," she said as she moved to the bed and placed a swift kiss on Gweneth's cheek. "I did not wish to disturb you, for you need the rest, but I thought, perhaps, you might feel up to dinner downstairs if you were awake. Renée is up and dressing."

Gweneth smiled happily and took her aunt's hand. "How can we ever thank you? This horrible nightmare seemed never to end. But for you and your husband, I do not wish to think what we should face."

Leonora's face was stricken with empathy as she replied, "Gareth arrived home more than an hour ago, and he has told me of your adventure. My dear, dear child, it is a miracle you are here at all." She reached up to brush aside a tear which spilled over from her brimming eyes.

"And, of course, we have spoken with this Captain Lavasseur," she said in a different voice. Her gaze slid from Gweneth's cheerful face, and she carefully compressed her lips before continuing. "The captain is a singularly striking man." A frail thread of laughter escaped her. "I must confess I find his devilish good looks rather more than a bit disturbing. A man like that—" She faltered. "I mean, such a man must inspire the worship of young women by the dozens. It would be understandable if one were to be led astray by his compelling ways and charming speeches, particularly in your case where he saved your lives. In wishing to afford him something in the way of . . ." But Leonora broke off again as a dark shadow crept up her neck.

She dropped Gweneth's hand and rose. "I told Gareth that this was not the time to press such matters, but he was so insistent," she murmured, and her eyes brimmed to overflowing once more, the brilliant drops falling on her heaving bosom.

Gweneth had sat in rigid silence, waiting for the question she knew was to come and gaining in resentment with every word. But, at the sight of her aunt's distress, she bounded from the bed to embrace her, the indignation forgotten.

"*Ma tante*, please do not be upset. The governor was concerned for our well-being, I am certain. Sit with me," she coaxed and patted her aunt's arm comfortingly. There was something alarming about the thin arm she touched, and when Leonora nervously smoothed the arch of her brow, the sleeve of her dress fell back to reveal one fragile, blue-veined wrist.

"What a ninny I am." Leonora gestured helplessly and wiped away the tears. "It is my recent illness, you understand. I do not care, Gweneth. It does not matter to me one bit what you have been forced to do. It is enough that you are alive. But if the man has taken advantage of you or harmed you, then do not be afraid to say so. You are protected, and Gareth has the authority to take the appropriate measures."

Gweneth's heart lurched. So Sarah had been right in

her estimation of the family's attitude. She hurried the words forth before her aunt could dectect her dismay. "Aunt Leonora, Capitaine Lavasseur has been nothing but kind, I swear it. He has never forced his attentions upon me nor sought to take advantage in any way. He is a fellow countryman and deserves my complete gratitude." Only a slight quivering of her voice disclosed her nervousness.

"I knew it. I told Gareth as much," Leonora sighed in relief. "It was just that with all those weeks at sea, four women alone, it is possible . . ." But she let the thought die. "You are not indifferent to this captain, though, are you?" She studied Gweneth's face, and nodded at the sight of her flushed cheeks. "No, I thought not. He is most anxious for you and has asked if he may call on you whenever he makes port. You would not object to this?"

Gweneth shook her head and whispered, "I am not certain of anything but that I should feel the loss deeply were he not to return. Is it wicked of me to express such things for a near stranger?"

"Why he hardly qualifies as a stranger, Gweneth, since you have spent nearly two months in one another's company. A ship is a small world indeed," she reminded her niece. "You must have been thrown together often on the voyage."

Gweneth's blush paled, for she had nearly let slip that her association with Captain Lavasseur was a bare week old. What would her aunt think if she knew the truth; that she had been brought to a brothel by another man and given to Lavasseur as a token of friendship, that she had nearly given herself to the stranger in a moment of weakness and then sneaked away with him in the wee hours? Leonora would have need of an inordinately compassionate heart were she to accept on faith the still respectable condition of her niece after having heard that tale.

"We shall speak of this later," Leonora announced and pulled Gweneth to her feet. "I have brought you a few things. These must serve until my dressmaker arrives. They are my things, and we seem to once have been of a similar size. They should be adequate for tonight."

"You must not feel that we are to be expensively clothed, Aunt. It is to my shame that we come empty-handed into your home," Gweneth replied humbly.

"Nonsense, child. Would you have me dress you in slave's rags? I shall have no more of this silly talk. Now—" And Leonora chose a gown from the pile of clothing she had dropped on a chair by the door.

Laurent prolonged his visit to three days. The luxury afforded by his hosts was a strong inducement to stall his departure indefinitely, but he knew he should leave. He had gallantly sought to turn aside the hefty purse forced on him by the governor, allowing that it quadrupled the amount in passage money he should have sought under ordinary circumstances. But the man was not to be denied and toasted him with lavish praise that first night to all gathered at the table.

"Captain Lavasseur, a man of inestimable honor and virtue," was how the governor phrased it. Laurent was somewhat embarrassed by the vision of moist feminine eyes which added their salute to this homage, but the winning smile upon Gweneth's lips set his mind at rest. This is what she had asked of him, and her gratitude was all he could have hoped for then.

The purse buttoned into his waistband made a conspicuous bulge under his sparingly cut coat, and he frowned again in annoyance. Gweneth lamented his decision to embark so soon but, as a man of infinite experience, this signaled the rightness of his purpose. How much more joyously she would receive him back into her arms when he returned.

Into her arms. Laurent savored the thought and then let his fantasies stray to the inevitable conclusion of that reunion. For a ten-day acquaintance he felt himself to have shown a restraint hitherto unknown in himself. She had come to his room a short half hour ago to say her good-byes in private, and he had let her go with no more than a lingering kiss on her fingertips. Had he allowed himself anything more, they might have found themselves entangled in the bedding of that magnificent four-poster which graced the room.

"You are a fool, Laurent," he chided the reflection in the mirror before him, "but ever a charming one." He laughed self-mockingly and swept his plumed hat and bag from the dresser.

It was good to be back aboard his vessel, Laurent observed as he stood watching Barbados fade on the horizon. A few short days and he would put to port again, for he dared not sail without a full crew into the ocean proper. Then there was that certain hand of poker he had left half played and was wont to finish, settling all debts. He barked orders for the trimming of a sail and turned his back on dreams to take up his duties.

Raoul waited with a set smile on his lips. The Frenchman had been gone long enough to reach Venezuela, but somehow he felt that the man's port had been the islands, Guadeloupe or, perhaps, Martinique. The tiny boat approached the *Cyrene*'s starboard side and each captain raised an arm in greeting.

Laurent boarded the ship quickly and met Raoul with hand extended. Raoul clasped it after a second's hesitation and pressed it in a viselike grip. If Laurent was surprised by the intensity of the pressure, it did not show, and he returned the power with equal firmness. Childish, primitive even, this display of aggression, but as their eyes met in subtle challenge, a glint of understanding passed between them.

"Welcome aboard," Raoul hailed as his grip slackened.

"*Mon ami*, Bertrand," replied Laurent and the tension between them vanished. The friendship remained.

Raoul gave orders for wine and cakes, and the two captains retired to his cabin to refresh themselves.

"I trust your voyage was successful," Raoul ventured when they had slaked their thirsts and sat regarding one another.

"Eminently so, Bertrand," replied Laurent with a smile and offered him an expensive cigar.

Raoul took his time in appreciation of its fine aroma. "And Mademoiselle Valois and party, they are well?" he questioned when the cigar was satisfactorily lighted.

"In the greatest of good health, I assure you." Laurent dug into his pocket, then spread several gold coins upon the table before Raoul. "The lady wished you to have this. I believe the amount will suffice for your trouble," he ended with high amusement in his dark gaze.

Raoul's mouth tightened at the gleam of money. He wanted no payment which might make him waver in his resolve to exact sufficient retribution of his own determination but, when his eyes raised to Laurent's face, he grinned and waved a hand of dismissal.

"The reward is yours, Lavasseur. I should not seek to divide the spoils. My consolation was conferred upon me before the fact."

Laurent met his look of self-satisfaction with equal facility. " 'Tis not a matter for debate, my friend, for I, too, found reward of another sort." He smoothed one edge of his moustache and considered the merit of the wine in his hand.

"You found the *jeune fille* a comfort on your voyage to wherever?" Raoul questioned with yawning indifference.

Laurent glanced away from the contents of his glass and across at the calm-sounding man. He arched a brow in surprise, having expected a very different reaction. "Bertrand, I possess a patient and subtle heart.

The mademoiselle entrusted herself into my care. Should I have portrayed the boorish manners of yourself? *Mais non*, once the cask is tapped and a quantity drawn to assess its merit, a rare vintage is to be sipped at leisure, savored and enjoyed." He raised an apologetic hand. "*Enfin*, that is the difference between us. I think the monkish exercise was not lost on Mademoiselle Valois." Laurent spoke amicably but found annoyance in the tiny wrinkles of amusement that now played about the captain's eyes.

"You are saying that Gweneth was yours only once, here in Road Town, Lavasseur?" asked Raoul and his humor was no longer veiled.

"I am saying that it is really none of your business, Bertrand," replied Laurent. His brow puckered in displeasure, for Raoul chuckled at his answer.

"Then, by all means, you deserve the gold, my Captain." Raoul swept the coins from the table to drop them in Laurent's lap. "You see, Gweneth left her dress behind and—wait, I have not yet finished," Raoul admonished the about-to-be-vocal man. "She also included a note. In it she begged me not to think ill of her, for it seems she was greatly distressed to leave me thinking she had wavered in her affection by allowing you to share her bed. I suppose it was foolish of me to ever think it otherwise." The startled expression on Laurent's face caused more laughter from Raoul but, oddly enough to his thinking, Lavasseur joined his revelry shortly.

The laughter died away as quickly as it had begun, and the two eyed one another in amused wariness.

"Lest the jest be all at my expense," began Laurent, "let me amend your thinking. Gweneth was spared my ardent attentions by confessing herself to still be a maiden. It was supposed that she had been yours repeatedly, and here I find myself abed with a half-draped virgin. *Morbleu!* What was I to do?" Laurent shrugged before the black stare accosting him. "Upon our slight acquaintance, the honorable thing seemed to be to acquiesce. So, there you are, *mon ami.* I, too, know the full tale."

The two sat in utter silence, each chagrined by the admissions of the other. At length Raoul lifted the bottle and served them both. "I believe a toast is in order," he said and cupped his glass. "To Mademoiselle Valois, a liar, a cheat, and a thoroughly irresistible creature. And to the man who lives to teach her the error of her ways!" The glasses tinkled in salute.

"And who shall this man be, Bertrand?" questioned Laurent when he set his glass aside. "It would seem that the hand is mine. Shall I remember to quote you as I bed her?"

"Not so fast, Lavasseur," advised Raoul, and he drained his glass. "By right, I have first claim on her. You have only her word that she spoke the truth to you, and we now know how well she weaves her deceptions."

"True, but it is I who know where she is to be found," answered Laurent smoothly.

"You think I cannot discover her whereabouts?"

"In time, of course, but by then she shall have been mine. That is the object of this little pledge of revenge, *mais oui*? The victory lies in deflowering the girl. What matter if you find her after that?"

Raoul's face hardened at the bluntness of his companion's remarks. If he had sought the same solution, it was different. The spoken words left a foul odor in the air.

"I do not believe I care for your attitude."

Laurent's gaze shot up to his companion's face, discovering disgust there. A flush spread over his cheeks, darkening them under his swarthy skin. He had meant no disrespect of the lady but was embarrassed by Bertrand's disclosures and wished to appear unconcerned. As it was, he was very anxious that Bertrand forgo his plans entirely.

For the time it took to count five heartbeats, Laurent toyed with the idea of accepting Bertrand's words as grounds for a duel. To kill him would remove the threat altogether, but that did not agree with his sense of competition. Besides, if he should lose . . .

"I apologize, Capitaine. In my spirit of the chase I spoke too frankly. I am as enamored of the mademoiselle as you. And therein lies the difficulty. It may be that I should choose to have her as my own. In such a case I am bound to protect her from you."

"Would you seek to marry the girl?" Raoul asked in amazement.

Laurent shrugged noncommittally. "I might know the same of you."

"I shall not marry again," Raoul stated flatly and found himself in need of more substantial fortification. This interview revealed more problems than it solved. The addition of Lavasseur as a serious suitor chafed badly. He jerked the cork from a rum bottle and poured.

"We have nothing to discuss in that case," answered Laurent, picking up the thought. "May the best man win and so forth," and he signaled for some of the same. Both men sank into their own thoughts till their glasses were emptied.

Raoul set his glass aside and rubbed his chin. "I suppose I could trail you around the Caribbean until we were sufficiently sick of it to come to violence, but that would be indulging in lunacy. We both desire the girl. What then is to be done?" He eyed Laurent intently. "An equal chance, a race perhaps? Each to the mercy of sea and wind. My ship is adequate to yours, I should wager."

"You forget we are in business, Bertrand. I have cargo that is weeks late of delivery. The way the *Cyrene* rides low in the water, I should say the same of you. Are we to throw our business to others while we cavort about on the sea like two love-sick seals in search of a mate? Non, not only our crews but the mademoiselle herself would divine the folly in that and laugh in our faces. She would win our livelihoods in place of—you understand. Also there is her uncle to be assuaged. So I suggest a truce for the time it takes to be free of our cargo. We shall meet—where?—in, say a month's time," reasoned Laurent and stubbed out his smoke.

Raoul approved this persuasive thinking, providing . . .

"You are wondering if I am to be trusted, *mon ami*. Not a very pretty compliment," cajoled Laurent in voicing Raoul's doubts aloud. "You have my word as a gentleman and a friend. My hand on it."

Raoul took the hand and held it. "I should rather know the whereabouts of the lady in question," he replied.

In the heat of the mid-June day Raoul had stripped to the waist while working alongside his men as they loaded rum and sugar bound for America in trade for tobacco and cotton bound for England. In the years following the overthrow of England's colonial government in the American states, trade had flourished between the new country and the Caribbean, giving merchant seamen like himself a chance to amass a self-made fortune. With another ship under his control, Raoul felt his dream of a shipping company would be a reality, and the funds for that purchase of a second vessel should be his with this next voyage home.

"Devil take this heat!" Raoul swore and rubbed the copious sweat from his brow with a forearm. He should have accepted Governor Dillingham's offer of a leisurely dinner as his was a nurtured friendship, but the month was nearly gone and he did not mean to give Lavasseur any excuse for setting sail without him. The delay had only whetted his appetite to renew his acquaintance with Mademoiselle Valois. No, he would set sail with the evening tide.

Raoul hardly noticed the black-clad figure who now gained the gangplank of his ship and only turned to the stranger when he heard his name called.

"I am Captain Bertrand," he replied wearily and set the heavy crate on the deck.

"Captain, my name is Bellefort, and I have letters for you." The properly dressed gentleman carefully sidestepped two burly men heaving aloft more cargo and ceremoniously handed over the mail.

By custom mail came through diplomatic channels to Raoul's regular ports of call, but he had been so busy these past weeks that he had neglected two opportunities.

"Thank you, my man," Raoul replied and replaced the mail with a coin on the man's outstretched palm.

The creeping flush on the stranger's face showed he interpreted this gesture as an insult. The captain must realize that he was not an errand boy but a man of some account in the governor's office. The secretary eyed the broad sun-bronzed torso of the captain in disdain but decided that a retort might occasion his being crushed by the force of those hard sinewy muscles. The swaggering fellow was doubtless a bully. Instead he bowed stiffly and left in a great hurry. He was heard to mutter something of the indignities one was ever subjected to in this savage land.

Raoul glanced down at the letters he held. A look of indifference swept the lot until his gaze fell upon the last. The sweat from his body turned to ice water on his skin and, without as much as a single word to the men about him, Raoul bolted for his cabin and set the lock.

Lavasseur waited one full week past the designated time for Bertrand. On the evening of the eighth day there came a man bearing a note from the captain, and Lavasseur tore it open in some anxiety when the man was gone. Had Bertrand found Gweneth and sent a note of victory? His frowning anger gave way to complete surprise as he studied the few short lines.

There had been a letter from Bertrand's father. The man was gravely ill and asked that his son come home. He had set sail for England more than a week past and asked that Lavasseur attend his cargo in Barbados which he, of necessity, had left behind.

Laurent read the note a second time, for the mention of Barbados jolted him sharply. But no, he was certain that Bertrand had not known of his nearness to Gweneth. Laurent threw back his head in a whoop of glee. Bertrand had missed the golden opportunity.

How unpredictable was that man. Never in their years of friendship had he betrayed the slightest interest in his natural father and yet, now, had cast all to the wind on a summons from the earl. Laurent sighed. He would never understand the man who played light with that which meant the most to him.

"Well, well, it seems I sail to certain victory," he murmured aloud. And with the best of excuses to return so soon, for a cargo waited for him. "The luck, *c'est fabuleux!*"

CHAPTER ELEVEN

The rainy season had come. Hardly a day passed when the ponderous thunderheads did not roll overhead, spilling their quotient of rain on sea and land.

Gweneth cast a curious glance past the canopy of trees to the sky beyond. The turbulence often would begin unexpectedly and end just as quickly, leaving the jungle sighing under its weight of generous moisture. And the heavy, close humming of the underbrush was a constant reminder of the nearness of yellow fever and malaria, just a breath away.

She walked in the dew-drenched garden of early morning. Her light green muslin gown barely swept the thick grasses, causing them to ripple in her wake. The heat became unbearable at midday, and she had chosen to rise early and take exercise before breakfast. Renée teased her eager sister and had been dubbed a lay-about in retaliation.

The house began to stir behind her, but Gweneth walked on. If she were late for breakfast or skipped it altogether, none would scold, for Leonora kept to her rooms till noon.

As she bent to pluck a hibiscus from its shelter of leaves, her arm brushed the generous, yet delicately laden bough of a bougainvillea, and the tiny lantern flowers scattered like confetti.

"*Nigaud!*" Gweneth chided herself as she jerked back her hand and saw the fine scratch that quickly filled with blood. She put the wound to her lips and, as a woman would, noticed with pleasure that the skin was smooth and supple. Gone were the last traces of two years' toil. Then a familiar pang of discomfort struck her. Renée might well give no second thought to the luxurious life which surrounded them, but Gweneth was still acutely aware of the burden they presented.

She approached her uncle that first week in hopes of being allowed to seek employment in another household.

"My dear child," Gareth voiced in scandalized tones. "Have we been so remiss in our attitude that you feel unwelcome and mistreated?"

"*Mais non*, Uncle. It is just the opposite. You and Aunt Leonora have been generous in the extreme," Gweneth replied as she sat before him on the broad veranda one evening.

"Then what is it? Why should you desire to become independent of those who love you?"

Gweneth felt flattered by her uncle's warm words, but she was disturbed by the long inquiring look he often gave her.

"Uncle Gareth,"—how strange the words were on her tongue—"it is the wish to ease the burden of our untimely appearance which urges me to offer myself for service."

"My dear. You are a blessing. Have I not noticed the quickened recovery in my wife since you arrived? Mere words cannot express my pleasure. And she's gained a French maid in the bargain. Nay, Gweneth, the thanks is mine. But, if it will ease your mind, I promise to approach you should an opportunity arise in which you might be of help." And he smiled away all further protest.

Thus assured, she had let the matter lie. Now, in the sweet cool air of morning, Gweneth wondered if the need should ever present itself. For weeks there had been little to do. Leonora was convalescing from a miscarriage suffered just weeks before their arrival, and the girls were left on their own for the most part.

In addition it had become increasingly clear that the society of these islands provided no place for employment. Who would seek to hire a nurse or children's maid when there were women to be had from their own slaves? Wealth was to be hoarded or spent solely for self-indulgence in this world where wages were seldom earned. Children of promise were tutored within the family to be sent abroad for final polishing when the time came. And then there was the consideration of her relatives' position.

It was not that there was no work to be found. On this island of thirty thousand souls the volume of work was astounding. Now that the late spring harvest was finished and a new crop sown, all hands were occupied with the processing of cane.

Not long ago Governor Dillingham had set aside a morning to accompany his nieces on a tour of his property.

The winding path followed by the open carriage brought them near the beach. The narrow stretch of sand was bleached white by the wind-driven Atlantic rollers, frosted with foam as they broke at the island's edge. From there they turned inland once more, to the soft fertile fields of the countryside interspersed here and there with brief tracts of palm, mahogany, and breadfruit trees.

As they passed the neatly furrowed fields, Gareth directed their attention with the tip of his gold-handled cane. He had discarded his velvet coat and wig on this occasion, substituting a tan riding jacket and soft, broad-brimmed hat over his short hair.

Surprised by the scarcity of laborers in the fields, Renée ventured to ask, "But you have so few slaves. How do you ever manage?"

Gareth's gray eyes sparkled as he said, "It is not as you expected, my dear? No throng of shackled savages toiling under the lash of the overseer's whip? Oh, I know of the heinous pictures painted by those humanitarians in Europe. So easily are we maligned when there is no proof to the contrary. Well, you may witness all and then judge for yourselves."

The cloying sweetness reached their nostrils long before the high roofed mills came into view as they approached steeper ground. Warehouse after warehouse stretched before them in the clearing and, here, the vastness of the governor's holdings became obvious.

As they alighted onto the hard-packed earth, heat combined with the sugar-laden smoke to stifle the clean scent of the wind, masking the sweat of the humanity all about them.

Within the walls of the mill they entered, huge crushing rollers made pulp of the stripped cane, spewing the sugary juice into large evaporation vats. Women, using heavy poles, stood on platforms above the cauldrons, stirring the foamy head until crystals formed at the bottom. From there the remaining liquid drained into copper vats kept boiling by well-stoked fires.

"Should bring ten thousand pounds in profit this year. A fine harvest by all accounts," Gareth commented of the method by which he amassed his fortune. "Of course, we've yet to weather the rainy season. Could cut my profits by half."

Renée looked at Gweneth and rolled her eyes, whispering behind her uncle's back, "*Enfin*, we have had nothing but bad weather. First it rains, then this detestable heat. What could be worse?"

"You are simply annoyed that your curls wilt out of doors, *ma petite*. For such a calamity, should even the heavens abate?" Gweneth teased as her sister swept a limp curl from her forehead.

Renée had used the excuse of the climate to cajole Leonora into allowing Amy to bob her tresses. The result, so much the rage on the Continent, gave her the look of a pampered poodle. But it suited her, calling attention to the delicate line of her cheek and chin.

A group of slaves, struggling under their loads of stripped cane, entered at one end of the mill where they traded this burden for kegs of molasses that would be converted into rum in the distilling house. Bare except for a sheen of sweat and filthy breeches of Osnabury linen, each man fell back as the governor passed, tipping his load quickly in a grotesque parody of a bow. Gareth strode before them without recognition.

"When the harvest is set and the hogheads filled for export, my people are free to tend their own needs. They are expected to keep a garden and mend their quarters," Gareth informed his charges. "They see to themselves, and I have gone far to keep them fit. Have you heard of the Code Noire? The French Indies made concessions to their slaves I have been eager to adopt. Can't go too far too quickly, mind you, but a bit of leniency here and quick final justice there keeps a firm grip on the reins and willing labor in my fields."

But as she watched the men and women toiling for no share and no profit, Gweneth suddenly wondered how long it might be before they, too, grasped the necessity of overthrowing the existing order. They were different, not truly of human stature, she had been told more than once since her arrival. But Gweneth knew those same desperate, hopeless expressions from long ago, on the streets of Paris, and understood from painful experience how rapidly they could be changed to ones of hatred and vengeance.

As they left the worksite, Gweneth was surprised by the vision of a bloody battered carcass that had once been a man strung in the fibrous boughs of a banyan tree. It gave lie to the governor's expressions of harmony. The crime, she was told, was stealing a cask of rum.

"But that is wicked, Gareth. Whatever are you thinking?" Leonora's eyes followed Gareth about the gold and white bedroom as she sat propped by many pillows.

"Of practicalities, my dear, a thing your feminine mind is wont to overlook at every point," Gareth replied. "We must settle the girls if ever we are to return to England."

"It is too great a cost. Poor little Renée. She will be desolate to find herself shipped to a convent. And what of Gweneth? She is too strong-minded not to balk at your attempt to separate them."

"True, dear wife, but I have always had a way with the ladies. Would you not agree?" A sardonic smile lifted his features. "I shall handle my niece as easily as I do all else. If you had but carried our child to full term, I should not be forced to engage in this dubious exercise in order to preserve our livelihood."

"That is not fair, Gareth," Leonora whimpered, but he turned his back. "No one longs for a son more than I. It is this merciless heat. How could anyone be expected to bear a child in these conditions?" she begged and lay another cologne-moistened handkerchief on her brow.

"Quite so, though it would seem you are particularly sensitive, for our last kitchen maid has birthed a fine daughter just this month," he said indifferently.

A strangled cry of pain broke from Leonora's lips. To have her husband flaunt his mistress's bastard and shame her was much too much. What beauty she still possessed dissolved before a flood of tears as deep, uneven sobs shook her.

Gareth shot his wife a contemptuous glance, then immediately divined the folly in making an enemy of his only means of securing the place he coveted. Had it not been for her weaknesses, they would never have met. Delicate health had sent her to the islands fifteen years before, and she had proved easy prey to the not inconsiderable charm of her father's land manager. The old man was horrified to learn of the marriage but, loving Leonora dearly, he granted her the plantation that she might not suffer too badly in her exile.

"There now, Leonora," Gareth comforted as he sat

by her side and drew her against his silk coat. "I spoke in haste. You must know that it is you I love. The other?" He waved a hand of dismissal. "A most unfortunate affair. I shall never mention it again. It is just monstrous that we who long so passionately for a child should be denied while others come to it so easily." Too damned easily, he thought irritably, for the bondswoman had been with child before he had shared her bed two months. Still a man must have some release, and he dared not touch his wife once a pregnancy was suspected.

"We must turn our backs on the past and seek the future with hope. You must go home if we are ever to have a child, but nothing will be gained there if these girls accompany us. I am not suggesting that they be cast into the streets. We shall select the very best school for Renée and a suitable arrangement for Gweneth. No father and mother could do more. In time we shall offer them a share of the inheritance, but even you should realize that we will lose the roof over our heads if either girl produces a son before we do. This is a delay, nothing else."

When satisfied that his wife was consoled at last, Gareth left her to search for his niece.

"Surely you understand the wisdom of this," Gareth urged. "Renée must complete her education, and we can offer nothing here." His argument had been presented smoothly and well as they shared a seat in the rear garden. As the yellow, pink, and purple blossoms nearby challenged and lost to the seductive perfume of the deep red frangipani flowers carried on the trade winds, Gareth became more aware with each second of his luck at finding Gweneth alone. The silent reflective mood he had found her in was quite suitable to his purpose.

"But Italy?" Gweneth cried in dismay. "It is so far away. Would it not be better for her to come to England with us?"

"Whatever are you saying, Gweneth?" Gareth asked.

"Aunt Leonora had told me that you are planning to return there once the spring storms abate. If we are to leave that soon, why cannot Renée wait to attend school? The thought of separation is terrible for me, Uncle, and so it would be for my sister."

Gareth's features remained impassive, but the gray eyes narrowed. That fool wife of his had spoken out of turn. "It would be best, of course, but I must point out several objections to so simple a solution." All sympathy colored his voice. "First there is the question of religion. You are Catholic. A convent would provide the proper spiritual as well as intellectual atmosphere for Renée. Then there is the difficult question of your citizenship. Here, in Barbados, I have the final authority to allow you to remain. In England I have no power. You have no papers, no visa, no rights. What if some zealous patriot should seek to deliver you both into the hands of the French authorities? In the murky ploys of political scheming I should be helpless to aid you." Gareth touched the bare shoulder exposed by Gweneth's summer gown in a gesture of comfort. "I should hate to see disaster fall upon your frail head, child."

"I am not a child," Gweneth retorted and turned an angry stare on him. "Could you not use your authority here to enable us to become English citizens?"

"Would you have me use my office as a tool for bribery and deceit?" questioned Gareth, his impatience with the girl lending his words proper affront.

"*Mais non*, Uncle," she answered contritely, immediately regretting her outburst. "I speak unwisely. I should not ask that of you. There must be some other solution."

"Dear Gweneth," Gareth crooned softly as he let his arm slip round her shoulders. Her scent stirred his thoughts to other directions, and he gazed long at her full trembling lips. If he could be certain of her feelings, perhaps she might be able to accompany them after all. But no, Leonora was the most direct path to his goal, no matter how sweet those young lips might prove.

"I speak harshly and frankly to bring you the realization of your situation," he said finally. "If you and Renée are to come safely into England, time must pass. This parting is no less dreadful for us than it shall be for you." He squeezed her arm gently, and Gweneth leaned her head against his shoulder, the blossom in her hair brushing his cheek.

"There, there. You must not despair. There are ways, but they require time. Why, if you were to marry a man whose nationality would protect you, then you would be safe."

Gweneth nodded slowly, and Gareth smiled above her head. How easily swayed were those who lived by their emotions.

"That is it!" he cried, as though the thought were new to him. "I know one or two Englishmen in these islands who would make an ideal husband for you."

Gweneth started in astonishment at this daring suggestion and turned to face her uncle. "Would you have me wed a man I do not love in order to save myself?"

Gareth smiled slightly. "The choice is yours, of course, but think on this. Renée will be away in school. As you have pointed out, you are no longer a child," he said as his eyes fell to her low neckline. "You are beautiful and old enough to be married. If the situation presents itself, why should you hesitate? A wealthy man might be able to bring Renée to England too. So lovely a bride as you should find any request answered by the man fortunate enough to wed you."

His silvery gaze rose to Gweneth's face. "The solution is in your hands, my dear. Would that there were a way in which I could fulfill your desire."

Gweneth stared at her uncle's enigmatic expression.

His words were warmly personal, but she must be mistaken. It could not be, and yet . . .

"Mademoiselle Valois? Mademoiselle? It is I, Lavasseur," called a voice which brought Gweneth to her feet in surprise mingled with relief.

"We are here, Capitaine," she replied needlessly, for Laurent was making long rapid strides in their direction. Gweneth put a hand to her hair to snatch the flower she had tucked behind her ear in the earlier solitude of the morning, wondering uneasily if the captain had seen her in the arms of her uncle. If he had, there was no effect of it in his face as he reached them.

"Governor Dillingham, I do not mean to intrude. Mademoiselle Renée told me that I might find Mademoiselle Gweneth in the garden, and I took the opportunity to seek her out for myself," Laurent said and offered a hand.

"So it would seem," Gareth replied dryly, not at all outwardly distracted by the man's sudden appearance. "You return so soon, Captain. Have you business in Barbados?" he questioned archly.

"Exactly so, monsieur. And with you yourself it would seem. I come to load the cargo left by your agent three weeks ago," Laurent volunteered with a smile.

"How did you know of that?" Gareth asked. "Well, no matter. At last the cargo will be moved. It has languished about on the docks for more than a month while that damnable fellow sails away with all the haste of a thief. Bad business, I say. It shall take some explaining before I entrust another cargo to Captain Bertrand."

At the mention of Raoul's name a tiny gasp escaped Gweneth, and she would have spoken had Laurent not caught her eye. Instead she turned away to hide the agitation in her heart.

"The capitaine is my good friend, monsieur. I assure you that only the most urgent of business sent him off so precipitously. And, as you see, he sent me in his stead. The cargo will take a few days to load, and then it will be on its way. I shall discuss these details with you at your convenience. But, with your permission, I should like to pay my compliments to your niece."

Gareth lifted a gold watch from its pocket and nodded. "The business of the day awaits me. Gweneth, you must think these matters through carefully, and then we will speak again before approaching Renée," he said and patted her arm. The distress on Gweneth's face he attributed to the subject they had been discussing. "Make our guest welcome, as I know you shall." Casting a speculative glance at the captain, he added, "Lavasseur, I shall expect you at midmorning. Good day to you both."

Laurent waited until the governor had disappeared from sight before speaking, letting his eyes fill with the vision of the woman at his side. In as little as two months' time she had grown more lovely. Her skin was paler but flushed with good health, and the skimpily cut gown revealed her so enchantingly that he was tempted to draw her close that he might kiss and caress her sweet silky flesh.

A deep sigh gave voice to his design, and he grinned broadly when Gweneth colored under his leer.

"Ah, mademoiselle, were we not likely to be interrupted, I should be moved to pay you the highest compliment a man may offer the object of his desire," he said wistfully and bowed low before her now scarlet face.

"Capitaine, for shame," Gweneth admonished but giggled in spite of herself. "Come, and give me your hand."

"I should give you so much more, *ma chère*, were you but to say the word. What, no word?" he asked in pretended regret. "A hand then, and no more."

Laurent took her hand and kissed it lingeringly,

turning it over to place a soft kiss on her pulse. "Your heart says yes, *ma petite.*"

"Hush, Capitaine. Someone may hear you," Gweneth replied and drew her hand away. The unexpected visit delighted her but also made her instantly aware that this was an ever disturbing presence to her emotions.

She turned and sat on the bench, beckoning to Laurent. "Tell me what—oh, but I know. You have seen Capitaine Bertrand. He has been in Barbados?" Her voice dropped to a whisper at the mention of that name.

"Do you fear him so much?" Laurent asked when he had seated himself beside her. "You have no reason, Gweneth. Bertrand is even now weeks at sea, headed for England." Laurent watched the quick rise and fall of her bosom.

"England? Are you certain?"

His gaze rose slowly to her face. "Quite. I received a note from him requesting that I secure and deliver his cargo. How fortunate for me that it was here. You see, we are destined to be thrown together." Laurent's brows drew together in a frown. "But you would have word of your capitaine still, *mais non?*" He lay his hand on hers. "He asked where you were that he might come to you."

"You did not tell him?"

"Non, *ma petite.* Your safekeeping is my concern, and I told him as much."

Relief flowed through Gweneth, leaving her weak.

"Enough of that man," Laurent counseled. "He has gone to his father's deathbed and will trouble us no more. Tell me how you have fared these last weeks."

The temptation was great to tell him of her uncle's plans for her sister and herself, but Gweneth decided that she should not burden her guest with any more of her troubles. Rather she launched into a gay story of her recent trip to Bridgetown.

* * *

Gareth paced the floor of his bedroom that night after all had retired. He must be careful of Lavasseur. It was a pity that the Frenchman was not in his pay, for he had seen how the man doted on his niece and her return of that interest. Who would not, for she tempted even himself to a natural lust. After all, she was no blood kin.

Gareth turned to stare out into the garden beneath his window. If Lavasseur could not be bribed, then he must find another who would consent to keep the girl out of England and thus assure his hold on Briarwood.

The door opened softly behind him, but Gareth did not bother to turn. "I was beginning to think you had forgotten me," he said quietly and laughed.

"*Mais non*, monsieur. How could I ever forget you?" came the amused reply as soft arms enfolded him from behind, and Gareth's attention found a more immediate interest.

CHAPTER TWELVE

The bottle-green waters of the lagoon lapped the grassy bank, slushing softly as sunlight dappled the shade. In this cool, breezy spot the basket had been opened and its contents distributed for a picnic. Gweneth's cambric gown billowed in the air, its sprigs of embroidered yellow daisies undulating on a sea of white cotton. The sleeves ended at the elbow, and the bodice was cut with the same low squared neckline as most of her summer gowns. It should have been filled with a handkerchief, but the sweltering heat had caused her to cast it aside together with her wide straw hat and veil when they paused in their walk to eat.

She glanced at the man by her side. Laurent, too, had abandoned his formal attire, doffing his frock coat and stock and rolling his sleeves to the elbow. Twirling a blade of grass between two fingers, he sat cross-legged on the bank. Gweneth's gaze lingered to study him, for his head was turned toward the distant shore. A fine sleek covering of black hair grew along the length of his arms to the fingers where they formed wiry tufts below each knuckle. The white lawn shirt appeared all the brighter next to his brown skin and, as the wind filled it, opening it to the waist, Gweneth's eyes were drawn to his smooth hard chest. But she wrenched them away immediately when he turned to her.

"How thoughtful of your aunt to provide us with lunch and the opportunity of finding ourselves alone," he said and raised a brow in amusement. "I had formed the conclusion that I was no longer welcome."

"What nonsense," Gweneth replied quickly, but she knew well the subdued attitude of the household that had fostered the captain's opinion.

While Laurent had attended to loading his ship these past two days, Gareth had taken the necessary steps to gain Renée's admittance to a convent near Venice. When she was informed of this, Renée balked in disbelief. Thinking Gweneth would champion her cause, she soon came to tears when Gweneth was forced to side with her uncle and express his opinions which she now shared. After their uncle departed, Gweneth was left to comfort her sister.

"I shall run away. Oh Gweneth, he cannot make me go. Not if you stand up to him for me. Make him change his mind, Gweneth. You can, I know you can!" Renée wailed and clung to Gweneth's skirts on her knees, the hysteria paling her cheeks.

Gweneth winced and turned away from Laurent at the remembrance. Since then Renée had not spoken a word to her.

"*Ma petite*, what is it?" Laurent flicked the bit of grass aside and moved close to put an arm around Gweneth's shoulders. "You are so sad. Come, out with it. How else may this knight aid his lady in distress?" he added lightly and put a hand, the gentlest of touches, to her chin to turn her face to his.

"This is serious," he said when he gazed long into her eyes. "Speak now, little one, for my time is short."

"All the more reason to keep silent," Gweneth replied but held her words with difficulty.

"I shall remain as long as it takes for the truth. Tell me."

Gweneth related the facts of Renée's being sent to school and her uncle's decision that Gweneth should find a husband. Laurent listened to every word as though weighing the merit of the arguments.

"Is that all?" he asked unconcernedly when the tale was done.

"It is enough," Gweneth answered shortly and pulled her knees up to wrap them in her arms. She removed her silk slippers and buried her toes in the grassy carpet.

"The solution is simple," Laurent said and traced a finger along her cheek. "Come with me."

Gweneth turned to stare at him in wonder. "Go with you? Go where?"

Laurent smiled indulgently. "To faraway places. To life, *mon amour*. I shall show you the world as few ever come to know it. I am bound for America and then England. After that," he shrugged and tightened the hand at her chin. "I would have waited until my return to approach you with this matter, but the time presents itself and answers all our prayers."

Leaning nearer, he bent to kiss the curve of her exposed throat. "We shall laugh and love and spend our lives to the fullest."

For an instant his confidence infected Gweneth, her eyes bright as she asked, "Are you certain, Laurent?" Then, "Oh, I am not so sure."

"I am, sufficient for the both of us. Chérie, listen to me," Laurent pleaded softly and cupped her face in both hands. "*Mon Dieu*, you are lovelier than anything I have ever laid eyes on," he murmured. "And you are mine, though it is a miracle to me." His face held such rapture that Gweneth felt dismay.

"Wait, Laurent," she begged and shrank back. "This is much too fast. I do not yet understand what you ask of me. 'Come with me' you say, and yet there is something which you do not say."

"What would you have me do, propose?" he questioned and came up on his knees before her. "Chérie, I do not know what awaits us. Give it time. Between us there is a quality of feeling, a need so strong that we are helpless to break its hold. It draws us to one another unerringly." He leaned over and would have kissed her lips, but Gweneth rolled aside and came to her feet.

"You offer me the life of a mistress, a kept woman, Capitaine," she declared frostily and folded her arms across her bosom. "I have been offered such before, by your friend. Should I answer *oui* to you when I have bade him *non*? What makes one the greater bargain?"

Laurent reached out and tugged her skirt but when she would not come forward, he rose. "*Mon amour*, we are the bargain. When you kiss me, I know there is a need in you which matches my own," he said warmly. "Never had I thought to possess a lady of your bearing and quality. Yet there is a desire, nay, a passion in you which beckons to me and asks me to answer in kind. Voilà, we are of a mind rarely met in this life." He wrapped his long arms about her waist and drew her near.

"Non, non, this is wicked!" and she sought to push him from her, but his embrace was not so easily denied.

"Do not fight me, Gweneth," he said silkily. "You knew that this time would come. The day, the place, it is all here. You knew it when you came with me." Laurent tightened his arms until her head was forced against his half-bared chest.

"You hear my heart, chérie? It beats with love for you, harder and faster than it has ever beat before. Listen, and know that yours responds."

Gweneth stilled within his embrace, her head awhirl with emotion. That he could speak so boldly of such things both alarmed and thrilled her. Still the hesitancy remained. Would it not be better for her to go with a man who declared his love for her than to marry another whom she did not desire?

Laurent touched her hair and forehead with kisses, closing his eyes to enjoy the feel of her in his arms and the sweet perfume of her body. Then he looked down, and when she raised her head with a question half framed on her lips, he bent and covered them with his own, drawing from her a honeyed kiss which stirred every fiber of his being.

"Oh Laurent, could I really come with you?" Gweneth whispered shakily. But Laurent, spurred by anticipation, bent lower to brush his lips over her throat and breasts. "Laurent, Renée must come with us," Gweneth continued, denying the sensations his mouth would force upon her. Her hands came up to hold his face and draw it up to hers. "You would take Renée also?" she repeated and noticed with misgiving the darkening in his eyes.

"What should she do aboard a ship?" Laurent straightened and shook his head, the raven locks whirling free about his shoulders. "This is for us. She is better off in a nunnery." He stopped to fasten his gaze upon her face, and Gweneth saw how those black pools shimmered at the sight of her. "We shall sail the wind, to be blown wherever it bids. It is not a life for a child. Lash your soul to mine, Gweneth, and we shall seek our destinies together."

Laurent pulled her closer and kissed her harder and more urgently than before, but Gweneth's lips held nothing. Drawing back, he stared at her in anger and frustration, for her eyes were as smooth and cold as glass.

"What would you have me do? Kidnap a babe? *Sacré Dieu*, the governor would set a price on my head so that I should be hounded from the sea," he scoffed, dropping his hands.

He thumped his brow with a palm and took several steps away before facing her. "This is madness. I want you with me, by my side, sailing with me. You would have me forfeit my life to set up housekeeping. Am I to retire to my house in New Orleans and sit about the grounds spinning yarns for brats in knee breeches about how their brave Papa once sailed the seas? Non, it is too great a price!"

Watching this irate man, Gweneth realized she knew nothing of him at all. He might want her, perhaps love her in his own way, but it was not enough. She could well consider his entreaty had it meant the safekeeping of Renée but . . . Her mind raced on to so many thoughts. Would that not mean that she was offering herself to him for her sister's sake? But no, she felt something for him, if only the weakness of the flesh whose pleasures she had only begun to understand. Yet it was not enough.

"I—I cannot do this thing," she said and dropped her eyes. "Renée is all I have left of my family. I must find someone who will help me keep her." The ache was so plain in her voice that Laurent nearly relented, but his pride forestalled to answer for him.

"So, you will not give yourself to me, but you would sell yourself to some rich plantation owner so that your sister might be spared a few years' education. That is what you say, Gweneth," he replied harshly. "You would accept the mauling attentions of some drooling old fool when you could have true love."

"Non—oh, I do not know," Gweneth said. Stamping her foot, she whirled away from him, for tears were rising fast to sting her eyes.

"Then you are a silly little girl!" And grabbing her roughly from behind, Laurent jerked her around, ignoring the damp streaks on her cheeks. "I shall prove to you that you could never endure the empty embraces of some feeble old man once you have known the passion of a hot-blooded lover." He yanked her fiercely to himself and whispered, "I promised to finish the lesson, *ma petite*, and this would seem to be the perfect moment."

Gweneth cried out, but his arm came around her head and clapped a hand over her mouth. Laurent smiled mischievously and bent her back until her knees gave way, sending her backward onto the grass. He fell over her, checking their fall with his free hand. She squirmed and tried to shove him off, but it only loosened his shirt, and Laurent released her mouth to press it to his naked chest.

"*Oui, mon amour*, kiss me," he murmured as he arched against her, his head thrown back to the sky. Gweneth struggled for breath against his warm hard flesh, but Laurent took her head in his hands and moved her lips in slow deliberate circles over his bronzed skin.

"Yes, yes, that is good," he whispered and looked down into her round frightened eyes. He slid lower and pressed his body along the length of her, urging his hips to fit hers. "It shall be so good for us," he said into her hair and teased the lobe of one ear with his teeth. "Do not be afraid. I will not harm you."

Tears blinded her until Laurent was but a vague dark form hovering above her. His head went lower, and long silky locks of black hair fell across her face. "Please, if you love me, you must not do this," Gweneth pleaded, her breath coming in quick shallow gasps.

"It is because I love you that I must. *Pardieu*, but you are exquisite." His black eyes kindled in lustful appreciation as he leaned down to one breast straining free of her gown.

Fighting for control of her body which was rapidly turning traitor under the sly touch of his lips, Gweneth screamed her denial of this intimacy.

"Hush, *ma petite*," Laurent cautioned with a gentle hand to her mouth. "We would not have anyone find us yet." He smiled wickedly. "It is not my wish to frighten you but rather to please you."

"If this is your idea of pleasure, monsieur, then I am certain to find the advances of my husband, whoever he might be, preferable to your mauling," she retorted proudly, but the whiteness of her lips confirmed her fear of him.

The muscles bunched and strained along Laurent's jaw as the smile eased from his countenance, leaving it chill. Gweneth turned from him, shutting her eyes. He was hot and heavy on her, but the burden of her terror weighed heavier by far.

"Is there nothing in your heart for me?" Laurent's husky choked tone caused Gweneth to look back. The anger was gone and sorrow lined the lean dark features. "Gweneth, chérie, am I wrong? I thought, I could have sworn upon all that I hold sacred, that you possessed deep, personal feelings for me. I would not have it like this for us. You force me to rash action."

He lowered his head to tenderly nuzzle one uncovered breast. "I am desperate for you, *ma petite*. Since that first night when you gave so freely of yourself, I have waited for that moment to return. Why do you hold back now?"

"Laurent, I was not myself that night. So much had happened." Gweneth sighed and touched his hair with her fingertips, feeling curiously calm now that he no longer compelled her surrender by force. "I know not how to answer you. Since those weeks I spent with Capitaine Bertrand, I have not—"

"Bertrand!" Laurent released her and raised up. "Always it comes back to your capitaine," he muttered and rolled off of her. The tense cords of anger flexed again along his jaw.

"That man has bewitched you." He cursed and tore a handful of grass from the ground by his boot. "You expect him to return, *mais non?*" Gweneth shook her head, but Laurent went on. "Then let me warn you what awaits should he find you. He shall come with one purpose in mind." And he turned with a slow, malicious smile teasing his mouth. "He wants revenge for the joke you played on him. If he should find you still a virgin, it will make his pleasure complete. You think me ungentle? You have no idea of the pain a man can inflict on a woman, particularly an untried maiden. It is not a pretty thought, and he will delight in every scream."

Gweneth shrank from his nasty grin and sprawled facedown in the grass. Laurent watched as her body shook with silent sobs and cursed loudly. He had hurt her deliberately, but the victory pained him the more.

Reaching out, he pulled her close, pushing the loosened cinnamon curls from her face.

"*Ma petite*, he is not the man for you. He was betrayed once by a woman he loved, and it destroyed all the feelings you and I possess. Come with me. Let me love and protect you always," he said gently and cradled her to his chest; the passion in his blood abated for the moment.

"I shall marry you in time, I swear it. But come with me tonight."

"I cannot leave Renée," Gweneth replied and pulled gradually away. "You are right. Renée does not belong aboard a ship, but I would not have my happiness at her expense."

"Always the same," Laurent said and rubbed his brow in vexation. "You would sacrifice yourself for her, but she cannot be allowed to do the same for you." He licked his lips, forcing down raging frustration with a gulp. Staring straight ahead, he said, "I shall not ask you again. Come with me, Gweneth. Come with me today. Look ahead, to the life before you, and leave behind all else."

Gweneth gazed at his profile, the sadness in her heart dragging all her dreams and desires into the murky depths of hopelessness. "I cannot," she said in the long silence between them.

"It is done," Laurent said softly and rose with graceful swiftness to his feet.

"Not that one, Gweneth," Renée declared scornfully.

"He offers much in the way of temptation," Gweneth answered noncommittally as she waved a hand toward the splendid house.

"Really, Gweneth, be serious. You would no more be content with that drab insignificant man than I with . . ." The metaphor failed her, and Renée giggled. "It matters not whom. You could not bear it. Admit it."

Gweneth turned to gaze out of the carriage at Aunt

Leonora who stayed behind to chat with Mr. Myers and his sister on the steps of their home. "It is a beautiful place. Not many young ladies in my circumstance could hope for as much comfort as Monsieur Myers offers. He seems quite taken with the prospect of having me to wife. He has been so bold as to mention that it would be his privilege to accept both of us into his household," Gweneth said but shivered slightly at the thought of the thin white hand he lay on her arm when voicing those terms.

"Gweneth, as though that should color your sentiments in his favor." Renée made a moue, but the taciturn set of Gweneth's chin changed her next words to ones of alarm.

"You would not consider it? *Sacré Bleu, soeur,* you would not marry that priggish Englishman to keep me from the convent?" Renée snapped her fingers. "School, what is that? But this, you would commit yourself forever. Oh, I should die of shame if you were to throw your life away so that I might be spared a few years' schooling."

Gweneth smiled at Renée's use of the phrase Laurent had spoken in hopes of swaying her affection, but Renée's fears increased as she perceived Gweneth's cryptic smile to mean that she would.

"Promise me that you would not," Renée begged and crossed the carriage to her sister's side, accompanied by a rustle of silken petticoats. "Swear it to me, Gweneth, here and now. You will not marry him for this."

Gweneth shrugged in annoyance that she had let slip the wanderings of her mind. "How silly this all is, Renée. Monsieur Myers has yet to even ask me," she explained, for to swear to such was beyond her ability to lie.

"But you say he spoke of it. You must know it will come," Renée objected stubbornly. "This is the third time in two weeks that we have come to tea. Such things are not done unless one is serious."

"Then I shall answer when it does come and not before." Gweneth could not tell her sister that their very lives might depend upon the discovery of a suitable champion such as Nathaniel Myers.

Mr. Myers was a colonialist like their uncle and reputed to be very wealthy. A widower of some twenty years, he was twice and half again her age of nineteen years. Though tall and slender, there was an indefinable womanish softness about the long pale face with its overly pink lips and its narrow nose beneath his powdered curls.

"That unfair opinion comes from the association with too many sailors," would have been Madame Bourgeax's scathing retort, Gweneth suspected. For all the attentive politeness he had shown on the occasions they had been thrown together, it seemed to Gweneth that his pale blue eyes studied her with the detached interest he might have displayed for a horse or some new bric-a-brac, assessing its merit and proper place in his household.

Once more Gweneth found occasion to regret the way she had summarily dismissed Laurent's offer. If he had not been so presumptuously assured of her, she might have pleaded for time to consider, but he had belittled her sense of honor and so placed his own on the line. He had seen her as far as her doorstep, curtly offered his farewell to her aunt, and marched out of her life without a backward glance, leaving Gweneth to explain in great embarrassment the grass stains on her gown.

Gweneth turned and was relieved to see Leonora standing by the carriage. The liveried, bewigged black footman bowed deferentially and helped her enter.

"My dears, what an afternoon," Leonora said and spread a pink silk fan to stir the overheated color from her cheeks. "You were both quite impressive. Mr. Myers and his sister were more than pleased by your company. And Renée, why have you waited all these months to allow us the pleasure of your lovely voice? It was just the right touch for the Myerses."

She stopped to sigh heavily in the thick, steamy air as the carriage sprang to action. "Dear me, this heat shall kill us all," she murmured and threw back her shawl. "As I was saying, Renée, your songs were delightful, and Gweneth's accompaniment quite effective. You naughty girls. I should have loved these long oppressive evenings to be colored by your talents." Leonora tapped Renée's knee with the edge of her fan. "Beginning tonight, there will be an hour after dinner set aside for music."

Both girls readily agreed, but at every glance for the duration of the journey, Gweneth met Renée's thoughtful stare and knew their aunt had succeeded in curtailing the talk but not the thoughts which ran through both their heads.

The next two weeks were crammed with preparation for Renée's departure and, if it were a sad task, at least it kept Mr. Myers from calling or the need for them to endure tea at his home.

Surprisingly Renée developed an enthusiasm for the venture as the time neared. "Who knows? We have been so fortunate in our capitaines, perhaps I shall find a new one whose affection I can claim as my own now that you won't be there to compete for him," she stated as she and Gweneth sat folding things into a trunk.

"At least remember that you are no swordswoman, Renée," Gweneth remarked wryly. "I made such a fool of myself. Capitaine Bertrand must laugh every time he thinks of it."

"Do you think he does that, thinks of you?" Renée ventured, speaking of the captain for the first time since they arrived in Barbados. "You have told me he did not touch you. Would that not make him remember you?"

Gweneth laughed aloud. "Mercy, I should hope not.

By now the capitaine has found other women to occupy him."

Renée carefully polished back a stray hair from her brow. "Gweneth?" She paused, as if considering her thoughts. "Do you ever think of Capitaine Bertrand, perhaps miss him?"

Gweneth looked up from her lap in surprise. "But of course not! Whyever should you ask? Bad dreams are best forgotten."

Renée cast a sidelong glance at her sister. "Oh, I do not know. It is only that . . ."

"*Oui, ma fille?* Out with it."

Renée dampened her lips with a quick lick of her tongue. "I did not think of it, even if you *have* called out his name in your sleep. It was Jo."

"Who? *Mais oui,* the house slave. Renée, have you been gossiping with the girl about matters you swore to me never to mention?" Gweneth's usually calm voice faltered in agitation as she violently shoved another garment into the trunk. "How could you!"

"I never but never break a promise," Renée cried in injured affront. "Actually it was Mama Theo who mentioned him, though not by name."

Seeing her sister's bewildered expression, Renée continued. "Have you not heard it said that there are those who can see into the future with powers beyond that of mortal men? Mama Theo is such a person. Jo knows all about her. The stories she can tell! Mama Theo is famous for her cures of every sort. Why, she can banish the curse of the evil eye and conjure a lover from thin air!"

"Or charm a gullible young mademoiselle into parting with something valuable in pledge of a rosy, romantic tomorrow," Gweneth finished dryly. "And which did she offer you, a lover or a blessed destiny?" Gweneth scoffed and shook a censorious finger at her sister. "And just how did you happen to meet this woman in the first place? Aunt Leonora warned you of the danger in venturing beyond the gardens without proper escort."

"I do not care a fig for danger," Renée declared unrepentantly and giggled. "Well, not that sort. Our future is so uncertain. We cannot remain here forever. I thought it wise to seek out someone who held the answers to what will be."

Undaunted by Gweneth's frown of disapproval, Renée carried on, warming to her subject with animated hands and face. "Yesterday—oh, you remember how I cried off from the trip to town because of the *mal de dents* That was so that Jo might bring me to Mama Theo's hut. She will not see just anyone. I had to send a pledge of good faith." Here Gweneth's eyes flew skyward. "And then there was the oath of secrecy. Such a hovel, Gweneth. I had expected—never mind that—the place was small and close, reeking of evil. No, perhaps it was the power," she amended. "Ah, no matter. We sat about the fire and, slowly, she began to mumble."

"Let me guess," Gweneth suggested and stood. "She cleverly described the voyage which brought us here and then, with a shrewd bit of guesswork, forecast romance in the shape of a sea *capitaine*." Gweneth concluded her narration by briefly dusting her hands together. "How credulous you are, Renée. All the island knows of our arrival, and the house is filled with servants who could easily relate any conversation overheard. Mama Theo probably knows more of us than we ourselves."

"I thought of that," Renée stated proudly, though her color had risen in response to Gweneth's derision. "And you are right, to a point. But she knew other things, things not another soul would know." Renée beckoned her sister to her side.

"Listen, Gweneth. She often spoke strangely and in rhyme so I scribbled down some of what I remember." She hastily snatched a note from her apron pocket and unfolded it. "*Voilá,* I have it!" Her voice dropped into a lower register.

> Danger you have fled,
> Danger you have met.
> Spawn of the sea . . .

"Oh, I can't read—"

> . . . Rascal in velvet cloth
> When safety it was found,
> Fled again but none to find
> Save more unhallowed ground.

Gweneth cocked her head. "A sorry rhyme, I think."

"There is more," Renée answered impatiently. "I do not recall the exact words, but it was a warning, of that I am certain. An event of great importance that would lead you back to the 'rascal in velvet.'" Something in Renée's voice halted Gweneth's next attack.

"It could be Capitaine Lavasseur she speaks of," she said as an afterthought. "He often wears velvet and has all but courted me to everyone's view." Gweneth shook her head. "No surprise in that. Besides, it was to be your future she read."

"Non, you still do not see. For me," Renée lifted her shoulders, "she could conjure nothing. But for you, Gweneth, she looked into her fire and saw a future."

"As I said, Lavasseur. I am sorry to disillusion even that dream for you, *petite,* but Laurent has gone, and he is not likely ever to return," Gweneth finished gently.

"Precisely," Renée nodded. "The man in velvet is Capitaine Bertrand. How dense you are, Gweneth. Capitaine Lavasseur may be a capitaine, but whose gaze is the color of the butterfly's eye?"

"Aha, now we come to it. You are ill. Either that or you have been bewitched. Butterfly's eyes, indeed! You should not have gone there, probably without your bonnet and in this heat. *Oui,* you do feel feverish," Gweneth said as she stroked Renée's brow.

"Stop that!" Renée demanded with a pout and slapped Gweneth's hand away. "You will not listen. Mama Theo drew the shades and poked about in the fire, using incantations to draw some sign of the man who is to be your savior. The tiny room grew quite thick with smoke, and just when I gave up in fright and ran for the door, the strangest thing happened. A huge white moth flew past my head and alighted on Mama Theo's arm. It was of pure gossamer white until it spread its wings. And there—*ma foi,*" Renée's voice faltered to a whisper. "Gweneth, there were two circles on its wings which shone of the deepest blue in the firelight. Blue, Gweneth, shimmering sapphire blue!"

Gweneth stood, nonplussed for a moment. She did not believe in witchcraft, but Renée's firm conviction was very persuasive. "I have it. The light of the fire drew the moth. Probably the old woman had it hidden away for just that reason. It was drawn to the flame."

"That does not explain her knowledge of Capitaine Bertrand's existence," Renée countered. "How would she know you had met?"

"Oh, I cannot tell," Gweneth replied crossly. "Perhaps some of Lavasseur's crew repeated what they knew of us to one of the people in town. Why, one of them nearly fought the capitaine for me. A poor riddle, a shabby lie, Renée. There is your witchcraft exposed. I would more readily believe Mama Theo capable of taming a moth than telling the future." But Gweneth's explanation brought new fears to her mind. If a slave knew of her encounter with Capitaine Bertrand, how many others would know, and how soon would some word of it reach her uncle's ear?

"Pooh, Gweneth. You do not understand because you will not. Mama Theo predicts you shall marry the English capitaine. You need not find it necessary to be courted by Myers after all." Renée's expression drooped. "And I thought you would be pleased. I was to leave knowing you would find happiness. Will you refuse Capitaine Bertrand when he comes?"

"He will never come here, Renée, and I do not want—" But seeing her sister's crushed enthusiasm, Gweneth bit off her retort and said, "*Eh bien.* Believe what you must. If it cheers you to believe that I shall find love, then hold that thought. We could profit by such luck, but do not ask me to share your faith. In any case no more talk of Capitaine Bertrand, ever."

A sudden windy squall from the summer-heated water struck the dock as they waited for the ship to weigh anchor. The cheery bon voyages and reminders that she sailed toward civilization could not stave the flow of tears and last-minute pleadings by Renée. Her chin trembled wickedly, and the exquisite porcelain features flooded with tears.

As Gweneth beheld her sister reluctantly dragging herself down into the waiting boat on Sarah's arm, she swirled round to pin her uncle with a defiant gaze, blistering in its mute outrage.

Gareth returned it with a semblance of regret, but his gray eyes were coldly hostile. Leonora dabbed ineffectively at her own brimming eyes and, in a quick misgiving for her health, Gareth put an arm around her to help her back to the carriage, an umbrella shared between them.

Yet Gweneth stood bareheaded in the drenching tropical downpour until the ship was but a tiny line of sail on the water's crest. Standing there with the warm rain streaming down her face, none would know the silent tears she wept. That Sarah had been sent to care for her sister was of little consolation.

"Should have gone with her," Gweneth murmured. But her uncle had adamantly rebuffed her request. He pointed to the fact that Renée's appearance at the convent would not seem nearly so unusual if she were to arrive with only a maid, reaffirming the need for discretion and circumspection. Nevertheless it seemed to Gweneth to be the willful act of a man determined to separate the girls.

CHAPTER THIRTEEN

One evening toward the end of October Gweneth strolled with Nathaniel Myers through the gardens surrounding his home. She had passed the early fall in silent mutiny against her relatives' anxious encouragement of Mr. Myers, but now that preparations for the departure to England had taken definite direction, her reluctance was tempered by concern for the future. The house and lands were about to be placed on the market, and while Mr. Myers had shown an inordinate interest in obtaining them, the governor was showing a strange reluctance to part with them just yet.

Nathaniel held himself stiffly in the severe gray frock coat and matching striped breeches, adding to Gweneth's impression of him as a thin, wraithlike creature. His limp blond hair had been tightly queued back and powdered, lengthening his extraordinarily lean face.

"My dear Miss Gweneth," he began when they were seated by the garden wall in the shade. "Your uncle, our illustrious governor, has made known to me the intention of his departure come the spring, and the extraordinary position this places him in where you are concerned. He divined my interest in your welfare and felt it necessary that I should be fully acquainted with the particulars." Nathaniel took one of her hands in his thin clammy ones, and Gweneth constrained with difficulty an outward shudder.

"Let us be frank, for there is so little time for the

sensibilities of civilized custom. You have come to be a very important interest in my life." Leaning nearer, his faded blue eyes sought her own. "I make so bold as to offer a solution to your situation by asking you to accept my suit and consent to be my wife."

Gweneth did flinch then and drew back her hand immediately. It was to be expected that he should propose, but not even the expectation dulled the revulsion which swamped her.

"There, I have been brutally presumptuous. But, with a little thought on the matter, I am certain you shall come to understand the soundness of the proposal," he murmured with a wan smile.

"Monsieur, I am grateful for your concern and regard," Gweneth replied, frantically casting about for a polite way to rebuff his request. "My uncle has unnecessarily alarmed you about my future, and I would not presume upon your kind nature by taking your proposal seriously."

"Dear girl, it is not pity that directs my actions. I have given the matter careful thought and find no alternative to your condition," he said complacently, folding those waxen hands in his lap.

Gweneth stared at him while repugnance welled up to replace the color in her pale face. "Monsieur, I could never—that is, I have no means, no dowry, and I should not seek such things at my family's expense."

"Ah," he cried, "but that, too, has been arranged. Your uncle has agreed to place his lands and house at your disposal. So, you see, you do not come empty-handed."

No, thought Gweneth, as the color rushed back into her face. I am to be the bile forced down your throat with the sweetening of the lands you covet. Barely able to keep her smarting pride from answering for her, she said, "My uncle had never mentioned these things to me and, that aside, I should not accept so generous a gift. The value of the land is too great."

Gweneth stood and took a few steps to prevent the

malice in her eyes from betraying the feelings which choked her with disgust. "And there is more, Monsieur Myers. Since you wish us to be frank, I must say that, though I admire you, I do not love you." She turned back to gauge the effect of those blunt words. Her eyes widened in surprise. Nathaniel was chuckling and shaking his long horseface.

"My dearest sweet lady, you are but a child, and the young often mistake love for those baser emotions which are fleeting at best and more often exist not at all, save in the heads of poets and the arms of those foul creatures of the night who ply that trade."

Gweneth recoiled as though he had touched her, and Nathaniel grew quite serious, realizing his fault at once. "I see I have shocked you. I wish you to become my wife and mistress of my household. Nothing more should I require of you once the acceptable demands of the marriage contract have been fulfilled. And even that could be delayed until such time as we are of a mind, for I can see that you share my revulsion of that odious necessity." His gaze flickered up and met the agitated countenance of the lady before him.

Gweneth remained speechless, unable to determine if she was more horrified by the proposal he made her as a means to gain additional land or the apparent loathing he confessed for the physical side of marriage. The urge to slap his face sent tingling shivers along her arm, but some cautious voice warned her that she must tread lightly.

"There. You may be at ease," he continued after a moment's pause. "The offer I make will serve both our needs well."

"But children?" It was the only thing which she could think to mention.

"Ah that," he answered and looked down at his hands. "That I leave up to your discretion. It is no great concern of mine."

Gweneth's knees shook beneath the light batiste gown she wore, but her words were firm in resolve.

"I must have time to think this through, monsieur, but do not be deceived. I am inclined to refuse you."

"Of course you must have time, my dear. There is one thing more I should like to add. I shall take the liberty of reminding you of your sister's present residence so far from you and promise here and now to send for her as soon as the ceremony has taken place." Nathaniel rose and offered his arm, bowing not quite low enough over her extended hand to touch it with his lips.

Gweneth reluctantly lay her hand on the arm and let him guide her toward the house. He had played his hand quite openly, believing she had no alternative but to accept. She did not have to look far to discover the author of this design. Monsieur Myers's very words were reflections of the sentiments her uncle had expressed.

Tilting her chin up arrogantly, Gweneth murmured, "*Mon Dieu*. Why was I fool enough to deny Laurent?"

"What is that, my dear?" Nathaniel asked pleasantly.

"A prayer, monsieur. Only a prayer," was the quiet reply.

Gweneth took to her bed for a week, pleading a queasy digestive condition, and Leonora, who was subject to the same malady, quickly accepted the excuse and shouldered the responsibility of caring for her. Plot upon plot formed in Gweneth's head only to be rejected for lack of means to carry it out. One could not simply run away on an island. Where could she go?

She even went so far as to pen a note to Laurent, confessing her regret for having spurned his proposal so arbitrarily and promising to agree to his merest wish if he would but return. Almost at once she crumpled and burned it. It was the mindless pleading of a weak soul and, more than that, an insult to the receiver. She would not stoop to such but, if she could locate him and urge his return, she would accept anything he might suggest. Yet there was no way to reach him with certainty, and Gweneth knew Gareth would never help her.

Still she wrote to him and bribed the slave girl, Jo, with one of her dresses to carry the letter to Bridgetown to be put aboard a departing vessel. If Laurent should have returned to New Orleans before embarking for Europe, the note might find him.

At the end of the week Gweneth appeared at the dinner table. Her cheeks hollowed and her expression sad, she knew her relatives would attribute her delicate complexion to ill health and not to the days of forlorn misery which led her to the inevitable conclusion that she must, indeed, marry Myers.

When the meal was done, Gweneth lay aside her napkin and raised her voice in the silence. "Monsieur Myers has made me an offer of marriage." Her gaze shifted questioningly from Leonora to Gareth, who set aside his glass and looked up in guarded expectation.

"And your answer?" was his quick demand.

Gweneth dampened her lips with a flick of her tongue as she stared straight ahead. "I find it necessary to accept," she replied without emotion.

"By God, well met, niece," Gareth answered jocularly. His delight was not reflected in his wife, for Leonora gave a small shudder and dropped her eyes beneath Gweneth's daring gaze.

"Come, Leonora. Shall you not be the first to wish your niece well?" asked Gareth in a harsh, demanding tone.

"Yes, Gweneth," Leonora said and raised a hand to toy with the lace edge of her collar. "I wish you every charity of fate and fortune." The miserable words conveyed sympathy and regret more eloquently than she imagined. A near smile hovered on her lips as she added, "At least you will be quite safe in Nathaniel Myers's care."

"Dear Lord, Leonora, but you make this happy occasion seem one for tears and condolences. This is a great moment. We must make haste to print the banns and inquire for a date." Gareth lifted his Madeira in a toast. "To the bride-to-be," he invoked in rare good humor.

Gweneth eyed the glass before her, picked it up slowly, spinning the crystal goblet so that a prism of color sparkled over the wine, and then tipped it suddenly into the vase before her. She rose, taking her leave of their company before either relative could voice disapproval, but over her shoulder she heard their voices.

". . . perhaps another man, Gareth. Not Nathaniel for so young and beautiful a girl," Leonora pleaded.

"Cease your sniveling, wife. The man will do well enough by her. Well enough," Gareth returned curtly.

Myers, aided by Gareth, pushed for an early marriage date, but a glimmer of hope came into Gweneth's eyes when Miss Myers insisted upon observance of propriety. "Goodness me, Nathaniel, the young lady must have proper time to assemble a trousseau. There must be a formal announcement, perhaps a ball," Miss Myers said during tea the following Sunday.

The day had no right to be quite so lovely, Gweneth thought remorsefully as she dressed earlier, and she chose gray in defiance of the burnished sunlight's crystalline glare.

"A delightful idea," Leonora concurred. "A betrothal ball and then two months before the ceremony so as to give us time to arrange the event of the year."

"Hum, I am not certain," mumbled Nathaniel, thinking more of the harvest to be lost than the girl sitting stiffly by his side.

"Let them have it, man. Nothing makes for a happier household than when its women are planning a wedding," Gareth replied. "The sum will be of no lasting damage." No, not with the winter harvest to ease the crunch, he noted mentally.

Three and a half months! Gweneth was curiously pleased by the luck. It was likely that Laurent would return before then if he meant to come at all.

"Now that that is settled, I'd best go and receive Mama Theo's blessing on the happy event," Gareth commented as the Myers's rose.

"Surely you jest? Ask that black skull rattler for her blessing?" Nathaniel scoffed, brought to a halt in the examination of his watch.

"You have yet to learn the benefits of such tactics, Myers. It's a handy device," Gareth assured him with a clap on the shoulder.

"I'll not have that voodoo nonsense peddled about among my slaves. It breeds insurrection and willful misuse of power."

"And fine handsome profits," Gareth finished. "She promises a bumper crop this harvest. She was right last year. Why should I not cultivate a benevolent presence among my chattel? She is paid generously to keep her people in my fields. I can spare my overseers the trouble of whippings with a pinch of harmless magic and save myself the need of doctor's poultices to cure the felons who might be flogged. How many laborers have you with raw backs when they could be in the fields?"

"Still this is a civilized business. It is my marriage, and I will have no spells cast over it by a dried-up old witch." And Myers shuddered delicately.

"'Tis a blessing I seek, no bane. You apply your methods, and I shall pursue mine. Harvest time will bear me out, I should think," Gareth answered agreeably and smoothly pushed on to inquire about Myers's new distilling house.

Despite Leonora's enthusiasm for the project, November passed into December with little cooperation from the bride herself. Gweneth made no effort to hinder her aunt's progress, but she did not bend to her aunt's entreaties to begin embroidering the fine linens bought for her trousseau. She was eager to help with the daily functioning of the household, so none could call her refusals the result of laziness, and it pleased her to know that even the maids recognized the source of her disinterest. If she could not prevent this calamity, she would not hide her contempt of it.

Only the nights were unbearable, and Gweneth often lay wide-eyed until near dawn. In those hours she swore silently against the evil overtaking her, remembering with bittersweet fondness the embraces of Laurent and how different it might have been. But, in the tortured labyrinth of her dreams, Captain Bertrand claimed her emotions, and she would awaken, acutely aware of his violation of her sleep.

December fifteenth dawned to a bright balmy day, easing Leonora's qualms that the frequent rains would spoil her plans for the large party spilling onto the rear gardens to take advantage of its sustained beauty.

Gareth was busy in his office at the usual hour, his white-peruked head bent upon a pile of writs, when his secretary interrupted him with the announcement that a Lord Avernon, Earl of Mochton, requested a word with him.

The visit took Gareth by surprise, for it was his part to know the comings and goings of all such dignitaries. He hastened the secretary to bid him enter. A quick straightening of his stock and a touch to the peruke and he was on his feet to greet his blue-blooded guest.

A tall, stately figure followed the secretary through the open door, and Gareth's keen glance noted the expensive finery of his visitor as he bowed deferentially. But his respectful smile faded to frowning confusion as he rose to meet the familiar face.

"But, what is this?" he stammered in slight annoyance. "I was told Lord Avernon wished to present himself."

"And so I do," came the man's reply, followed by deep humorous laughter. "Does my appearance startle you, Governor? I am nearly accustomed to the change myself. Lord Avernon, alias Captain Bertrand, at your service," Raoul said and bent slightly.

Gareth recovered his manners at once and offered the man a seat. Madeira and biscuits were sent for immediately, then he leaned back in his chair to contemplate the figure before him.

"Well, well. How has all this come about? Why have you never presented yourself to me as your title deserves?" Gareth asked, mentally recounting their numerous dealings for some breach of form which might account for the abrupt change.

Raoul smiled lazily and draped an arm over the back of his chair. "Let me just say that I have suffered a change of fortune."

"A most favorable change, I should venture," Gareth replied and reached out to serve them from the tray now set before him.

"Yes and no," Raoul answered, suddenly sober. "The death of my father forbids me to think of the change in wholly gainful terms."

"Aha, I quite understand. But what brings you to my tiny island? This new position must not find you in need to ply the trade heretofore required."

"Yes and no again, Governor. It is my own choice to continue in shipping and now the means of that enterprise have come to hand so that I may expand. It is to that end I seek you out, for a purely personal transaction." Raoul absently fingered the ribbon of his tricornered hat. "I shall need a post here in the islands, and I understand your lands are for sale."

"Were for sale, would be more precise," the governor corrected with a regretful sigh. "As it is, my house and lands are committed as a dowry for my niece who is to be wed. In fact the announcement of the betrothal is to be made tonight. I must reluctantly refuse your interest."

"Your niece?" Raoul questioned conversationally. "I

have never heard you mention a niece as a member of your household."

"That is because she and her sister are newly arrived this summer past. Some poor relations who managed to escape the Revolution in France." Gareth heaved a sigh and continued in distaste. "They have taxed my patience and purse sorely, I can tell you. These French, ever in need of some new frivolous luxury. One would think my resources were unlimited. The younger girl is in a convent, so much for her." The gesture was one of dismissal, and Raoul's eyes narrowed in response, but Gareth missed this as he fingered the charm in his pocket.

"And the other?" Raoul inquired.

"She is to be wed, thank the saints. I would have her off my hands all the sooner. A reluctant, petulant child, but then, what can one expect of such a creature? Proud and vain as a peacock, that one," Gareth said and sipped his refreshment.

"As to the business, if I may change the subject. I do not require the lands but would rather have the house. I need a residence for my stays here and have seen that yours is the best to be had."

"That is so," Gareth nodded in satisfaction. "However—well, perhaps we could come to some agreement. After all, the girl has nothing of her own, and the man she is to marry is wealthier by far than I. The details are not final, and it is land he desires. Mayhaps there is a bargain to be had here." He smiled in pleasure that the cost of ridding himself of Gweneth might yet have a profit to be made in it. He begrudged the tough bargain Myers had driven in return for the girl, and he did not need the house since his own residence was of equal value.

"May I be so bold as to inquire as to the name of the groom?" asked Raoul. "It may be that I know the man."

"You do. It is Nathaniel Myers."

"Myers?" Raoul was clearly startled, for the man's

reputation was a constant source of rude jests among the population.

"I see you have heard the unfortunate gossip surrounding the man," Gareth said smoothly. "It is a sorry thing that when a man chooses a single existence, others pin odious labels on him. Well, this ceremony should bring an end to their scathing taunts."

"Of course," Raoul agreed, though he knew the rumors to be founded in more than the twisted imaginations of idle chatterers. "I must present my congratulations to the happy couple."

"You are in luck, then, my lord. The engagement ball is this very evening. Could I prevail upon you to make an appearance, however brief? It would add to our little occasion to have so important a guest."

Raoul grinned and accepted the artfully wrought means to renew his acquaintance with a friend.

The seamstress was all aflutter over this new sheath style which was becoming the rage of Europe. "It is just the thing for you. Your figure was meant for it," she had assured the young lady. But as she stood quizzing her reflection in the mirror, Gweneth was aghast. The sheer blue gown of Oriental silk shot through with gold thread just restrained her well-endowed bosom, and the soft folds clung seductively to her hips and thighs, revealing more of her than any nightdress. The gown, caught up under her breasts with a gold velvet ribbon, fell to the floor where it formed a short train in back.

Gweneth shook her head slowly, the strands of pearls adorning her cinnamon curls swinging freely, and wondered to what purpose her uncle had commissioned such a gown. Her betrothed was not likely to be enticed by this flirtatious array. He kept to his odd aversion of not touching her more than necessary and never took the liberty that was his to steal a kiss or bestow a leering glance on her. Gweneth grimaced. It was better that way than to have his long face drooling over her flesh. She pulled on long taffeta gloves, commanding herself not to think beyond the next minute.

"Dear child, what a vision you are," exclaimed Leonora as she entered the gold and white bedroom. "You have always been a beauty but, dear me, I believe I shall be entirely neglected this evening, as shall all the other ladies who will have the misfortune to be compared with you."

Gweneth laughed gently, fully enjoying the flattery. "You are beautifully dressed, too, and I am certain all shall mistake us for sisters."

Leonora wore a brown silk chemise with long taffeta sleeves and a beige silk scarf tucked into the low neckline. Her auburn curls were lightly powdered, turning them a pale strawberry, and upon them sat a lacy confection topped by a pair of ostrich plumes.

"We will dazzle all eyes," was Gweneth's final comment.

Gareth paced the hall in blue satin tailcoat, complete with sash and gold epaulettes announcing his rank, while his black patent, gold-buckled high heels rang sharply on the parquet floor. At the sound of feminine voices he looked up the garlanded stairway, his expression severe beneath the elaborately clubbed wig. The wheels of the first carriage were crunching to a halt outside, and he meant to deliver a brief reprimand for the ladies' tardiness.

Instead his mouth fell open a little, and a swift jolt of pure lust jarred his loins at the sight of Gweneth. Every curve of her delectable form was barely clothed in the silky fabric, and her slightly flushed cheeks added allure to her attractive face. There was nothing ordinary about her beauty; its very attraction poured from the vivid aura of her vitality.

He tore his eyes away and let the lascivious look come to rest on his wife. At six and thirty years she was still a handsome woman, but the strain of three miscarriages had drained the pink from her delicate skin, leaving it sallow, and her once firm proportions had withered to bare the bones of her face and shoulders. Compared to Gweneth's radiant youth, it seemed cruel that they must be made to stand side by side.

Gareth had just time to praise both ladies and place an impersonal kiss on his wife's cheek and a more lingering one on Gweneth's. "After all, we are family," was his defensive reply when Gweneth's eyes narrowed at this sudden familiarity.

The door opened to admit Mr. and Miss Myers, and Gareth went forth in welcome with the gardenia scent of Gweneth's perfume still enveloping his senses. He watched in envy as Nathaniel bowed over his niece's hand, regretting that such a tasty bit of flesh should be wed to so insufficient an admirer.

"Mercy me, I knew we had invited many guests, but my hand is shriveling under such constant attention," observed Leonora behind her fan to Gweneth when a lull in the entrance of new guests came. "You must be as stiff as I, Gweneth. Let us snatch a chance to refresh ourselves. Every male here is lounging nearby in hopes of earning your favor. Oh no, go ahead, dear, for I hear footsteps on the porch and we will soon be plagued with more bowing and kissing."

Gweneth slipped gratefully away, but Leonora's prophecy held true; no sooner had she escaped one menace than did she find herself assailed by a crowd of prospective partners. She smiled at them all but accepted the hand of the eldest gentleman, Mr. Lollings, whose old-style periwig jostled about his frail old shoulders as he lead her in a quadrille.

No lack of partners and the need to cloud her senses with thoughts other than those of the forthcoming announcement kept Gweneth busy until the dinner hour. Though she sat with Nathaniel during supper, he barely spoke. His disapproval of her gown caused his lips to tighten into a thin white line whenever he found another man's eye upon her.

With a perverse sense of humor aimed at abetting his choleric disposition, Gweneth now chose to dance and coquette with the youngest and boldest of her admirers. As in most colonial outposts, there was a surplus of men, most of them young soldiers, and they made the best of every opportunity afforded them in female company.

"Where's the governor been hiding such a fetching bit of womanhood?" grumbled one among a group of red-coated officers as they stood envying the luck of the comrade who had claimed Gweneth as partner.

"Damn if I should know," replied another. "'Tis not right. Been bowing and charming to enough ill-favored old matrons these past eighteen months to suit me a lifetime while under my very nose Aphrodite has resided."

"Damn waste, her marrying old man Myers," added still another, dipping discreetly into his snuffbox.

"Hear she's poor and needs the match," volunteered the first.

"She shall be in need of something different if what I hear be truth. I don't fancy a wife but, wed to Myers, the girl will soon come to seek a paramour and that, me lads, is an office to which I shall aspire. Such as she will not be content with gold's cold touch to fill her arms." High laughter followed as all eyes turned back to the blue-robed lady.

Not even Gareth's scowl of disapproval intimidated Gweneth as she danced a little more provocatively and sipped another glass of champagne to prove her lack of concern. Soon the room began to spin slowly, shimmering warm and glaring with the dazzlingly colorful spectrum of the gathering.

Lead onto the floor once more, Gweneth spied a newcomer. His back was to her, but her gaze lingered appreciatively on his broad back and tapered waist fit snugly into a black velvet frock coat embroidered in silver. The clipped dark chestnut head was bowed away from her, but the rich deep voice carried over the music to pronounce him English. She curtsied automatically to her partner while vowing to herself to take the next pause to make the gentleman's acquaintance. A little dalliance with such a handsome figure should make complete her mockery of the occasion.

The dance ended to find her within an arm's length of the man's back, and she reached out to lay a light hand on his shoulder. The stranger turned to face her with a questioning look and then a full sardonic grin.

Gweneth gave a frightened gasp, her heart stilling within her breast for an instant, and she swayed visibly as he caught her by the elbow.

"You!" she whispered in choking disbelief.

"Your obedient servant, mademoiselle," Raoul replied easily, taking pleasure in the livid shade of her face. But Gweneth backed away as though his was a ghostly presence, and turning sharply, fled the room.

The crowded dance floor protected the observance of her headlong flight, but Gweneth was hardly aware of her actions. The sight of Captain Bertrand obliterated all else, and even as she plunged into the thick undergrowth toward the lagoon, his face was ever before her, his handsome features alight with mischief and devilish high humor.

When the dark, star-flecked night at last closed in upon her, Gweneth stopped, holding her sides and gasping for breath. It could not be and yet it was. He had touched her, he was real. The elegant clothes and new, shorter hair could never alter him, for his eyes were the same arresting, penetrating sapphire that taunted her dreams. He had found her!

"*Sacré Dieu!* What shall I do?" she sighed to the silent black water before her. She sank weakly to the ground and covered her face with both hands. There was nothing he could do, she told herself. Her uncle would protect her and, if need be, she would tell the tale of how they had met.

"I am safe. He cannot harm me here," she said aloud after some minutes.

"Now who would ever wish to harm Venus?" came a reply.

Gweneth did not bother to turn to her unbidden companion, for she knew that voice from times ago.

"Here. You shall ruin that gown," Raoul said when he came to her side. He bent down to lift her without incurring resistance. "'Tis not much of a frock, but what a vision you are, *ma belle*."

Gweneth stared up at his eyes gleaming in the dark and the shadow of a smile that shone from his parted lips. "You are most accommodating. First you approach me unsummoned and then you find a private moment for us. Had I known how welcome I should be, I'd have come all the sooner."

His mockery gave Gweneth her voice, and she jerked free of the hands still holding her arms. "How dare you come here. You risk your neck for nothing, monsieur. My uncle, the governor, will not take kindly to your presence," she retorted and backed away.

"He knows? I should think he would have mentioned it when we met this morning," Raoul answered, not at all shaken by her threat.

"Non. He does not know of your rascally behavior," Gweneth admitted reluctantly. "I sought to spare myself that indignity. But I shall not hesitate to bring the matter to his attention should the need arise."

At his laughter Gweneth shivered, unreasoning fear tingling her scalp. "You may find humor in the situation now but—"

"My dear mademoiselle," Raoul interrupted. "Shall you forever be threatening me with one violence or another? You have proved how deadly you can be." He put a hand to his once-wounded shoulder. "Let us leave this debate and speak to the present. I understand you are to be married."

"*Oui*, that is so," she said and stepped a bit farther from him. In a quick dash she might escape through a break in the foliage if she put enough distance between them first.

Raoul guessed her thoughts and, in two long strides, covered the space between them, linking his arm through hers. "We must talk. We will walk if it will steady your nerves. You are shivering, *ma belle*."

They strolled along the bank of the lagoon but never nearer the house. "This man you are to wed, could you do no better? Damnation, why would you throw yourself away on a prig like Myers?"

Gweneth groaned in fury and tried to twist free, but Raoul only chuckled softly and caught her wrist in his firm fingers. "Careful, sweet lady, or what little there is veiled shall come undone."

"I will not remain here to have you swear at me and belittle my fiancé. Now, if you will kindly give me my hand," she replied disdainfully and tossed back her curls to stare at the arrogant set of his head.

"Not yet. You must tell me why you have chosen this man. He is old enough to be your father. Why, I would guess your uncle to be ten years younger and a sight more taken with your charms."

"Monsieur Myers is a respectable gentleman who honors me with a proposal of marriage. He is well educated and wealthy," she said and made another useless attempt to free her arm.

"All you say may be true, but I cannot find a reason in it for your acceptance. Unless—could it be that his charm lies in his purse?" Raoul asked in a voice thick with sarcasm.

"You are hateful, Capitaine. Let me go. I wish to return to the party before I am missed." Gweneth did pull free this time.

"With so many guests, two will not be easily missed. Now answer the question. Is this man your choice?" Raoul leaned nearer to catch a glimpse of her expression.

"It does not matter whose choice it is. I shall marry Monsieur Myers," Gweneth replied weakly. She could not tell him how much she detested the thought and, instead, turned away.

"Then we are likely to become neighbors." Gweneth whirled round to face him, her pulse galloping uncontrollably. "I thought that might please you," he said evenly. "As it happens, these grounds and this house are soon to be mine. They adjoin Myers's property, do they not? What cozy neighbors we shall be."

"That is a lie. My uncle is giving this house and his lands to Monsieur Myers as a dowry on my behalf," she retorted, but her sense of things began to jumble as the rushing blood sped her amply imbibed supply of champagne through her veins.

"The property, yes, but I have a bid in on the house, and your uncle has agreed to consider it just this morning. I say again, quite a cozy arrangement. And, if you are determined to marry that milksop, you shall shortly be in need of a lover."

"And you would put yourself forth as a candidate," Gweneth jeered, trying to adopt his careless tone. She could handle the antagonism between them easily and set her guard.

"But certainly. I have had occasion to sample the wares and find that they suit my needs admirably."

"You are incredible," Gweneth breathed and light laughter shook her shoulders. "To what purpose should I require a lover, Capitaine? After all, I shall have a husband."

"More need than most, mademoiselle, for the man you wed will never be amenable to begetting you a child. In me, you shall find an ever-ready servant." Harsh mocking laughter disrupted his speech, but Gweneth had grown quite still. How had he come to know of the matter she had not even been able to think on herself?

"Do not hide behind stiff maidenly modesty, *ma belle*. Your practical French nature could not be shocked at the suggestion. Many of your fellow countrywomen have thrived on such associations for centuries. Marriage is a sensible contract for mutual benefit. But romance? Ah, that!

"Of course, you shall be constrained to bring Myers to your bed a few times so that the paternity of the child cannot be called into doubt. He is a pale, thin-blooded weakling but, perhaps, you can overcome his reluctance toward women.

"We are of much the same coloring, you and I, and should the child bear a striking resemblance to his sire, all shall say he takes his looks from his mother. If, however, the child should inherit my distinctive eyes, I may be persuaded to find room in my heart to recognize the bastard as my own."

Gweneth moved so quickly, Raoul did not realize she had acted until he felt a hard, stinging blow on his cheek. "You vile, infamous—" But her words were checked as Raoul grabbed her by the arms and brutally shook her.

"I have yet to teach you who is master," Raoul growled and raised a hand. "No, not violence. There is a better way to correct your behavior. Come here and let me offer you a taste of the joys you can expect as my mistress," he crooned, drawing her trembling body into his embrace.

Scarcely a sound passed her lips before Raoul covered them with his own, his arms crushing her to his velvet coat. The flaming brand of his touch seared her lips. She pushed against him repeatedly, but she was locked in his arms, one arm across her shoulders and the other about her waist.

It seemed his mouth would devour hers, but her frantic squealing and pounding on his chest were answered only by a rumbling chuckle. "This is what you want, what you have always wanted," Raoul muttered into her mouth and twisted his head around to fasten his lips more firmly over hers.

"Non, non," Gweneth screamed within as his mouth moved confidently, endlessly over her lips, parting and drinking their sweetness. But it was herself she denied, for the touch and taste of him assailed her senses with slivers of half-remembered dreams, turning her shivering into a trembling of a very different nature. He was angry and insulting, daring her to find any warmth of feeling in his lust. She must not give in to his demand. And yet she knew she would.

The pounding ceased, and her fingers curled round the collar of his coat until she was clutching it in desperation.

She loved him, and with the admittance of that loving came courage. She reached up higher, running her fingers through his thick ruffled hair to pull him closer, swaying against him to offer herself as freely as he took of her. The certainty with which her body exclaimed her desire of him frightened her, but she needed this physical touch more.

Raoul tempered his embrace to let his hands roam caressingly over Gweneth, and the feel of her beneath the gossamer gown gave his desire bodily reality. He did not want the sensual pleasure she aroused in him, for he meant only to tease and embarrass her with promises of things to come. But the enjoyment of her eagerly returned kisses nearly overthrew his calculations.

Reason tore at him, though his body ached with yearning. Amid the swirling lure of her perfumed softness Raoul wondered if she were hoping to move him to betray by some word or sign the thoughts that were forming in his fevered mind: words of desperate longing, words of love. He must not, would not have that confession wrenched from him by this scheming girl. If he could not remain indifferent to her response, he would bend his passion to another fashion.

His fingers dug savagely into her tender flesh, and Gweneth moaned with pain, but she did not back away as he expected. Not even when he roughly forced a hand down the front of her gown to knead a breast with his strong fingers as he slid a knee intimately between her thighs did she seek to prevent him. Then, so be it. He would satisfy himself with her here and now, then sail away before his cause was lost. She would learn that he was not a man to be trifled with and that no woman would ever hold him to account.

Gweneth did not hear the voices calling to her at once, unaware of all reality save that of her lover's lips and hands and body. But, when she recognized her uncle's voice, she pushed away and quickly adjusted her gown. Breathless and dizzy she pushed the hair from her eyes with a tremulous hand.

Raoul came to his senses too, and laughing low in swift calculation, he pulled her back into his arms and forced her mouth against his. Several buttons of her gown ripped loose as he jerked at the neckline to expose more of her.

The shubbery crackled in parting and then a bright ring of light sprang up over the entwined couple. Raoul looked up in startled surprise and backed away, freeing the girl.

"What is the meaning of this?" thundered Gareth as Gweneth spun around, clutching at one shoulder of her gown as she squinted against the lantern light. It was then that she discovered that he was not alone, for a shadow stepped into the circle of light revealing itself to be Mr. Myers.

"I say, Gweneth, that I will have an explanation," repeated Gareth.

It was Raoul who answered. "Are you acquainted with this lady?" he asked in all innocence. "If she is yours then I apologize."

"She is my niece," Gareth answered cold voiced.

"Your niece?" Raoul swung round to Gweneth. "But why did you not say so, *ma belle*? You are the bride-to-be?" He chuckled self-deprecatingly and faced the gentlemen. "Dear Lord, I did not know. We met again by chance just now and came for a stroll. I had no idea!" He spread ten fingers of dismay.

"Met again? Gweneth, do you know this man?"

came a question from Nathaniel whose face was a ghastly yellow in the amber light.

"Why, we are old and intimate friends," Raoul offered and half turned to smile at the victim caught in his trap.

"I see," Nathaniel said in flat tones and turned on his heel to melt into the shadows.

Gweneth breathed barely at all, both hands pressed to her heart. Her attention was wholly for the lover turned traitor by her side. She gazed at the figure in the darkness, his expression mildly humorous, and knew that he had baited her. He had not felt any of her love. He meant merely to seduce her and then depart had they not been caught, and this unexpected turn of events provided him with a more devastating and complete revenge.

Utter weak shame engulfed her as she stood between the two men and she bit her tender, swollen lips. Clenching her fists, she forced them to her sides and glared at Raoul's smug grin to wish him in hell.

"You win, Capitaine. I hope this is sufficient repayment. I should have known better," she said at last in a dull, emotion-shattered voice. She stepped past him and faced her uncle. "No explanation could ever satisfy you. Simply understand that an old debt has been paid," and she moved quickly out of the light into the dark.

CHAPTER FOURTEEN

Sudden illness was the byword for the evening but, when Nathaniel Myers left abruptly after closeting himself with Governor Dillingham, there came a sprinkling of rumors that the engagement had been broken by unexplained events.

Gweneth shed her finery and climbed into bed more than an hour before the last of the guests departed. Yet, when Leonora appeared with a swish of her skirts and tiptoed to the bedside, Gweneth lay fully awake.

"I have not killed myself," she said dryly when her aunt peered timidly through the bed curtain.

"My dear, dear child. What is this I hear?" Leonora reached out and took Gweneth's hand. "The ranting and swearing behind the library door all but turned out the affair. Your uncle and Mr. Myers came nearly to blows. What is this talk of your shameful behavior with Lord Avernon?"

"Who? My behavior was shameful, though for reasons you could not suspect," she answered wearily and sat up, curling her legs under herself.

"What happened, Gweneth?"

"I was discovered in the embrace of Capitaine Bertrand. A small thing really." She shrugged and rested her chin on her hands.

Leonora gasped. "Then it is true?" She shook her head sadly. "Whatever possessed you, Gweneth? It is not such a trivial matter. Nathaniel marched away after informing your uncle that the engagement is irrevocably broken."

Gweneth gave a hiccup of amusement and then bubbled over in near-hysterical laughter, high and strident. "*Mon Dieu*, the *capitaine* has helped me where no one else could. Perhaps there is something to thank him for after all."

"Take yourself in hand, girl," commanded Gareth, his face purple with rage as he stood firmly planted in the doorway. "Will you tumble in the grass with every hot-blooded rogue who happens your way? I will have an explanation if I need thrash it out of you, you wanton chit!" he shouted as he crossed the distance to the bed.

Gweneth paled to instant sobriety and recoiled at his approach until Leonora stepped bravely between them. "Merciful heavens, Gareth. You will frighten the wits from the child."

"No child that one!" he roared with an accusing finger at Gweneth. "She flaunts her charms for every man's view and then picks the lustiest to satisfy her bold harlotry."

"Not true!" Gweneth cried. "I have never—"

"Do not speak lies to me, girl. Why, another minute and I should have caught you pleasuring that stud Bertrand, or Lord Avernon as he now calls himself. To think that I have harbored a slut under my roof these many months. First that libertine Lavasseur is drooling about your skirts and now Avernon."

All Gareth's frustrated jealousy vented itself. She had played the innocent so well whenever he had attempted the slightest indiscretion. Now it seemed that she but chose her lovers and, for reasons unknown, he had been found wanting.

Gweneth drew the covers over her nightgown and stared at her uncle in stony silence. She could not say what might have happened had they not been interrupted, and there was a great possibility that he was correct.

"Have you nothing to say? No sorrow, no pleading

for understanding? God, but you are a brazen whore to boot!" Gareth thundered.

"Please, Gareth. Let the girl speak," Leonora begged, settling herself uncertainly on the edge of the bed.

"Monsieur, I wish to speak privately with my aunt. It is to her that I owe my explanation," Gweneth answered defiantly. Angry flames of green fire leaped in her eyes as her gaze met and held the brittle steel in Gareth's. His face darkened further, but after a minute's hesitation Gareth turned and walked out, slamming the door.

Gweneth sagged back on the pillows, a quiver of pain pulling at the edges of her bruised lips. From somewhere deep within her the protective shell of shock began to crumble, its fissures seeping with the bile of delusion and deceit. "I am so ashamed," she murmured.

Leonora did not reply but gathered Gweneth to her and let the girl cry onto her shoulder till all the pain and guilt were shed in the flow of those tears. She stroked her niece's hair and rocked her comfortingly. The words tumbled forth, thick with sobs, as Gweneth poured out the story she had held too long. She told the truth, omitting only the self-confession of her love. Leonora listened, her face now pale, now angry, but she heard it all.

"You should have told us in the beginning, Gweneth, and we might have spared you this anguish. This man, Bertrand, is a devil. I will speak with Gareth. He will know best how to deal with him." She set Gweneth from her and pulled the covers over the girl's frame. "Rest now, darling. It is finished."

Gareth did not waste time pacing the hall while the women spoke together but headed with deliberate strides for the servants' quarters. If this Avernon were an old acquaintance, then there was one who should know something of the relationship. Another catch in his carefully wrought plans, Gareth thought with an oath. The girl was nothing but trouble, yet he could not afford to have her spirited away by Avernon, if only as his mistress. He must find some way to salvage his months of maneuvering and plotting.

"Your Excellency, is this wise?" asked the young girl beyond the door.

"Open the door this instant, you little fool. I must have words with you." Gareth replied, loud enough for all ears cocked in their direction to hear. The door opened slowly to reveal Amy in a nightdress.

"Grab a dressing gown, girl, and follow me down to the library, for I am not of a mind to be kept waiting. Hurry along," he commanded and stomped down the hallway.

"Monsieur, what is it?" Amy asked when he had shut the library door to insure privacy.

"Am I not to be greeted more warmly?" he asked impatiently and pulled Amy to his broad chest, kissing her roughly. All the lust he held for his niece he bestowed upon this substitute, delighting in the shivering fear he invoked. She was a fetching piece who played the wanton well, but even as she strained against him, the image of Gweneth locked in Avernon's violent embrace turned his own passion sour.

"Ease your lewd affections, girl," he said sharply and pushed her aside. "Another time I shall satisfy your urge, but now I shall have your answers to a few questions." He grabbed her wrist and squeezed until she cried out. The fright on her face relieved his need to inflict pain, and he dropped her arm in distaste, dusting his hands together.

"That is but a sample of what you can expect if you lie to me now. Tell me what you know of Lord Avernon and Mademoiselle Gweneth."

"Monsieur, I know no Lord Avernon," Amy whined and chafed her bruised wrist.

"Ah yes, perhaps he went by the name of Captain Bertrand to you. Well, what do you know of the man?"

Amy's story was the same one that Gweneth allowed her to believe aboard the *Cyrene*, but Captain Lavasseur's appearance was a mystery. Still Amy managed to convey that both captains' interests were not limited to the temptations of Gweneth's beauty but had driven them to seek her own favors as well.

"So you have bedded both men in your mistress's wake?" Gareth's self-esteem smarted doubly with that bit of information, and he scrutinized the girl before him with disgust. "Whoring wench," he mumbled.

"*Mais non*, monsieur. I but express their interest." Amy sidestepped a little closer and smiled sweetly. "Neither of them is half the man you are, monsieur. A woman would know that immediately."

Gareth laughed contemptuously, but her wit helped appease his wounded pride. He indicated the whiskey decanter, and while she poured for him, he loosened his stock, letting his mind shift through the muddled tale to cull the important details he could use. "You say Captain Bertrand raped your mistress. Are you certain it was against her will?" he questioned presently.

"*Mais oui*, monsieur. She fought him most bravely I am told but, afterward he kept her locked in his cabin for days. When he did let her go, so great was her shame, she would not speak to us of her experience but wept in her bed each night."

"And this Lavasseur, did he, too, rape the girl?"

"Monsieur," Amy smiled and shrugged. "I do not know how they met, but if they succumbed to the temptation, I believe it was of mutual desire."

"What of the other men in her life before this?"

"There were none, I suspect. If you have ever heard the stories they tell of Madame Bourgeax, then you would not need to ask."

"Yes, yes, come in," Gareth waved to Leonora as she arrived at the door. "That is all, Amy. Do sit down, Leonora, and let us hear Gweneth's defense."

* * *

Gareth nodded at last. "The stories are the same, save for the crucial point. Gweneth does not admit that she was attacked, and yet she let her companions believe that she was."

"What difference can that make to your demand for satisfaction?" Leonora replied. "The intent was there, and he came here to our very home to perpetrate another villainy. That leaves nothing to be done but that you should challenge the scoundrel."

Gareth's laughter was short and cutting. "How very dramatic you are, my dear. Would you have me surrender my life to a superior blade? The man's ability is well respected. I should be a fool to cross swords with that miscreant. I hope I have more sense than to expend my life for a miserable child of your sister's." Gareth paused to expel a deep breath. "No, there is another way out of this tangle, a way to salvage the marriage and save all our plans. The man ravished the girl. There were plenty of witnesses, Amy for one. And then, one of his own crew might be persuaded by a coin or two to give evidence. Bertrand shall be brought to trial and the case made public. Then Nathaniel can accept the girl with a clear conscience that her honor is intact and his pride salved."

"But think of the scandal, the shame it shall cause!" cried Leonora. She made as if to rise, clutching the silk-covered arms of her chair so that it puckered.

"A duly applied cautery has saved many a limb, my wife. It must be done," Gareth replied, waving her back into her seat. "Enough. I shall attend to the matter at first light."

Afraid, but more fearful still of her husband's curious solution, Leonora found the courage to ask, "What if Captain Bertrand is innocent?"

Gareth swung round with a furiously dark look. "Gweneth has shared the man's bed, of that I am certain. It remains only for her to admit it."

* * *

SILKS AND SABERS 255

The message arrived shortly after breakfast, a note from Governor Dillingham summoning Mademoiselle Valois to present herself at eleven thirty that very morning. An urgent matter required her cooperation, it said. Thus Gweneth found herself jostling along the road to Bridgetown within an hour of the note's receipt.

She shifted several times on the leather-covered horsehair seat to relieve her tender backside. The driver sped the team at a maddening pace and the bouncing, smacking rhythm of the carriage meted out severe punishment to her nether regions. There was no use in admonishing Jonathan to slow his pace. All the household was aware of the black temper that had descended upon the master the night before and she would not be the cause of a whipping.

Gweneth gritted her teeth and held on with both hands. Surprisingly she was not apprehensive about the interview to come. She had endured the depths of despair as she stood gaping in astonishment and horror while the capitaine ground her reputation beneath his heel. Her uncle had said his worst last evening. Anything he might think to add could render no further harm.

Looking much cooler than she felt in her light green chemise and straw bonnet, she stepped down into the white, sandy street and adjusted the wide sash beneath her breasts. Her footsteps sounded lightly but decisively on the marble floor leading to the governor's office, and she showed neither alarm nor dismay when she was ushered into his presence without any introduction. Her calm, self-assured expression was her shield of dignity as she stepped inside that room.

Gareth rose swiftly to his feet at her entrance and Gweneth braced herself for his first volley, but no words were spoken until the secretary had departed, closing the door after himself.

"Dear child, you have come," Gareth greeted her with warmth.

A pucker of bewilderment creased Gweneth's brow as he came to take her hand and lead her to a chair. "I feared the events of last night had overwhelmed you," he said in concerned tones.

Gareth leaned back against the front of his desk. His face was grave, but there was an unusual softening in those cool gray eyes as he clasped his hands before himself as if in supplication. "I hardly know where to begin, Gweneth. That I owe you an apology for my gross mishandling of a most sensitive issue goes without saying." He paused to adjust his posture and clear his throat. Apologies were alien to his nature, but it served his needs in this instance.

"The explanation you wove for Leonora demanded a certain amount of collaboration but, thankfully for us all, such an instrument was readily within our grasp. Your maid, Amy, was of such an eagerness to vouch for your tale I am amazed we had not heard something of it before now."

Again he paused, and the intent look in his eyes showed that he expected some word from Gweneth. But she remained silent with the first stirring of hope that she would be believed.

"Do not worry, child. Justice shall be done, and you need not go in dread for your person a moment longer."

"Uncle, I fail to understand your meaning. I have no qualms where Capitaine Bertrand is concerned." Gweneth sighed and bit her lip which had begun to tremble with the utterance of that name. "The deed is done. There is nothing which can retract it," she added and flushed under Gareth's watchful regard.

"What's that?" His expression altered to one of consternation. "Confound it, Gweneth! What of your reputation which has been spattered with the slime from that jackal's boots?"

"It concerns me little," she replied truthfully but dropped her eyes to her lap where the removal of her gloves became a self-absorbing interest just then.

"And what of your marriage? Mr. Myers was scandalized, perhaps beyond all reconciliation," pressed Gareth as he rose to his feet.

"It takes very little to scandalize Monsieur Myers," she said tartly, "and his feelings concern me not at all." Tiny crinkles formed in the corners of her mouth as she drew off the last glove.

Gareth's gray eyes flashed silver in an instant of warning, but she had not looked up to catch it. Quickly he dissembled his annoyance, saying, "'Tis a matter of concern to your aunt and myself." He swung an arm out dramatically. "Once the tale is loosed, and soon it shall be, the stench of it will spare none of us. Think of your family if not yourself."

Gweneth raised confident eyes to her uncle. "I have done nothing which requires me to go in fear of people's opinion. I have more faith in their charity, Uncle. For, if the truth is to be known, I should become something of a pitiable figure, I imagine. The capitaine shall reap their scorn. That shall be my satisfaction."

"Pshaw, girl. As your guardian and only male relative it is left to me to seek amends. The scoundrel has distressed his last maiden, by God, or I shall know the reason why," Gareth finished with a slamming of his fist on the desk.

The vehemence of his action startled Gweneth. "Monsieur, I fail to see what can be done. It was a small thing really. Only the circumstances made it seem infamous."

"Do you consider kidnapping and rape mere trifles, my girl? Well, I do not. And, as an administrator of justice, I cannot do otherwise than see to it that the offense is punished."

"*Mon Dieu*, what are you saying?" Gweneth cried and rose. "There was no rape, only the folly of a few kisses."

"There, there, Gweneth," he soothed, putting a paternal arm about her shoulders. "We are family and must speak frankly to this misdeed. Amy has told us all. I can understand your reluctance to speak of the humiliation that has been forced on you by this fellow, but you must take heart. The man can no longer harm you."

An icy knot of fear curled and settled in Gweneth's chest. "She told you—but it is a lie. He never—oh, monsieur, you have not killed him!"

"Of course not, Gweneth," Gareth answered in irritation. "That is for a court to order and execute, but the man has been taken into custody, and I shall see that he does not lack for reason to wish for the hangman's knot."

Far from the reassuring look of gratitude he expected, Gweneth answered him with a stormy green glare. "This is unjust, monsieur. The man has done nothing to warrant his arrest, and if you thought to gain my support in this, then you are mistaken." Gweneth moved away and raised her hands in a gesture of helplessness. "I have woven such a tangle of half-truths these many months that I can appreciate how difficult it is for you to believe me. But the man is not guilty, and I could never accuse him falsely in a court of law."

Gareth rubbed his thumb back and forth over his fingers thoughtfully. This was something he had not credited, that the man was of worth in the girl's eyes. Still he held all the cards, and she must come to realize it.

A small smile tightened his thin lips. "Am I to understand from this emotional display that the man is something to you? I should have suspected it when I found you and the captain, ah, *flagrante delicto*—"

"Monsieur!"

Gareth's smile deepened. Yes, this was the method. To insult her honor would move her to protect it. "The man took you by force and kept you locked away aboard his ship for days. He is not an unattractive figure. Perhaps, with repeated—entreaties, he conquered your aversion," he suggested with a smirk.

"*C'est mensonge!* A lie, I say!" she retorted, her emerald gaze scathing in its affront. "I am a maiden still. You have no right to arrest an innocent man."

Gareth's brows peaked in amusement. "Innocent, is he? I should like to know how you kept that rutting stag at bay all those weeks at sea," he jeered and turned his back to walk to the front of his desk. The girl's stubbornness had provoked him to a momentary display of the enmity between them. Best to press the issue before he sparked further bad feeling.

"This is of no consequence, for the course is set. I need only your signature on this paper to complete our business," he said after a moment and lifted a sheet from his pile of papers.

"If it is a deposition against Capitaine Bertrand, I shall not sign," she answered firmly. "*Mais non!*"

"You shall sign," he replied flatly and dipped a quill in the crystal inkwell before offering it to her. "Sign it with a steady hand, my little niece, for there must be no doubt as to the signature."

"*Pourquoi?*" she persisted. "He cannot harm you, and I do not care."

"Yet I do, you foolish chit," Gareth hissed, goaded again to temper. "You have made a mockery of all my plans. You think I did not notice you playing the coquette last evening with every pair of breeches under two score years? You fancy yourself a fetching piece, and so you are, but you shall not escape marriage to Myers. This exercise is for his benefit. I could have you shut away for the shameless scandal you have caused. Yet I offer you the freedom of marriage. Which shall it be?" A faint tinge of color brightened his cheeks, but he ended his tirade on an aloof, practical note.

Her uncle was provoked, and Gweneth certainly dreaded the workings of his mind, but her answer was plain. "I cannot condemn an innocent man, whatever benefit it might be to me."

Gareth leaned forward over the desk, bracing himself with both hands. "There are other ways," he said pleasantly, but the cords in his neck stood out under the pale skin above his stock. "Do you not think I can wrench a confession from that man? He went far to incriminate himself before Myers last evening. With a little prodding, who knows?"

His expression hardened as he went on. "We are a primitive society here. None should care a whit for the screams of a man in agony. It is a common occurrence behind prison walls. There may be little left to hang and your stomach will retch at the sight, but it can—it will be done, if you do not sign."

Waves of nausea swept Gweneth. Compared with the satanic plot unfolding before her, Capitaine Bertrand's revenge was but a lark. She tore at the ribbons of her bonnet and removed it to give herself more air. Fear for the captain replaced all else in her mind as she struggled to fathom the depth of the danger in which he lay. There must be a way to appease her uncle and spare Raoul, but her reasoning was paralyzed with fatigue from a sleepless night.

"And, if that is not enough inducement, think on this. You have a sister on your conscience. What is to become of her if you are not wed? We cannot care for her indefinitely. How long do you suppose she will fare safely once she is abandoned?"

"You would not dare! Aunt Leonora would never allow it," she replied, but her voice quavered with uncertainty, for she knew how easily he maneuvered his wife.

"I should not have it come to that," Gareth admitted in seeming regret. "We speak of ugly possibilities which need never come about." He sighed and walked briskly over to the bell rope. "But I can see that you demand further proof of my determination." He yanked the bell roughly.

In a few minutes the sound of footsteps caused Gweneth to turn to the door. There, being shoved through the entrance, was Captain Bertrand, his wrists and ankles linked with heavy chain. He stumbled over the ungainly weight but recovered his footing, straightening up to glare at the guards who accompanied him. His shirt was ripped, and one bloody sleeve hung about his wrist; but it was his face which brought Gweneth none too steadily to her feet. His hair fell in wild disarray over his brow, and a large bruise swelled one cheek grotesquely. Above it the flow of blood from a cut at his brow had crusted that eye nearly shut.

Gareth approved the look of horror on his niece's face. "There you are, Mistress Gweneth. My men paid a visit on the captain quite early this morning. I am told he gave them a time of it, but, as you can see, he was finally subdued."

Gweneth did not reply, held in check by the damning gaze of the prisoner. Until this moment she had never thought to face him again.

Raoul studied her carefully before speaking. "So you had not realized the consequence of your spiteful action, mademoiselle," he scoffed. "Well, I hope you are amused. Your servant," and his chains rattled as they scraped the floor when he bowed condescendingly.

"Still the swaggering cock, what, Bertrand?" Gareth asked with a sneer. "We have ways to chasten that admirable spirit of yours. Why, I was just explaining to my niece—"

"Non!" The choked-back scream startled both men. "Non, Uncle. I beg of you," Gweneth cried, not caring for the scene she created as she ran across the room to clutch Gareth's arm. "However much displeased you are with me, you cannot do this."

"How wise of you to realize it," Raoul said with a chuckle. "Come, Governor. The girl is properly frightened and contrite while I am duly humbled. Now, if you will be so kind . . . ," and he held out his manacled wrists.

Gareth merely smiled and signaled to the guards who pinioned Raoul between them.

"Is the decision in your hands, mademoiselle?" Raoul questioned, but a blow from a muscled fist sent him to the floor with a grunt of pain.

"Take him outside," Gareth ordered. "And you might have preparations made for a flogging while you wait," he added as they dragged the prisoner from the room.

Gareth shut the door and turned to his niece. "He is mine. What shall you do?"

"I must think," Gweneth stalled. The captain's appearance had pricked her protective instinct, and she pushed from her thoughts the sickening possibilities as to what methods her uncle might employ to reach his aim.

"Very well," Gareth sighed. "And while you deliberate, I shall pursue my own methods. I will have your statement or his confession. It matters not which." He turned and reached for the doorknob. "If you care at all for Captain Bertrand, you will choose to spare him the indignity of torture."

Gweneth remained silent while he spoke, but a cry of denial burst from her when he opened the door.

"Aunt Leonora shall not allow you to do this once she hears what I have to say."

Gareth smiled slightly. "Do not force my hand, girl, or it shall fare so much worse with you. It will take time to fetch your aunt. By then the deed will be complete. With a confession I need not wait for a court to condemn him. Prisons are not without cutthroats who might well kill one of their own for the simple pleasure of it."

"The same may be said of holders of high office, monsieur," she rallied but shrank back expectantly as Gareth moved from the door, his face livid. Then, as suddenly as it had risen, the anger faded.

"No, I shall not force you." Gareth stepped round

her, striding to the desk. "This is all I require," he said and held out the paper.

Gweneth swallowed hard. The most she could do was hedge for time. "Capitaine Bertrand will not be further harmed in any manner if I sign?" she asked in a clear voice not measured by the painful thudding of her heart.

Gareth's ear was alert to this wavering of her defiance. "You have my word on it. Merely sign. What you do after that is up to you. You may salvage your engagement by playing the wronged woman in court or weep for your lover and lose all. I care not. My responsibility to the family honor will have been discharged."

His smooth words were couched in a suggestion of how the captain might be freed, but Gweneth doubted the sincerity of it. But her immediate concern must be for the safety of the chained man beyond the door. "You must send for a doctor to tend the capitaine. Swear that he shall be treated decently."

Gareth glared at the impudent young woman but caught just in time the meaning of her words. She was ready to capitulate. What difference if the captain should face the gallows in the full bloom of health if, by his death, the way was cleared for Myers to keep to the bargain between them?

"Sign and I shall send for a doctor before you depart."

"Send for the doctor, monsieur. Then I shall sign." The insult wrested no visible evidence of anger from Gareth this time, for he heard only her promise to affix her name.

A messenger was sent forthwith to the doctor and, when he arrived, Gweneth scratched her name at the bottom of the page with a surprisingly steady hand, ignoring the sense of foreboding pressing in on her.

CHAPTER FIFTEEN

Feelings of guilt nettled Gweneth for having affixed her name to a document scarcely read. Not until common sense intervened to remind her that, in doing so, she had spared Captain Bertrand the certainty of torture, could she draw a deep breath. The results of a whipping she had once witnessed in the early days of the Revolution when the cat-o'-nine-tails were routinely applied to any party suspected of disaffection with the cause. Such a fierce shuddering overtook her for a moment that her teeth danced a lively measure before Gweneth clamped them shut and forced the ghastly memories aside. The fates of members of her family were too closely bound up in those reflections for her to ever willfully recall the horror and frightful misery of that time. She crossed herself in a quick prayer of hope that her menfolk were safely beyond all agony.

The carriage wound its way more slowly homeward than the murderous pace of an hour ago, but now it was Gweneth who urged Johnathan on with cries for speed. She must seek out Aunt Leonora and explain to her the captain's innocence and how and why she had been driven to sign the complaint against him. It was a pitifully weak hope that Leonora could stand up to her husband, but it was the only hope Gweneth had.

Hardly waiting for the carriage to halt, Gweneth jumped down and hurried up the steps into the house. *"Un moment,"* she called to the slave girl disappearing round a corner of the great hall. "I would speak with Madame Dillingham. Where will I find her?"

The tall sloe-eyed servant turned back abruptly, her short, parti-colored skirt swishing softly in her wake. "Mistress Dillingham gone, missy," she replied with a smile. "She gone to town to see the governor."

"*Diable!*" Gweneth scowled and bit her lip. Who could she turn to now? "Have a horse saddled for me, then, while I change. Oh, please hurry," she said impatiently and wiped her damp brow with a gloved thumb.

"You not well, missy?" the girl questioned, noting how pale Gweneth had become. "It is the heat."

"The heat?" Gweneth asked with a puzzled look. "*Mais oui,* I suffer *mais affreusement,* most horribly," she murmured absently as she turned away toward her room.

Quickly stripping off her gloves and bonnet, Gweneth dropped them carelessly on a chair. Her gaze flickered about the tidied room and came to rest on the blue gown from the night before which had been repaired and hung by the window to air. A dull ache throbbed where her heart should be as she marched over and caught up the dress to stuff it into the armoire in quick angry movements. She needed no reminders of her folly. Had she but followed her head and not her treacherous heart, none of this would have occurred.

Miserable tears prickled her eyes with the recall of unyielding muscular embraces and hard, merciless kisses. How could she have not realized that his whole manner bespoke contempt and dislike? There was no need in him for her beyond the selfish determination to ridicule her, and she had complied by offering herself willingly as a victim.

"*Moi faute,*" she said aloud and rubbed an impatient hand over her eyes as she sank into a velvet chair, kicking off her suede slippers. Almost at once she rose. Crossing the room, she drew a sheet of paper from the desk drawer and began writing. She would ride into town and send a message to Daniel. The captain's crew would not stand idly by and let him be hanged.

The tingling sense of warning stole slowly through her until its insistence caused her to jump and turn round. "Amy, you scared me witless," Gweneth cried and leaned back against the desk in relief.

"Pardon, mademoiselle. I saw that you were busy with a letter and did not wish to disturb you. I have brought lemonade." Amy offered the tall sweating glass of liquid garnished with lemon slices and a sprig of greenery on a silver tray. "Cook put a finger of rum in it to cool and relax you."

Gweneth accepted the glass in one hand and slipped the scrap of paper into the drawer with the other. "Let me unhook you," Amy offered. "I know of the trouble you are in, and I think it most infamous that the capitaine would abuse you so!" She drew the sash from Gweneth's dress. "I will stand by you and tell the truth, no matter what."

"Tell me what you have said to the governor, Amy," Gweneth answered and shrugged off the gown. "Just as you told it to him. It is of the utmost importance." She slipped on the dressing gown held out. "Capitaine Bertrand has been arrested, and I fear my uncle shall seek to have him hanged."

Amy's expression brightened with anticipation. "*Vraiment!* Because he ravished you, he must pay."

A chilling touch traced Gweneth's spine. "That is a lie," she corrected coldly. "It is a confusing truth, Amy, but I tell you the capitaine never touched me. If I could simply prove it!" She jerked the ribbon from her hair, sprawling on the bed.

Amy turned to flee from her upset mistress, but Gweneth forestalled her. "*Non*, stay and tell me all that you have said to the others. I must know which lies to answer." There would be time to contact Daniel afterward.

Amy approached reluctantly and picked up the glass. "But first you must drink this, mademoiselle. Cook made it particularly for you."

Gweneth pulled herself to a sitting position and took a few sips. The lemonade was pleasantly cold on her tongue but slightly bitter. Rum did not find favor with her; but Gweneth obligingly swallowed a little more.

"Now, Amy, speak to me plainly and thoroughly."

The maid stood respectfully and repeated most of what she remembered, but she stopped and corrected herself so often that Gweneth soon set the more than half-full glass aside to give her full attention to the rambling story.

Amy's smooth voice was vaguely comforting, for the French tongue was seldom heard on the island. Capitaine Bertrand had spoken to her in French the night before, Gweneth remembered now, and his deep vibrant voice wafting through the dark came back to her with bittersweet clarity.

The room seemed to grow misty and cool as Amy's story became lost in the pulsating drone of bees hovering and swooping in the tangle of orange and scarlet blossoms flourishing just outside the window. Gweneth opened her mouth to urge the girl to raise her voice, but the effort was beyond her and a lazy smile formed on her parted lips. The sweet promise of sleep beckoned, and Gweneth murmured inaudibly for the girl to leave. The blessed release which eluded her for weeks now came stealing softly, a velvet muffler of unconsciousness.

"It is poison? Can you be certain?" The strident lament roused Gweneth, but she fought the person shaking her to wakefulness, for the dimly lit room held not the serenity of her dreams. "Let me be," she muttered thickly and closed her eyes.

Leonora stood by her niece's bed, helplessly wringing her hands. "Gareth warned me of the girl's distraught state, but I never imagined—" And she gave way to a pitiful sob.

"Mistress Dillingham, it's best that you wait outside," the physician instructed and waved the woman toward the door.

Dr. Birney picked up the glass on the commode and examined it. The flowers were dreadfully familiar; thornapple blossoms. It was a slow, drugged death the girl had chosen.

"Damn foolish child," he muttered and shook his grizzled head. The rumor of the broken engagement had reached his ear this morning, but that a lovely girl like this should seek to end her life was incredible. The doctor fumbled with her clothes, the better to hear her faint heartbeat. She was a beauty, he thought, remembering her as the dazzling lady of the ball. Myers was an idiot to spurn such an exceptional creature, whatever the reason.

He had just concluded his observations when there was a quick intake of breath at his elbow. He swerved round to find Governor Dillingham standing at the bedside. His piercing slate eyes were riveted to the girl's half-naked body.

Dr. Birney cleared his throat and brought the sheet discreetly over Gweneth. "She has tried to end her life," he said simply and stood to shield the girl from her uncle's obvious interest. "I said—"

"I heard you," Gareth snapped and fixed his gaze on the tiny man before him. "Will she—I should like to know if you can save her?" He had not meant to betray his interest in Gweneth, but neither had he expected to trip upon the sight which greeted him.

Dr. Birney adjusted his glasses over his stubby nose. "It's difficult to answer with any certainty. We have no way of determining precisely how much poison she ingested." He indicated the glass by the bed. Gareth's sharp gasp of breath in recognition of the deadly blossoms made Dr. Birney nod in agreement. "It shall require several bleedings to let the ill humors—"

"No leeching," Gareth imposed abruptly.

Dr. Birney sucked in his lower lip. "Why, sir, of course she must be bled. If the poison is not drawn from her veins immediately, there is very little hope indeed."

"My command remains," Gareth replied flatly. "The girl is subject to fainting spells, and my wife is certain that her blood is too thin."

"Well now," said the doctor, tugging furiously at his waistcoat, "were you to hear a physician's opinion on the matter, it would be this," and he tapped his spectacles with a forefinger. "The child's blood is too thick, too thick by half for this climate. Thick blood for chilly climes, thin blood for the tropics. She has not made the necessary change. Why, I thought the very same thing just last evening when I met her, all pink cheeked and rosy lipped. Too much bad humor there, I said to meself, I—"

Gareth raised an imperative hand. "I've heard this lecture before, Doctor, and I am still unimpressed. My wife has lost three children to your infernal meddling. She's as pale as a sheet from you physics, and still she does not produce." The doctor's lips twitched, but Gareth had not finished. "This time you shall do as I say. But before you drag out your odious nostrums, there is another matter I require you to acknowledge." Gareth lowered his eyes to the bed. "The poor girl has suffered a vile misfortune. No doubt, it led to this tragedy. The man is in custody, caught just this morning. There is no need for you to examine her for evidence of violation, for the dear child has signed a written accusation. I'll need simply your collaboration to put the rope securely about the culprit's neck." Without waiting for the doctor's reply, Gareth strode from the room.

Dr. Birney's distracted gaze fell on the girl. Rape. That would explain the suicide attempt. In his experience it was not unusual for gently bred ladies to consider death when confronted with the unspeakable alternative of memory. The doctor clucked his tongue in misgiving but decided it was healthier for his professional life to follow the dictates of his employer rather than face possible slander if the girl should die under his own prescribed care. Leeching was the preferred method, but there were other ways of ejecting the poison.

Gweneth gasped and choked on the scalding hot liquid forced down her throat. She would surely drown, she thought, wildly fending off the strange hands which sought to hold her aright. Voices droned and roared in her ears, but the words were gibberish. The hot, bitter vetch churned in her stomach and soon spasms of nausea bent her double as she was sick again and again. White-hot pains cut through her like steel, laying her open to an agony beyond any she had ever known. And still she was helpless to the continuous plyings of fluids down her inflamed throat. Try though she would, none would answer her hysterical pleas for help.

An eternity passed, weighted in deliberate, viscous beads of minutes. Whether day or night she could not tell, awakening only to blinding light as the candelabra blurred and multiplied themselves. Her words tripped and twisted on her tongue, spilling out in a senseless jumble. She struck out at the phantom figures clothed in gleaming white. Grotesque figures of childhood nightmares became reality, pawing and dragging their clawed hands over her skin till she was flayed.

". . . observe the twitching . . ."

" 'Tis a sure sign of the poison."

". . . periods of delusion."

"If her heart withstands the shock, I cannot hope to know the results of the hysteria to her mind."

". . . a matter of hours."

Corporal O'Grady followed the orders, however distasteful they were to him personally, and shackled his prisoner hand and foot. It ain't as if he could escape through a window or even had the time to burrow his way out of this dungeon, he reasoned as the cuffs snapped closed over the man's wrists.

"Sorry, Cap'n. Them's me orders," O'Grady said with an apologetic smile. "Don't seem right. Leastways, you should have your last night in peace."

Raoul grunted and squatted down on his heels. "Perhaps the lady above us still fears for her virtue," he spat.

A grin creeped across the corporal's ruddy boyish face. "Well met, Cap'n. It do stretch the sense of things to bring you here, but I suspect it has to do with the ruckus kicked up after you were sentenced."

Raoul looked up in surprise.

"I see you ain't been informed, Cap'n. Seems some of your crew took the news right poorly. Threatened the magistrate, they did, and vowed to wreck the town. Of course the governor done away with that straight off. Told them they was no longer in your employ, for your ship had been confiscated and all cargo therein."

Raoul's face darkened dangerously at this reminder of his vessel, and the young guard took an instinctive step back toward the musket he had left leaning by the doorway. But Raoul made no move and, after a moment, bade the corporal finish his tale.

"If you can bear the hearing of it, certainly. The governor said that your crew was discharged, and unless they could affix themselves to a new ship by day's end, he'd have them arrested on vagrancy charges. A wily one, that governor, for no sooner had he smote them with the back of his hand than he turned it palm up in offering. Said there was a ship in port in need of a crew, and if they were of mind, he'd sign them on, just so they set sail at first tide. That gave them a bit to chomp." O'Grady gave up a chuckle but checked his mirth on sight of the man at his feet.

For all that the captain had ill chosen the object of

his seduction, he was far from presenting a ridiculous figure. Lucifer himself could not have looked more proud and vengeful, O'Grady reckoned and crossed himself for insurance.

Raoul threw back his head in laughter at the young man's superstitious alarm. "Faith, sir, tell me what you find to fear? Were I able to summon demons, it would not be to your hazard I should wield such a force. But there, we stray. What of my crew and ship?"

O'Grady removed himself a step from the man crouching at his feet, glad now for the precaution of chains. "Well, to a man they accepted the governor's offer. All except one old sea dog who said he'd just as soon be jailed as in the pay of the devil, but the governor had him taken into custody aboard the *Jamaica Rummer* with the others." O'Grady brought the captain a dipper of water while he talked, and Raoul drank thirstily, cradling the utensil in his manacled hands.

"That be the whole of it, Cap'n. By the by, I'd take no solace in the thought your men may yet save you. The governor set a guard on the wharf to keep them on board, and you are not to hang till hours past the tide. Guess that explains the change in your jail. If your crew should attempt to free you, they'll not be afinding you, now will they?" O'Grady took the empty dipper and slung it over the pail.

"A pure shame, this business. Did you not offer to marry the lady, Cap'n? It were a far sight better to— well, I saw her once. You could do lots worse, to be sure."

"Leave me, man, and keep your plaguey advice for others," Raoul answered and swore under his breath. "Hold fast, there. I could do with a bottle from the shelf yonder." Raoul pointed to a wall lined with dusty bottles. "And make it the best."

O'Grady scanned the cellar. It was not likely one bottle would be missed among so many, and he nodded and dragged a bottle of brandy from one shelf. He picked the cork with his knife and handed it over. "To your health, Cap'n," he said and departed.

Raoul took several long pulls on the bottle and placed it on the floor beside him in the dark. "Marry the girl? Damn it, she had not the gall to even set foot in that hall of deceit to speak her own lies," he grumbled aloud. He had set himself up to be freed after observing the horror in Gweneth's eyes as she beheld him battered and chained. Then, too, a doctor had arrived so quickly and he had been kept decently after that, having been allowed exercise and full meals. But now he knew that he waited in vain for the visitor who could set him free.

"What fool I," Raoul sighed and hoisted the bottle again. Not until Gweneth did not appear at his trial had he known an uneasy moment. Her signature to the complaint had shaken him, but it was with the testimony of the doctor that she had tried to take her life "after having been accosted by the prisoner" that he finally realized the full peril in which he stood.

Gweneth's attempted suicide—if it were to be believed—sat unhappily in Raoul's mind for it invoked the memory of another woman's success. Was it that Gweneth found herself in like circumstance? That would explain her acceptance of Myers's suit. Perhaps she was driven to find a father for her unborn child.

"Lavasseur!" Raoul groaned in certainty as his mind rushed ahead to the conclusion. He had won the girl and then left, unaware of the deed he had perpetrated. For, surely, he would have made some arrangements had he known. So Gweneth had sought to save herself by marrying.

Still that would not explain her willing compliance with his own abruptly determined lovemaking. "Mayhaps the lady had developed a taste for the exercise," Raoul mused. There was little hesitancy before she had abandoned her protests to press on him the most ardent kisses ever rendered from her lips. Aye, there was passion in that soft sweet mouth and a skill she had not possessed months before. Damnation, but he might, indeed, have found a mistress in that coquetting petticoat had he only stifled the urge to humiliate her before her uncle.

Of all the rash actions that were ever his undoing, this had cost him most dearly. It made no sense that she should suffer him to pay with his life for such a trifle unless there were things to which he was not privy.

Raoul sprang to his feet. "Corporal, Corporal O'Grady!" he shouted. "I will have a word with the governor. Now, if you please." No answer came in reply and though he called again and again till he trembled with rage, never was any answer returned.

"No light!" came the shrill cry from the figure on the bed as Amy entered, and she quickly doused the lamp she held. Good, Mademoiselle Gweneth was alone.

Amy edged closer to the bed and called softly, "Mademoiselle, oh, mademoiselle. Pardon, but I must speak with you."

"Come closer, Amy, but no light. I beg you," Gweneth said.

Amy ran the rest of the distance and fell on her knees by the bed, sobbing loudly. "Mademoiselle, I prayed you would not die. He said it could not harm you, but it did. *Mon Dieu*, I nearly killed you!"

"How long, Amy? How long have I been like this?" Gweneth asked weakly and pushed up on one elbow to reach out and touch the maid's head. She ran her fingers through Amy's pale hair to make certain that this was no shadow. So often she had spoken to one or more of her visitors only to discover that they were manifestations of her illness. "How long have I been ill?" she asked again.

"Two weeks, mademoiselle. It is my fault. I should never have listened to him. He is a wicked man. He said it was an accident that you were so sick, that the measurement was in error, but I do not believe him."

Gweneth barely heard the distraught girl, for there had been only one thought in her mind since regaining her senses. "Capitaine Bertrand, he has gone?"

Amy raised her head and caught Gweneth's slender hand in her own. "*Mais non*, mademoiselle. There was a trial, and he was found guilty. Oh, Mademoiselle Gweneth, he is to hang on the morrow!"

"Non! That cannot be." Gweneth struggled to sit. "I heard . . . or was it a dream? So many dreams, so many illusions; but no, this was real. It must be real," she murmured in confusion. She could nearly remember all her testimony, orderly and thorough, and blessed Daniel's avid collaboration.

Amy came to her feet. "*Mais non*, you must rest. Lie back, mademoiselle. You are still ill."

But Gweneth grasped Amy's arm in a firm grip. "I must speak with my uncle. He must be made to realize his error before an innocent man dies!"

Amy pulled away, daunted by the urgency in her mistress's voice. "Non, my lady. Monsieur Dillingham must not hear you say such things. We are in danger, such danger. You do not understand." Amy took Gweneth's hands in hers and held them tightly. "You are weary, and there is so little time. No one must find us together, but I must make you understand. The governor said that you must be kept safe until he could seek the justice you would deny. He said we must spare you the humiliation of the trial or, in your tenderheartedness, you might destroy yourself by lying to aid the capitaine. You know I would never hurt you, after all that you have done for Sarah and me. But the governor spoke so convincingly of what should be done that, God save me, I believed him!" Amy's voice trembled with tears as she buried her head in her lap. "It was only a sleeping potion, he told me," she whispered faintly.

Gweneth passed a cool hand over her sore eyes. She

had not spoken to anyone since regaining consciousness at dawn, not to answer the doctor's questions about her sight, not Aunt Leonora's emotional entreaties that she get well. The day had passed in tranquil silence troubled only by her inability to have gained Captain Bertrand's forgiveness. Now, listening to Amy, the shadowed comfort of her imaginings failed. She had become ill before she could set the captain free.

Gweneth moved suddenly, swinging her feet over the side of the bed. "I will go to the prison and speak with the magistrate. The capitaine is not guilty, Amy. I will find someone to hear me and believe." Gweneth freed her hands and put her feet to the floor, but the quick moment of rising pitched her into a dark, spiraling dizziness which dragged at her consciousness. Only Amy's alarmed cry kept her from fainting, and she sank back onto the bed.

"Mademoiselle, you do not know what you are saying. Your uncle will never allow you to interfere," Amy warned as she helped her mistress back onto the pillows.

"Then I will see Capitaine Bertrand."

"It is hopeless. You do not know all that has happened. Why, your uncle has brought the capitaine here for protection. He is locked in the wine cellar at this very moment, and there is a guard," Amy explained and supplied the details.

Gweneth listened intently. It would take all her strength to achieve the execution of the plan forming in her head, but it was of no consequence to her that the risk was great.

"Amy, it is God's hand which brings the capitaine within our reach. Go now, but come to me again when the house is asleep. I cannot act alone. Therefore I shall depend on your loyalty." She stopped and searched the maid's face which was bright with tears. "You say you meant me no harm and I believe you, but you must prove your devotion now by keeping faith. If you do not, we are all lost. Do not be afraid, we will find a means to right this wrong."

Amy trembled under her mistress's touch. The governor had threatened to accuse her of the crime if it were to become known that Gweneth had not poisoned herself, and his intimidation was so complete that Amy had greatly dared even to enter Gweneth's room. But now that she saw in this lady of her own age a determination and will equal to his, she could do naught else but follow her lead. She had not the slightest belief that two women could prevail, but that her mistress could seek that end with such confidence was enough.

CHAPTER SIXTEEN

"I am here," Gweneth called when her door opened. She slid from the bed. Weariness had crept up through her body as she lay waiting, but she shoved this enticement aside at the sight of her cohort.

Amy moved slowly forward until she could make out the figure of her mistress in the shadowed room. Gweneth was fully dressed beneath her dressing gown. "What are you doing, mademoiselle?" she asked in disbelief.

"It is my plan, or part of it, Amy." Gweneth came round the corner of the bed, shielding her eyes from the pale candlelight. Illumination in any form had afforded her nearly intolerable pain since the first day of her illness. She quietly revealed to the maid the details of her design.

"But it is much too risky, mademoiselle. If you should be caught and brought before the governor, *Sacré Bleu*, what will not happen?" Amy whispered in reply. "If this thing must be done then, I beg you, let me run the gauntlet. You are too weak."

"Precisely why it must be I," Gweneth answered matter-of-factly as her pulse quickened in anticipation. She had ever loved the thrill of a challenge. "No one will ever suspect me if I am successful. And that is the part I have devised for you. You shall take my place in this bed, and should anyone come to check on me, you must feign sleep or, if a light is struck, protest weakly that it is intolerable and that you wish to be left to rest. None should think to search for a servant if the house is roused to the suspicion of an escape."

"What if you should fail?" Amy persisted.

Gweneth shrugged. "What can they do to me? I am disgraced, and nothing more would my uncle dare than that he has already attempted. Kill me he would not, and any scandal would bring my protest to light. We have all to gain and nothing to lose."

"This capitaine, he is very important to you, *mais oui?*" Amy questioned knowingly.

"There is no time for discussion," Gweneth replied shortly, dismissing the subject. "Get into bed and, here, put on this nightcap to cover your blond hair. None must know it is you, Amy. No one."

Gweneth spread a shawl over her head and tied it under her chin, pulling it close over her face and hair. "I should return within the hour. If not, you must seek your own bed and never tell anyone that you have helped me in this. God be with you," she added and kissed Amy's cheek.

The dark hallway provided thankful relief for Gweneth's eyes as well as concealment, and she sped along its length toward the servant stairs, stopping just long enough to draw a sword from the coat of arms hanging at the top of the main staircase. The cold steel seemed warmly alive in her hands, and the thought of the defense it offered spurred Gweneth on. The stairwell was empty and shrouded in velvet black, but Gweneth's strangely altered vision found the merest vapors of light to guide her down the rough wooden steps, and she came to the first floor without mishap. The stairs to the kitchen lay to the left, but Gweneth paused to press her cheek to the cool stone wall for her breath now came in slow, painful gasps and her hands were numb with fatigue.

The rapier slipped from her stiff fingers and slithered across the stone floor, its sharp clang echoing up the stairwell. Gweneth caught her breath and wriggled back into the darkest corner, waiting for some inspection to follow the racket. Her head swam in a fog, but the rest of her body seemed weighted, and her courage fled in the wake of her increasing stupor. Once before she had plunged into folly only to have it recoil on her. What more was this than the delirium of a half-blind girl? she asked herself. She was ill, more so than she had realized.

The rough-hewn stone scraped her cheek as she sagged onto the steps to await certain detection. She could not go on, and she was too sick and afraid to care.

"A soul without fear is a fool," a voice whispered inside her. Where had she heard that? Courage without respect for the challenge was a valueless armor. Yes, that, too, was true. She needed not the strength to battle her foe, only the cunning to disarm him.

When no one investigated the disturbance, Gweneth cautiously raised herself and advanced across the floor to retrieve the weapon. When her hand tightened on the hilt, a purposeful frown knit her damp brow. Surprise was her best weapon, and surprise she would use. Quickly she moved forward before second thoughts could rob her of this new resolve.

Wan light filtered up the kitchen stairs, and Gweneth's eyes began to stream as she reached the lower level. If the guard were posted in the servants' hall, she would be helpless, blinded by a thousand points of splintering pain. But she stumbled on, forcing a knuckle between her teeth to bite off the cry of agony swelling up in her chest.

A single lantern gleamed above the common table, but the noonday sun had never seemed as bright to Gweneth as she groped her way past the chairs, fingers splayed in defense. No one waited here and, if Amy were correct, she would face one sentry. The blood roared through her head with each pulsing beat but she reached the entrance to the cellar hall without notice.

The light was fainter here, and long shadows danced along the floor before her. She caught up the edge of her shawl and wiped the water from her face. Raising the rapier, she peered hesitantly around the edge of the doorway. Fifteen feet ahead, the guard stood, shoulders braced against the wall and a musket draped loosely over crossed arms. The man's chin rested on his chest. Gweneth smiled at his dozing form. Here was her one chance.

"Pardon, monsieur, but I should remain quite still if I were you," Gweneth cautioned and reached out for the dark barrel of the musket.

O'Grady jerked awake and half turned but checked himself as the tip of a blade pricked the skin of his neck.

"Not another inch, *mon ami*, or I shall be forced to pierce your throat," Gweneth warned, pushing the barrel aside.

O'Grady blinked once and then again at the slight feminine figure before him. "Saints preserve us, now if it ain't an angel I am beholding," he exclaimed and grinned at the girl.

"Careful, monsieur, my hand trembles wickedly, and I'll not hesitate to improve on your smile if you so much as breathe too deeply," she answered to a softly blurred silhouette. His features were lost on the white oval of his face, and the red uniform formed the mere image of a man.

"Well now, darlin', what do you think you be doing here? Is it the captain you come to see?" he asked in amusement.

"The weapon, monsieur." And her hand tugged at the musket. O'Grady's fingers moved, and Gweneth heard the trigger cock. "Would you shoot me, monsieur? It won't do, you understand, for should I not run this dainty blade through your neck in reply, you may offer it up to the hangman when the governor discovers that you have killed his niece." She had hoped to avoid giving herself away, but the words gave the corporal pause as she hoped. He stared round-eyed at the lady before him.

"The devil, you say. And here I am protecting the very scalawag whose life is forfeit because of you. Well now, if this not be a puzzle," he said thoughtfully.

"The puzzle is that you have not yet released the weapon," Gweneth replied and increased the pressure of the point at his throat. "It is very foolish to keep a lady waiting. Where are your manners?"

O'Grady relaxed his grip on the musket slowly. After all, she was but a girl, and he could easily overpower her without help. Indeed it might go ill for him should he do more than that. "At your service, miss, though I doubt your uncle would approve," the corporal rallied.

Gweneth cast the gun behind her without looking back. "Turn, *s'il vous plaît?* And slowly for I should hate to damage that uniform. But make no mistake, monsieur, I can and I will if necessary."

O'Grady began turning away, then swirled back to catch the blade in his hand, but Gweneth had expected some attempt and fell back to circle the steel out of his grasp and lunge forward at the dark form. It caught him in the right forearm, and he yelped and leaped away.

"Now what you be doing that for, darlin'? Would you maim a man who's doing no more than his duty?" he asked and clapped a hand over his freely flowing wound.

Gweneth brought her blade up again and with her other hand felt for the solid comfort of the wall. Her breath was ragged with the effort to control her fright for, when he had grabbed for her, she had not known whether her blade would find him. If he perceived her poor sight, she was lost.

"The key. That is all I require of you," she said boldly and advanced again.

"He'll not get far, darlin'. Have you had a change of heart for the poor captain? Is that it? Best go see your uncle, lass, and let him decide. 'Tis a devil of a chance you are taking this way," the corporal reasoned, but he kept a respectful distance from that yard of steel flickering before his face.

"The door, monsieur. Open it now."

O'Grady reached for the keys at his waist and surveyed them. "And if I'll not be doing your bidding, miss?"

"Is the answer not flowing from you now?" Gweneth questioned saucily. But the giddy-headed feeling was returning, and she knew she must hurry.

"You are a stouthearted thing, I credit you that." O'Grady laughed good-naturedly and put the key in the lock.

"Open the door an inch, monsieur, and no more. That is fine. Now turn your back on it and kick it open."

"What?" O'Grady shook his head. "No, I'll not be suspecting the workings of your mind, darlin', though I'd purely like to know."

"Capitaine, are you—" But Gweneth needed say no more for the prisoner grabbed the corporal from behind, encircling his neck with the length of chain between his wrists.

" 'Tis a fine thing you've done—" Raoul halted in mid-sentence at the recognition of his rescuer. "Gweneth!" He had heard the voices beyond the door but, until it swung open, he had not realized a plot was afoot. Before his stunned gaze Gweneth swayed and leaned weakly against the wall as her knees gave way.

Raoul was brought back to business by the struggling man in his grasp. He jerked the corporal inside the cellar and butted the man's head against the wall. The corporal fell slack within Raoul's shackled embrace, and the captain lowered him to the floor, dragging him clear of the door.

When Gweneth regained consciousness, Raoul was pressing his dampened shirt to her face. Her cool green eyes regarded the man above in bewildered tenderness. His face was pale and stern.

"You silly little fool," he said brusquely but smiled in relief for she had only fainted. "You have yet to finish what you begin."

"Capitaine, you are safe?" she asked uncertainly.

"Thanks to you, *ma belle*. Well done. But why, after all this time, have you come to me?"

"I—I have been ill," she answered softly and put a hand on his bandaged brow. "Are you well, Capitaine?" She could not tell his features any longer and saw only the white linen wrapped about his dark head.

Raoul swore impatiently and lifted her into his arms. "Gweneth, I thought you—but, never mind. You have been ill. I should have known that yours is not a vindictive heart. You sweet silly girl, you might have been killed."

"You are safe. That is all that matters. Oh, but you must go quickly. If we are caught!" Gweneth whispered frantically and struggled to her knees.

"You are in no condition to look after yourself. Come, I will take you along with me," Raoul answered and reached out to collect the weapons once he had steadied Gweneth on her feet. "The corporal is under lock and key. It will be some time before anyone looks for us."

"Non, you must go alone, and swiftly, Capitaine. I would only encumber you," Gweneth countered. "They will believe you have kidnapped me if I leave. I will stay behind to clear your name." Gweneth put out her hand as Raoul turned back to her, but she missed the steady anchor of his arm and stumbled.

"Dear Lord, what is it?" he whispered and cradled her protectively.

"My eyes. I cannot see well in the light. It will pass, the doctor has said so," Gweneth replied but snuggled closer to the warmth of his bared chest. This is where she wanted to be, and as his arms held her tightly, she could not keep the tears from coming. The feel of him had been the only comfort in her dreams, and now he held her in truth.

"Gweneth," Raoul said softly into her hair. "I was told what you tried to do. You must never repeat this nonsense of attempting to do away with yourself. You may come with me if it will spare you the shame of remaining."

Gweneth closed her eyes and swayed into him, her arms going around his hard frame. If she wished it, she could go with him. There was nothing she wanted more, and the impulse to lift her lips for his kiss nearly succeeded. But no, this was not meant to be. Too much pain, too many betrayals lay between them to ever hope . . .

She pushed roughly out of his embrace and lifted her trembling chin proudly. "I have given you your freedom, Capitaine. It is yours to take and leave."

For the few long seconds he stood staring down at her, the wild expectation that he would argue sprung to life within her. But then Raoul smiled—it seemed so sad—and said, "We were ever an ill-matched pair, *ma belle*. Curse the fates that have entangled our paths. I shall go, but first you must be made safe." His hand brushed her cheek, and then he scooped her up and began his trek up the steps.

Gweneth directed him to the first floor, then slid from his arms. "There is a door at the end of this passage. It leads out into the gardens beyond the stables. From there you should be safe."

"And you, Gweneth?" he asked gently.

"I know my way. The darkness is a blessing, and none shall know I have helped you."

"Farewell then, *ma belle*," he said and turned away abruptly. "Gweneth?" Raoul paused but did not look back. "Promise me that you will not marry that Myers fellow. If it is Lavasseur you desire, then wait for him. He will return."

The husky whisper in the cloaking dark left

Gweneth breathless, but before she could reply, a door opened at the end of the hall and the silhouette of the man she loved was gone.

"Who's there?"

Gweneth had turned down the hall of the main floor, thinking it better, were she to be seen, that she should be discovered in the main quarter of the house. The reasoning proved wise, for she had but passed the library doors when they opened to admit the person of her uncle.

"Monsieur?" Gweneth questioned timidly and threw up a hand to protect her eyes from the glare of the room beyond. His sudden appearance made her skin crawl in apprehension, but she moved forward.

Gareth halted in astonishment. He had not expected the nightwalker to be his niece. The doctor had pronounced her through the worst of the illness but said that it would be weeks before she recovered sufficiently to be about. The fact that she had been left without any remembrance of the events surrounding her sudden sickness greatly relieved his anxiety. With proper encouragement she should be made to believe that she had sought to take her own life, and none would ever be the wiser. Still the French maid must go. He could not expect her to live in fear of him forever and, when she no longer pleased him, she would be dealt with.

"What brings you here at so late an hour?" Unable to sleep himself, Gareth had sought the comfort of brandy and a book. Tomorrow would see the accomplishment of a deed he found distasteful but necessary, for it removed the last obstacle to his goal.

Gweneth shivered. The captain had just left, and he would require time, perhaps an hour, to make good his escape. He knew of the ship leaving port at dawn and had said his crew would welcome his company.

"What is it, girl? Are you seeking someone?" The words gave Gweneth's frantic, unfocused thoughts an anchor. "*Oui*, Uncle. I wish to speak with you. You were not abed and I came in search of you," she replied and advanced toward the library.

Gareth fell back and waved her in, watching as Gweneth felt with searching hands her way into the room.

"May we have less light, monsieur?" She could no longer stomach to claim him as kin. "My eyes are so sensitive." She found the support of a leather wing-backed chair in a darkened corner and sank gratefully into its soft cushions.

Gareth doused all but a single candle and came to stand over her, his hands tucked behind his back. He was dressed for bed in a red velvet dressing gown and turban which covered his clipped hair. "It is late for such a meeting. Can your visit not wait until daylight?" He frowned over the slumped form in the chair, noting with suspicion that she was dressed. "Why are you abroad just now? Where have you been?" Suspicion became alarm and he bent down and roughly dragged her from her chair.

"Were you skulking about, seeking your lover?" he shouted and shook Gweneth until her head snapped back and forth drunkenly.

"*Oui, oui,*" Gweneth murmured when he released her and shoved her back into the chair. The room reeled wickedly, but she fought the nausea to mutter, "But do not worry. You have found me out. All is lost!" She bent over her knees sobbing.

A grim smile of satisfaction thinned Gareth's lips. His restlessness had served him well. "How came you to know that the captain is here? Answer me, my girl, or you shall know a full measure of my wrath. Curse it all! You deserve a thrashing for your impudence," he thundered as she continued to weep.

Time, she must give the captain time. "A drop of brandy, *s'il vous plaît*? I feel dizzy. Please, monsieur, I shall speak but—oh, I . . ."

Gareth grumbled blasphemously but poured a glass

and brought it to her as Gweneth counted off the seconds with the pounding of her heart. She did not fight her hysteria and many minutes, precious minutes, passed before she could bring the snifter to her lips. The liquid fire braced her shivering as she prayed silently for the man rushing through the night. The moon would be rising now, bringing the tide. Could he make his escape on the departing vessel? She drank slowly, letting the time slip by.

"Let's have it, Gweneth. The truth," Gareth demanded when he had stubbed out his cigar. He had nearly gone below to check his charge, but the complete misery of the girl's tears convinced him that she had been thwarted in whatever she intended. Instead he chose to enjoy the fine Carolina tobacco and his victory.

"I heard the servants talking in the hallway by my door. That is how I know the capitaine is here," Gweneth ventured between sobs. "Oh, monsieur, you must not hang the man!" She came away from her chair and flung herself at his feet. "Have mercy, monsieur. I shall do anything that you ask, anything at all. You may send me away, I do not care, but you must not hang Capitaine Bertrand!"

"All this for a man you claim to despise?" Gareth asked skeptically. "Why do you prostrate yourself at my feet and offer anything—was that not your plea?—in order to serve him? He cares nothing for you. Any other man in his place would have begged to be allowed to wed you," he threw at her contemptuously. "He would rather swing from the gallows than bed you again. It speaks very poorly of your skill, my dear." The sardonic laughter stung Gweneth, but she could not afford to answer his insults in the manner she desired.

"He must think that I would not accept him since I was not present at his trial. If you let me speak with him, I can change his mind. I know I can." She kept her head meekly lowered so that he would not see the hatred burning so steadily in her eyes. He would never agree to this, and she knew it.

"That is what you would like to believe," Gareth chuckled and turned to pace the room. "You believe yourself undeniably attractive, that any man would give all to fondle you freely. You have much to learn, my dear." He half turned to eye the pathetic figure on the carpet. "Would you offer yourself to the guard? Was that your plan just now? Would you offer yourself even to me for a promise of the captain's release?" Insulting laughter filled the room, and Gweneth shuddered involuntarily, but she bit off the derisive reply that leaped to her tongue.

"Monsieur, you mock me pitilessly and, perhaps, with cause. I do not know what I would not do to free the man. If I were not so sick in mind and body, my answers would be more rational. As it is, I have depended on my emotions."

Gareth sniffed rudely. Emotions always ruled foolish heads. "Enough of this. The court found the man guilty and rightly so. It is not within my power to alter the judgment. You would do better to gather your strength for the ordeal ahead," he replied, enjoying the torment of this proud spirit. "I have secured Mr. Myers's consent for an immediate ceremony. The scandal caused by this sordid business deems it prudent that you should wed hastily and set this misadventure behind you. Rise, girl, and calm yourself. Your illness makes you ridiculous. Go back to bed and stay there until you are sent for. My wife shall be awakened to attend you."

Gweneth rose and wiped her damp face. With a half-hour's start the captain should be well on his way. The search would begin with the grounds and spread out from there. It would take time to muster a search party and by then the captain would be beyond their reach.

"I shall await your pleasure, monsieur," she said and

returned to her seat. "My aunt may decide that I should be allowed to visit the capitaine after all."

Her strangely confident tone brought Gareth round, and the hair raised on the nape of his neck as he stared at the scant smile hovering about Gweneth's mouth. "Liar!" he raged and swooped down on her.

Gweneth cowered in fright, raising her arms protectively. "Liar!" he repeated and grabbed a handful of her hair. "You have betrayed me!" He struck out and slapped her full across the face. The stinging pain rendered her senseless, and the following punishment was not felt.

Raoul made good time. Once past the garden he plunged into the undergrowth, waded the lagoon in several powerful strides, and then skirted the slave settlement by threading his way through the impenetrable dark of a grove of banyan trees. Beyond sight of the house he headed away from town only to double back when he reached the edge of the jungle. The sand glowed iridescently under the indigo sky while a golden arc at the farthest edge of the water heralded the rising moon. His boots sloshed noisily on the damp grasses, and he slipped more than once, but he forged on. If Gweneth had been discovered or his escape found out, the hunt for him would begin on the road to town. It was less likely that they would search for him on the shore.

Raoul halted to catch his breath, gasping in the salt-tinged air that ruffled his hair and whipped his wet shirt. He shivered, but not from the cold. He had left a woman behind to brave the fury which would accompany his flight.

"Damnation, why would she not come with me?" he muttered through chattering teeth. Yet he knew the answer. She had saved him through a sense of duty, a righteous chivalry, no doubt learned at her father's knee. For one fleeting moment he had held her, felt her arms go about his waist, and he had rejoiced in her need of him. How close he had come to forcing her to accompany him, but the hesitancy in her eyes smote that resolve. She loved elsewhere, and he could only want her happiness. That, and a safe harbor.

When he had spied her beyond the cellar door with an unhealthy paleness to her cheeks and lips but with eyes bright in determination and anger, something within him changed. There she was—that magnificent head of hair billowing about her shoulders—alone, afraid, but with the courage to strike out even when backed to the wall. He saw no longer a mere woman of desirous proportions and temperament, no more the worthy opponent or spirited filly to be tamed, but a single fragile, very human creature not unlike himself. Whatever she had done, there was good cause. He was certain of that, and all his own anger had died in tribute.

He would find Lavasseur and send him or bring him, kicking and screaming if need be, back to her. Whatever lay in his power, he would do to make certain that she would never again be left to meet life alone. In a world gone mad with cunning and treachery, she could not last forever with the sweet gentle courage which was her nature.

The pale opaline crescent climbed silently into view as Raoul mulled over these thoughts. He shot one quick look over his shoulder in the hope that she was abed at this moment and pressed ahead. The light gave him speed but also signaled that his time was shortening.

Bridgetown lay to his right as he ducked again into the jungle and came over the ridge of a hill. His eyes scanned the harbor and came to rest on his vessel. She rode the anchor proudly and a lash of fury curled about his heart with the knowledge that he must leave her, too, behind. There was another ship he must board, and he heaved himself down from his rocky perch without another look and scrambled to the edge of the shimmering white stretch of road.

Nothing stirred on the path, and he traversed the stretch of road to town at a quick jogging pace. His years of vigorous sea life had adapted him to long endurance, and he accomplished the five miles in less than thirty minutes. He darted between the closely built shanties, his boots crunching softly on the pathway. The wharf lay ahead, but he turned off and headed for the jungle to the left, staying well within the tangled shelter until he was far from the dock.

Raoul studied the harbor at close range and found that he had chosen correctly; the *Jamaica Rummer* was anchored near this beach. He walked casually across the sand, stopped to pull the boots from his feet, and dived cleanly between the swells of the foaming surf. The water warmed and soothed his aching limbs as he swam purposefully toward his beacon. His men were aboard, and he did not doubt that they would welcome him.

The first fingers of gray streaked the sky as Raoul reached the hull. He dug into the barnacled, worm-riddled timber with his fingers, absently deploring the wretched heap he must captain. It would drag badly on the ocean and probably leak. He would have his fine ship back at all costs, the pride of his life. Curls of pitch edged under his nails as he searched for a hold on the slimy side, and he swore mechanically as he floundered in the sea and bashed his head against the side.

It was ridiculous to pursue this course, he decided and swam round to the other side in time to spy the anchor line as it strained against the force raising it, sleek and dripping from the bottom. Just in time, he thought, and kicked off for the sinuously twisting cable. It was treacherously slick, and Raoul scrambled desperately for a firm grip, churning the water into a foam-flecked cauldron. The coils writhed under his grappling hands, but he seized it securely just as the anchor broke water. He wrapped his legs about the heavy thick braid as he was hauled out of the sea and sent spiraling upward toward the deck.

The two men who were guiding the line over the railing raised a cry upon sighting a man hanging on to the line. They brought the line up more slowly and grabbed the drenched figure by the shoulders, heaving him over the side when he reached the top.

Raoul sank to his knees on the deck but raised an exultant face to the two sailors at his side. "Much obliged, mates," he rasped and took the hand offered to hoist him to his feet.

"Avast, me boys. What goes there?" called a voice from the quarterdeck. Captain Willows lowered his lubberly form down the ladder and strode over to the dripping wet man.

"Captain Bertrand!" he cried in amazement. "Here, you there," he pointed to the two seamen. "Seize the fellow. He is an escaped prisoner."

Neither man moved.

Raoul ran a hand over his face to dry it and grinned broadly at the squat, barrel-chested man staring up at him.

"Beg pardon, Captain, but you seem to overlook the fact that these are my men," he returned and placed his fists squarely on his hips.

"We will see about that," Willows retorted and turned to cry a note of warning to the two soldiers lounging about the foredeck. But Raoul shouted his presence to the men coming forward, and they easily overpowered the armed soldiers.

"It would seem we have one captain too many, Willows. Though I hesitate to label you my equal. This garbage scow deserves no better than a bilge rat for a skipper. However, 'tis my lot to pilot this sorry craft. Now, if you will be so good as to disembark." Raoul laughed and indicated the water.

"You are mad, Bertrand. You'll not get away!" Willows cried in impotent fury, his slack mouth quivering in affront.

"You think not?" Raoul arched a brow in amusement. "I have come this far with none the wiser. Of course, by the time you reach the shore, the tale will be out. Hurry now, and be about your civil duty."

Willows's bristling black moustache twitched in agitation. He could do nothing, for the crew was loyal. Until now he had kept to his cabin awaiting the moment of sailing, fearful of urging his authority on these men. Willows wet his lips and eyed the men pressing in on him warily.

"Over the side, my lads, and gently now. We would not have it said that our hospitality is lacking," Raoul rallied. "Ah yes, one thing more. Your boots, my captain. You'll find a fine pair lying on the beach."

One, two, three. The splashes counted off the deposits into the sea.

"Look sharp, lads, we had best be off before the din begins," Raoul shouted and leaped up on the pilot deck by the wheel. "Make fast that anchor and spread all sheets. We'll be needing every inch of it to take this rotten hull out to sea. Away and no dallying."

The men answered with laughter and scrambled to their posts, scaling the rigging and unfurling the remaining frayed canvas. Their captain was aboard, and there was no reluctance to do his bidding.

"Cap'n, it's a pure delight to see you," hailed Peckcum as he came to shake Raoul's hand. "We been afearin' the worst. Had us battened down tighter'n a ship in a storm. How did you manage to flee the gibbet, sir?"

"The deed of an angel of mercy," Raoul replied darkly as he stood with his face to the shore. Somewhere behind the town he had left his soul or, at least, all of it that mattered. "To your post, mate, or I'll deliver you over the side myself," he said tersely and tore his eyes from that dark hump of land.

* * *

A violent shock brought Gweneth to her senses as she was roughly deposited on what felt like a bed. Her eyes flew open, and fresh terror gripped her as she awoke to total blindness. The scream she pushed forth stayed in her throat. Her tongue was dry and clung to the roof of her mouth. She swallowed hard only to strain against the tight binding over her mouth. Caught and tied, where was she and who was there in the dark?

Low angry whispers wafted about her, and she struggled to sit but discovered her arms and legs were securely bound.

"You blundering idiot! I'd slit your throat if I had not need of you." That voice. It was her uncle. "You had best not bungle this business or I'll have your head, you scurvy spawn. I possess enough evidence against you to dangle you by the neck twice over."

A grumble of denial answered the virulent pronouncements, but it was lost in swearing.

"Here is your commission. The girl goes to Cairo and see to it that she is handled with care." Low harsh laughter deepened Gweneth's terror. "'Tis a sultan's gift you bear and, mind you, the price she'll bring will depend on her condition. I have promised to deliver an exceptional beauty. If she is put upon by you and your men, you'll answer to the new owner. The girl is worth her weight in gold, pure gold, and the coin is yours if you deliver her unscathed. Best keep her fit, for every ounce she loses will be so much less in your purse. Keep faith with me, and our long association will continue to both our profit." A ready oath of solemn pledges answered this bribe.

Gweneth cried out, but a mere squeak escaped the filthy rags as she twisted frantically within her bonds.

"The girl's awake," Gareth chuckled. "'Tis a pity, for I would have you gone by now. But, look you here, she is only one of those French maids to whom I generously offered the luxury of my household until she was caught thieving. She lies without a blush, and I would have strung her up had I not found her comely enough to pay an old debt. Heed not her lies, but deliver her quickly. The sultan shall receive you well and, who knows, if the chit pleases him, he may double the price. I go and you must cast off at once."

Gweneth rolled onto her side, but the ledge of the bed disappeared and she tumbled into oblivion.

CHAPTER SEVENTEEN

"Take it easy, missy. Easy there, I say," his high, thin voice pleaded as the cabin boy gingerly pushed the portal open. His wide brown eyes flitted uneasily about the darkened room, but nowhere was the lady to be seen.

"It just be Peter with yer supper," he ventured and stepped fearfully into the cabin. Many was the time since the voyage began a mere week ago that he had begged the captain to send another man to tend to this prisoner; but he had always been denied with the crude reminder that the boy's fourteen years were the skipper's best protection against the lady's virtue.

"She'd chew ye up and spit yer carcass to the four winds afore she'd allow a skinny stripling the likes o' ye to mount her," was one of the captain's lesser taunts.

The farthest thing from Peter's mind was the seduction of that beauteous lady, but he believed full well that she was capable of defending her honor against all takers. Did he not still bear the black eye from one of her well-aimed slippers? He faced the weeks looming ahead with the abysmal certainty that this was not his last badge for having braved the lioness's den. Why just this morning she had emptied a bowl of porridge on his head and then kicked both shins while he attempted to wipe his sodden face. Yes, sir, the lady was a wildcat.

Peter set his tray on the table and was reaching for the tinderbox when a figure shot from the corner near the door and sprinted up the steps. Peter let loose with a yelp and clamored up after her, but the lady had a head start he could not overcome.

Gweneth ran across the empty deck and headed for the railing, her long hair flying in the sea-freshened breeze. She had climbed the rigging to hoist herself overboard when one of the crew leaped on her and dragged her back.

Gweneth thrashed out with arms and legs, screaming to be let free, but the swarthy, bearded man's grasp only tightened about her waist as they reeled about the shifting deck.

"Let me go, let me go!" she wailed, kicking and clawing the man who held her.

An oath of astonishment issued from the seaman even before she sank her teeth into one of his dirty tar-blackened hands, and Gweneth's head snapped up to meet his bewildered dark gaze. The recognition was swift and certain, buckling her knees with the shock, and she slumped forward into his arms.

The man pulled Gweneth hard against his chest and whispered quickly into her ear. The words were all but inaudible, yet she knew he told her to swim for her life in familiar, intimate French. Stunned by his presence, she barely felt the stinging slap which sent her backward into the bulwark. The sailor came at her again but now she tore her terrified stare from the bearded face and, taking a firm grasp on the railing, swung herself over the side.

The water swallowed her completely, but Gweneth was swimming before she surfaced, holding the hastily gulped breath until the sea broke over her head and she could refill her lungs.

She shot one furtive glance over her shoulder as she treaded water. A crowd was gathering on the deck, and lanterns were being swung over the side to aid the cries for a search. She wriggled free of her gown, having doffed petticoats and shoes in anticipation of her flight, and struck off into the dark as the voices carried with frightful clarity on the water giving orders for the lowering of a boat.

The black water melted into the dark outline of land ahead, giving no hint of the distance to shore. Gweneth swam on, fighting the swells of an ebbing tide and straining an ear for the splash of swimmers. They would not find her easily once she left the meager light surrounding the ship, she told herself, and she could stay afloat for hours if they reached shore before her, swimming round the tip of the island if necessary. She had watched through the porthole as the ship came into the bay, noting as much detail of the land as possible. And when the ship dropped anchor just before nightfall, she made her plans.

The tepid water kept her from a chill, but in straining against the tide, her arms and legs began to tire. She was still sore and awkward from the beating meted out by her uncle, but there was no turning back from her course now. The salt water stung her eyes and made the back of her throat ache. An hour sooner and the tide would still have been with her, Gweneth thought bitterly, but came to the alert with the splash of a boat into the water.

She increased her stroke, but her limbs balked at the exertion, turning jellied with fatigue. Trapped. That was the word that had burrowed through her every waking thought since she regained consciousness. So close had she come to escape that she would rather drown than be captured again.

Voices, loud and wrathful, drew nearer, and lantern light sparkled the backs of the waves before her. Anxiety wrestled fatigue as Gweneth swung to the right, away from the craft gaining on her but also from the shelter of land. Closer and clearer came the sounds of her hunters till she could hear the scraping of metal on wood as the oars dipped rhythmically into the sea. Gweneth's flesh creeped with the nearness of those sounds and, in her thoughts, she saw them overtake and pluck her from the water.

The boat, when it passed, came within ten yards of her and Gweneth flipped below the surface with a kick. Yet the effort of breathing which plagued her brought her involuntarily to the surface more quickly than she wanted. The rasping sound of her own burning lungs filled her ears as they glutted their starved passages, and she was sure her stalkers would follow the noise to their prey. But, when she shook the sopping masses of hair from her eyes and turned a fearful stare on the sea, the boat had slipped beyond her and was heading straight for the shore. They were not hunting her in the water after all but planning to lie in wait on the beach where she would be helpless to fend them off.

A blubbering sob mingled with the briny water as Gweneth's anguish overcame her, and it seemed she could fill the harbor to overflowing with her disappointment. She knew she had lost. Still she swam on in the mindless toil to which there was no longer any purpose.

The minutes passed with excruciating languor, and Gweneth gulped and swallowed more and more of the bay. Her stomach turned queasy with spasms of rejection while her weariness sank her again and again. In the final moment of resignation the apparition of the grimy, beard-masked face rose through her draining senses. Those deeply saddened eyes were those of her brother.

Raoul set back his chair at the entrance of Peckcum. "We espied 'em, Cap'n, just like you predicted. You've more lives than a cat and the second sight o' a warlock. Bless me, I be thankin' me lucky stars I'll not be comin' up against you tonight," the first mate declared.

Raoul's eyes twinkled as he rose. "'Twas not only luck which brought us here. Good Captain Willows left behind a very detailed account of his past voyages when he so promptly took a bath in Carlisle Bay." He smacked the log lying open before him with the flat of his hand. "A most interesting history. The man is nigh to illiterate, but I've had little else to do this past week but study his records, and there is aplenty written on these pages to scuttle finer craft than he. But, see here, you are certain the ship you have sighted is the *Cyrene*?"

"Am I not to know me own home?" Peckcum asked indignantly and drew his broad frame up to its full height with a hitch of his breeches. "It's the *Cyrene* and none other. Like you figured, they disembarked after dark. Heavy laden they be, too. Must be some celebration they plan. It were enough to make me hanker after a slice of the spoils."

Raoul's shoulders shook in silent laughter. "Well, when this deed is accomplished, you shall not find my gratitude to be stingy. But now, to the business before us. Keep close watch with several men until their camp is laid for the night. Well into their revelry we shall pay a social call on Captain Willows, but not before the demon black rum has addled their heads and slowed their limbs."

"Aye, aye, Cap'n. I'm a lovin' the sound of it and itchin' for the sport," Peckcum replied and departed.

Raoul sat back and surveyed his quarters for the last time. With disgust he observed the floor and walls whitened by a thorough scrubbing of lye which had been Daniel's first task. The lingering putrid smell was now overlaid by the sharp sting of alkali, but the ragged bedding and heap of filthy clothes in one corner was a strong reminder of the wallow in which its owner had lived. Daniel had tossed what seemed to be a ton of rotting scraps of food, empty broken bottles, and other trash, including several rat carcasses, into the sea.

If cleanliness was next to godliness, then Willows ran true to form, for the pages of misspelled words delivered up to Raoul's intelligence a wealth of skulduggery. Smuggling, marauding, white slavery, and all other matter of underhanded piracy filled the thick volume. Even his cache, this island, was marked on a scrap of paper.

Raoul slammed the book shut in revulsion, wondering if Willows had yet realized the loss. Oh, he had left behind gold and silver in the strong box and a rope of fat creamy pearls whose clasp was studded with diamonds but, to Raoul's mind, the prize lay in the logbook.

He dug into his pocket and lay the heavy strand of pearls over one palm. He could afford gifts like this many times over now that he claimed the title of earl. But what was privilege when it had been won at such a cost? Did he yet forgive his father? No, that would take more time, but neither could he sit by the dying old man and not pledge that forgiveness. It was not the title and fortune that spurred his words. The title was an encumbrance, and he had proved to himself that he could succeed on his own. But, with his last words, his father had given him the one thing he never thought to own.

Still fortune's fool, he heeded his father's summons and returned home for the first time since his eighteenth year. And, in doing so, Raoul discovered bitter but, perhaps, redeeming truth. His father had a few hours left in this world, but he won back his son in some measure, for he told Raoul that he had, in truth, married his mother but that her parents had seen it annuled. It was the one thing he could never forgive her. The parting was painful, but to know that she would allow their love to be wiped away without protest was more than he could pardon. She never even told him of the child until it came time for her to send him to England, and he had struck out at the boy as his only means of punishing his lost love.

The boy was quick witted and grew strong and straight, yet none of his accomplishments ever elicited the loving response he strove for in his father. There grew respect and always there was a bit more than tolerance but, to a young boy deprived of maternal love, it fell far short of his expectations.

Then, in his twelfth year, Raoul was sent home from school for fighting. When his father learned the reason for it, he sat the boy down and calmly and completely broke his heart. Bastard, the boys at school had called him, and that was what his father confirmed.

Raoul's hand clenched over the pearls as he remembered how he struck his father that day and, though the blow must have hurt him, his father merely smiled tightly and said that the boy was well on his way to understanding that he must fight for his life and take what he would have from it.

All his attempts to run away were frustrated until his eighteenth year, and this time Raoul chose the sea; it was too broad a distance for even a father to span. But love eluded him even there and, when his wife betrayed him, Raoul stopped looking.

It was not until his father became ill did he realize that, in denying his son, he had lost more than he could ever regain. A sheaf of papers were signed on the deathbed, and his son became Lord Raoul Avernon, Earl of Mochton. If his father found peace in that hour, Raoul still searched in vain for his.

"Gweneth," Raoul murmured low in tortured memory of heavy burnished curls that filled his palms and slid effortlessly through his fingers. Something snapped in his hand, loosening from his grasp a shower of pearls which bounced and skipped across the deck and fell rolling across the boards. Raoul sprang up and reached down to scoop them from the floor, jamming them deep in his pocket.

"Confound it!" he muttered impatiently and passed a hand before his eyes as if to physically sweep Gweneth's vision aside. "She is behind me," he said when his arms fell limply to his sides. He must be realistic. There was his ship which he could and would have back. With the information in hand and money aplenty to cock the right ears in his direction, he would clear the slate and return to England, there to grapple with Gweneth's ghost until victory was his.

Late into the night, with starlight softened by wisps of pewter clouds to guide them, Raoul and a small band of men climbed the hill separating their harbor from Willows's cove. He halted at the top, and a tremble of delight sped through him at the sight of the *Cyrene*. The gale of three days ago had missed her, and he gave thanks in his heart, for the *Jamaica Rummer* had floundered badly in the midst of the storm, taking on water and nearly cracking her hull on the shallow inlet bottom. Raoul's stern insistence kept the crew from abandoning ship and seeking shelter on the island after she lost her foremast to a splintering crack of lightning and, miraculously, she stayed afloat to the end.

All eyes swung to the beach below where high ribaldry issued up from the throng of drunken sailors lounging about driftwood fires.

"I could use a bellyful o' that," Peckcum allowed, smacking his lips and pointing out the spit where a boar turned over the sputtering fire that lapped at the fatted juices. "They came well stocked. Might be a lesson there, Cap'n," he hinted with a roll of his eyes in the captain's direction.

"Were we to fill the hole with meat enough to tide you over a voyage, there'd be naught left over for cargo," Raoul answered softly lest his voice carry on the wind. He retreated a step and looked to where most of his crew had disappeared round the point of land separating the two ships. With muffled oars they were to sneak up on the *Cyrene* while Raoul dealt with Willows. He gave them a few minutes more and then plunged into the jungle thicket toward the shore.

Willows hoisted a keg above his head and lapped up the spirits falling freely upon his face and neck.

"E'gord, Cap'n, yer be fairly bathin' in good rum," commented a compatriot.

"Aye, laddie, and the taste was never sweeter on any man's tongue," he replied after sluicing a mouthful about his teeth and spitting a long drizzle on the ivory sand. He ran his tongue over his wet lips and wheeled about to peer into the jungle. A loose-lipped leer parted his mouth as a tempting idea wriggled its way into his soused brain. " 'Tis only the company o' a particular sort we come sorely deprived of," he said and belched. "There comes to mind, me fine lads, the vision o' the sweetest piece o' womanflesh I ever clamped eyes on, and she be just out o' sight," he continued, laying a stubby finger alongside his nose and squeezing shut an eye.

"Not the prisoner, Cap'n?"

"The very one, lad," he answered the cabin boy. He straightened up and tugged his weskit over his broad pouch. "The girlie must feel neglected, seein' us make merry while she lies alone. 'Tis a dire shame, that it be, and I figure the little kitten ought not be left out."

Willows had planned to wait for the dawn to begin his hunt, but now, if she hadn't drowned, which was in itself probable, he wanted her found and pressed tightly in his embrace. Dillingham's black heart could shrivel in hell for all he cared, Willows vowed, and took a long swill from the barrel. There'd be other maidens one place or another, and he'd swipe one in trade for the sultan. This bit o' petticoat was rightly his if he trapped her. A full belly, a slaked thirst, and a soft mount, all the pleasures of life in a single night. Now that was heaven!

" 'Tis the wench I want and to the man who finds her, I'm a mind to award him a tumble with the prize," Willows bellowed. "Mind ye, she's to be mine first."

The thunderous cry of a free-for-all rose from his men. They scattered like a disturbed hive of bees, swarming out in widening rays as the drunken horde surged up the beach and into the midnight-blackened underbrush.

Raoul's men paused at the edge of the beach, surprised that their approach had been detected so readily, but the shouts of the chase reaching their ears gave notice that the melee had begun for very different reasons. A tiny smile crept over Raoul's features. The ship was theirs for the taking and Willows would be none the wiser.

They held back until the camp cleared, then headed with weighted footsteps onto the sand. The men rowing for the *Cyrene* had sneaked up on the skeletal crew unawares, and Raoul paused as noise of the confrontation reached him. His luck of the past few days held. He needed simply to heave the two beached boats at the water's edge into the surf and join the rest of his men.

"Cap'n! Cap'n Bertrand, over here!" The explosive cry came from Peckcum, and Raoul swung round, straining his eyes to see the bulky figure of his first mate bent over a dark form at the shoreline. Peckcum dragged a body from the surf and flipped it over at Raoul's feet as he raced up.

"Dear Lord!" Raoul dropped to his knees in the shallow water swirling in around them. It soaked his breeches and billowed up the short chemise to completely expose the girl's body.

Time suspended its forward flow, coiling back on itself as he gazed at the once beautiful face and lustrous hair that now writhed about like inky strands of seaweed. The sea-jade eyes were plastered shut by long matted lashes, and below her shadowed face the once provocatively lush lips that he had often savored against her will were ghastly white and drawn with flecks of spume.

Sickening thuds hammered his chest as Raoul lowered a trembling hand to feel for a pulse along the curve of her jaw. It throbbed, weakly but steadily. Quickly he stripped off his coat and wrapped the nearly drowned girl in it, ordering Peckcum's coat from his back to finish clothing Gweneth's body from the curious stares of his crew.

"That be the French girl, Cap'n," Peckcum said as he tucked his coat under her hips and drew it down over her knees. "Blimey, Cap'n. What the devil is she doin' amongst this swine?"

"Shut up and get those boats launched," Raoul roared, his face a granite study in wrath as he met Peckcum's gaping countenance over the limp girl.

"Aye, Cap'n." He hoisted himself to his feet and sent the men scurrying over the sand while Raoul lifted Gweneth carefully into his arms and followed.

Peckcum's cries brought several of Willows's crew back to the beach, but even as they ran toward the thieves making off with their craft, Raoul's men yanked pistols from their belts and laid them out on the sand.

Raoul braced Gweneth's flaccid body between his knees to free his hands for rowing, but he was forced to abandon his chore in order to bend her head over the side as her retching began and she spit back into the sea a good deal of its contents.

"Easy, my lady. 'Tis good you rid yourself of the brine. Let it come," Raoul urged, but his softly spoken assurances were not answered, and Gweneth lay unconscious in his arms when the shudders quieted.

Raoul brushed the wet hair from her face, and a quiver of savage rage pierced his bowels at the sight of dark bruises on her face. He swore viciously under his breath, knowing full well the atrocities she must have suffered at the sadistic hands of Willows's crew. But how came she to be here? A spasm of pain crossed his features, for he knew intuitively that he must be responsible, that whatever had occurred had its cause in his escape. Not until he tasted blood did he realize that he had bitten through the inside of his lip to hold back the shivers of disgust threatening him.

A cry of "All secured, Cap'n" rang out as they

neared the *Cyrene*, and Raoul shouted back orders that any prisoners taken were to be held fast to await questioning. He must know who to blame for Gweneth's wretched condition, and then he would punish them all.

Gweneth trembled and stirred. Arms held her firmly, and even before her eyes opened, she knew she had been captured. "*Mon Dieu*, I should be dead," she moaned feebly and stiffened but made no effort to shrug off the arms enfolding her.

"Be easy, my lady. You are safe," Raoul whispered in French, and she relaxed against him saying. "*Oui*, Benoit. *Merci*."

Raoul's whole body jerked at her words. She thought him someone else and was comforted by that. He bent near her to speak his own name, but her lids fell shut and, to his dismay, one hand came up and rested quietly on his shirtfront.

"She be comin' round, Cap'n?" the first mate asked. "Aye, that's good news. Poor lass, beaten and ditched most likely. Damn, but there's a blackhearted bunch for you. I'm a mind they used the girl—"

"Stow it, Peckcum. You run on at your own hazard," Raoul muttered in that menacingly low voice his first mate knew always forwarded a foul temper. There'd be the devil to pay this night.

"Aye, Cap'n, I hear you," he replied respectfully and reached out for the rope being thrown from the ship.

All hands were aboard in a matter of minutes and hardly had Raoul planted both feet on the familiar deck than he commanded the anchor raised and the sails unfurled to catch what tide there was left.

Gweneth remained unaware of her surroundings or even of the man who held her, but she leaned against him as Raoul carried her to his quarters and she whispered in protest when he lay her gently on his bunk.

Daniel hurried in behind his captain but beat a hasty retreat when he was met by a volley of oaths.

Raoul stripped away the jackets and soaked chemise though Gweneth moved restlessly to prevent him. He poured a stiff measure of whiskey, stopped and gulped half of it, and then brought it to the bunk with an armful of blankets. Lifting her head, he poured it between her stiff blue lips and slapped her smartly on the back when most of it belched forth in choking.

"Drink," he commanded and forced another few swallows down her throat. The bruise on her cheek was less startling in better light and it would heal quickly, but there were other, older bruises ringing one eye in a greenish-yellow hue and several purplish weals marked her arms and shoulders. She had received severe punishment at someone's hands, and he vowed through profane rumblings to avenge her with ten lashes for every injury he discovered.

"Non, non! Please, I beg you!" Gweneth, roused to wakefulness by the feel of hands on her body, lashed out at the man hovering above her.

"Gweneth. 'Tis I, Raoul," the man said, and her hands were grasped tightly but kindly. "Be easy and know that no more harm shall come to you. You are safe with me."

Scalding hot tears obscured her vision before she could clearly divine the truth of his words, yet the voice was familiar and the sapphire eyes unforgettable.

Gweneth awakened, instantly alert, and jumped from the bed. A sky of dazzling cerulean greeted her sore eyes at the porthole. Gone was the island beyond the wide expanse of foam-flecked sea, and its absence left behind the shavings of a nightmare all too real.

She clutched her throat nervously and discovered the stiff lace-trimmed collar of one of Captain Bertrand's shirts. Her eyes swept down the length of her to the breeches tied about her waist with a sash. Too she was dimly aware that she no longer smelled of the ocean and that someone had braided her hair.

They could not wait to be on their way and deliver the prize before any more damage could be done, she thought bitterly. Well, sooner or later she would effect another escape, and this time the sea would claim her completely.

The roll of the ship left her sensitive stomach somewhere near her throat, and she prudently turned from the view to relieve the sour taste on her tongue with a drink. As she put the glass to her lips, the door swung open.

"Feeling better, I see. You really shouldn't be about yet, though it is a pleasure to behold you, mademoiselle," Raoul greeted as he stepped inside, closing the door. His step was brisk, but when he put out a hand to her, Gweneth shrank away and dropped the goblet.

"Do not fear me, Gweneth. I mean you no harm. My God, what are you doing here?" he asked, but his hand fell to his side as he watched her expression change from fear to astonishment to mistrust.

"I might know the same of you," she replied in a tone which sounded disapproving, for it was beyond reason that he should be here in other than her dreams.

" 'Tis my ship, and I have every right to her," he answered testily. Damn the luck, she did not seem overly pleased to see him, he thought. He stared at her pale calm countenance, noting that though she was some the worse for her ordeal, whatever had happened had not broken her, for the emerald eyes thrust at him a thousand questions and challenges.

"Come, my sweet, and let me tend your bruises," he said encouragingly, but when his hand touched her cheek, she backed away again.

"I—I need to take the air," she said uncertainly, edging toward the door. "I may be sick—oh, please!" she wailed and bolted past him.

When she reached the deck, her eyes darted everywhere until they came to rest on the man for whom she sought. Raoul hurried after her to see one of the prisoners on the foredeck rise to his feet at the sight of her. She gave a little cry of what seemed delight and ran with open arms toward the grimy sailor who stood forward.

The shock of her demonstration added fresh insult to his poor reception, but Raoul waved aside the guard who moved to prevent her from reaching the prisoner and ordered the man's chains struck. "Let them be," he directed, but a deep frown of aggravation pleated his brow as Gweneth fell headlong into the man's arms.

The man had been brought from below after Raoul boarded the *Cyrene*. He was the only one to ask if the invaders had discovered a girl on the island but, when pressed, remained stubbornly silent as to the reasons for his concern. He would answer with neither name nor information about himself or the girl but sighed in relief when told that she was safely on board.

"Benoit, Benoit, *mon amour!*" Gweneth cried breathlessly.

Raoul watched impassively as the tall dark seaman wrapped her in his eager embrace. "Look how she clings to him," he grumbled, and the gleam of her joyful tears forced a hard smile to his lips. In all the days and months he had known her, he had never seen such tender regard in her expression. By God, this man, Benoit, was the luckiest man alive. He wrenched his head away as the dark head bent to kiss Gweneth's radiant, upturned face and spun sharply on his heel. He would not torture himself by witnessing the action of these lovers.

"Benoit, *est-ce que c'est tu?*" Gweneth whispered as her fingers brushed over his tousled head and thin face.

"*Ma fille*, you are so big," Benoit teased in French, but the tremble in his voice underscored the return of her joy. He bent and kissed her cheeks, once, twice, three times before quickly brushing his lips over hers.

"You are alive, Benoit. You are perfectly, wonderfully alive," she cried, but when she dropped her hands to his shoulders to emphasize her statement, they became slick. "Oh Benoit, you are bleeding. You are injured!" She grabbed his arm and turned him around. The thin filthy shirt covering his back had been slashed repeatedly by the administration of a whip. "*Morbleu,* Benoit!"

The anguished voice brought Raoul around, and he flinched at the sight of the man's back, knowing how it must seem to her. He had seen the effects of the whip the night before but, as the man would offer no explanation, Raoul decided to let him suffer, thinking his discomfort might prompt him to a freer tongue. Now he gave rapid orders that sent Daniel scurrying for medicine and bandages before he came to assist Gweneth with her paramour.

Benoit's gentle expression hardened in anticipation as the captain approached him, and he stepped deliberately between his sister and the man in challenge.

Raoul slowed his step in response to this silent display of enmity but Gweneth took Benoit's hand and pulled him forward.

"Capitaine Bertrand," she greeted, "I have found him! This is my brother, Benoit." And she impulsively reached for his hand to bring it to Benoit's. The two men exchanged curious glances.

"Brother?" Raoul's frown faded. "Monsieur Valois, I am honored."

Benoit shook the proffered hand in bewilderment, searching his sister's face for some explanation. "The honor is mine, I believe, Capitaine, if you are responsible for saving my sister," he replied firmly but swayed unsteadily when the captain released his hand.

Raoul put a hand under his elbow, saying, "Monsieur, there will be plenty of time for amenities once your wounds are dressed." His gaze shifted to Gweneth's doubtful look. "This is none of my handiwork, mademoiselle. He shall be fine, I promise you. Ah, here is Daniel. He will see to the necessities."

"*Merci*, Capitaine," Benoit said graciously. "You will forgive me if I am somewhat confused." He turned to Gweneth. "I was not certain that you had recognized me last night." He touched his scraggly beard. "I knew there was a woman aboard, but I had not known it was you. Then last night when I caught you in my arms, I saw your face reflected in the moonlight. *C'est incredible!* I must be mad, I thought, but it was you. And such a beautiful sight, *soeur*." A smile crinkled his weathered skin. "Unfortunately Capitaine Willows saw you get away from me, hence my stripes," he shrugged.

"But, you should have told them who I was, that we are—"

"Gweneth, do you really think that would have spared me?" Benoit shook his head. "Non, more likely my throat would have been slit before I was tumbled overboard. They would not have wanted any witnesses to the business of that ship, particularly by a member of your family. Someone paid a great deal to make certain you reached your destination unharmed. There was talk, you understand. Capitaine Willows himself feared to go near you." Benoit paused, taking in for the first time with full understanding her battered condition. His fingers curled about her chin, tilting her head back for better light. "I hardly touched you," he murmured with a frown. "Who did this? If Willows so much as—"

"Non, non. It is not what you think," Gweneth quickly broke in with a fleeting glance of embarrassment at the captain. "I will explain everything later only, please come . . ."

"Yes, monsieur," Raoul interrupted gently. "Let Daniel take both of you below." His glance shifted to Gweneth with an enigmatic look. "You may be needed to help, but I should like a word with you when you have a moment." He bowed and left them.

For nearly an hour Daniel and Gweneth worked on Benoit's back, applying ointment and bandages before he stretched out on his stomach to rest. When they were alone, Gweneth sat down and held his hand while she told Benoit of the fates of his brothers and sister. When that was done, Benoit put many questions of his own to her.

"This Capitaine Bertrand, you are certain that we may trust him?" Benoit asked at length.

Gweneth shifted uneasily and looked away from his penetrating gaze. She was not yet ready to explain this particular association. " 'Tis a long story, Benoit. He saved Renée's life and mine when Adolphe was lost, as I have said. There is no need to say more now. I believe him trustworthy."

"Yet he calls you by your given name, and he is English, is he not?" he questioned. The words seemed ones of accusation, and Gweneth's look was instantly guarded.

"I do not see that one has anything to do with the other. We are something less than friends if it comes to that. Had he not been the swaggering, arrogant braggart he is, then none of this—"

"Enough, Gweneth, enough," Benoit interrupted wearily. "I can see that your jade eyes still turn to emerald when you are excited. The story of your capitaine can wait, for it is obvious that you harbor as much feeling for this man as he does for you."

Gweneth jumped as if stung. "Whatever makes you say such a thing?"

Benoit arched a brow. "He saved your life a second time, did he not? Do you not feel that is proof sufficient?" A warming tingle of affection stirred Gweneth as she received his smile.

"Now go and thank him for both of us. I am tired, but you may wish to warn him that you now have a protector on board who will see to it that he brings you to the altar quickly."

Gweneth sprang to her feet, a fist poised on each

hip. "I do not need nor do I desire to see Capitaine Bertrand brought to the altar for my sake. You are very much mistaken if you think I possess even the tiniest bit of tender affection for that—that Englishman!" Her brother's indulgent laughter shamed the color a deeper shade in her cheeks as she realized that she had protested much too much.

"Ah, *ma fille*, you have not changed. *Mais oui*, you are more beautiful and intractable than ever. I can see you have sorely missed the steadying influence of three older brothers." He smiled still, but his voice broke over the last words, and Gweneth was instantly on her knees by his side.

"Oh Benoit, I am a thoughtless idiot. We must not quarrel. I am so glad to see you. I had thought you dead for so long." She lay a comforting hand on his bearded cheek. "Close your eyes and sleep. I will come back soon."

CHAPTER EIGHTEEN

Raoul paced the deck, his thoughts centered a few feet below where Gweneth was closeted with her brother.

"Brother," Raoul said aloud and found an unsought smile tugging his mouth. He had not believed the extent of his jealousy when she had flown heedlessly into another man's arm. It was more than that of a rival favored. She had been so blasted reserved and unimpressed by his own presence, as though she had granted him a favor in saving her, as though she had expected him! Damn her conceit! Had she known that he could not forget her in spite of all? Had she read him more clearly than he had read himself?

Raoul pushed a careless hand through his hair. He had hardly been able to bear the thought of her in another man's arms. And all these days he had been like one insane, thinking her in the merciless hands of her uncle. And a right concern it proved. Now that the prisoners feared no retribution, they were more than willing to claim that the girl had not been kidnapped but sold, sold by her own flesh and blood.

Daniel looked up at the captain as a stream of the bluest oaths he'd heard in many a day poured from the man's lips. Chuckling to himself, Daniel wagged his head. "That little French dolly has got him by the throat. I do hope she will be charitable." But even as he spoke, Gweneth appeared, and she looked anything but merciful. In fact she looked mad enough to barrel down on the poor captain and blast him broadside out of the water. This was going to be too good to be missed, and Daniel intentionally spilled his load so that he might lag about a minute or two longer.

Daniel doffed his cap as she passed. "Good day, missy. Glad to have you aboard."

Gweneth paused before her old friend and held out both hands which he readily accepted after a hasty wipe of his own on his breeches. "Monsieur Daniel, *mon ami*. You are well, I trust?" She smiled, and Daniel basked in the glow.

"I be fine, missy, but I do worry about the cap'n," he said quite seriously. Perhaps he could soften her attitude a tat.

"*Vraiment?* Why, whatever ails him?" she asked scornfully. "He seems the same strutting peacock he ever was." Her eyes went up to where he stood scowling down at her, and she knew the captain had heard her. Straightening under his appraisal, she sought Daniel's attention. "What is this great distress, Daniel?" she whispered.

"You, missy," he replied softly with a grin and bent before her startled expression to scrupulously set his spill aright.

Gweneth turned to the captain but saw that he had given her his back. Seized by an undeniable urge, she leaned forward and stuck out her tongue at that imperious figure. The answering laughter was totally unexpected since she had not noticed the two seamen beyond the captain staring at her. She hurried forward, head bent, before Raoul spun around.

He came to stand by the steps and offered Gweneth his hand in assistance as she climbed up to him, but she held it so short a time that she nearly fell backward when the ship dipped into the back side of a swell.

Raoul grabbed for her, his grip digging into her upper arms. "Silly fool! Would you dash your brains out rather than have me touch you?" he grumbled but dropped his hands as though she burned him.

Gweneth felt sillier than ever but could not force a thank you to her lips. Instead she rubbed her arms. It was some moments before she could think of anything to say, for he stood staring down at her with murderous intensity.

"My brother is resting well. I thank you for that, Capitaine Bertrand," she managed at last.

Raoul grunted noncommittally. "And have you been filling his ear with a complete defamation of my character?"

"What makes you think I would care to speak of you to my brother?" She looked away from his skeptical expression and down at her hands. "I have thought him dead these two years. It was more important that he learn of the loss of our father and Adolphe and Phillip. Besides Benoit has formed his own opinion of you quite without my help." She shot him a defiant glance.

"Really? And what does he think of me?" Raoul questioned with a mocking tone, but it had suddenly become important that he should know the opinion. As ally or adversary, Monsieur Valois lay between them.

She took a step from the captain's side. "He thinks you are a brave man, a hero, if you will." A grunt of cynicism answered her. "Oh yes, his words to you were that you should be warned that I now have a protector on board and that—" Her memory got ahead of her tongue, and she could not finish the declaration.

"Yes, mademoiselle? Surely there is more." A glint of derisive humor in his marine-blue eyes accompanied his urgings.

"Benoit does not understand our situation, and the rest is better left unsaid," she owned reluctantly. If her feelings were so obvious to Benoit, how much more readily might the man of her desire recognize them.

"Then, perhaps, you will explain to me how you

came to be aboard the *Cyrene*. I had expected difficulties but nothing so controversial as your own sweet self."

Gweneth shaded her eyes against the sun with a hand as she looked up into Raoul's grinning face. "So, you did not know I was aboard. That explains your gallant attempt. More piracy, mon Capitaine?" She hated the spitefulness in her voice, but his nearness brought forth all her antagonism. He did not want her. And, if she could not fly into his arms with a shower of kisses as she ached to do, then she would thrust him into the role of opponent to save her sanity.

Amazingly he did not rise to the taunt. "I would not have left you behind had I ever suspected that—that scrap of filth Dillingham would take his rage out on you!" The viciousness of his words surprised her.

"I suppose that is my fault too," she replied defensively, thinking his anger must in some part reflect on her mishandling of the deed. "Benoit and I suffer from the same affliction. We trusted where there was no faith to be had."

She told him what Benoit had related of his surprise release within sight of Madame Guillotine two years before. He had been swept up in the riotous crowds which stormed the tumbrels on that particular day. They had wanted one of the prisoners for their own pleasure, and he was freed in the melee. Shelter was afforded first in the overgrown banks of the roadsides and then in various barns and lofts now empty while the once prosperous fields lay dormant. Like Adolphe his thoughts and actions were aimed at conducting his sisters to freedom, but, unlike the more relaxed days of the recent year, Benoit could find no help. He hired himself out as a seaman, intending to smuggle Gweneth and Renée aboard when he could. But his plans fell to nothing when he was drugged one night and awakened aboard the *Jamaica Rummer* to discover that he had been shanghaied. And so he remained till now.

"You see, he trusted the devil's own, and, like me, he was betrayed," she explained softly. "The governor found me abroad in the house only minutes after you had gone. At first he believed my lies, but he became most angry when he realized that I had tricked him into delaying his search too long."

She touched her swollen cheek gingerly and grimaced. "Mercifully I was so weak from my illness that I fainted before . . ." She sighed and dropped her hand. "Your freedom shall be short lived, I fear. It will bode ill for you because of me," she announced with a direct look at Raoul.

"Not to worry, *ma belle*. Nothing has gone as planned since the very first time I fished you from the sea. But I wish you would alter the circumstances of our rendezvous after this. You make a most provocative sea nymph, but you nearly drowned, my sweet," he teased. "But do go on. It was Dillingham who beat you?" The smile turned down in displeasure.

"*Oui*, Capitaine, but I do not blame you. Never that! He has hated me from the first. I see that now, but I do not know why. 'Marry Myers, marry Myers,' it was all he said to me for months. So much seemed to depend on it. When he found me with you," she said unsteadily, "Myers revoked his proposal, and I must suppose he sought to punish me through you."

Gweneth's hand closed convulsively on Raoul's sleeve, and she looked deeply into his eyes. "I did not tell him that pack of lies which brought you to trial. You must believe that."

Raoul heard her words and believed, but his heart had begun to pound when her fingers curled tightly on his arm, and he could not trust himself to reply lightly. Gweneth saw this hesitancy as reluctance to give his pardon and, releasing him, turned to study the distant reach of the water.

"The day is so beautiful. I never thought to see another like it," she murmured to herself. In a louder voice she said, "Before I conceived the idea of escape,

I thought of suicide." She stared down at the series of scratches crisscrossing the pulse of each wrist. "*Eh bien*, I find I am a coward."

"Gweneth, do not!" he ordered brusquely and covered the telltale marks with his fingers. The anger in his voice was overlaid with concern. "I would have come after you had I known what was to be done to you." He paused, and when he spoke again, his voice was mellowed with good humor. "I still owe you, *ma belle*, for you have saved my life twice. I hope you will give me no cause to find the debt owing once more."

Gweneth gazed down at the strong brown hands clasped over her wrists and hoped that he could not feel the racing of her pulse. But he did feel the quickening beneath his fingers and, before either of them was aware of it, she had turned into his arms. "None of it matters any longer, Gweneth. You are safe. I have my ship, and Benoit lives. It is truly a beautiful day." He put a hand under her chin and lifted her face to his, tracing the bruises with his thumb.

Gweneth gave up to the gentle pressure of his lips, but the pleasure of it was sweet misery for she knew he meant only to comfort her.

Raoul was startled when she suddenly bolted from him, but he did not follow her. She had betrayed enough of her feelings in her kiss that he was satisfied to let her go for now.

He turned to the men nearby and ordered full canvas. There was the little matter of an account to be settled in Barbados.

The men snapped to attention at his command, but the pleasant expression on his face was not lost on them. The captain had won his lady back, and their lives were bound to be a great deal easier because of it.

"*Ma pauvre petite*. Of all the men in the world, trust my sister to fall in love with a profligate," Benoit said in exasperation.

"I did not say I loved him," Gweneth protested.

"Did you need to, *ma fille?* It is written in your eyes, your tears." He beckoned to her from the bed and drew her into the curve of his arm.

They had talked often in the past three days while Benoit recovered. He was on his feet now and could even stand the friction of a shirt over his dressing. Gweneth had been reluctant to confide in her brother, but they had soon fallen back into the pattern of their childhood, and little by little she told him everything.

"There is but one thing to be done," and Benoit smiled. "We must—"

The knock was followed by a hail of greeting. "Come in, Capitaine," Benoit replied with a wink at Gweneth. "*C'est très bon.*" He rubbed his hands together as he walked toward the opening door.

Gweneth's eyes followed her brother. His shoulders were stiff, but his stride was long and graceful. He had lost the slender supple figure of a fencing master, but the long hard muscles cabling his arms and back displayed a strength he had never before possessed. The beard was gone, and she could not refrain from commenting on the pale jawline below his walnut-stained brow and cheeks. "A half-baked loaf of bread, you are," she teased.

Raoul entered, his figure neatly dressed in formal attire, and Daniel followed laden with trays. "I bring dinner in hopes of sharing your table, monsieur. Mademoiselle," he said warmly with a special smile for Gweneth who had risen at his entrance. She put a self-conscious hand to her hair and wished for a gown instead of the captain's shirt and breeches.

"You are more than welcome, Capitaine. My sister and I had just spoken of you. Be seated, by all means. What have we here?" Benoit asked and peeked under one napkin as Daniel set the table.

Gweneth hardly touched her plate, for the captain's

presence and his frequent long looks across the table made her uncomfortably aware of Benoit's recent observations. He was more than alive, she thought. Her every breath seemed to be drawn from his. Even the clothes on her back would seem to caress her with the knowledge that they had once draped his masculine frame. He will consume me, she thought wildly and edged her chair a little closer to her brother's.

"The best meal of my life," Benoit declared as he broke the silence which had hung over the meal.

"You were ravenous, Benoit. Have you been starved?"

"Nearly so, little one, but that is of no import. Now, Capitaine, if you will permit, I have certain questions to put to you," Benoit said as he leaned forward over the table. "Gweneth has told me all, and I should like to have your version."

Raoul shot Gweneth a glance that made her shiver. "She has told you all, you say. Then did she tell you that I have treated her both callously and dishonorably and that she most likely detests the sight of me?"

Benoit made an impatient gesture. "This antagonism between you is not my concern but, if what she tells me is true, you have a great deal for which to answer."

"Perhaps," Raoul replied offhandedly as he continued to trace imaginary circles on the tabletop with the tip of his knife. "I am at your disposal should you wish to settle the grievance."

"Do not be absurd!" Gweneth cried and rose to her feet. "Your flippant attitude has—"

"Sit down, Gweneth," Benoit demanded and reached out to tug her into her chair. "I can speak for myself. Capitaine, my sister's life has been threatened, she has been beaten and her reputation—" he snapped his fingers—"it is nonexistent. You are a fugitive from the law, and she is to blame for that." Gweneth groaned impatiently, but Benoit kept her silent with a look of annoyance. "Some of these things will require time to right. But, in your case, at least, I can offer a rapid solution. Marry her, Capitaine, and you are a free man."

"Marry?" The sharp breath of astonishment issued from Gweneth as she turned a horrified stare on her brother. "Are you mad?"

Raoul glanced at her and smiled briefly. "You have not yet put this to your sister, I see. It may be that she prefers another man. In fact I am certain of it since she has offered him all the benefits of a wife without yet securing the title."

"What is this, *soeur?*" Benoit asked harshly.

"I—I cannot think what the capitaine means," she stammered. He was toying with her again, and this time with her brother as the audience. She raised a scathing glance to Raoul. "You love the jest, monsieur, a fact that I can attest to most knowledgeably but, I beg you, do not make a mockery of me before my brother."

"It was not intended as a jest, mademoiselle. Your brother would have come to know in time. All of Barbados is aware that you are a maiden no longer. Such evidence was brought forth at my trial by a physician. After your conduct in Tortola, it was not hard to guess the rest," Raoul answered with a sharp edge to his voice, but he looked from Gweneth's frozen stare with the thought that perhaps he should not have chosen to throw his rival's shadow across the proceeding. Instead he finished his explanation for Benoit. "The man's name is Lavasseur. I know him well and am certain that he can be persuaded to marry your sister. Her affections are his. So you see, your suggestion does not signify."

That the discussion was decidedly distasteful to the captain both the Valoises understood, but only one realized why.

"This man, Lavasseur, you love him, Gweneth?" Benoit asked quietly.

"Must we speak of this before *him?*" she cried in

frustration. "I will answer nothing but to say that he was not my lover." And she sought Benoit's eye with a silent plea that he would say no more.

"Then you are free to marry Captain Bertrand and rescue him from the gallows," Benoit persisted logically. "It is so obvious a solution that I do not understand that you two had not thought of it yourselves." He shook his head in bafflement.

"I have never been asked," she muttered through clenched teeth, wishing this disastrous audience would end. Could her brother not see that his assumptions were totally in error?

"Is that all, *ma belle?*" Raoul questioned with irony. "That is simply arranged." He rose to round the table and pulled her from her chair.

Clasping both her hands determinedly over his heart, Raoul bent close to her saying, "Mademoiselle, this poor pitiable wretch of a man looks to you with a pure and simple heart, to bind the wounds of misfortune which have occasioned his life to be held forfeit to the hangman's knot. Spare him that horrendous fate by answering in the affirmative that you will bless his humble existence with your companionship for this, the rest of our lives."

"Capitaine, this is unworthy of you. Do not do this!" Gweneth angrily snatched her hands from his.

"Perhaps a few moments alone," Benoit suggested and was through the door even as Gweneth called him back.

"Now," Raoul said unpleasantly as he turned back to her. "I know you care very little for me, but it would greatly enhance my chances of reversing the sentence against me if you would marry me. I am not your choice, that I understand plainly, but it would answer your slim hopes of finding a husband should Lavasseur not be amenable."

Gweneth returned his glare with equal enmity. "Capitaine, this will not serve. You care nothing for me, and I cannot imagine a more horrible fate than for a woman to be trapped in a loveless marriage. Surely we can find another solution." She marched to the door and swung it open. "I bid you *bonne nuit.*"

But she had not reckoned with her brother, and for most of the night, he pleaded his case. First reasonably, even cajolingly, then stormily and demandingly until she finally broke under his badgering and gave up to tears.

"Ah, Gweneth," he said sympathetically. "You love him. Admit it. What better reason can there be for you to say yes?"

"He does not feel the same for me, and I am too proud to have him on any terms but those," she objected mournfully.

"Too proud. *Mon Dieu,* you are that! But listen to me, you difficult girl. He has feelings for you. Did you not see how his eyes kindled with interest when I put the subject to him? Everything you have said of him leads me to believe that he would not feel fettered by the contract between you." His black eyes gleamed impishly. "You are beautiful. What man could resist you if you plied those womanly charms to their fullest? *Ma fôi,* you should be able to tame that proud arrogance of his with a lingering kiss or two."

"Benoit!" Gweneth cried in embarrassment. "How dare you say such things to me. Why, you are little better than he with your indelicate assumptions."

"Be honest, Gweneth. You would have it so. I would not counsel you thus if that were not true. And the capitaine? He pants for you. He is willing to have you. *Vraiment,* may have you in spite of me. He has given me sufficient reason to call him out before this. Marry him, Gweneth. It is best."

"He believes me to have been another's mistress."

"Then tell him it is he you love."

"Non!"

"Then I shall."

"You would not dare!"

"Then simply prove it on your wedding night. A

man must believe his own eyes. I'll not force you. *Enfin*, I could not. But if you do not marry him now, you will have lost him forever," Benoit advised gently.

Gweneth closed her eyes and drew a long breath. The desire to belong to Raoul, to share his bed, had tortured her for so long that her whole being quivered at the thought. To be his, ah yes, that is what she wanted with desperate certainty.

With a slowly nodding head, she said, "I relent, Benoit. I hope to God that this is not the final folly of my life."

For reasons other than her lack of proper clothes, Gweneth never ventured beyond the door. The captain often joined her for meals, but she never addressed him and spoke only when questioned directly. He did not make mention of the betrothal, as if the fact were of no import. If he would speak one word of tender feeling, she told herself, she would pour out her heart and give voice to all those emotions which made a maze of her mind and kept her from sleep as long as she heard his voice above her in the night or his footsteps as he prowled the deck till dawn. Yet it never came. His scowls increased until, by the time they reached their destination, she was frantic with the desire to cry halt to the entire affair.

Raoul saw only the once proud, defiant girl he reveled in contesting now subdued as if her very nature had altered. The blue crescents beneath her eyes darkened with each day, and her helpless fear at the sight of him marked how great her misery was.

His own temper burned within an eyelash of detonation, and more than once he punished a man with the abandoned fury he could not heap upon his rival. "'Tis Lavasseur she pines for, by thunder. Lavasseur with his honeyed tongue and courtly manner."

Increasingly the memory of Gweneth's scantily clad body in Lavasseur's bed crept back into his mind. Had they tricked him in Tortola? Were they lovers even then? Or had— Bah, there was no comfort in those speculations. That she had accepted his love was enough. Damnation, too much!

From blinded wrath to morbid remorse, he wrestled the jealous demon with taunting green eyes, Gweneth's eyes. At long last, the day of docking, he took firm control of himself and swore not to touch his bride until she felt bound to honor their marriage ties. Once the words were spoken and she was his, at his leisure he would destroy her defenses one by one until she asked, nay, begged for his love and Lavasseur was a neglected memory.

Gweneth twisted the braided rope of gold round and round the third finger of her left hand. It was heavy, of ancient design, and it seemed to strangle her finger to numbness. Yet it was actually much too large, and she kept impatiently sliding it back toward her palm with her thumb.

"My mother's ring," Raoul had informed her under his breath when he plucked it from his pocket during the ceremony. Gweneth's gaze swerved up from under the corner of her lashes with a look of disbelief, but the padre had continued to murmur the words of the service in Spanish and she had kept silent.

She understood nothing but the ritual as she repeated her vows parrot fashion, and she began to suspect Raoul's motives in choosing a place where the language was unintelligible to her. At least it was a Catholic service, and that the captain had chosen such was surprising. Why, he could have performed the ceremony himself aboard his ship with Benoit as proxy groom. But no, he needed witnesses, and a priest would record the marriage in the church documents, she reminded herself. He was only protecting himself. And the brief joy she had known in marrying before the eyes of God vanished.

There was a series of surprises that morning, not the least being that she had not, in fact, married Captain Bertrand but Lord Avernon, earl of Mochton.

"One of the many delights this marriage has in store for you, *ma belle*, for you shall become a countess when the hour is out," Raoul replied when she balked at his signature to the marriage contract.

Gweneth stirred and looked up from her hands to the man across from her. He was dressed just as he had been the night of her betrothal ball. The velvet coat fit the broad shoulders precisely and the froths of lace at his throat and wrists were spotless. She grimaced at the drabness of her own attire. Thoroughly French in her love of clothes, it was depressing to know he outshone her. She had to fashion her own wedding gown from a bolt of navy linen which she was given by the captain some days before. She had borrowed a length of lace from one of his shirts but the effect was very uncertain. "Quaker," Benoit had pronounced the results. Well, at least her injuries had healed, and her face had returned to its natural shape and color.

"We leave at once," Raoul declared, breaking in on her thoughts, and Gweneth met his eyes for the first time that day. Not even when he had kissed her so heartily that the sound of it reverberated through the tiny stucco church had she given him more than a glancing flicker of acknowledgment.

"The ceremony has made you safe enough, sweet wife, but I remain an outlaw, and I do not want to be trapped in the bay by a British frigate. On the sea, our chance of eluding them is much greater." He grinned broadly, eyes wide in speculative humor, then turned from her to gaze at the horizon. Wife. Yes, he liked the sound of that.

A whirl of gulls cartwheeled about the tall spindly masts of the *Cyrene*, but Gweneth looked neither to them nor to the sea beyond as Benoit helped her from the carriage. The tiny port on the coast of Venezuela was safe for the moment, but to delay for even a night would be foolish, Benoit explained.

Gweneth stepped down reluctantly and bit her lip

in vexation. She would have liked nothing more than a decent meal and a properly anchored bed which did not pitch and roll to the rhythm of the ocean, but not even that bit of comfort would she be allowed.

"*Mon Dieu*, Gweneth. Have you some malady?" Benoit asked when she had come to stand within the protective circle of his cloak as it began to rain.

"*Non*. It is only that I am far from certain that this marriage was a good thing." She sighed and turned her eyes to the retreating figure of Raoul. "He is not pleased with me. *Quant à ça*, the capitaine, too, appears to regret the decision."

"You have given him very little reason to feel otherwise. One would think you were seeing him off to the gallows. This fault you may readily amend tonight," he reproached but with a chuckle.

Gweneth shook off his arm with an annoyed shrug. "Men! Is there nothing else you think of?" The chuckle became laughter and her scowl increased. "*Eh bien*, I hope the capitaine has no such illusions. The alliance of convenience holds no such bargain with it." Her slender shoulders lifted eloquently as she flounced away toward the ship.

"A word with you, madame," Raoul called when she had boarded the vessel and turned abruptly away as he came near. "A word now, my wife, and in my cabin." He detained her with a hand on her arm, saying, "Unless you would prefer to entertain my men with our first proper acquaintance as husband and wife."

The blood flared in Gweneth's cheeks, for he had spoken loud enough for those nearby to hear, and a rumble of whispered words and snorts followed.

"Damn, you'd think he ain't mounted that little filly afore," laughed one seaman with a poke at another's ribs. "Moreover, though she may be a sweet bit o' flesh, I wonder what treasures lie beneath them petticoats that the cap'n can't wait to tumble her on her arse and toss them over her head?"

A moaning wail of despair erupted from her throat as she swung round, slamming with full force against Raoul's chest before she pushed past him. Head tucked to her chest and arms curled over her ears, she ran blindly from the sound of further words.

But hear them she did. The loud whack of muscle on bone and then the hollow thud as a body met the deck reached her ears almost at once.

" 'Tis my wife you speak of!" Raoul thundered with such ill-tempered wrath that Gweneth halted her flight. "And, if any one of you dares look upon her again without the utmost respect, I'll quarter him with my bare hands and feed his entrails to the sharks!" He hoisted the fallen seaman by his belt and tossed him over the side. "All hands, to posts. Prepare to cast off."

With a fleeting look of anguish at Benoit who had come to her side, Gweneth brushed past him and left the deck.

Raoul chafed his scraped knuckles with the palm of his hand as he entered the cabin behind her. His face was lined with displeasure, stirred by his own ill-chosen words before his men and the fact that she had been subjected to their brutally crude reaction. Slowly he walked over and took her trembling frame in his arms for, though he could not see her tears, he knew she wept.

"A damn foolish business, Gweneth. I apologize. A ship is not a gentlemen's salon, but you shall hear no more of that, I swear it," he crooned into her hair. She twisted out of his arms, her cinnamon hair flying back from her face as her head snapped up to meet his.

"Perhaps I shall not hear it, Capitaine, but I shall always know what they are thinking, *n'est-ce pas?* I am no better in their eyes than any of a dozen harlots you have bedded before," she spat at him, her sea-flecked eyes agleam with tears. " 'Tis a whore I am to them, thanks to you, and 'tis a whore I shall remain."

"Gweneth, Gweneth, it does not matter. They will

keep a good distance. I know you are a lady," he answered with arms outstretched to bring her back.

"Do you? Do you really when you so readily admitted to my brother that you believe me to have been Lavasseur's woman? I wonder that you do not offer your crew a chance to share your 'treasure.' Surely they are entitled to a cut of all your profit at sea."

"My God! Do you think me so foul a rogue?" he hissed, for she had pricked the one sore spot in his joy at having wed her. "You are mine now, and Lavasseur had never dare so much as smile in your direction if you should meet again, or I'll offer him the same I would any man." He grabbed her by the arms and jerked her to his chest. "You forget that man, I demand it!"

Gweneth shuddered at the violence in his voice, afraid to speak, and his arms tightened about her as he bent in search of her mouth through the veil of her hair. A shiver spread through her as his lips touched hers, brushed over them to sweep away the tendrils of hair, then greedily fastened on them, pressing and nibbling with his teeth.

Kiss upon kiss he forced on her full, unresisting mouth until the heat of his passion urged him to forget his vow of patience. He hooked the tip of his boot about the leg of a nearby chair and dragged it under him without releasing her mouth.

"Please . . . oh please," she begged, but his artfully wrought embraces were fast melting her resolve to hold separate from him.

"Be still," he muttered against her lips and sat down, drawing her into his lap. His fingers searched the front of her gown, and when it opened to his hand, they slipped inside the bodice to find the full curve of softness they sought.

"You are so lovely," he murmured in a long husky sigh. "The very sight of you is a sore ache in my loins. Ah, Gweneth, it has been a long time in coming, this hour," and he lowered his head to salute that tender swelling of flesh with a kiss. His voice broke the spell holding her entranced with the seductive enticement of his caresses. Not one word of love had he spoken. She gave his ear a vicious yank and jumped from his lap when, in his momentary surprise, he released her.

"Always your pleasures, monsieur!" she raged at him, unaware that her open gown revealed his plunder. "Always it is 'my need, my desire.' May the aching in your loins seize you with such excruciating pain that your—your manhood shrivels with the agony and ceases to give you either pleasure or torment!"

When he did not respond but sat gaping with eyes held below hers, Gweneth looked down. With a groan of exasperation, she roughly jerked the bodice together, fumbling the buttons closed with anger-cramped fingers.

Raoul licked his lips and crossed his arms over his chest, stifling the need to rip the gown from her and take what belonged to him. "Why must you forever fight me, *ma belle*? You want me. Both of us are aware of it. You are fully woman and the passion which frightens you could give you such rapture. Why, the mere brush of my lips upon your skin leaves you sobbing for more. You are my wife, Gweneth. Let me service you as is my right."

She put up both hands in denial. "Yes, we are married. You have the papers in your possession to secure your freedom so this '*marriage de convenence*' has been fulfilled. Now you have had your little game of pleasure with me. If you require more, *eh bien*, search out some *chère-amie* to satisfy your lust for I'll not bear a brat of yours, sired in a moment of carnal intrigue." When the last button was affixed, she reached out, grabbed a tankard of ale, and sent it at his head, delivering him a glancing blow. *"Libertin!"* she shouted and escaped through the door.

Raoul sat a space of seconds in silence, then threw back his head in laughter. "The devilish vixen," he declared at length. "She will know the full strength of my manhood one day soon." It was enough for now that she trembled with delight at his caress. Raoul frowned. What had he said this time to spark her displeasure? Mayhaps the lady was more shy than he thought, and his vow of passionate yearning unsettled her. No matter. On the next occasion there need not be words. Nay, only a night of long breathless kisses, sweet yielding flesh, and roistering climaxes as he joined her body to his.

"You shall desire me, lady. Aye, indeed, you do already. How can I not know it when your eyes meet mine with such taunting dares?"

She had broken from her shell of silence with a hurricane's turbulence of feeling, and he would not allow her to enter it again.

CHAPTER NINETEEN

Benoit threw up his hands in disgust and marched away from the rail, leaving Gweneth to her stubborn, childish pout. "Let her stew," he muttered angrily, for all his arguments met with the same cold rejection.

The days had stretched to the full string of a week, and nothing had changed. Gweneth glared at the captain in icy fury, never allowing by any word or sign that her temper had lessened.

The days were balmy and clear, the sea of smooth and even temper, but the air aboard ship was charged with thunderous portent. Even the noonday watch went about their tasks in hushed voices. No song or lazy laughter lightened the hour, though a few grumbles were heard.

"A man ain't even free to take a leak with the missus about," one man complained.

"More agitating is this wretched garb that chafes and binds a man. I'd be stripped to me skin ifin' it not be for the company o' the fairer sex."

"Belay that, seaman," Peckcum ordered and shoved the man along. "Best keep out o' the lady's sight. The cap'n don't appreciate so many greedy eyes on his wife."

"Wife?" the seaman snickered, but he choked on his next words as a meaty fist forced them back.

"Like I'm tellin' ye, keep them eyes of yer's lowered," the first mate advised.

Raoul acknowledged his brother-in-law's greeting as he passed the quarterdeck with a curt nod. His eyes were on the slender figure he saw so rarely. She suffered his company only in the hour when they dined, and even then Benoit's presence forestalled any overture on his part. Why, she still slept in her brother's room. For all the weight carried by the papers in his drawer, Raoul noted with aggravation, she might as well belong to another.

Daniel watched his captain with a sympathetic eye as he paced back and forth. They had come this very day to anchor off the coast of an uninhabited isle to take on water. Though they kept off the main shipping lanes for reasons well known, this particular island was familiar to the steward and the idea it inspired might prove fruitful to the captain's desires.

"E'scuse me, Cap'n, but might I have a word with ye?" Raoul looked round and nodded, but Daniel beckoned him aside. "It be a particular sort o' matter I ken ye might not want overheard," he advised as they strolled out of earshot.

"Now, Cap'n, I ken ye not be likin' another man muckin' about in yer business, yet hear me out and ye'll most likely be humored," Daniel confided in hushed tones. "The mistress don't like the idea o' all this company about, and I do believe she'd set her brother on ye ifin' ye was to—well, ye be seein' how it is between them. I overheard her roundin' on him smartly for suggestin' that she make peace with ye, and he finally come to admit that the marriage seemed a mistake which he could only rectify by standin' betwixt ye."

Raoul's lips curved in a sneer but, when he shot a meaningful glance over his shoulder at the solitary lady on the far deck, his shoulders slumped and the anger faded. "For once I'm at a loss, Daniel. I've wooed many a woman to good effect. What does she want of me?" he asked dejectedly.

Daniel smiled inwardly. Poor Cap'n, smitten but good. "Well now, Cap'n, if ye be askin' . . ."

Raoul gave him a rueful smile. "Out with it, man. You long ago passed the boundaries of respect."

Daniel did grin then. "It comes to me, Cap'n, that gently bred folk expect too little and too much of their womenfolk. If a maid blushes and flutters her lashes at the least sign o' boldness on a gentleman's part, then she's to be praised a virtuous lass. The man tumbles heels over heart in love and then hopes to meet a siren over the marriage bed.

"Yet the girl who shows uncommon spirit and fire is classed a tease or worse. They be given impossible choices, Cap'n.

" 'Tis much simpler for common folk. A lad marks a maid as his, and they do what comes natural, with or without the holy words. The mistress's been given too many choices. Ye branded her a harlot once when she met you squarely. She ain't likely to invite more of the same. The trick, it comes to me, is in narrowin' the choices. Not yea or nay but willin' or un, Cap'n."

"A philosopher as well as a steward, Daniel? Is there no end to your talents?" Raoul asked, clearly intrigued by this logic.

" 'Tis only a bit o' livin', Cap'n, and a man learns much. For instance, there's this here island . . ." And Raoul bent closer to hear Daniel's suggestion.

Next morning the captain invited Benoit to accompany him while he scouted for fresh water, suggesting that perhaps Gweneth should come along so that she would not be shut up in her cabin until they returned.

The day shone with exceptional brilliance, the cerulean sky a magnificent foil for the verdant isle and turquoise waters of the cove. Even Gweneth's troubled spirit floundered in the tropical splendor and submerged, leaving behind the girl who once flirted with her brothers' gallant friends in the cool of the Valois's formal garden. She fell to laughing and teasing with Benoit and Daniel and, on Raoul, she bestowed a smile the likes of which at once kindled his hopes that Daniel's ploy would succeed.

"The isle, *c'est magnifique!*" she purred in pleasure as the sweet-scented trade winds ruffled her unbound hair and brushed her cheeks to pink warmth. With shoes in hand and her skirts hiked above her knees, she jumped from the boat into the shallows and splashed through the surf to the shore. The sand clung to her damp feet, covering them in a crumbly hot powder as she plowed up the beach toward the jungle.

"Best not, mistress," Daniel called after her. "Leastways not alone. There be ten dozen kinds o' beasties in them wilds."

Reluctantly Gweneth turned back to join the men dragging the dinghy to a secure beaching. She squatted down on the scorching sand to pluck up a fluted shell, turning it over and over in her palm. She had so longed to escape for a short while, to be alone with none to please but herself.

"If it is adventure you seek, *ma belle*, I have just the item," Raoul offered, dropping the oars by the boat and extending his hand to her.

Gweneth eyed him speculatively, a frown between her brows, and then rose, dusting the sand from her skirt and clasping her hands behind her back. "Unnecessary, Capitaine. I shall do nicely right here," she answered primly and looked away.

Raoul's mouth twisted in a wry grin. "Husband is my title now, madame, and I have very little patience to argue with you over the matter. Do not tarry, or I'll heave you over my shoulder and have done with all requests."

Gweneth's face set in a determined sulk, but she cast a pleading glance at Benoit for guidance.

"It will do you good to have some exercise, *soeur*. Go ahead," he replied and shrugged noncommittally.

There was no help to be had there, Gweneth decided, and turned up the beach, pointedly sidestepping Raoul's offer of assistance.

The captain's stride was long and rapid, and he

soon outdistanced her, but never did he even once glance back to concern himself with her ability to follow. Gweneth kept her eyes on his back and swore more than once when, in her haste to keep apace, she stumbled over a gnarled root or vine in the path.

Palm leaves raked her face and dragged at her hair and skirts, but she pressed on through the thick jungle growth for fear that, should she lose sight of him, he would leave her to stumble along blindly.

In the thrashing caused by her passage, Gweneth gave flight to a large chartreuse parrot who skimmed by within inches of her nose, and she shrieked in a most undignified manner. Fast on its heels came loud, insulting laughter.

Raoul had spun about at her cry but spotted the winged creature, and his apprehension gave way to humor. He stood his ground until Gweneth reached him, then took her none too gently by the arm. "Must you be forever lagging about?" he asked and hurried her forward. "It is not much further. Ah, here we are, darling. Our own private chamber," he announced as he lifted the broad green frond of a palm to reveal a clearing.

The wide expanse of grass ran to the banks of a shimmering pool, fed at one end by a narrow trickle from the rocky cliffs above. The sun shone with honeyed brightness on the scene, lending it an unreal quality, and Gweneth stepped into it before she was aware that near the edge of the water wood had been laid for a fire and several blankets were neatly piled by a basket.

A private chamber, he had called it, and Gweneth shot the tall impressive man beside her a wary glance. Had his patience found its limit just when she had become sure that he had given up?

As if she had asked, Raoul said, "The time has come for this distance between us to end, madame." A sudden smile revealed even white teeth. "You are a wife and owe your man the pleasure of your company."

Gweneth halted her step, but he jerked her forward, not sparing her a look.

"The method is yours to choose. I can make it an extraordinary experience for you or, if need be, take my satisfaction on your writhing, protesting frame. I would have the former but—" He checked his step and turned to her, his eyes a vibrant, wicked blue. "Alas, the choice is to be yours."

His chuckle of amusement rankled, and Gweneth drew a quick breath in resentment. "Your methods show no variance, Capitaine. Must you forever be bullying me with the prospect of your ungovernable lust? I would have believed your success with women allowed you some self-assurance." She smiled sweetly and shrugged free of his touch. "Alas, it seems I am mistaken," she finished in the same mocking tone he had chosen.

The sapphire gaze narrowed in irritation, but Raoul kept his temper. He started forth only to pause when Gweneth did not follow. "I was wont to refresh myself before turning to other considerations but, if you insist—" And he turned to her.

Gweneth fell back a step and then darted past him in a perfectly faked maneuver, recalling to Raoul's mind her expertise with a blade. She hurried over to where the supplies were laid and came to her knees before the basket. In it she found bread and cheese, a bottle of wine and, tucked into a checkered cloth, a little bird, freshly turned on a spit and still crisply warm. Food for the savage, she thought shrewdly and spread out the repast. Anything to buy a reprieve from the trap he had sprung.

Raoul sat beside her and busied himself with the corked bottle but, under his lowered lids, he admired her slim graceful hands, the blush of pink on her soft cheeks, and the swift rise and fall of her breasts. Unable to stay the impulse to see more, he reached out and whipped the kerchief from the front of her gown.

Gweneth gasped in alarm, but he simply dropped

the ruffle and returned to the bottle. Even so, his eyes strayed to the tender expanse of rounded flesh above the low neckline.

Her brows rose in disdain, and she reached to snatch back the garment, but Raoul trapped her hand in his. "Please," he whispered as his wide, half-foolish gaze met hers. Her gaze faltered before his oddly gentle expression, and she withdrew her hand to complete her task.

The meal was eaten in another of those ever-present silences between them. Gweneth kept her eyes on the shimmering silvered surface of the pool while Raoul gazed in discomfort at the exquisite woman soon to be his. The wine sang through his veins to be echoed in every inch of his being, and he shifted awkwardly to relieve his distress.

Gweneth nibbled the final crust of bread and sipped a last taste of wine before coming to her feet. "I believe it is time for us to return, Capitaine. The others will wonder what we are about."

Raoul looked up from where he lay leaning on one elbow. "The others know what we are about, *ma belle*. Only you seem still in doubt." He smiled lazily and curled up to unfold on his feet. "I could use a dip in that pool. Come along, wife, and if you behave, I'll let you scrub my back." He bent over and retrieved a cake of soap from the pocket of the jacket he had tossed aside.

Gweneth was amazed by the quietude with which she watched him cross to the bank of the pool and begin drawing off his boots, but a flush of embarrassment spread over her as he removed his shirt and loosened the knee strings of his breeches and unbuttoned the waistband.

"You are not ready," he called over one brown shoulder and Gweneth replied, "I do not care to bathe," conscious then of his intent. She took the opportunity of his turned back to scan the jungle for the opening they had used before.

"Thinking of escape?" he asked in her ear as his arms came round her. "You must realize there is none," and he spun her around. His fingers loosened her gown before she could stop him, and it was in vain that she struggled to keep it about her shoulders, for he pulled it to her waist and plucked the strings from her corselet.

"Step out," he commanded. With shaking fingers she let the dress slip to the ground. Raoul slid both arms around her narrow waist and felt for the fastenings to release her petticoats. She suffered in silence this intimacy but gasped when his cheek brushed her breast. The petticoats slithered to her ankles, and he stood back to observe his handiwork.

Raoul whistled through his teeth and grinned approvingly. "It would be a shame to spoil that bit of silk," he said as he fingered her chemise, but Gweneth grabbed his wrist with both hands and held it away.

"Why so reluctant, sweet one? It will come off soon enough," and he reached up to caress her silky mane. The heavy auburn tangle fell in thick luscious waves to her waist, and he wound a curl about his hand and brought it to his lips. "The fragrance of your hair has always been a great attraction to me," he murmured huskily. The mixture of tenderness and desire lent his eyes a smoky hue, and she bowed her head in confusion.

"It is a shame I am not the only man to share your favors," he muttered abruptly and shook the hair from his hand. "You play the blushing maiden effectively, madame, but do not tempt me to anger with this false modesty." He pulled her roughly into his arms, thrusting his face close to hers. "I had nearly forgotten how easily you lie."

" 'Tis you who lie, Capitaine, but I have no defense to offer," Gweneth answered coldly, but the thudding of his heart under her palms warned her of his rising temper.

He hugged her tighter, lifted her off her feet, and

covered the distance to the water swiftly. He threw her from him with the taunt, "I trust you swim, my lady?"

The water broke and swallowed her but, far from the icy shock she expected, the liquid flood was cool and welcome on her hot skin. Her toes touched the rocky bottom, and she was propelled upward instantly to break the rippling surface.

Raoul stood above her, hands on hips, and he nodded in satisfaction as she gulped in fresh air. "I should have known a witch would float," he commented and bent to strip off his breeches before her surprised face.

Gweneth turned away in disconcertion but not before she had glimpsed the narrow waist and hips and marblelike muscles of his untanned thighs. Raoul's laughter was a deep throaty rumble, and then the water heaved, erupting in a cascade of crystal drops which descended on Gweneth's head.

Raoul caught her about the waist and lifted her high to toss her from him. Gweneth shrieked and plunged in over her head to find him again at her side when she surfaced. He drew her in with one arm and swam toward the shore. When he released her, they stood in water reaching only waist high.

"I would not tire you too soon, *ma belle*," he said against her ear. "Take this," and he handed her the soap. "Now be a dutiful wife and scrub your husband's back."

Gweneth snatched the soap from him and nearly tossed it as hard as she could but decided that he would only make her pay for the show of defiance, and so, curbed the impulse. When he turned his back, she smoothed the moisture from her face and adopted an indifferent expression. He would get no further rise from her, regardless of what he did, she assured herself. She lathered the broad hard flesh and poured handfuls of water over him to rinse it away.

"The front, if you please," he said politely and faced

her. Gweneth continued her vigorous scrubbing, ignoring the tingling sensations which ran the length of her arms with each touch, and scowled hard on the job before her. She would not give him the satisfaction of knowing that he could provoke her to either joy or fear.

The view of her well-molded breasts with their taut peaks thrusting proudly through the drenched silk sent white-hot shafts of delight through Raoul and all but scuttled his desire to make her fully aware of his masculinity before he took his due. Reluctantly he shut his eyes to her smooth, velvet touch.

Gweneth screwed her mouth to one side, observing this picture of indulgent leisure and, reaching down quickly, she struck him sharply behind both knees. He buckled under to come up snorting, but she was yards away, laughing heartily at the prank.

Far from being annoyed, Raoul cleared his throat and laughed with her. Her beauty was unmatched when she was happy, he thought, feeling his own inadequacy. This wondrously lighthearted mood was all he ever wanted for her, but it was the one thing he could never seem to bring her. He was ever moved to threaten—aye, and bully her into submission. She laughed with everyone; Benoit, Daniel, and even Lavasseur. What was it he lacked that so many others accomplished easily?

He finished his bathing and hoisted himself up on the bank while rivulets of water coursed down his lean frame as he shook dry. Gweneth looked away as he turned to her and offered a hand. "Allow me, my lady," he coaxed, but she kept her head bowed. "Not yet," she replied and concentrated on making soapy froth of her shampoo.

Raoul laughed and bent to splash a handful of water over her back. The chemise clung like a second skin, and a smile settled on his features as he watched her full breasts, buoyed by the water, bob gently as she scrubbed. He must allow himself the privilege of observing her bathe often, he decided. It was a most excellent prelude to the drama which would follow.

Springing easily to his feet, he walked over to the blankets. Gweneth watched from under her cover of suds and into the fear she knew crept a new sensation. His masculine nakedness was an enticement which troubled her, but it pleased her, too, to observe the obvious assuredness with which he carried himself. Godlike? Perhaps not, but certainly a splendid male.

Raoul lifted and spread a blanket in the half shade, stretching out on his stomach with his head resting on his arms.

Gweneth ducked under the surface to rinse her tresses and felt again the strong need to escape. Several strokes brought her to the far shore, but as she would have sprung from the water and bolted into the jungle, common sense checked her. She could not go back to the beach without her clothes, and when she cast a wary eye over her shoulder she saw that her gown lay practically at Raoul's feet. *"Diable!"* she murmured and grudgingly swam back.

The sun dried Raoul's skin, leaving it smoothly taut. He watched Gweneth's graceful form slice through the water and savored the passion that swelled within him. "Not much longer, sweet wife," he said to himself.

Gweneth reached the near bank and timidly eased herself up into the grass, turning her back on her audience of one. Using her fingers as a comb, she dragged the tangles from her hair and spread it over her shoulders as a protective veil. Bending her head over her knees and closing her eyes, she let the sun bake and steam her hair dry. It did no good to contemplate what was to happen, but it was impossible to quiet the anxiety which threatened to sweep forth and engulf her. Gweneth hugged her knees tighter, furious that Benoit had left her to the fate that awaited half a dozen yards away.

"Gweneth."

The word, spoken so softly it might have been whispered in her ear, brought her head up sharply and she slued round. Raoul now lay on his side facing her, an arm draped discreetly before his groin. "Come to me, Gweneth," he said.

The water felt suddenly cold on her skin, and she shivered. A fearful tightness seized her throat and became too great to swallow down. He did not move, but as their eyes met, Gweneth seemed to be drawn to him, his superior will conquering all reluctance, and she rose to close the distance between them.

Emotions warred within her as she gazed down at him. He could force himself on her, of that there was no doubt, and that he had brought her here for that purpose he had made plain. She could fight him or remain impassive, either way he would win. But there was one thing he would not expect.

She dropped to her knees and, taking his warm smooth face in both hands, leaned forward and put her lips to his. She heard his faint gasp as their lips met, but she closed her eyes and moved her mouth over his, not drawing away when his lips parted and his tongue darted between. His arms came round her as he lay back pulling her down on himself and Gweneth's fingers slipped through his damp curls and laced themselves behind his head.

Raoul stroked her shoulders and back lightly, then lowered his hands to cup her buttocks and hold her hips to his as he moved rhythmically under her. Fear gave way to vague sensations of exhilaration as she pressed his warm sweet mouth to her own and, when she felt him swell and harden against her thighs, absurd feelings of triumph mingled with her excitement, and the last of her reluctance faded to longing for the experience ahead.

Raoul's senses swam with the unexpected eagerness of her demonstration. Yet, into some tiny corner of his mind seeped the nagging, jealous doubt that she was a stranger to these intimacies. The seed took root instantly, and he muttered an oath and pushed her off, rising up to catch her by the wrist.

"In whose bed did you learn that trick, dear wife?" he drawled. His eyes, darker by far than the azure sky overhead, narrowed accusingly, and Gweneth shrank back in astonishment. This is what he wanted. Had he not proved it with every gesture, every word?

"This is to be my pleasure, madame. We will attend your wanton desires on another occasion," Raoul warned, grabbing her by the shoulders and pushing her down under him. "Your lover, Lavasseur, may have schooled you well, but learn that one man's needs are not always like another's."

He snatched at her flimsy chemise and grinned when it rent to expose her full, pink-tipped breasts. One arm slid under her to arch her upward, and the other hauled her wrists over her head. He bent, pressing his lips to one peak to groan aloud when it became firm and swollen under his careful tutoring. Then his lips caught at the other, and it was Gweneth who whimpered as he teased it to response.

Hot, searing kisses he spread over her breasts and sleek stomach before he took her mouth again, forcing her lips apart to taste a full portion of her unique sweetness.

"You are mine from this day forward. Mine alone," he growled through clenched teeth, and he moved to bruisingly force a knee between her locked thighs.

Gweneth struggled wildly, wanting to take back every instant of her surrender, but the effort was useless. She collapsed with averted face to await the abuse which was to follow, consoling herself with the knowledge that it was he, in the end, who must apologize.

Raoul rose up, a dark silhouette against the frond-shrouded sky, and thrust deep, his way unbarred. Gweneth's half-cry died on her lips, the hurtful pressure's momentary discomfort nothing compared to what she expected. Mystified and suddenly cold with fear, she looked up to the man above her.

"What? No more denials, my not-so-virginal wife?" he voiced sarcastically.

Gweneth's eyes grew until the white shone all around. Bewilderment became disbelief followed closely by horror as his meaning became clear. *"Mon Dieu!"* she moaned and brought a freed hand quickly to her mouth. "It is not possible," she said in a choked whisper. "Who could have—?" And her fevered thoughts hurried back to Captain Willows, to the cabin boy, to all those days in Barbados when she had lain ill and at the mercy of any man—even her uncle.

Raoul stared down at her pain-ravished face, and the blood stilled in his veins. Could it be that she was innocent, that she had willingly lain with no other man and thought herself untouched? Or was this more treachery? But no, he was a man of the world, and no maiden pure could be more horrified by what had happened to her in these few minutes. Raoul swallowed and felt a great disgust rising from the pit of his stomach.

Brilliant tears edged from under the sweep of Gweneth's lashes and slid slowly from the corners of her eyes. Raoul swore once and then again. "Gweneth, look at me," he pleaded, but when she did not answer but to stare blankly, he moved to leave her.

"Non, do not," she whispered and clutched frantically at his neck. "Please, it is done, my lord. Do not fail me now." Just once, her heart cried, to be his once would be enough.

Raoul froze above her and felt again the overwhelming need in himself that nothing, no one but she could fulfill. Laying a sweaty cheek to her heart, he began to murmur hoarse words of tenderness. Then, with as much restraint as his passion would allow, he started to move against her, uttering softly rendered words of encouragement into her hair and kissing the salty dampness from her lids. But the exquisite manipulations of their bodies soon overrode him, and his release burst forth with a violence he knew hurt her.

Gweneth wrapped her arms about him to hold him close and let the shuddering force of his body carry her beyond the pain.

Raoul lay quietly above her for a long time after, his joyous satisfaction at odds with the stupid, senseless method he had chosen to that end. He kissed her cheek and throat and sought for some means to express his regret, but words were useless, empty noises against the accusation of what he had done.

Gweneth felt the fluid ease of his body tense under her hands still clutched to his back. Her fingers lightly stroked him, feeling the hard flexible strength of the muscles, and she marveled that such power as was his had not battered her but, with passionate direction, had given her an awareness of a pleasure which transcended the need for words or excuse. She had wanted him and had been totally shameless in that need. Would he understand that it was the first time she had ever done such a thing?

Raoul raised up at last and rolled onto his back, pulling Gweneth into his arms. He knew he must say something, but he was not at all certain that the course he was choosing was wise.

"Gweneth, you must listen to me," he said quietly, "and God forgive me for what I am about to say. There is something which you have a right to know." He took a deep long breath. "I thought you knew but dear Lord, how could you? Your lover was I. That first day so long ago, the day we met. I took you while you still swooned."

Every fiber of her being stiffened. "Non! Not you?" she cried as a frigid emptiness seemed to open under her to suck dry the last of her illusions about him. A convulsive spasm rocked her, but she could not utter a single sound.

Raoul tightened his arms about her, but she lay

limp, giving no response when he called her name. He groped for words to fill the dreadful silence. "Let me try to make you understand," he pleaded hoarsely and, for the first time in many years, he spoke of Marianne, sparing himself none of the humiliation the telling cost him.

On and on the words spilled forth into the lazy heat of afternoon until he had related even the circumstances of his birth and childhood in the anxious need to share her shame. When he finished, she did not move, and they lay silently in the shade until sleep claimed them both.

Perhaps it was the droning of a fly or a bead of perspiration gliding across Gweneth's sleek stomach to where her skin met his, but, as though touched by an invisible hand, Raoul awakened. The sun was slanted under the trees where they lay and spread its full light on their intertwined bodies. He slid his leg from where it lodged between her thighs and her eyes flew open.

He rose quickly, unable to face whatever Gweneth's reaction might be, and pulled on his breeches with the experience of years of hurried dressing. Turning to hand Gweneth her things, his gaze avoided the depth of hers.

In time, he told himself, she would forget this. For, in spite of her fear, she had shared his need in those final moments of lovemaking and that must speak to his plight. Or had his confession afterward awakened in her a shame and disgust which could well destroy the tenuous threads of her feelings? He contemplated the frail girl kneeling in the grass beside him and came to know the meaning of pity.

Dry eyed, Gweneth flung her dress carelessly aside and stepped to the edge of the pool to plunge in and extinguish the fevered blush of her skin. The water soothed and drowned her thoughts until there was only the sky above and the plaintive cry of winged terns to fill the void. When she was done, she gathered her clothes and dressed slowly and without shame before her husband's troubled gaze. Sick at heart, she left it to the stranger by her side to lead her to the beach.

Daniel and Benoit sat cross-legged round the late-afternoon fire but came to their feet as the couple approached.

"There ye be, Cap'n. Another hour and we'd o' come after ye," Daniel greeted as his keen kindly eyes roved from one to the other.

"We are ready to cast off, Daniel. Man the oars, if you will, while I launch the boat," Raoul returned. Turning to Gweneth with a warm glow in his eyes, he said, "Be good enough to wait with your brother while preparations are made."

Gweneth nodded but dodged his inquiring look. She dropped to the ground by Benoit and hugged herself against the cooler breeze now skimming the water.

Benoit watched his sister some while, marking the wistful expression on her face that was in contrast to the sad slant of her eyes. "Gweneth, there is trouble for you?" he asked gravely and set a brotherly hand on her arm. "I made an error in bidding you accompany the capitaine, *mais non?*"

"Non," she answered, her voice a bare whisper. "We now have no secrets between us."

"Ah." Benoit smiled knowingly. "I thought something of the like was to take place, and I should say by the manner of your husband that the matter was discussed at length and to his complete satisfaction."

"Benoit!" Gweneth cried angrily, but her scarlet complexion betrayed her.

"Little one, save your shame for, truly, you are man and wife. None should think it otherwise between you. *Mon Dieu!* I had begun to wonder if the capitaine were half the man I charged him to be. His patience has been far greater than mine would be in like circumstance. It was not to be endured forever."

He leaned closer and lifted her chin with a hand. "I understand your reluctance to speak of these things with me. You should be counseled by a mother or married aunt, but there is only me, Gweneth, and I would not mislead you. You have tested your man's spirit and honor to its limits. He lacks nothing for courage and strength of purpose. He is able to provide generously for you. And his regard for you is easily measured by the freedom he has allowed you. If he pushed the conclusion, it is because he knew, as I did, that there was no other end to be made. Be happy, *ma chérie*, that such a man loves you."

Gweneth scanned her brother's confident face. "But does he?" she wanted to ask. No, she need not ask that which had been answered with the breaking of her heart.

Dinner aboard ship was a noisy affair. Raoul's singularly jocular mood was shared with easy camaraderie by Benoit and Daniel, but Gweneth kept her eyes on her plate, raising them once, when Raoul asked if his wife's things had been brought to his cabin. A comb and a pair of sandals were such a meager trousseau that she would have laughed on any other occasion.

Daniel nodded vigorously but caught the look of apprehension in her eyes and scratched his ear, wondering anew at the lady's strange behavior. The captain was so pleased, and here she was showing the fear he had never before seen when many's the time in the past when it would have been more understandable.

Raoul withdrew two cigars from his pocket and offered one to Benoit. "I have a better idea," he said as he was about to light it. "Let us seek the night's air and spare my wife a room reeking of tobacco." He rose and leaned over to kiss Gweneth's brow. "You must be tired, *ma belle*. I shan't be long." A tender smile touched his mouth and then he followed Benoit topside.

Daniel cleared the dishes while Gweneth sat glumly. When that was done, he sprinkled a fine black ash over some coals he had pulled from the stove. "Incense, missy," he announced when his actions brought her attention. "There ain't much to be said for this place as a bridal chamber—" Gweneth's suddenly guarded look brought a pucker of concern to Daniel's old brow but he continued. "I did change the linen. It be the best on board, and if ye was to take a peek in the chest yonder, ye'll be a findin' a gift." He winked and pointed to the captain's trunk.

"From you, Daniel?"

"Nay, missy. The cap'n bought it in England, but I reckon he had ye in mind right along." He stood awkwardly, wishing he could find the words to reassure her but figured that was her husband's place. "I best be goin'."

Gweneth went over to the chest when Daniel had gone and opened it to reveal a nightdress of the sheerest mauve silk.

Raoul stepped into his cabin and found it dark but wonderfully fragrant. He mentally blessed Daniel for the thought and turned his attention to discovering Gweneth. At first glance she appeared to have fled, and a deep cleft formed between his brows. Just as he turned to bellow for Daniel, a shadow stirred on his bunk.

Shoving the door shut, he sighed in audible relief. So she had not run from him. He knew she was troubled and, though she had not raged at him as he had expected, that she had remained was sufficient.

Doffing his boots and clothes on the floor, he hesitated above the bed to trace the seductive lines of his wife's back, and a delicious shiver enveloped his body. She had found and donned the gown he had bought for her. Quickly he knelt on the bed and rolled her over and into his arms.

"I see you discovered my present." He stopped. Gweneth's shadowed face gleamed with copiously spilt tears, and she trembled uncontrollably under his touch.

"What is it? Are you ill?" he asked and gathered her closer.

Gweneth shook her head but when he pulled her into his lap and she realized that he was naked, she pushed against him frantically. "Let me go! Let me go," she moaned and shrank back into the corner of the bunk. "Please, do not touch me. I can bear no more pain," she cried between lessening sobs.

Raoul frowned and wet his lips. "Because I hurt you today, you fear I shall do so again?"

"Oh yes, you have hurt me, many times. But never like this!" She wailed, and all the wretched misery of her soul poured out. "All these months you have known and let me believe a lie. I nearly married! How you must have relished the thought, knowing that I would someday be found out and suffer the humiliation without ever understanding how it had come about. *Mon Dieu*, you are a vile, contemptible man. And to think I actually begged you to— Oh monsieur, you planned well your revenge!"

Raoul's neck warmed to the flush of his embarrassment. "Was it so infamous a lie? I thought you knew, must have suspected as you led me to believe," he said gently.

"Suspected what?" she shrieked. "When I regained consciousness, I was sick with grief for my brother and numb with the shock of having nearly killed a man. The terror I knew when I thought you might die! Oh, but I'd have watched and rejoiced in your agony had I known. You thought! *Sacré Dieu*, what did you think?"

Raoul checked the impulse of his thoughts. He could not turn back now. "I think that I am a great fool," he replied flatly and gripped his hands between his knees. "I did not consider my actions infamous at the time. I am an arrogant man. What I want I have always taken, and I wanted you. And then, you goaded me into making a spectacle of myself in full view of my crew, so when I had you alone and helpless, I took my chance to even the score.

"I was a rogue, I fully accept that, but I could not know that I would be the first, and it was not until the deed was accomplished that I realized what I had done. It did not sit well with me to know I had debauched a maiden, but I never intended to abandon you. I meant to keep you, to take you under my protection."

"As your mistress," Gweneth added dully.

"It is the usual thing in such cases," Raoul allowed candidly. "I should have let you go, but I could not. You were a challenge, a prize to be won, and I wanted to know what it was to have you return my desire, to feel the racing of your heart against mine and know that your ecstasy was of my making. Ah, but gentle lady, your head was full of fanciful dreams of romance, and from the first, such an alliance between us was impossible. The callous attempts at seduction, the trip to the brothel in Road Town, even my bedding Leila with your knowledge were all part of my effort to strip away your idyllic dreams. You had to see life as it often is, brutal and swift. But it recoiled on me, Gweneth. I only drove you to hate me."

"What else? I let you believe that—oh, what is the use?" Gweneth stammered, choking on her rage. "All the time I held my head high, ignoring the leers and obscenities of your men, you were laughing up your sleeve. You'd have done better to stay away and hide your secret, for the hangman still waits with a true and legal debt for your neck."

"You forget that we are married," Raoul objected

politely. "Today I have made you mine, truly," he continued in a tender, caressing voice which flowed though the dark.

"Non! No more of your lies. I am a mere convenience until the next woman comes along. You will use me and then discard me like all the rest," she spat at him. "I'll yet see you hanged by the heels." And she reached out and slapped him hard across the face.

"Oh non, let me be!" she cried when he grabbed her by the arms and pulled her against his chest. "I did not mean it. Please, you must not do anything that would force Benoit to challenge you. I will keep my silence. I have told him nothing. Only don't hurt me so that he will know. Here," she cried, tearing at the front of her gown. "I offer freely what you want. Just don't take my brother from me. Please, anything but that!" Tears spattered Raoul's chest as she leaned forward to press frantic kisses on the wiry tangle there.

"Damnit, Gweneth! I do not deserve such fear," he exclaimed, chagrined by her hysterical reaction. He set her away and pulled the front of her gown closed. More words poised on his tongue, tarried there, and died unsaid. God, how she must despise him, he thought again with shame. How could he expect her to believe him now if he said he loved her. His every reckless attempt to ensnare her was spawned by that love which gave his selfishness a cruelty to rival the ruthlessness of her uncle. Oh, he knew her well enough to fashion such words as would bend her selfless nature to his will, but she would come to him in dread, and that he could not stomach.

Raoul stood, feeling for the first time a shyness at his unclad state before a woman. Crouching down, he swept the floor with a hand to search for his breeches.

"I shall not disturb your rest again," he said, his tone harsh and cold to Gweneth's ears. "I'll never again ask anything of you."

"You are leaving?" she asked.

"That is what you prefer," he replied and swore when he stubbed his toe in the dark while his breeches escaped him still.

Giving up for the moment, he wandered aimlessly about the cabin, delaying that moment when he must shut the door between them forever. He crossed over to the porthole and gazed out at the indigo sea. He should never have returned to the islands and certainly not into Gweneth's life.

Gweneth wrapped the nightgown over her nakedness and sank back on the bed. She had won. Never again need she go in dread of his temper or his lust. This is what she wanted. She had spent every drop of her venom on him, and he had acquiesced to her wishes without so much as a struggle. She should feel relieved and thrilled by the victory. Why, then, was there this terrible sense of defeat?

Gweneth wiped her teary face with a corner of the sheet and tucked her legs up under herself. She hated him. What else could she feel? He was guilty of a crime punishable by death and, if justice were done, he would meet that end. And, if she were swamped with reasons for her hatred, where was there a single support for the love she had so jealousy guarded all these weeks?

Her love, she had called him in the sheltered recesses of her mind as she lay in this very bed while Willows piloted the *Cyrene* beyond her last hope of ever finding him again. She had cried for that stupid proud woman who had shoved him from her arms because she was too vain to offer her heart where it might be rejected. And, all the while, he was a parvenu and a cheat. How blind she had been to fashion a lover from this bitter, barren hulk of a man. He was a stranger to love and nothing he had ever said or done belied this reality. She had only herself to blame for falling in love.

The fire behind the grate hissed and sputtered as

the last log crumbled to ashes, throwing a kaleidoscope of shadows up over the room before leaving it in complete darkness.

Empty and void like her captain's heart, Gweneth likened the ship's cabin. Then, in answer to the aching measure of her pulse, the memory of Raoul's voice, painful and throbbing in the heat of the afternoon, returned. If he knew naught of love, was it his fault?

Without realizing it, she had listened, and her heart had gone out to that child, neglected and abused. Who was to blame for the small helpless boy who had become a cold unfeeling man? Would she have been different had her life of loving comfort been traded away?

But she was different, different altogether from this man. She knew what it was to be happy, to have the security of a family's acceptance in love for simply being alive. And if she could hold back that gift of love merely because her chosen one did not meet the standards of acceptability, how then was she different from any of the others who had wounded and repudiated him all his life? Had he not more to lose in his fear of love than she? And, merciful heaven, she wanted him, wanted him more than her own self-respect.

"It is no good, Gweneth," Raoul said in that uncanny way he seemed to have of reading her thoughts. His voice was calmly dispassionate as he kept his eyes on some distant spot. "I am not a fit companion for any woman. My heart has long since beat to a leaden measure, and you are right in every bitter judgment you have ever formed of me."

His voice deepened, colored by an emotion Gweneth had not heard before. "You are vibrantly alive and so filled with that fragile gift of love that I must hope you shall never understand the sort of man I have become.

"I have made you my wife against your will, and I suppose I could spare us both by keeping that long overdue appointment in Barbados, but I am a scoundrel fully, and the price is too dear. You are free to leave me. If you wish, you may live on my estate in England. I will never venture there, I promise you. It is the best I can offer until the sea claims me, as one day it surely will. And, God willing, you will one day find a man worthy of you."

He was not aware that Gweneth had come to his side until he felt her breath, sweet and cool, on his shoulder. "Raoul," she whispered, and he stiffened. When her arms slid round to encircle him from the back, he gasped and his head slumped forward against the bulkhead.

"Raoul, let me stay," she pleaded so softly. "I fear you only when you heap your anger and disdain upon me. If you will give me time, I shall forget the past." She rubbed her cheek against the smooth hardness of his back. She would forget, she must. "Let me into your heart as I so long ago opened mine to you. I shall be glad of whatever you have to give. Show me how to love you that I may earn your trust."

"Dear heaven!" Raoul uttered hoarsely, shuddering within her embrace as emotion such as he had never known gripped him. A sob escaped him, hardly more than a muted sigh, and then he was turning in her arms.

"Oh love," he whispered and reached out to accept her as Gweneth fell into his arms. "You are my love, Gweneth. Let me love you if only for this moment," he pleaded and hid his face in the lush fall of her hair.

He wept then. Tears glided freely down his proud features as he crushed Gweneth so tightly that she felt a part of the storm setting him aquiver. And she rejoiced!

He called her his love and she could forgive him all because the defense of pride was no longer a barrier. She cradled his face in her hands and kissed his eyes, his cheeks, and then his lips, murmuring his name over and over with incredible tenderness.

"Hush, hush, *mon chérie*," she whispered and lay her cheek to his wildly thumping heart. "This is all I ever need, to hear your words of love."

"I do love you. So long I have loved you and been helpless to break free," he answered. Bending down he lifted her into his arms with an ease which still surprised her. She threw her arms around his neck, pulling his head to her breast, and he burrowed into that delicious warmth, kissing each velvet mound in rapture. The bed was but a few steps, and then they lay together.

In the silence after, Raoul pressed her to his side and listened to the slow even breathing of his wife. She had given of herself as no woman had ever offered him, and he had answered her with a vulnerability never shown. His sighs echoed hers, and he had shivered under her shy, delicate caresses as she did to his bolder, self-assured stroking. And, when she hesitantly reached down between them to quest the nature of his manhood, it had left him gasping with the knowledge that her mastery over his was complete.

She had cried when they were done, and he had not fully understood why but berated himself for failing to subdue his body's mounting thirst which drove him over the brink of restraint to a flood tide of unbridled passion. Yet, when she spoke, it was not in reproach but with such sweetness that it fashioned a silken lasso of love about his heart to hold him to her forever.

"I have dreamed of you but the imagining was a pale, sad thing when compared with the magnificence of your body's touch. As you are a man, so you have made a woman of me." She leaned over him then and kissed him with soft, trembling lips.

CHAPTER TWENTY

Gweneth slept soundly, unaware that Raoul had slipped from her side during the night to pore over his charts on deck where the light would not disturb her. He returned near dawn and once more made her his in the dusky light of night's end.

When she awakened, the cabin was awash with fingered streaks of daylight. A new and delightful contentment pervaded every limb as she raised a lazy hand to stifle a yawn. She came slowly to consciousness, savoring the fluid ease of her body. The band of gold gleamed brightly on the hand held to her mouth, and she smiled.

Raoul stirred restlessly, rolling onto his stomach as she moved by his side, and threw an arm about her waist, but he did not awaken.

Gweneth inched up, propping her chin on one hand, and sought with a finger to trace the lines of her husband's half-hidden face. She fingered the lightly furrowed forehead, the thick, well-defined brows, moving on along to the wrinkles at the corner of one sleeping eye, down the bridge of his nose and, pausing, she gazed wondrously at his wide, finely sculptured mouth, soft now with sleep.

How well she had come to know the texture and taste of those lips. The kisses offered by them in these last hours acquitted the bruising punishment of all those past. They had been seductively tender, spreading a fluid fire to whet her appetite, and she had sampled the ambrosial banquet in enchantment.

Her eyes strayed down over his naked shoulders and back, firm and dark as oak in the filtered light, and on to the pale, compactly rounded buttocks where began the light tawny pelt reaching to his ankles. Afraid she would disturb his slumber, she held back from touching his manly nakedness which beckoned a woman's hand and contented herself with lingering, caressing glances.

He was not a savage lover but neither was he as gentle as she dreamed. He had made love to her twice, quickly and fiercely, driven by the eagerness to know her and the many months of denial. Yet, just before dawn, he had banked the flames of his passion against the third encounter, urging her on with the most persuasive of caresses and kisses till her breath came in short, quick gasps and her body strained instinctively against his.

Raoul's laughter was deep and joyous as he gently teased her, using words to describe his pleasure at her response which would have shocked and embarrassed her in any instance but this the privacy of their bed. Still he denied them both until the hungry aching racing along her raw nerves bordered on pain, and she reached out for him, drawing him onto her with the urgently whispered plea that he take her then.

He came to her swiftly, shattering the barrier of physical separateness, and forging them as one. She cried out at the near-violent nature of his hunger, but the release, when it came, splintered the aching with a torrent of blissful warmth that left them shuddering in shared consummation.

Gweneth ran a finger under the feathery edge of curls along the nape of Raoul's neck. How strange, she reflected, that from her experience of a carefully nurtured childhood she should discover that he was her choice and her pleasure. For, even in the first hours of their union, she knew no other man would ever replace him in her heart.

The floor was slick and cold under her feet, but the

longing for warmth drove her to the sea chest in search of Raoul's nightshirt. Silk bedclothes were all very fine for sultry tropical nights. But when the wind rose off the cooled sea in summons from the rising sun and one's husband seemed negligently contemptuous of the chilling breeze, anchoring the bedding and his wife's gown under his hips, 'twas but one thing to be done.

"Wife. I do not recall giving my leave of your company."

Gweneth craned her head around to look over her shoulder as she squatted before the chest. Raoul leaned on an elbow with a mischievous grin on his handsome features.

"I awakened you. I am sorry," she replied and drew the nightshirt over her head.

"What? Are you cold, *ma belle?*" he asked, but his attention fastened on the sensual lines slipping beneath the folds of his garment. "If 'tis warming you seek, madame, you need look no further than here," and he adjusted his position to leave an inviting space.

Gweneth hid her contented smile and answered sotto voce. *"Mais non, mon seigneur.* One may grow indifferent to the same feast laid too often upon the palate."

"Ah, love, just lay this banquet upon my pallet and allow me the indiscretion of gluttony," he returned warmly.

She shook her head quickly, but a giggle bubbled up from the depths of her happiness.

Raoul sprang from the bed and placed his fists on his hips. "Woman, to deny me is to ask no quarter. I shall scuttle your protests, weigh anchor under your laggardly keel, rip that negligently spread cloth from your exceptionally proportioned hull, and beach you upon my berth with a well-aimed broadside," he thundered, but his face and eyes were awash with mirth.

"Hush," she cautioned, her eyes flying wide with scandal. "Someone may overhear you."

"Hear me? My dear sweet wife, after having been subjected to your shrieks of delighted transport this past half hour before dawn, I doubt my crew would take notice of a few well-chosen words by your husband."

"Oh?" Gweneth's face flamed crimson. "Was I so very loud?" she asked in the barest whisper.

Confronted by this sudden vision of virtuous shyness, Raoul roared with unfettered laughter. "Aye, *ma belle*, loud you were. So very much so that I was deaf to all but your rapturous cries and the surging cradle of your velvet thighs. But fear not, for your lips lay against mine and what was not lost in their embrace found expression elsewhere." He indicated his chest where a fine tracery of red scratches intermingled with the furring there.

"Oh!" A finger edged its way between her teeth as Gweneth struggled with the meat of the conversation. "I should not have . . ."

"Should not, my love?" he questioned softly and came forward to cup her scarlet face in his broad brown hands. "Should not have been a young woman in the throes of her first passion? Nay, Gweneth. I would have it none other. 'Tis proof of my—our achievement."

The laughter in his eyes sprang up and vanished. "But, if you would do penance, then by all means apply the succor of your kiss else I should die from this brutal mistreatment," he urged in such mournful voice that Gweneth gave way to laughter and, reaching up on tiptoe to lay her arms about his neck, placed a kiss on his lips.

Raoul's embrace was ironclad, and they kissed and laughed in one another's arms until a more serious but definitely more absorbing interest claimed them both.

Astonished and delighted beyond measure, Raoul directed the eager pupil in his arms to the heightened pleasure of them both. And when they lay panting and surfeited in one another's embrace, he spoke that amazement.

"I shall never understand the puzzle that you are." His whole face shone with loving contentment as he kissed her long and deep before letting her reply.

"*C'est bon*, monsieur. Then it shall be a while ere you tire of me," she teased. But his wonder was no less than her own, for the blooming passion between them gave new bliss with each encounter.

"I can never grow tired if your ardor remains," he replied and kissed the tip of her nose. "I should not have guessed that such ecstasy owes itself not to experience but to the joy of love freely given. Saints above, I have never been happier!" His gaze held hers, and a wicked grin lifted his features. "I have learned, too, that you do purr when sated and, if it is within my power, you always shall."

Gweneth closed her eyes as a rush of blood flamed her cheeks, but she was pleased as only a woman can be whose man rejoices in her display of passion. "Raoul," she murmured and opened dreamy eyes, "*Je t'aime.*"

Gweneth pulled a row of stitches from the frayed collar of one of Raoul's shirts and bent over it with a critical eye to determine the extent of the repairs required. Raoul spent most of his hours topside, and the time weighed heavily on her with only the creaking of the ship and the mournful soughing of the wind through the rigging for company. She did not begrudge him his duty but, as the days passed in this sanctuary on the seas, she began to long for a home where she could be as much a wife as a mistress.

"Why did you not tell me that Dillingham tried to murder you? God's blood, woman, you stayed behind when you knew he wanted your death!"

The strangled bellow of enraged fury bolted Gweneth from her chair, and the scissors and bobbin of thread slithered from her lap and rattled across the floor. One moment she had been alone and the next she was confronting the infuriated stare of her husband. No, the wrath of the master of the *Cyrene*.

"Mercy, Raoul. Look what you've made me do," she replied smoothly, but her hand shook as she bent to retrieve the tools. He strode up and kicked the scissors away within an inch of her grasp and, taking her by the shoulders, raised her up to her full height.

"Answer me, Gweneth. What mad scheme kept you in Bridgetown when you might have escaped with me?" His voice quavered with anger till the sight of Gweneth's unblinking gaze made him realize that he had unduly frightened her. More calmly he said, "You might at least have told me the truth of your illness. I would not have left then without you."

"Exactly so, Capitaine," she answered and tapped his chest lightly with a finger. "You really should not use that gruff, bawling voice below deck, *mon amour*. It rattles the timbers, and I will certainly be deaf by the voyage's end," she scolded playfully. But when her smile was not returned by those grim features, she bit her lips and shrugged.

"I did not tell you because I could not have gone with you. I was dizzy and weak, nearly blind. You would have had to carry me more than half the way, and it was easier for you to travel alone," she explained softly.

"Damn your arrogance!" he cried and threw up his hands in exasperation.

"Arrogance?" she echoed.

"What else? You steal through a house thick with pitfalls, challenge an armed guard with an ornamental trifle—a hatpin would have been more deadly—and then play the self-sufficient female, all for my benefit." He turned from her and slapped his thighs with the palms of his hands. "If you ever try to make things 'easier' for me again, I'll paddle that fetching posterior of yours so smartly you will be taking your meals at attention for a week!"

The blustery tirade ended as it had begun, but Raoul's heaving back betrayed him. Gweneth caught his arm to bring him round and saw the silent mirth hovering about his twitching lips.

"Gweneth, forgive me. If I had given a single rational thought to your well-being, all of this could have been avoided," he acknowledged when his humor subsided. He enfolded her in his arms and pressed a kiss to a curl at her temple. "I did not know what to make of the story of your illness when you did not appear at my trial, and I'm afraid I suspected the worst. Either your sudden sickness was a convenient lie because you feared to face me or— Damn, but I'm weary of being in the wrong with you."

He dropped his hands and glanced at her briefly before looking away. "I thought perhaps you were with child, Lavasseur's child. That, at least, would have explained that travesty of a marriage planned with Myers."

"Oh no, Raoul. You did not?" Gweneth cried and, unexpectedly, she laughed, clear, beautiful laughter that set Raoul's frown aside.

"Confound it, Gweneth, but you've led me a merry measure. My wits addled with jealousy, met at every turn by your cool manner, I was like a man possessed. That is why I acted the jackanapes where Lavasseur was concerned. I thought that you had been his all those months I was gone when once you might have been mine."

"Why, Capitaine, you do care," she murmured against the sleeve of his coat.

"Do you not yet believe me? I am ever eager to prove it," he answered in a hushed, suggestive tone as he pulled her closer.

"*Mais oui*, husband. I must believe it when the evidence announces itself so boldly," she said with a giggle for, pressed so intimately to his masculine frame, there was nothing to disguise the probing hardness in his loins.

"Jade," he taunted with a chuckle and pushed her gently from him, "but I will not be so temptingly swayed from the issue. You must realize, as Benoit does, that you were always in danger, that my appearance was incidental to the reason."

Gweneth turned away and resumed her chair. "I have no wish to remember any of that," she said calmly, but a coldness crept through her happiness at the mention of her uncle. "We are beyond his control. It cannot matter any longer what the reasons were."

"There you apply a quick but dangerous logic, Gweneth." Raoul squatted on his heels before her, taking her hands in his. "Have you thought that it was not only you Dillingham wished to be rid of? There was Renée as well. He does not yet know that Benoit lives. If so, then his danger may equal your own. You gave Benoit no reason to believe that you alone merited Dillingham's hatred. No, there is some other explanation. Renée was disposed of simply—"

"*Mon Dieu!* You do not think my uncle shipped Renée across the sea to be sold as he intended me to be?" Gweneth cried out, and her nails dug sharply into the palms of Raoul's hands.

"Nay, Gweneth. Think. You saw her board the ship in the company of other passengers, and it was a proper British vessel. Now listen. Benoit and I have talked—"

"Hence the lecture," she noted aloud.

"Listen, Gweneth. It has been decided that he will secure passage for you and himself to England when we lay in port at Tortola."

"But what of you?"

"Ah yes, that." He smiled. "You will fight no more battles if I can help it, and that is why I am putting you beyond the temptation."

"You are going back to Barbados!" Gweneth voiced in alarm as she tumbled to her knees beside him. "He will kill you, Raoul. He will not give you a chance to clear yourself if I am not there to avow the truth of our marriage."

A ripple of annoyance flowed over Raoul's features. "I will not abide your interference this time, Gweneth. You are my wife, bound by your oath of obedience, and I shall have my way in this."

Her delicate brows rose skeptically. "*Vraiment?* Did I promise such a thing?" she asked. "How remiss of me. Just what else did my vows contain?" And the loving tenderness in her bewitching green gaze set Raoul once more aquiver with yearning.

"Confound it, woman! Isn't it enough that you have succeeded in unmanning me once? You shall not be hearing my words of love nearly so often if it prompts you to make mock of them. I shall be no quivering lump of desire to be molded to your scheming designs. A firm hand, a rigid taskmaster, is what you shall reap for all your pliant ways," he warned even as he drew her in to kiss the soft, parted lips she raised in answer to his reproach.

"A strange hour for prayer," Benoit remarked from the door where he lounged against the jamb. The picture of kneeling lovers had its charm, he admitted, but turned a discreet back on the pair until they had righted themselves.

"I dropped my sewing and Raoul was kindly helping me regain it," Gweneth explained and carefully shook the creases from her skirt.

"What else?" Benoit answered as he picked up the scissors. "I must remember this lesson in seduction when next I trip upon a beautiful lady at her needlework. Most educational, this husband of yours, Gweneth. *En effet*, there lurks an unclaimed Frenchman beneath that Anglo-Saxon exterior." His laughter was that of genuine approval.

A glow of happiness warmed the smile that she offered the two men in her life. They had become friends, sharing more than the ties of marriage, and Gweneth welcomed the alliance for their sakes as well as her own.

She sat and resumed her mending while Raoul turned his attention to his brother-in-law, but his fingers curled about Gweneth's slender neck in possessive pride.

"What is the verdict, *mes amies?*" Benoit questioned.

"Gweneth goes to Tortola," Raoul exclaimed flatly.

"Under protest," Gweneth amended as she caught the material with her first stitch.

Benoit chuckled. *"Tant mieux."*

"Matamore!" she returned tartly.

"Enfant," Benoit rejoined.

"Ingrat."

"Ungrateful? Me? *Ma foi!* Was it not I who brought you to heel for your beloved capitaine when no one else could? I make you a wife and in return you defame my character."

"You speak too freely of things best kept quiet," Gweneth admonished.

"You were wrong to try to keep this from the capitaine," Benoit answered. "I will not have you within Dillingham's reach again. *Merde!* I myself would have the honor of dispatching that—" Though Gweneth remained ignorant of most of the blasphemies uttered by the English-speaking crew, Benoit's virulent speech in their own meticulous, Gallic tongue scorched her ears and brought an appreciative whistle from Raoul.

"Exactly my sentiment, monsieur, but I claim the right to meet Dillingham," Raoul replied. "Besides Gweneth needs an escort. She has fallen into the hands of too many scoundrels ere this, and it is beyond belief to suppose every man who succumbs to her charm will show the restraint of her earlier conquests."

Raoul's easy grin worked its full effect on Gweneth's upturned face, and she busied herself quickly over the work in her lap. Oddly enough, however, the mention of his impropriety no longer rankled but fled before the wind with the realization of his love.

"And just how do you propose to make my uncle listen?" she asked and pulled the length of thread tight. "He is not likely to welcome you into his presence. Who will protect you?"

"Impertinent chit," Raoul teased and pinched her upper arm sharply. "I am not so much the blunderer as you would seem to believe. My actions are rational enough when there are no bewitching green eyes about to distract me. And that is why you shall be securely stowed away. Dillingham will want no witnesses to the words we will exchange. A quiet little visit in the middle of the night should suffice. I hold a deadly hand, and he will soon come to know it."

"You will not kill him?"

"What? Challenge a cravenly misbegotten cur like that? God in heaven, I'll thrash him trice over for having laid a hand on you."

"But you will not kill him?" Gweneth pressed, her work now forgotten in her lap.

Raoul tugged a curl. "Marriage has tempered you, *ma belle*. I can remember a time not so long ago when you were hot for blood. Mine, if memory serves."

Gweneth sniffed indignantly. "That was different. It was in defense of a loved one."

"And this?" Raoul invited encouragingly.

Gweneth felt the edge in the battle slipping from her. "Adolphe had just died. I am not dead."

"No thanks to Dillingham's care," Benoit introduced.

"That miscreated slug!" and Raoul's temper roared off in a fit similar to Benoit's.

"Careful, *mon ami*," Benoit interrupted. "Another outburst such as mine will scandalize Gweneth completely."

"Aye, 'tis rightly so," he agreed. "You have my leave to weigh anchor at eight bells, monsieur."

Benoit inclined his head and sauntered out.

"Benoit is to sail the *Cyrene*?" Gweneth asked in a puzzled voice. "You are giving up command of your ship?"

"Yes and no, my love." Raoul removed her sewing from her lap and cast it aside. "My ship was impounded by the authorities. If, by chance, she is recognized, she had better have a new skipper. Benoit has put his years of bonded service to good use. He knows much of the ways of the sea and, with time, could make a first-class captain if he chose." He lifted Gweneth from her seat and sat, settling her on his knee.

"The trip is short and should be uneventful. With Peckcum as first mate, he will be fine. If we are boarded before we reach Tortola, they will find that the *Cyrene* has a new captain and two passengers on holiday. It is unlikely that Willows has scampered back to Dillingham with the news that he has lost a second ship to me. None will question the change.

"I really do despise this gown," he continued conversationally as he toyed with the buttons of Gweneth's only dress. "It does no justice to that which it covers." His fingers worked swiftly and certainly.

"And then there is my own selfish need to spend what time there is with my bride." The dress slid from Gweneth's shoulders and his hand on her back arched her to him. "Oh, yes, I have such a need, wife."

The date on the calendar made it early spring, not that any indication of the change showed itself on the endless blue-green waters of the Caribbean. But where the sun usually drew Gweneth from below to bask in its golden haze, crisping the tendrils about her face and toasting her cheeks, today it clammered closely in about her. Drops of perspiration raced down her face, leaving sticky trails. She smoothed the salty flecks of spume from her lips with a languid hand as she watched the undulating horizon. The rise and fall of the ship, which often lulled her peacefully, made her recent lunch seem too gross a burden and even though she swallowed back the temptation to be ill, the lightheadedness prevailed as she clung stubbornly to the railing.

"A fine time for *mal de mer*," she murmured, gripping the brass rail until her knuckles whitened. "I shall not be sick," she insisted, but the ship's very next dip into the backside of a wave found her retching over the side.

She cast a furtive glance about and wiped her flushed face with a handkerchief from her pocket. Thank heavens, she thought, no one had noticed her weakness. Raoul would expect his wife to be a proper sailor after two and a half months at sea. Even she could not understand this recent weakening. She had been perfectly healthy until a few days ago but, perhaps, her uneasy state was the result of Raoul's insistence that she leave for England without him.

That had been the cause of the first battle between them since their reconciled marriage. Raoul was implacable; she was furious, and they had quarreled. But it did not surprise Gweneth to learn that they could not carry that anger into the small confines of the bed. There she became as eager as he to draw the limit of their disagreement to a simple difference of minds, not hearts. It was a lesson she would not forget. Tempers would flare again and again, her Gallic pride and his innate arrogance made that a certainty. Yet the sparks of a healthy clash only added to the assurance that theirs was an enduring relationship. Raoul could be as angry as ever and she might be an exasperation, but it in no way threatened the solidarity of their partnership.

Gweneth was tucking the handkerchief away when the deck again buckled beneath her feet and, just in time, she grabbed at a line to keep from being dashed against the boards.

"What ho, missus," hailed Peckcum as he caught her under the arms from behind and set her firmly on her feet. "Ye ought have yer sea legs afore now."

Gweneth looked up into the first mate's broad face and her lips parted in reply before she hiccuped and clapped a hand over her mouth and swayed against him.

"Careful there, missus. What ails ye?" But the sickly green complexion of the lady's face told him all he needed to know. "Ye'd do better to take to yer bed a spell. It'll soon pass. The cap'n is right wise to put the land under ye. I did wonder . . ." But Peckcum stopped, realizing that his familiarity bordered on insubordination. "Well, I'm amind from where the wind blows," and he winked and grinned. "Here, ye take me arm as anchorage, and I'll steer ye below. 'Tis a hot brick for yer feet and a dram o' spirits under yer belt what'll tide ye over."

"*Merci*, Peckcum. I cannot think why I should become ill. It is foolish of me. Perhaps something I ate," Gweneth answered, but she did not withdraw at once from the solid comfort of his impersonal embrace.

Peckcum glanced down at the head bent below his chin and wondered afresh at the ignorance of proper young ladies. Still it was not his place to amend her lack. After all, he reasoned, if the lady had not yet come to an understanding of her condition, the cause would not go unknown for long.

"Whatever it be, missus, ye can be certain it shall pass."

Gweneth took the arm offered and forced her rubbery legs to obey her command that they carry her forward.

"Cap'n, ye certain about Lady Rachel?" Daniel looked from the note in his hand to his captain. "What if the lady—excuse me, Cap'n, but what if she should mention your former affection to yer wife?"

Raoul looked up and laughed. "I could have you

thrown in the hole on a dozen different occasions each day, your respectful tone aside, Daniel. Why I do not is beyond me. I doubt Rachel gossips about her former escapades. She's married these two years to a proper sort of fellow and, if she has not yet given up the sport, at least she has the sense to be discreet."

"Ifin' you be sayin' so, Cap'n. Still ye might want to put a bug in yer lady's ear afore she comes to hear of it from other quarters. She'll not like it one bit."

"Still her confidant, Daniel? I'd have thought her brother was privy to all her complaints these days." Raoul scraped back his chair to rise. "I will consider your advice, but it is my inclination to disregard it. Gweneth has been sulky as it is without putting additional worries into her head."

"What worries?" Gweneth questioned at the threshold and the two men started guiltily.

"What is it, Peckcum? Has my wife come to some harm?" Raoul quickly inquired as he noted how heavily she leaned on the first mate's arm.

" 'Tis but a spot o' the plaguey seasickness, sir. Like as not, it will pass in a matter o' weeks." A sharp look from Daniel told Peckcum that his suspicions were probably correct.

"*Le mal de mer*, is it?" Raoul asked. "We shall soon take care of that."

"Cap'n, sir, what o' this?" Daniel questioned and thumped the pocket where he had hastily deposited the letter at Gweneth's appearance.

"You have your orders," Raoul answered with finality. "See to it that it is delivered as soon as we reach port. Leave us now. I shall call when I have need of you."

"What troubles Daniel?" Gweneth asked when the two seamen had departed.

Raoul pressed her back against the bed where he had guided her. "Nothing that needs concern you, *ma belle*. Daniel is an old fool who worries for naught. Rest, my love, and we shall talk later." He pulled the slippers from her feet and tucked her under the covers.

"I wish to speak of it now, Raoul. Tell me where you are sending me. I should know that at least." Gweneth closed her eyes for a moment to shut out the giddiness which skirted her senses.

Raoul sat on the ledge of the bunk and brushed her cheek with his fingertips. "Aye, Gweneth, if you promise to be quiet. You are going to stay with Squire and Lady Nicolson on Tortola. You will remember them as our hosts of the ball last spring. Daniel bears a request that they take you into their home until you are able to find passage home. Now go to sleep and not another word on the subject," he added, watching the tiny furrow deepen between Gweneth's arched brows.

A faint uneasiness hovered about her eyes, and Raoul was reminded of a stretch of sea off the North African coast whose smooth green shimmer was a sure indication of treacherous currents beneath. A feeling of contentment spread slowly through him. "How easily she is read," he thought in amazement. "How could I have been so blind to her love that night I found her in Barbados and she held me in her gentle embrace and offered up her lips to my brutal treatment?" It was there in the depths of her eyes even then. It was there now, with concern for him, and the knowledge of it humbled him.

"I remember Lady Nicolson well," Gweneth replied after some thought. "A great horsefaced woman with sad cow eyes and a figure to match."

Raoul's laughter was quick and sharp. "Nay, Gweneth. I do not recall such a guest for there were so many, but Lady Nicolson is quite the opposite. Charming, poised, something of a flirt—"

"Something of a beauty with the kind of heavy dark hair a man longs to veil himself in and generous, pouting rouged lips which beg to be kissed and a body that—but you would know better than I what her body promised and delivered," Gweneth finished for him in terse, caustic tones.

Raoul gave her a narrowed look and then whistled. "So you heard. Damn Daniel's presumption to teach me manners." He rose from the bed with his back to her. "I will not spend the rest of my life apologizing for what occurred in the first thirty years. You knew me when you accepted me. Knew enough to guess what sort of life I've led." He spun around to face her. "A man, Gweneth, not a blasted saint, not even a faithful lover. But I never lied for what I wanted. I never promised anything in return for favor, only mutual enjoyment. And that, I believe, I gave in abundance." He stopped and smiled that familiar, infectious grin that always tugged at Gweneth's heart. "You are my only, dearest, most precious love."

"Then do not send me from you like some worrisome child. I will not go to one of your former women, shepherded by a brother as though I am too stupid to manage myself." Gweneth wet her lips, seeking for the strength to maintain her dignity, for she felt like nothing so much as a hurt child.

"I do not want to know who the women were in your life; keep me ignorant if you can. But neither will I go smiling in humble need to one only to be fed gossipy stories of your prowess in bed. I do not wish to know if the phrases of love you speak to me have been used before to kindle the fires of a thousand other lustful couplings. I do not want to hear your praises dripping from the lips of another who knows your body as well as I and, perhaps because of experience, has given you more—"

"Silence!" Raoul commanded and the sound of his wrath brought Gweneth out of her reflective stupor and, quailing and pale, upright in bed. "No more! Not another single word if you value what is between us. I have stood more from you than anybody has the right to expect, and you will not belabor me for my failures a moment longer." Raoul drew a deep breath summoning all his restraint to keep from allowing his temper full vent.

"If you will not accept the arrangements I make for your own good and comfort, so be it. You may fend for yourself in Road Town, and I wish you good sport of it. But, by God, you will not speak to me like that again!"

He stood staring down at her, his features dark with rage, but the plea in his eyes was plain. Gweneth scrambled from beneath the bedding and ran to him.

"Raoul, please come with me!" she wailed and flung her arms about his neck. Not even her promise to herself not to repeat this request could stay the sobs which racked her body as she clung to him. "You say you love me. We must not part like this. It is not enough for me, these few weeks. I want more. It is selfish, I know, but I want it all, not simply a few weeks of perfect love. If you do not return, you will have killed us both.

"How should I live on after so brief a glimpse of happiness? We've only begun. Where are my memories of you with our first child? I want to watch you grow old over the seasons of life, to see your temples flecked with silver and your features mellowed with the span of good years. It is heartless to deny me this. I shall never ask another thing of you, I swear it. Please do not go to Barbados!"

The catch in Raoul's throat grew in the moment of silence between them. He did not deserve such love. But how could he explain to her the need to clear his name, the name so newly his and one he would fight to keep at all costs?

"Gweneth, dearest sweet wife," he whispered hoarsely. "Ask anything of me but this. You must know I would let nothing stay me from your side that was of less importance. It is for you that I do this thing, for us. The matter must be settled, or we shall ever live in some fear. I must know why Dillingham plotted so vehemently against you. If it was the mere capricious whim of a mean spirit, I shall make it plain to him that he must select his victims with more care in the future." His hands flexed into fists on her back. "If there is more, it is better I should ferret it out in his own territory. A few months, Gweneth. That is the length of our parting. Then nothing will keep me from your side."

"If I were as certain as you . . . ," Gweneth began slowly.

"You may swear by it, *ma belle*," Raoul returned against her ear and nibbled the soft curve of her neck. "Now, lady of mine, press upon me kisses such as will seal the oath between us and hasten me home to you."

Gweneth held still under his kiss, the fervent longing in that touch missing this once to spark off a returning warmth. For all the others she could present a fearless disguise of self-possession, but the anguish flowing through her now could not be cast out, and it deadened every other impulse. There is death in Barbados, her heart whispered, and she had lost the gamble too often not to know dread.

But Raoul could not hear that whisper and knew only that his wife had rejected him. He pushed her quickly away to the full distance of his reach. His eyes narrowed. "So, it is to be like that," he muttered ominously. "It is too bad you are not my mistress for then you would realize the danger in such a maneuver. We are bound, yes, but be careful that your pride does not wreck even that."

His words struck and lacerated Gweneth's already sore heart, but she was unable to reply when he turned and strode from the cabin, slamming the door behind him. And she ran to the basin, there to be sick when he had gone.

CHAPTER TWENTY-ONE

It was very late when Gweneth rolled over at the sound of the cabin door's opening. The formidable shadow of Captain Bertrand loomed before him as he strode through. She had been abed for hours without bothering to rise for the supper she could not endure, but she felt better now and welcomed the sight of Raoul's nakedness when he had shrugged out of his clothes and came toward the bed.

"All will be forgotten," Gweneth whispered to herself but, when he had blown out the candle and settled himself beside her, he did not lean over to kiss her or pull her close.

"I am cold," she said next to his ear, but he gave no sign that he had heard. Undaunted, Gweneth reached out for him.

Raoul did not move when her feathery light touch settled on his face. "No, no, my love. It shall not be so simple for you this night," he decided in thought and heaved a sleepy sigh. Let her learn what it is to earn a man's desire.

When her caresses were not answered in kind, Gweneth paused, squinting against the darkness to catch a glimpse of her husband's face. He does not want me, she realized with a jolt. I make mention of his mistresses, and he prefers the escape of old dreams to me!

The thought smarted as she chewed her forefinger in confusion and embarrassment. I am pleasing as a wife but not so exciting as a mistress, mon Capitaine?

she thought silently. One would never know what to expect with a mistress. The thrill of adventure and loss lurked behind every last embrace. Would she be there in welcome next time? Would he come again? Yes, Gweneth had to admit, perhaps there was something in that to spice a man's passion.

Eh bien, then I will not play the wife. If it is a mistress you dream of, then that you shall have. We shall see then, my fickle husband, if your thoughts stray for long. She turned her eyes, now accustomed to the night, on the long masculine body uncovered beside her.

What touch or caress inflamed a man to the best advantage, she wondered thoughtfully? Everything pleased him at any other time, but then he was always the aggressor, she the imitator. Now she must learn for herself and Gweneth realized that the prospect did not displease her.

Slowly and uncertainly she stroked his closed face, straying over the outline of his features as though she were blind, and behind each caress she left the soft impression of a kiss.

Raoul remained still, though the latent flame in his blood leaped instantly when she placed several light kisses at the corners of his mouth before pressing down full until his lips parted to her teasing probe.

Good, a good beginning, he thought, but now, what will you do? I shall not unbend to mere kisses, *ma belle*, and you are still ignorant of much of love's delights.

Gweneth's lips followed her fingers to the curve of his ear, down his neck, onto his chest. Her playful nips and tugs sent the blood scalding through his veins, but the rigid control Raoul demanded of his body held till her hands and face lowered to his belly and descended.

"Oh—love!" The gasp of astonished pleasure escaped, but Raoul dared not move, afraid that the moment would vanish.

The instinctive passion which spurred her was unlike anything he had ever experienced. So this, too, need not be taught, he mused through the veil of strangely sweet, exquisite torture to which her fingers and lips put him.

With a rapturous groan, he reached down and lifted her up until her breasts rested upon the mat of hair at his chest. The full length of her curving, clinging, womanly body unashamedly expressed her desire.

"My lady, we are even at long last for, truly, I have been seduced," and he laughed softly into her deep emerald gaze. "I am yours, a mettlesome impatient stallion, a worthy mount for so capable a mistress. Tonight, you ride."

"I am a marvelous mistress, non?" Gweneth questioned from within the comfort of her husband's arm in the dream of love's aftermath. Raoul's immodest laughter sent her out of his embrace.

"No, Gweneth, you would not last a month as a mistress." Then, because he read insult in the rigid column of her back, he wound a length of her hair about his hand and dragged her down against him. "Do not despair, *ma belle*, for you need never ply that trade. 'Tis a compliment I gave you." Still no reply. "You give too much and ask nothing in return. That is your endearing failure," he murmured and nuzzled her ear.

"But I—" Gweneth shut her mouth. She had been flushed with her victory and overeager to pronounce upon it.

"A woman who preys on men takes, not gives," he said. "She demands much for her service and never but never offers her love, *ma chérie*. Such a woman must use the promise of her body to barter for jewels, a house, perhaps even a coach. All you asked of me was a return of your love. That is the payment you exacted and that you have in generous supply. While it is the treasure of a wife, it is the plague of a mistress. And that, my love, is why you are not at heart a harlot."

"I think I am complimented, my lord," she said grudgingly, "but I am not certain."

Raoul rolled her over onto her back, his gaze a smoky midnight blue. "Would you prefer that I shower you with gifts and trouble you with my presence a mere once a week?"

"I would die of so little attention," she replied sincerely.

"Ah, now that you have had a taste of love's heady brew, you're caught, my Cyrenaic of the *Cyrene*. Is it the man you crave or simply his skill, I wonder?"

"Now you are being purposely unkind," she scoffed, wiggling free of his embrace. She sat up and flung her hair over one shoulder, primly crossing her arms over her bosom.

"I do not believe it, you know," Raoul said, indicating her posture. "The prim maid becomes you less that that of a daughter of joy. You must be content to be the wife of my table and hearth, joy of my bed, and guardian of my heart. And—in time, mother of my children."

Gweneth's look was suddenly guarded. "Mother, in time, you say. Then you do want children?"

"Yes, that too," Raoul admitted, quite astonished at the conviction in his own voice. It had never occurred to him before that he should desire sons and daughters of his own. At least he had not been a total profligate, indiscriminate in whom he bedded; but none of the women of his long acquaintance had ever laid the claim of paternity on him.

A weak, uneasy sensation skirted his gut. Suppose he could not sire a child? His eyes ran briefly over Gweneth's lovely slender form, not thin but without an ounce more than beauty would allow. She would bear fine strong children and, if he could plant a child within a woman, it would be with her.

"In a year or so, we shall attend this business of

children. Give it time, Gweneth. That I have you is more than I could hope for. Children are none so important next to that," he said, mostly for his own benefit.

He is uncertain, Gweneth decided, and hugged her arms closer against the chill. He had not given her the answer she hoped to hear, not quite. There was still much of him that remained a secret, and his life had given him no ready assurance that childhood could be a joyful secure life. She must not hurry him into such a commitment.

Still the signs were there. Her monthly flux was three weeks late. And now there was this nausea. Even she had been able to figure it out while lying in the darkness before his coming.

"I shall wait," she promised herself. The responsibility of marriage was yet strange to him. He needed time before plunging ahead into other uncharted waters.

Raoul sat up and, treading lightly to his desk, he lifted a ring of keys from his coat pocket and fitted it to the lock. The drawer scraped open and shut, but Gweneth could not tell what he withdrew. Settling in the bed once more, his arms pulled her upright in the bed, leaning her back against the paneled wall.

"Since you insist on playing the wanton, I thought I should pay the price." He put his hands under her hair at the nape of her neck, and when they fell away, Gweneth felt the weight of a necklace as it slipped down to hang from her throat.

Raoul touched the shimmering pearls, large as grapes, where they nestled in the hollow between her breasts and shook his head. "They seem so much the less lying next to your own secret treasures," he said and slipped a breast into the palm of his hand, squeezing gently.

"I love you!" Gweneth cried immediately and flung herself out across him in a crushing embrace that offered affection not passion, and Raoul felt the sly prickling of tears behind his closed lids.

The cannon blast, meant as a salute and warning, thundered overhead even as the mizzen lookout's bellow of "Sail ho!" carried below deck. Raoul was hardly out of the bunk and into his breeches before Peckcum's knock nearly unhinged the portal.

"British frigate, sir, and mean company by the looks o' 'em," the first mate roared.

Raoul swore to himself and affixed the last button before drawing the bolt. "How many and at what distance?" he asked calmly, but his gaze raked the man's features in savage intensity.

"There be only one, Cap'n. Sail's not more'n two leagues out. Damn jackass—" Peckcum's glance shifted to the bunk and the lady who had burrowed low in the covers on his entrance, and he swallowed back his deprecating thoughts. "The lookout must be moonmad not to 'a spied her afore this."

Raoul tugged on his boots. "Can we run before her and slip the trap?"

"A half hour earlier, we'd a stood a chance," Peckcum answered grimly. "As is, the sea's smoother'n a babe's arse. Nary a wind nor ripple. She's comin' up afore us. In the time it'll take to heave us about, she'll be up our—well," Peckcum grunted and wiped his mouth with a massive hand. "We'd best stand and prepare to fight."

"Speak sense, man. We carry not the shot nor cannon to meet her equally. Douse the lanterns fore and aft and prepare to hoist full sail, but await my order."

The first mate saluted, little more than a nod, and turned toward the deck. "And, for God's sake, keep the silence. We've an hour before dawn. Perhaps we've only not to draw attention to ourselves, and they'll be off after other prey," Raoul added.

Gweneth craned forward over the rail to better her

view, but the distant ship remained nothing more than a vague gray shadow on the vast black water.

"She's maneuverin' to come about and meet us afore the wind, Cap'n. Permission to hoist sail, sir?" Peckcum asked.

The maneuver was clumsily handled, and the sails sagged curiously before billowing out feebly. Raoul ground his teeth as he all but heard the timber on that far ship scream from the blunder. "Of all the addleheaded nonsense," he groaned. "Does she have witlings for a crew?" he questioned at the poor handling of that superb vessel.

"What does that ship want of us?" he muttered and sent a quick appraising glance at his wife. For himself he would not fear the decision to fight but, for her, there might be disaster.

"Peckcum, give the order for the raising of our flag." She had not fired again. It might be that she only wanted to know their ship's standard.

"And which one would that be, Cap'n?"

Peckcum's sly wink was answered in kind, but his captain said seriously, "Why the true one, of course, His Majesty's colors. Will our minor alterations give them sufficient doubt as to our identity?"

"Could be, Cap'n. A fine bit o' wisdom in that," Peckcum answered.

Gweneth had watched from the shore some weeks earlier as the crew removed the *Cyrene*'s figurehead and, with block and tackle, lowered it into the hole. The name had been whitewashed on the hull. Now the precautions made sense, and Gweneth prayed behind clenched teeth that the ruse would hold as she watched her husband with bright clear eyes.

"Best get below, missus. One glimpse o' that bright head o' yers and we're done for," the first mate advised from the corner of his mouth. His eyes were fixed on the seamen scurrying about the yardarms freeing the ratlines.

"Go, Gweneth," Raoul added from behind her.

"They may be simply flexing their muscles, the bastards, but we'll chance nothing."

"Will you surrender rather than fight?" she asked, giving nothing away in her voice.

Raoul did not answer but propelled her below. If he surrendered, it would be like slitting his own throat. No captain ever gave up his ship without a fight, did she not understand that? But could he allow her to be blasted from the water for the sake of his own stubborn pride?

"Stay below with me," she urged and held Raoul's arm. "Do vessels not routinely hail one another at sea? Could it not be simply that? If you are not recognized—"

The hail from the British man-o'-war could be heard in the hallway, and both Gweneth and Raoul turned abruptly toward the steps, but it was Benoit's voice that answered the cry, forcefully and boldly. Standing in the shadows, Gweneth could not tell the expression on her husband's face, but his fingers closed tightly over hers as they waited.

The words were muffled and unclear, but as the hail and return of words filtered below, it slowly became evident that they had not been purposefully singled out for attention.

"Yes, we are bound for the islands," Benoit cried in the pause. More voices, stronger now as the ship neared them, bawling out questions and answers.

"We are losing our advantage with every minute," Raoul groaned, for it was obvious that the *Cyrene* was not yet free of the drag line which kept her from drifting in the becalmed sea.

Peckcum's boots fell heavily on the steps as he marched below. "They are bound for Barbados, but there be sickness on board. The cap'n and first mate be both abed, and there's none to pilot the ship," he announced with a broad grin. "They are requestin' permission for an escort to port."

"She's helpless. We are free," Gweneth breathed in relief and hugged Raoul's arm.

"What is the sickness, mate?"

"Sounds suspiciously like food poisonin', Cap'n, what with the cramps and vomitin'. O' course it could be somethin' worse."

"She needs a pilot, Peckcum," Raoul replied flatly.

"Aye, Cap'n, that be the truth o' it. Only, if it ain't too serious, don't it seem best to—"

"She's marooned, seaman!" Raoul hissed low. "Don't attempt to teach me the code of the sea. Take two men and what supplies you will need, then it's over the side with you. You will have ample opportunity to revise your harsh opinion by the time we reach Barbados. If it's a true sickness, just remember your life depends on bringing her through."

Peckcum's ruddy color had ebbed. There was nothing a seaman feared more than illness, unless it was drowning. "Me, sir?" The big man shifted on his feet. "Aye, aye, Cap'n. Will do."

Raoul turned to Gweneth, his eyes coolly neutral as he took in her tremulous smile. "I'll be believing you a witch, woman, if you continue to gloat. So it's Barbados for us all. I hope m'lady does not have cause to rue this turn of events."

"Another hour before we can run with the tide," Benoit said. They had come to lay off Barbados earlier in the day, and all hands stood by for the piloting of the coral reefs which ringed these islands and made the passage into the harbor risky at best. It was early evening now, and the sun would soon dip below the horizon carting the brief twilight rapidly behind it.

"*Peste!*" Gweneth replied with oddly violent strength. "Can we do nothing but wait?"

"Little more. The fact is, there is a vessel ahead of us. We must give her time before we follow."

"Another ship?" she asked, having paid no attention

to the waters around them, for her eyes stayed steadily on the dark green land ahead of them.

"Cap'n Lavasseur's *Christobel*, missy," supplied Daniel. "She's been within hailin' distance this past half hour. He appears as anxious as we to run the reefs but not afore the tide. O' course, none knows ye be aboard."

Laurent. Gweneth felt suddenly discomforted. Had it taken all this while for her message to reach him, or was he making a business call on the island as usual? How could she explain her marriage if he had received her plea and come back expressly to help her? What if Raoul should discover that in her note she had practically promised to . . . These thoughts and more ran through her head at the unhappy news.

"Reckon Cap'n Bertrand will have a right pleasurable time of it breakin' his news to his friend," Daniel mused aloud with a quick grin.

Of course, Gweneth thought with an abrupt lessening of her guilt. Raoul would put it to him plainly and Laurent, as a gentleman, would hold his tongue. Gweneth's brow wrinkled. He would, wouldn't he?

Raoul strapped the rapier to his belt and looked down at the brace of pistols in the open case before him. They were primed with shot, but that would be of little use if he were drenched. He was not about to wait for the *Cyrene* to drop anchor in Carlisle Bay before setting foot on land. That circumstances had forced him to bring Gweneth along was an irritation in itself. He would hate to bind her hand and foot to the bunk while he went ashore. Therefore he planned to leave her now. Wildcat though she was, not even Gweneth would be so reckless as to plunge into the Caribbean in an attempt to follow him to shore.

He came on deck, dressed only in shirt and breeches. His boots hung casually from one hand as he came up behind Gweneth and encircled her waist with the other. "Would you not care to go below, love, and arrange your toilette? Within the hour we shall be entertaining guests in the bay," he said as his eyes tracked hers to the black and gold *Christobel*.

"You are only half dressed yourself, sir," she answered when she had turned in his arm. "No stock nor stockings, no coat nor waistcoat, are you not a trifle casual, my lord?" she inquired with a mocking, critical gaze.

"I have things to do before I greet Captain Lavasseur. And with you to fill his eyes and stir his loins, he shall have no interest in my attire." The tone was light, but Raoul withheld any expression from his eyes.

Gweneth blushed and inwardly damned the scarlet flames licking at her throat and cheeks. She should not have shown any interest at all in the mention of Laurent. "As you say, Capitaine, it is time to don the role of temptress." But when she moved past him, swinging her hips in taunting invitation, Raoul clapped a hand on her bottom.

"Steady there, *ma belle*, or that dangerous wamble of yours may land you a stint in the hole for the time we are in port." He caught a handful of her skirts and pulled her back into his arms for a quick, hard kiss. "Now, about your business, madame, but lightly and ever so demurely."

Gweneth smiled at him and hurried below. When she was out of sight, he jerked a thumb toward the dinghy waiting to be launched. The men who hoisted the craft would pilot the reefs for him and then he would wade ashore. He stuffed his feet into his boots, swung over the side into the tiny boat, and gave orders for its lowering. It was a devilish trick to play on her, but there was no other way to protect her.

Gareth sat back in a red leather wing chair in the empty library and propped a leg up on the cold hearth.

"Damnable heat!" It was not possible for a man to

enjoy the merest comfort in this sweltering inferno, he reflected irritably. Still . . . he sighed heavily and dropped his coffee cup into its saucer with a jarring rattle. Leonora was no longer here to fly into a fit of hysterics for the fortieth occasion since the disappearance of her niece, and that was some small respite.

He rubbed away a trickle of moisture from his brow. Every reminder of those hours after Captain Bertrand's escape still squeezed fresh sweat from his body. His actions were those of a sleepwalker as, for the first time in his life, he had acted on impulse. And, as to be expected, it served him poorly, for no sooner had he begun to take his rage out on the girl than he was interrupted by Amy. Fool that she was, she had come in search of her mistress. A few sharp slaps and she had spilled the entire story of the rescue, and he had not hesitated to choke the life from her with his own deadly, beringed hands. She knew too much and what she had just witnessed made the abrupt silencing necessary.

He gagged and bound Gweneth, then carried Amy's body up to Gweneth's room before trudging down to the wine cellar to the soldier whom it was necessary to dispatch with a wine bottle. What a help it was that he had locked out all his slaves for fear they would learn of the captain's whereabouts and talk. There was no one to see or hear his movements but Leonora, and she had taken a sleeping draught before retiring.

A wrinkle of distaste flowed over Gareth's features. So much violence and death. The good captain had not even bothered to kill the guard. No, he himself had had to do it all. He had carried Gweneth's inert body out to an abandoned shed and arrived back at the house just as Captain Willows and the constable rode up with news of the captain's escape. Yes, Gareth answered, he had just made the same discovery and, what was more, his niece had disappeared. From there, the quixotic wheels of justice began to turn, and he was spared explanations. The shocked and swooning Leonora freed him from examining the bodies and conjecturing about what had taken place. The constable assumed that Gweneth had been abducted, despite Willows's claim that the captain was alone. Either the captain had dragged off the girl and killed her in some particularly fiendish way, or he had smuggled her off the island, the guardian of justice maintained.

Later in the day, when Gareth could spirit Willows away, he had delivered to him the extra cargo. Willows was no fool, but he was not particularly bright and seemed to see no connection between the escape and the bundle aboard his ship.

"The gleam of gold has blinded keener eyes," Gareth muttered and chuckled without mirth. He should hate to exchange places with Bertrand were he foolish enough to be caught. No explanation he could speak would ever unravel the tangle of this trap. Yet, though the risk was great, Gareth could not force himself to kill a third time, but Gweneth's fate was certain.

Gareth fingered a tassel on the sleeve of his lounging jacket while the clock on the mantel chimed the hour. On the morrow he, too, would sail for England. Leonora had departed some weeks ago, much to his insistence and relief. The house was closed, and the shrouded rooms echoed with the stillness of uninhabited ground. He sent the last of the house slaves to Myers only this afternoon but some unreasoned urge kept him here tonight when he might have accepted Myers's hospitality. It was as if all the ghosts were to be faced tonight and the victory savored in the silence of their defeat.

His hand went instinctively to the pistol under his coat at the sound of rattling glass. "Steady there, old man. 'Tis only the wind," he cautioned himself, but the nerves which had never failed him would not marshal themselves into order, and it was with dreamlike awareness that he watched the sheer summer-weight curtains over the terrace doors part.

Raoul was surprised by the empty, dark vision of

the house but the sight of Dillingham's saddled mare on the carriageway convinced him that the man he sought was still within. He drew his blade from its scabbard and gently pushed the unlocked windows open.

"Who goes there? Speak or I'll fire," Gareth roared and sprang from his chair.

"Will you, indeed? And here I have come all this way to propose a chat."

"Bertrand!" Gareth's voice was dry as he felt his pulse throb at his temples. Immediately he stuck his pistol out of sight.

"None other," Raoul replied congenially and stepped into the room. "A little light, perhaps, Governor?"

"Bertrand," Gareth repeated in astonishment but when he had struck a spark to the lamp on the nearby table, a strange sardonic smile lit his features. "You show a deplorable lack of sense in returning here. But you did say a chat. Is the hardware necessary?"

"A precaution, no more," Raoul returned and lowered his blade. "The same as your pistol."

Gareth's hand had crept up the bulge of his coat, but he let his fingers slide easily down his belly as if to smooth the material. "You refer to my challenge, of course. A precaution," he rallied, and his smile deepened although Raoul's concentrated look had not left the telltale lump.

Taking his cue from the lack of aggressiveness on the other man's part, Gareth struck a defiant pose. "See here. What brings you back? You've debauched my niece and God knows what else since you abducted her. The authorities have been alerted in every port of these islands. How dare you show your face in my house?"

Raoul's gaze shifted, and in the insufficient lamplight he saw the room was empty. All but the heaviest furnishings had been removed and dust covers blanketed nearly every other piece. Raoul slipped forward a pace and whipped the sheet from the other fireside chair, seating himself.

"Suppose you begin by explaining why you trusted Willows?" Raoul said suddenly. Gareth's face twitched, but he remained silent. "Tell me about the night I escaped. Tell me what happened to Gweneth." The voice addressing Gareth grew colder with each word, but he could not discern anger in the captain's face.

"Who helped you escape?" Gareth asked finally.

"Gweneth, of course."

"And you abducted her."

"You know that is a lie," Raoul replied shortly.

Gareth's temper lowered as his opponent's rose. He could not guess what Bertrand knew or had heard, but an enraged man made mistakes and when he made that unguarded error, he would be dead. "Can you prove it?"

Raoul relaxed against the chair back. "Send for Amy or Corporal O'Grady."

"Dead."

The single word hovered in the air between them. Raoul's fingers locked on the hilt of his weapon. "You killed them."

"My dear fellow, the authorities see it otherwise. You overpowered the corporal and struck him a fatal blow with a full bottle of wine."

"A lie."

"You then crept up to Mademoiselle Valois's room, surprised her with the maid Amy and, having strangled one girl, you made off with my niece."

Raoul struck the carpet with even raps of the tip of his blade. "I'll say this much. I have Gweneth."

"Do you really?" Gareth questioned with disbelieving laughter. "And what do you propose to do with her?" He had remained standing till now but seated himself casually. "Am I to suppose that is why you come to me? A proposition of some sort, is that what you have in mind?"

"Something of that nature, yes. I want you to write a retraction of my sentence, restoring to me my ship and liberty."

"Nothing else?" Gareth's tone was one of mockery. "How do you suggest I grant such broad amnesty? Two murders and a kidnapping, surely you must remember your crimes. How will you deal with these?"

"I have a witness."

"Ah yes, the undoubtable Mademoiselle Valois." Such a flimsy lie. Gareth had expected much better of the man.

"Make that Countess Avernon, or Madame Bertrand, if you please."

"Of course, you have married the lady. No doubt there is a child on the way, and for that highly plausible reason she is unable to accompany you just now," Gareth declared willingly. "What sort of fool do you take me for, Captain? I'll vow you have some trumped-up papers which attest to your supposed marriage, but I do not believe you can produce the lady herself."

"You seem rather certain of that," Raoul observed calmly. "What if I produce the contents of a certain logbook by one Captain Willows? Half literate, I fear, but passably legible to even the most casually interested reader. One is supplied with dates, cargoes, maps, and—names," he added with special emphasis. "I wonder that my transgressions won't be overshadowed by your own."

Relief sighed audibly from Gareth. So this was his ace. "A good try, but it does not signify," he explained slowly, his mind racing forward to the time when the captain lay dead and he must summon the authorities. "You found Willows's logs when you pirated away his ship." Gareth looked up. "Another felony, Captain? My, but you compound your villainy at every turn. And we must add to this the death of my niece since, of course, she cannot be produced."

"The log and my—ship are both in the harbor at this

moment. If I do not return soon, my men have their orders. You will not take my vessel before they reach the captain of that British frigate coming in behind them."

The movement was swift, more rapid and smooth than would have been expected from a man who spent his days behind a desk. Raoul leaped to his feet, overturning his chair, but Gareth's pistol was directed at his heart.

"You understand that I may not allow you to leave here," Gareth drawled in nearly regretful terms.

"Quite."

"Whatever charges may come to light as a result of Willows's logs, 'tis best confronted without you. Despicable rogue that you are, you came back on the off chance of blackmail, to strike a bargain to buy your freedom. My answer: your death. I'll hazard the rest," Gareth explained and stepped slowly behind his chair to lengthen the distance between himself and the captain's blade.

"What of my position as a peer of the realm?" Raoul asked, glancing about for a means of protection.

"Yes." Gareth frowned. "That is inappropriate. It should be so much simpler if you were a mere privateer, *un chevalier d' industrie*, as Mademoiselle Gweneth would have phrased it. Still there must be some blot on your record, some indiscretion of your earlier years which sent the heir of Mochton out to sea. Of course whatever it is will be brought to light after your demise. A crime of passion and violence, I should think, quite in keeping with your nature."

"You can be rid of me, perhaps, but what of my wife and child?" Raoul asked in an effort to confuse the man.

"Child?" Gareth echoed blankly. "Is the mythical Gweneth with child so soon? Well yes, I can believe it. She looked to be a prime breeder." Gareth pondered this bit of news and then a thin-lipped smile appeared. "I can almost believe you have truly found her. If so, then you have told me where she is."

"Have I?" Raoul's voice was calm, but his head cocked to the sound of carriage wheels on the drive. That would be Peckcum and Benoit. He stared hard at Gareth, but the man had begun to speak again and seemed unaware of the noise.

". . . have sent her to Mochton Court. I have all the time in the world to rid myself of her and your offspring. Young girls often lose their first. Without you there will be less chance that she'll produce a legal child, though I wonder if she won't drop a bastard or two in her haste to be consoled in her grief.

"She's a delectable bit of flesh, and there will be many a young stallion sniffing about her skirts before long. Well, 'tis no concern of yours." Gareth was enjoying himself hugely at the captain's expense, delaying and giving over completely to this bit of fiction in order to increase the man's humiliation. He wondered absently if he should tell the captain the truth of the girl's fate but no, this served as well.

More movement outside. Raoul spoke suddenly and loudly to cover the disturbance. "One question, Dillingham, a last request you might say. Why do you so hate Gweneth?"

Gareth's brows rose in an exclamation of genuine shock. " 'Twas never a question of hate, Captain. The girl and her sister presented a mere inconvenience." His hand wavered slightly but did not move from its target.

"They were an obstacle to my wife's inheritance. That is why I needed the girl married off to Myers," he said as though willing Raoul to see reason. "I needed time to produce a son to inherit. With Myers there'd have been no heir, no legal one. Your untimely arrival presented a problem. Even that first night it was plain you meant destruction to my plan. Gweneth would have run away with you to England and maybe you would have married her. A son with you? There would have been dozens, I've no doubt." Gareth sighed, wearying of the conversation. Yet he had reason to be proud. He had come through this entire ordeal without once losing control, the pure and proper gentleman.

"She gave me some bad moments with that Frenchman Lavasseur, I can tell you. Even I was tempted, more than tempted." He watched as Raoul's face visibly paled in even this poor light. "Never mounted her, did you? Imagine my surprise when I exacted that payment for having allowed your escape. I can tell you that she was worth—"

"Shut your damnable mouth!" Raoul bellowed and lurched forward, but the priming of the gun checked his movement. "All this for a few pieces of gold!" he spat out, trembling with rage and the fear that they had been overheard.

Gareth glared at his victim. "Not money. For title and respectability! My mother was a strumpet who married a bondsman, a derelict and rapist. Respectability means more to a man like me than it ever could to those like you who have known your worth from the moment of your birth." Gareth shook his head. This was off the subject. "I've not found so many deaths appealing, yours least of all. You must realize that you engineered your own death in coming back. Now I can bind the last thread of my tapestry with your end. *'Pas à pas, on và loin.'* Totally appropriate, my motto. Step by step, I have gone far."

The shadows in the doorway behind Dillingham rippled as one separated from the rest and came forward.

"Good God, Gweneth!" Raoul cried in strangled fury. "Get the hell out!"

"Very good, Bertrand. You really could have made your mark on the stage," Gareth rejoined approvingly. "For a moment I nearly believed you had seen someone."

"You do not believe in avenging angels, monsieur?"

Gareth jumped and nearly turned but saw the threatening gleam of Raoul's sword from the corner of his eye and scotched the curiosity to make certain that he had heard aright. "Well, well, this is a pleasure, my dear. So Bertrand was not lying."

"Think, monsieur. Which of us do you want dead?" Gweneth asked unsteadily, for she could not draw her attention from Raoul's face.

"Both of you, naturally. As it is, I prefer to kill you, dear niece, before turning my pistol on your husband." Gareth braced himself with a hand on the chair back. There was no exit for him now. It was but to make certain he killed them both and, if he survived, to flee.

"As you turn to fire, I'll cut you dead, Dillingham," Raoul warned, shaken to his boots by Gweneth's appearance. Where the devil were his men?

"But not, I think, before I have widowed you, Captain, and that is a chance I prefer to take. Your thrust may not be as clean as you desire, and then you, too, shall die. On the other hand I could weigh the odds in my favor by disposing of you first," and Gareth raised his weapon, aiming the deadly barrel of steel at Raoul's head. "Your wife will not grieve for long. I shall send her after you to the sweet reward of a grave."

The distinct sound of a drawn spring on metal was heard in the silence. "I, too, have a pistol," Gweneth announced bravely, but she had never fired a shot in her life and knew not if she could even aim one.

"She's deadly with a blade and a crack shot as well," Raoul lied, begging silently for time. It did not matter that he could die, but he damned Gweneth for choosing to die with him. You brave, beautiful fool, he thought with a curse. "Come, make your move, you scurvy swine," Raoul rasped out, dropping the formalities. "Show yourself for the lowborn, blowby you are," he jeered, hoping to goad the man to some false action. "You will have one shot, you baseborn craven. Use it before I slice you to ribbons."

Sweat ran and gathered in his brows, but Gareth could ill afford to move, however cautiously. "The girl won't shoot," he said to no one in particular, "not at a man's back. Her integrity is too great for that. She must know that you have fallen, Bertrand, before she will act." His voice rose and strengthened, as if he drew courage from his own pronouncements.

"I know you too well, little niece. Does your hand not tremble dangerously at the thought that you must kill? To take a life, can you do that, I wonder? I doubt it," he continued to taunt the girl at his back while he mentally calculated the distance between them with the sound of her sharp, uneven breathing.

It may have been a trick of light and shadow or it might have been the fear which quickened every sense of Gweneth's being to the slightest suggestion of movement but, as Gareth's finger seemed to close over the trigger, Gweneth's fingers responded in kind and a deafening explosion of light and fire shattered the night followed by another and another until the very room was lit with flame and the stench of gunpowder.

All the figures stood for an instant, frozen in tabloid against that background of light and smoke. There, in that fractional eternity when Gweneth's eyes met Raoul's over Gareth's shoulder, she saw the blood well at his brow and the senseless surprise in his face, and she knew it mattered not that she might have struck her uncle, for he had not failed to strike with lethal effect.

Her head swam dizzily and as she slumped forward, a paper character in a shadowbox of toppling figures, she wondered fleetingly how her uncle had managed to return her fire without so much as moving, for the sharp cold pain shattering her heart must certainly mean death.

CHAPTER TWENTY-TWO

Gweneth awoke with a start, the acrid smell of gunpowder lingering in her nostrils and throat. She no longer lay on the carpet of the dimly lit library but rested on a bed in the shimmering pink and gold bedroom that had once been hers. Fear, so acute she was unable to move or cry out, gripped her when a man stepped back from the windows and turned.

"Laurent!" The pitiful cry burst from her lips, freeing her limbs from paralysis, and she stumbled from the bed and met him halfway with outstretched arms.

The sobs came with long gasps, and she trembled so hard that had not Laurent held her upright, Gweneth would have been at his feet. He half carried, half pulled her across the floor to the bed and gathered her gently to his body with soothing hands.

"Ah, *ma chère*, if you do not cease, you shall break my heart. The man was not worth even one of your tears."

Gweneth jerked back. Instantly she sprang for him, kicking and scratching like some cornered wild thing. "*Menteur!* I hate you! You are . . . nothing compared to . . . *Mon Dieu!* Why Raoul? Why not I?" she shrieked.

Laurent gave up defending himself and sprawled on the bed in laughter while Gweneth flailed overhead. "*Pardieu!* Give over, chérie. I believe I prefer Bertrand's wrath to yours, though what he shall do to me if he should find us like this I dare not ponder."

Gweneth sat back on her heels, nails poised in challenge. His gentle teasing and wickedly amused expression were completely unfathomable as Laurent's gaze slid over her in lazy appraisal. "I have always regretted not completely undressing you when the opportunity was afforded. *Merci*, madame, for the display. *Ma foi! C'est perfection.*"

Gweneth's hands fell to her breasts, failed to entirely disguise her nakedness, and gave up the effort. The tears held by her momentary anger flooded her eyes and spattered her breasts with tiny jewels.

"*Bien amie*," he whispered softly and, raising up, caught her again against his chest. "What stupidity! Why had I not realized it? You do not know that your *capitaine* lives." Her chin lifted swiftly, her gaze a dazzling green, and Laurent could not resist lightly kissing her cheeks moist with tears. "He lives. Of course he lives. You do not think I should permit anything else?" he announced dramatically. "Why, I shot the poltroon between the eyes."

"But Raoul? Who shot—?"

Laurent smiled smugly. "You did, I suspect. No, there was little harm," he added quickly to expiate the horror in Gweneth's face. "A neat parting of his hair, nothing more."

The feel of his warm lean hands on her bare shoulders brought back some semblance of sanity, and Gweneth prudently wrapped the counterpane over her nakedness. "Where is my husband?"

Laurent smiled but the disappointment was apparent as she hid from his sight that lovely, lithe sun-browned body. "Then the marriage is a true one. So many things were said on that hell-bent ride from Bridgetown, but the truth of your marriage—*Eh bien*, for you I am glad." A puzzling frown puckered his brow. "Bertrand has owned up to his feelings? It is more than . . ." And his hand made a sweeping gesture to include not only her but the bed.

"He loves me," Gweneth returned simply without

looking directly at him, for his frank inquiry brought several problems to her mind.

"It is well that you know it. When you fell, he cried out in such agony that I thought at first one of us had wounded you. *Morbleu!* He waded in on us with such vile oaths and blows that I thought your brother and I would be bludgeoned to death." He laughed in memory. "Have a care, madame, your husband can be a savage. Non, *le diable l'importe;* I should offer my sympathies to him," Laurent amended and put a tentative finger to his left cheek to examine the scratch from her nails showing a faint trickle of blood.

"Poor Laurent," she murmured and added her hand to the fingers at his wound. "Forgive me, only where—"

"Ah, *ma petite*. A single kiss from the fair bride and I shall collect your ill-tempered husband who is closeted below with the authorities."

Not waiting for her approval, Laurent initiated what became so thorough an embrace that Gweneth began to suspect the outcome. Just as she began to struggle in defiance, he was plucked from her with such unexpected swiftness that she lurched forward onto her face.

"Damn you, Lavasseur! Dare you make love to my wife before my eyes?" The explosive words were barely sounded before Raoul landed a powerful fist to Laurent's middle that sent him crashing against the nightstand and onto the floor.

"For pity sakes, woman, cover yourself!" he bellowed in accusation, and Gweneth scrambled for the cover she had unknowingly lost in her surprise.

Laurent swept the dark hair from his eyes and smiled disarmingly but made no move to rise from his rather ridiculous position. "Perhaps I deserved that for what I was thinking, nothing else. It was quite harmless, I assure you."

Raoul stood, fists poised and legs apart though flexed for another attack. "Not so harmless that my wife has not left her mark on you. I should know better than to leave a picaroon with another man's riches. On your feet. Hell, but I am going to enjoy bashing in that handsome face of yours!"

As he moved toward his reluctant opponent, Gweneth interposed herself between them, dragging the cover from the bed. "Laurent has done nothing—oh, it's a *mesintelligence*—a . . ." Her voice failed as she stared with joy and thanksgiving at the man she loved.

"A mistake," Laurent offered from the floor.

"That's it, a mistake!" she cried gratefully. "I thought I saw you murdered, and Laurent made some comment—oh, I do not remember—but it seemed to be about you. I attacked him, do you not see? The kiss, it was nothing," Gweneth finished in an airy dismissal that brought an injured glance from Laurent.

Raoul's glare examined one, then the other, and he lowered his fists, forcing the fingers straight. Still he answered roughly. "Damn, Gweneth, you stand there and defend him! Time was when to kiss you was to invite attack and not vice versa."

"Ah, that sounds like my presence is no longer required," Laurent interjected and rose guardedly.

"Stay where you are, Frenchman," Raoul ordered, and Laurent merely came to his feet.

"*Mon ami*, will you never understand?" Laurent indicated Gweneth with a jerk of his head. "See how the girl dotes on you? I for one have known how it would end for both of you from the beginning." He cocked his head with a quirked brow. "*Enfin*, it was against my nature to resist the temptation to try to woo her from you, for all that. Do not blame me too harshly for stealing a few kisses when you were not about."

What Raoul might have answered was forestalled by the collision of a slight frame against his as soft slender arms wound themselves about his neck. The delectable, tantalizing pressure of parted lips drowned out any reply and only just in time did he reach to grab for the coverlet snaking down Gweneth's form, leaving her back and hips displayed for Laurent's view.

"Gweneth!" The high-pitched cry could belong to only one person, and Gweneth pirouetted about to confront her sister.

"Renée? How can it be? Where have you come from?" she asked incredulously as she took charge of the bedding and almost tripped as she ran to the door. The hugs and kisses interspersed with quick exclamations completely excluded for once the dominating presence of the two sea captains.

"What happened? Why are you not in Venice?" Gweneth questioned. In as little as seven months Renée had changed considerably, the promise of maturity of last summer now bore fruit, and her slim young body showed new and softer curves beneath her bottle-green velvet gown.

Renée blushed prettily under her sister's appraisal with a sidelong glance at Laurent through her lowered sooty lashes. "I never went to Venice. Oh Gweneth, you are so stubborn and practical that I did not trust you," she said impatiently. "If I'd told you what I planned to do, you would have stopped me."

"Of course," Gweneth nodded. "But what did you do?"

"I did not believe for a moment that you could outwit Monsieur Dillingham." A spasm of pain flitted over her features, but she hurried on with a slight toss of her blue-black curls. "You needed help and someone to get you out of the mess you are forever stepping into."

"Amen," Raoul grumbled to the room at large.

"I knew you would not be sensible enough to search for Capitaine Bertrand yourself, so it was left to me to find him." A dimple appeared in the corner of her mouth as she smiled at Raoul. "You told me, Gweneth, that Capitaine Lavasseur's home was New Orleans and after that, it was simply a matter of going there and seeking him out to help me discover Capitaine

Bertrand's whereabouts. Oh non, do not ask me to explain how it was accomplished. It was ever so easy to convince the people aboard ship that I wanted desperately to visit old family friends in the New World before leaving for Europe. Capitaine Lavasseur's family is quite well known, and that is why we are here."

"Not quite that simply," Laurent amended, now standing by Raoul. "I was at sea when your sister arrived on my doorstep, and by the time I returned home last month, she had completely won over my parents and siblings." A speculative smile spread across his lips as he held Renée's gaze. "She may be young, but your sister has a way about her that had even my brothers vying for her affections long before I arrived. Naturally I could not refuse the challenge." His gaze swept back to Gweneth. "You are a trial to any man's peace of mind, chérie, but there is something to be said for the helpless female—especially when you are holding her exquisite little form in your arms and she clings to you, begging so sweetly for your help and comfort."

Gweneth's startled expression swung from Laurent's complacent grin to Renée's crimson cheeks. "Oh, do not look at me like that," she objected saucily. "Surely you cannot be jealous of my little adventure. You have your capitaine, why should I not have the same?"

"Is there to be another marriage in this family? *Morbleu!* Is a brother to have no peace of conniving females?" Benoit questioned from the doorway. "So, you are awake, Gweneth. I cannot decide between hugging you to pieces for being alive or turning you over my knee for bolting from us at the dock when you did."

"Well, I, for one, can," Raoul thundered, and Gweneth turned back quickly to see him touch the red mark at his hairline. "Confound it, woman, you snatched away half my life appearing in that room when you did. How did you manage to escape Benoit and Daniel?"

Gweneth shrugged airily but took a hesitant step

back from the man scowling above her. "I know my uncle. Your sword was no match for a gun, and when I realized that you had left yours behind, I knew what had to be done."

"You could have waited for aid."

"They were taking too long," she mumbled. "Laurent reached the dock before us, and Peckcum thought he should come with us. They just stood there talking at cross-purposes and waving their hands about."

"Bertrand, *mon ami*, I wish you had been there to see the look in Monsieur Myers's face when Gweneth jerked him free as he descended from his carriage at the dock. She sprang into his seat with the reins in her hands," Laurent commented with an amused shake of his head, "and vanished before we realized that she would not wait for us."

Gweneth looked up timidly through the veil of her lashes. "I am sorry I shot you," she whispered in agony.

Raoul studied her harshly for a moment. "I am tempted to let you believe that lie. Humility sits well on your features. But that is not the case. Dillingham struck me and, if you had not caught him in his right shoulder as he fired, I'd not be standing here now."

Gweneth tried to smile, but the effort trembled uncertainly on her lips as gathering tears mirrored the distress in the depths of her jade eyes.

"Out of here, all of you," Raoul declared firmly. "I plan to leave Barbados at the first opportunity, and I do not want an exhausted, hysterical female on my hands." Though the words held no comfort, the strong gentle arm he put about Gweneth's shoulders denied his anger.

"Raoul," Gweneth began when the others had gone and he lay her back on the bed, "is it over?"

He sat down beside her and tucked the covers protectively around her. "Yes, my love. Dillingham got no more than he deserved, and there is collaborating evidence to justify my action. My mistake was in not thinking him the desperate, cold-blooded killer he was. Forget him. He stopped at nothing, not even where you were concerned." Raoul threaded his fingers gently through the cinnamon curls tumbling across the pillow. He had come so close to losing her that the icy knot in his entrails had not yet vanished.

"Raoul, I heard," Gweneth murmured faintly and turned her face away. "When I think of the awful things I said to you, I could die of shame. It was better when I believed that you raped me. Then, at least, I was yours alone. What must you think of me now?"

Her voice throbbed with an undisguised ache, and Raoul swore and pulled her into his arms, knowing where her thoughts had strayed. "I love you," he said in a choked breath, and Gweneth raised apprehensive eyes to his face. "Nothing you have ever suffered could change that for me." He cradled her to his chest, pressing so hard that she could hear the rapid sure strokes of his heart. "I am a man driven by ten thousand kinds of demons, most of whom seem to delight best in the agony of my jealousy. But this is different. I lied to you for the best of reasons. Not, as you may suspect, because my pride suffered as a result of your misfortune and not because it was easier to soothe my anger by making you think I was responsible for your fate. For once in my life someone else came first. I knew even as I uttered the words that I might risk losing you. If you could have seen your face—well, there was no other way of giving you back yourself.

"I think I always believed your innocence. You told me the truth, and I knew it to be such, and yet . . ." Raoul sighed philosophically. "There it is. My emotions are not rational. I want you. I need you. You are in and of every breath I take. And whenever someone else draws from you that unexpected intensity of your gaze, I am lost. If nothing else, I have learned this.

"I need to see your face in every morning's light and feel your warmth in the last dregs of my consciousness each night." He tilted her chin up and ran a thumb with a loving touch over her soft full lips. "Perhaps I shall continue to make a fool of myself upon occasion, but only—Lord, to think I'd ever come to this because of a green-eyed slip of a woman!" he said hoarsely, capturing her lips in a fierce, demanding embrace.

"Do not mistake me, I'd have ripped out Lavasseur's heart had I suspected for one minute that his attentions were serious or that you welcomed them. The violence is real, the anger is strong, and the temptation to tease me could prove dangerous." Raoul shook his head slowly, and the sudden change from grim seriousness to boyish grin was complete. "Now, if there are no further topics of discussion," and he leaned over to press Gweneth under him onto the bed, but she held him off by the shoulders.

"Just one thing more, mon Capitaine." She moistened her lips nervously and smiled. "I meant to wait until I was certain, but since you need so very much assurance. Oh—I know that there is no one who can part us. Still and all it is only fair to warn you that in the coming months it is quite likely that someone shall be quite obviously between us. That is, until he or she can be laid in its own little bed."

"Dear God!" Raoul's voice was thick with amazement as understanding crept slowly into his face. Reaching down between them, his hand slipped with infinite care over her slightly swollen belly, undetected till now. He swallowed hard and blinked. "You mean—you are certain? Oh, God in heaven be praised that he should see fit to offer a miracle to an idiot the likes of me!" he cried and swept her once more into his arms.

"Raoul," Gweneth whispered with tears of relief as she held his face in her hands. "I want to go home now. I think we have earned our passage at last."

Second Generation
Howard Fast

THE SECOND TRIUMPHANT NOVEL IN THE TOWERING EPIC LAUNCHED BY

THE IMMIGRANTS

Barbara Lavette, the beautiful daughter of rugged Dan Lavette and his aristocratic first wife, stands at the center of *Second Generation*. Determined to build a life of her own, Barbara finds danger, unforgettable romance, and shattering tragedy. Sweeping from the depths of the Depression, through the darkest hours of World War II, to the exultant certainty of victory, *Second Generation* continues the unbelievable saga of the Lavettes.

A Dell Book $2.75 (17892-4)

At your local bookstore or use this handy coupon for ordering:

| **Dell** | **DELL BOOKS** SECOND GENERATION $2.75 (17892-4)
 P.O. BOX 1000, PINEBROOK, N.J. 07058 |

Please send me the above title. I am enclosing $ _____
(please add 75¢ per copy to cover postage and handling). Send check or money order—no cash or C.O.D.'s. Please allow up to 8 weeks for shipment.

Mr/Mrs/Miss _____

Address _____

City _____ State/Zip _____

Dell Bestsellers

- [ ] **TO LOVE AGAIN** by Danielle Steel $2.50 (18631-5)
- [ ] **SECOND GENERATION** by Howard Fast $2.75 (17892-4)
- [ ] **EVERGREEN** by Belva Plain $2.75 (13294-0)
- [ ] **AMERICAN CAESAR** by William Manchester ... $3.50 (10413-0)
- [ ] **THERE SHOULD HAVE BEEN CASTLES**
  by Herman Raucher $2.75 (18500-9)
- [ ] **THE FAR ARENA** by Richard Ben Sapir $2.75 (12671-1)
- [ ] **THE SAVIOR** by Marvin Werlin and Mark Werlin . $2.75 (17748-0)
- [ ] **SUMMER'S END** by Danielle Steel $2.50 (18418-5)
- [ ] **SHARKY'S MACHINE** by William Diehl $2.50 (18292-1)
- [ ] **DOWNRIVER** by Peter Collier $2.75 (11830-1)
- [ ] **CRY FOR THE STRANGERS** by John Saul $2.50 (11869-7)
- [ ] **BITTER EDEN** by Sharon Salvato $2.75 (10771-7)
- [ ] **WILD TIMES** by Brian Garfield $2.50 (19457-1)
- [ ] **1407 BROADWAY** by Joel Gross $2.50 (12819-6)
- [ ] **A SPARROW FALLS** by Wilbur Smith $2.75 (17707-3)
- [ ] **FOR LOVE AND HONOR** by Antonia Van-Loon .. $2.50 (12574-X)
- [ ] **COLD IS THE SEA** by Edward L. Beach $2.50 (11045-9)
- [ ] **TROCADERO** by Leslie Waller $2.50 (18613-7)
- [ ] **THE BURNING LAND** by Emma Drummond $2.50 (10274-X)
- [ ] **HOUSE OF GOD** by Samuel Shem, M.D. $2.50 (13371-8)
- [ ] **SMALL TOWN** by Sloan Wilson $2.50 (17474-0)

At your local bookstore or use this handy coupon for ordering:

Dell | **DELL BOOKS**
P.O. BOX 1000, PINEBROOK, N.J. 07058

Please send me the books I have checked above. I am enclosing $_____
(please add 75¢ per copy to cover postage and handling). Send check or money order—no cash or C.O.D.'s. Please allow up to 8 weeks for shipment.

Mr/Mrs/Miss_____

Address_____

City_____State/Zip_____

A beautiful woman at the pinnacle of power can commit many sins. Only one counts— getting caught.

INDISCRETIONS

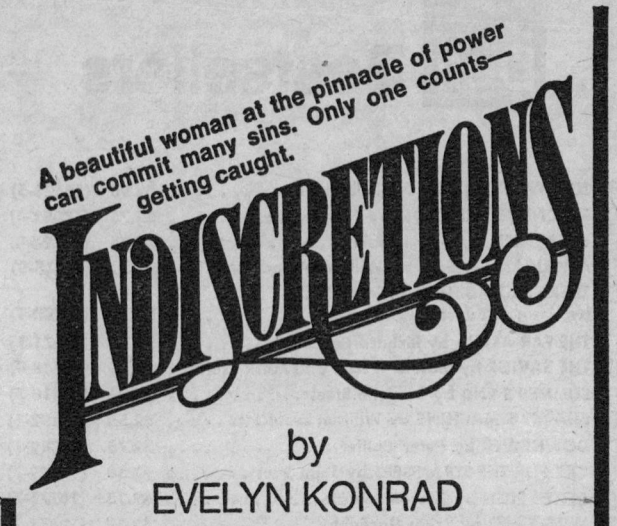

by
EVELYN KONRAD

"Sizzling."—*Columbus Dispatch-Journal*

"The Street" is Wall Street—where brains and bodies are tradeable commodities and power brokers play big politics against bigger business. At stake is a $500 million deal, the careers of three men sworn to destroy each other, the future of an oil-rich desert kingdom—and the survival of beautiful Francesca Currey, a brilliant woman in a man's world of finance and power, whose only mistakes are her *Indiscretions*.

A Dell Book $2.50 (14079-X)
At your local bookstore or use this handy coupon for ordering:

Dell	DELL BOOKS INDISCRETIONS $2.50 (14079-X)
	P.O. BOX 1000, PINEBROOK, N.J. 07058

Please send me the above title. I am enclosing $ _____
(please add 75¢ per copy to cover postage and handling). Send check or money order—no cash or C.O.D.'s. Please allow up to 8 weeks for shipment.

Mr/Mrs/Miss _____

Address _____

City _____ State/Zip _____

THE PASSING BELLS

by

PHILLIP ROCK

A story you'll wish would go on forever.

Here is the vivid story of the Grevilles, a titled British family, and their servants—men and women who knew their place, upstairs and down, until England went to war and the whole fabric of British society began to unravel and change.

"Well-written, exciting. Echoes of Hemingway, Graves and *Upstairs, Downstairs.*"—*Library Journal*

"Every twenty-five years or so, we are blessed with a war novel, outstanding in that it depicts not only the history of a time but also its soul."—*West Coast Review of Books.*

"Vivid and enthralling."—*The Philadelphia Inquirer*

A Dell Book $2.75   (16837-6)

At your local bookstore or use this handy coupon for ordering:

| **Dell** | **DELL BOOKS**   THE PASSING BELLS $2.75 (16837-6)
P.O. BOX 1000, PINEBROOK, N.J. 07058 |

Please send me the above title. I am enclosing $_____
(please add 75¢ per copy to cover postage and handling). Send check or money order—no cash or C.O.D.'s. Please allow up to 8 weeks for shipment.

Mr/Mrs/Miss_____

Address_____

City_____State/Zip_____

**Sometimes you have to lose
everything before you can begin**

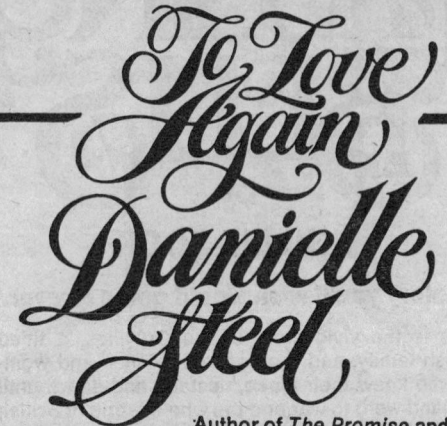

To Love Again
Danielle Steel

Author of *The Promise* and
Summer's End

Isabella and Amadeo lived in an elegant and beautiful world where they shared their brightest treasure—their boundless, enduring love. Suddenly, their enchantment ended and Amadeo vanished forever. With all her proud courage could she release the past to embrace her future? Would she ever dare TO LOVE AGAIN?

A Dell Book $2.50 (18631-5)

At your local bookstore or use this handy coupon for ordering:

Dell | **DELL BOOKS** | To Love Again $2.50 (18631-5)
P.O. BOX 1000, PINEBROOK, N.J. 07058

Please send me the above title. I am enclosing $ _____
(please add 75¢ per copy to cover postage and handling). Send check or money order—no cash or C.O.D.'s. Please allow up to 8 weeks for shipment.

Mr/Mrs/Miss _____

Address _____

City _____ State/Zip _____

SHARON SALVATO
co-author of *The Black Swan*

Bitter Eden

**He taught her what
it means to live
She taught him what it means to love**

Peter Berean rode across the raging landscape of a countryside in flames. Callie Dawson, scorched by shame, no longer believed in love—until she met Peter's strong, tender gaze. From that moment they were bound by an unforgettable promise stronger than his stormy passions and wilder than her desperate dreams. Together they would taste the rich, forbidden fruit of a *Bitter Eden*.

A Dell Book $2.75 (10771-7)

At your local bookstore or use this handy coupon for ordering:

Dell	**DELL BOOKS** Bitter Eden $2.75 (10771-7) **P.O. BOX 1000, PINEBROOK, N.J. 07058**

Please send me the above title. I am enclosing $ _____
(please add 75¢ per copy to cover postage and handling). Send check or money order—no cash or C.O.D.'s. Please allow up to 8 weeks for shipment.

Mr/Mrs/Miss _____

Address _____

City _____ State/Zip _____

8 MONTHS A NATIONAL BESTSELLER!

EVERGREEN
by
BELVA PLAIN

From shtetl to mansion—Evergreen is the wonderfully rich epic of Anna Friedman, who emigrates from Poland to New York, in search of a better life. Swirling from New York sweatshops to Viennese ballrooms, from suburban mansions to Nazi death camps, from riot-torn campuses to Israeli Kibbutzim, Evergreen evokes the dramatic life of one woman, a family's fortune and a century's hopes and tragedies.

A Dell Book $2.75 (13294-0)

At your local bookstore or use this handy coupon for ordering:

| Dell | DELL BOOKS
P.O. BOX 1000, PINEBROOK, N.J. 07058 | Evergreen $2.75 (13294-0) |

Please send me the above title. I am enclosing $ _____
(please add 75¢ per copy to cover postage and handling). Send check or money order—no cash or C.O.D.'s. Please allow up to 8 weeks for shipment.

Mr/Mrs/Miss _____

Address _____

City _____ State/Zip _____